Susan Johnson was born in 1956 and spent her childhood in St Ives, Sydney. She moved with her family to a pineapple farm on the coast north of Brisbane and in 1975 began a cadetship on the Brisbane *Courier-Mail*, attending the University of Queensland part-time. She did not complete her Bachelor of Arts but began full-time work as a journalist on publications including the *Australian Women's Weekly*, the *Sydney Morning Herald* and the *National Times*.

Susan is the recipient of several fellowships from the Literature Board of the Australia Council and now writes fiction full-time. She is the author of *Messages from Chaos* and *Flying Lessons*.

susan
johnson

a big life

PICADOR
AUSTRALIA

First published in 1993 by Pan Macmillan Publishers Australia
This Picador edition published 1994 by Pan Macmillan Pty Limited Australia
63-71 Balfour Street, Chippendale, Sydney

National Library of Australia
cataloguing-in-publication data:
Johnson, Susan 1956 - Dec. 30 -
A big life
ISBN 0 330 27438 4
I. Title
A823.3

Printed in Australia by McPherson's Printing Group

For STEVE FALLON and JANET JOHNSON,
and in memory of
JACK (BRAD) and SCOTT MORONEY

Acknowledgements

This novel was written on a fellowship from the Literature Board of the Australia Council.

With special thanks to Mary Jane (Molly) Campbell, Johnny Hutch, Beryl Kaye for their reminiscences, to the Acromaniacs (Barry Phelan, Karl Magee, Peter Hill and Gary Cross) for their time, and to Barbara and Gregg Moroney for their kind support.

With love and gratitude to Barbara Johnson and Margaret Connolly for keeping the light shining.

'. . . to be nothing more than innocent!'

HERMAN MELVILLE, *Billy Budd, Sailor*

'People will soon get tired of staring at a plywood box every night.'

HEAD OF 20TH CENTURY-FOX, 1946

'Great ideas originate in the muscles.'

THOMAS EDISON

PART 1

Sydney

Madhouse

In the house at 61 Allen Street, Sapphire Hayes was birthing the baby who would grow up to look into the eyes of the King. She liked to suck the leaves of a mint plant while her body went about its business, and was concerned now with prising free a large leaf from the roof of her mouth with her tongue. 'Mum,' said Ethel. Saph Hayes opened her eyes and said, 'What is it, love?' Ethel, who always tried to look as if nothing could surprise her, was standing at the foot of the bed, her face tight. 'Do you want some more mint?' she asked, but Saph Hayes only closed her eyes again, and rubbed her infamous Hayes nose. 'Outside now, Eth,' said Saph's fat sister Eva, 'there's a good girl.'

It was a light spring day, a slice of moon was visible. Lightning did not strike the sky; no birds flew in celebration. Yet the world was alive and rippling, the air was young, it had plans. Ethel sat beneath the frangipani tree in the front yard, breaking off the flowers for the pleasure of seeing them leak white blood. Flowers spilled on the ground; Ethel dug a a small hole and buried them, then lay back on the wet grass.

Inside, Saph Hayes thought of her husband, who was away somewhere, she forgot where. She was rolling now, rising and falling, she was trapped in her own skin with no escape. She remembered the pain all over again, she remembered its rhythms and terrible shape. She tried to concentrate on the mint leaf, but her tongue swam against it like an alien creature, twisting and turning, straining at its root. '*Jesus*,' she said to the ceiling, and fat Eva patted her hand and said, 'Now, now.' The waters of Sydney Harbour were not parting, a comet did not pass across the sky. Outside in the street walked free people, inhabiting a different world without pain.

At half past ten a miracle happened: a living boy passed from one world to the next. The angels did not sing; his mother cried. The child was her sole creation, a fatherless production to whom she was God. She kissed him, patted her hair, then sat up and asked for a cup of tea and a corned beef and mustard sandwich. When Eva had cleaned up the baby and left the room, Saph Hayes opened his fist, and found it empty. For the first time she looked fully into his face: he was fresh from heaven and instinctively she drew him closer, already sensing he would need it more than most.

Saph Hayes kept all her babies dangling from a sugar bag on the wall. She made sure the nail was secure before hanging them, and balanced them carefully, cradling them with cushions when they were small and placing their legs through the holes she had cut at the bottom when they grew. They were happy enough swinging in that rough hessian bag, knocking their heels against the wall. It kept them out of mischief, and left her arms free, so that she did not have to rediscover her own limbs after twelve months. Saph Hayes had enough to do at the cake shop without carting babies from pillar to post, but she kept a close eye on the sugar bag all the same. She had given birth to seven children now and six were still living: she must be doing something right. She looked over now at her latest: he was asleep again, he was dreaming, away.

William Sly Hayes was perfect, for he still dwelt in an unearthly place. He lived in that strange land between the born and the fully conscious, yet knew how to suck without lessons. He could not cry like an adult at happy endings, for happiness did not yet remind him of the loss of happiness, and he could not weep for its memory. Where he dwelt, happiness and all things were still possible: he puckered his mouth and there was nourishment, he lifted his fist and there was comfort. Billy Hayes was a blissful grub inhabiting a safe cocoon, the whole world was his secure and delicious foundation. He did not yet distinguish himself from the atmosphere: he was water, matter, spirit. Billy Hayes *was* the world, the lifeforce, pure and straight.

He did not think as he hung in his sugar bag, for he was not yet truly among us. When he was not sleeping, his eyes contained nothing but a dreamy blankness, for intelligence had not yet been ignited. The world claimed him slowly, as is its fashion, so that he did not even notice his own fall from grace.

But one day Billy Hayes woke up and recognized his mother.

That is, he saw in one moment that she was different from himself, as he himself was distinct from the world. He did not know that this was the first mark on the canvas of his life, a mark that was necessary to make but which also contained his fall. He did not feel grief but jubilation: he grabbed at once at his mother's hair, her teeth, her infamous nose. Saph Hayes laughed and jiggled him, she seemed to meet his recognition and, placing him on her shoulders, ran giggling about the room. The other children joined in and ran with her; they squealed and fell and cried, all at once. The noise was so loud Eva ran in from next door to see what was happening and stood in the doorway shaking her large fat head. What she saw was Saph and her usual madhouse: the children hysterical, Saph giggling, the baby Billy high on her shoulders, his head perilously bent. 'Saph, the baby!' Eva called, fearful of his still frail neck. But Billy Hayes was spinning, his clothes flying, Billy Hayes was flying about the room, a baby king! He knew the shock and joy of being alive in mid-air, reeling dangerously yet at the same time feeling safe and wholly loved. He spun on his mother's shoulders, his mouth wide and screaming. His eyes rolled, his neck arched, he felt the earth's great pull. It was his first conscious moment and it entered his nerves and his blood. Later of course he forgot this moment, yet it was his, Billy Hayes's whirling start.

Sapphire Hayes was an odd sort of mother: she swung from lamp-posts and called all her children Tom. 'They come when I call, don't they?' she said to Eva when Eva suggested Saph call them by the names they were given. And indeed all of them did answer to Tom, even Ethel, who was the oldest and often embarrassed by her mother, frequently walking a good distance from her in the street. There was also Mary, Cecil, Ellen, Bede and baby Billy, but none of them cared to be called anything else by their mother but Tom.

Sapphire Hayes didn't swing from every lamp-post: she only swung from one if she was particularly happy or if it was the right kind of day. She was a tiny thing, with thin wrists and short, fine legs. Her expression was kindly, so that people frequently smiled at her in passing or felt they could tell her their stories if given half a chance. Her nose was her most prominent feature, and she claimed it arrived in a room a full minute before the rest of her did. It was a whopper, rolling down from her forehead with abandon, before stopping with a bang at the end. It blossomed into a kind of knob there, so that what it resembled most was a false nose. Yet Sapphire Hayes was known as a looker, and was proud of her pretty ankles and handsome face. She liked a nice dress, a well-made hat and clean gloves; she had good posture and instructed all her children to walk tall.

Saph Hayes was also a fine whistler, and could whistle any tune you might want. Hers was no ordinary whistle but high and throbbing, a theatrical falsetto which ran with wild emotion, staggering into grief or surging heavenbound with joy. She whistled in the kitchen in the mornings, a popular love song or most often a hymn: she whistled so loud that Eva and Arthur heard her from their bedroom next door. Eva and Arthur lay in bed listening, for her whistle told whole stories without words. The only time Saph Hayes's whistle failed her was when she got the giggles, and when she got the giggles she might never stop. She was a top giggler, worse than the children, and when she got the giggles, the whole tribe would soon follow. 'She's off again,' Eva would say when she heard the din, often finding all of them collapsed in a heap on the floor. 'Oh, stop them, Eva,' Saph would beg helplessly, wiping tears from the end of her nose. 'My stomach hurts!' somebody would cry, and that would send the lot of them into fits again.

She had an absent-minded, haphazard way of loving, a wandering hand that patted a child's head or shoulder with the familiar rhythm it had learnt burping infants. The child would stand beneath her gently beating hand, hypnotized by the rhythm, while Saph whistled softly or smiled vaguely into the child's hair.

She had an acute way of telegraphing her emotions, so that when she was moved by something, you could feel the great rush of excitement through her. She held your hand so tightly you feared for your bones, and she need only place a hand on your shoulder for you to feel all the life in her.

Saph Hayes's discipline was erratic and unpredictable, so that what a child could get away with one day, he might be punished for the next. She tended to punish by withdrawing her attention, ignoring so completely that the child began to wonder if he was there at all. Once Cecil had been rude to her and when he came home from school in the afternoon, she pretended not to know him, calling to the other children that here was a little boy who was lost. 'Where do you live, dear?' she inquired blandly, while Cec stood crying, pleading to his mother that it was he, Cecil Hayes. She expected nothing less than magnificence from her children and each strove to lay their best selves at her feet: they would have done anything to win her admiration, to have her look at them as if they were the best thing she'd seen all day.

She had a great natural gift for making all her children feel special, so that each child secretly believed himself or herself to be her favourite. It wasn't that she gave any of them an extra potato or listened harder to one child than the next, it was a particular way she had of bestowing her attention, as if you alone were her singular joy.

Yet of all her children Saph Hayes felt Billy was different. It was not only that she had carried and delivered him fatherless, that he knew of no other parent but her. For the first time she had clearly heard the sound of crying from her womb, and had rocked the child within her own flesh. Out in the open this baby needed all her comfort, for there was something too tender about him, and she keenly felt the duties of her eyes.

That he was her last child she was also certain: she looked upon him as her final great act. She was careful, however, not to show this, and to each of her children she seemed likely to personally hand down the sun.

On certain nights in Allen Street, happiness gave out its soft throb, and children wrapped in blankets believed the world could do them no harm. On other nights they all lay with their heads beneath pillows, listening for sounds in the dark. For Saph Hayes was also unaccountably timid, scared of murderers, ghosts and moonless nights. 'I've been frightened all my life,' she confessed to Ethel, as the two of them crept with a candle to the outhouse. 'What was that?' she whispered as she held tightly to her daughter. 'Did you hear something move?' She would make Ethel stand guard at the door while she hurriedly made her ablutions: Ethel trembled in the night air. Then the two of them ran like billy-oh back to the kitchen, where Saph would bolt the door and once again check all the windows.

It was the dark which frightened Saph Hayes most, the endless black which robbed her of her sightful skills. She felt unarmed against it, as if it were some cruel trick to deprive her of rights. It annoyed her, not being able to see the world clearly, the frangipani tree, the fingers of her own hand. She felt the night gave unseen forces an advantage, as if they could see her but she must live blind, afraid. All sorts of creatures came alive in Saph Hayes's nights, and all her life she felt saved by the first light of morning.

It was morning when she whistled loudest, feeling safely delivered into the clear light of day. It was the way all the children came to consciousness, rising out of sleep to the tune of a psalm. Saph Hayes wasn't particularly religious, but she found a psalm or a hymn best suited mornings. Sometimes she'd whistle a tune she'd heard only once on Eva's piano: she had a good ear, a mimic's unschooled skills.

They always ate porridge in the mornings, cooked for half an hour using water, never milk. Cecil was chesty, given to flu, so there was often a bowl of boiling water with eucalyptus oil for him to stick his head over, to help his congestion. Billy sat on his mother's lap, being spoonfed, but sometimes Mary would feed him, or Ethel. Ethel tended to miss his mouth, so that porridge hardened against his cheek; she was rough, the spoon hit his gums.

After breakfast Billy was hung again in the sugar bag, while beds were made and plates washed. His mother worked at the Ivy Cake Shop, a neat place on Glebe Point Road inherited prematurely by Eva's Arthur after his poor mother had inadvertently walked in front of a horse. Saph wore a little lace cap and an apron, and brought stale cakes home as a treat. She kissed Billy and his brother Bede goodbye every morning, then waved as they cried in the restraining arms of Auntie Eva. Eva did not have her own children and Saph's believed she did everything wrong: she didn't hold them right, and pressed their noses too hard against her large bosom, speaking to them as if they were deaf and dumb. Eva came every morning through the gap in the side fence, which Arthur had inexpertly cut with an old saw. All day she played with Saph's babies, placing the older child Bede in a kind of

8

wooden cage. Because he was walking, he was more trouble: in his wooden environment he was hemmed in and safe.

Billy rolled on the grass on a blanket and knew himself to be low on the ground. He felt thick Sydney grass with his fingers and ate small rocks and the cracked empty shells of snails. 'Dirty!' Eva cried if she caught him, holding him over the sink and clearing his mouth. He mainly rolled on his back in the sunshine, smelling earth, frangipani, the clean autumn air. One morning he saw the roots of a tree rising up from the ground, a vegetable muscle breaking free of the earth. He pulled himself toward this and levered himself up. Suddenly he found himself standing on his own legs: Billy Hayes, with his own private shadow!

Peter Gillespie

To all intents and purposes, William Sly Hayes left home just before his fifth birthday. It happened the day the stranger came, when Billy removed himself to his own head as if to a distant country. He was small for his age, a pretty child, with a fine head of curly blond hair, which sometimes showed glints of red and gold. He was the only Hayes child with this colouring and was already conscious of himself as an outsider, that in some inalienable way he stood out. His eyes were an unusual olive green, ringed with dark lashes, so flattering it was sometimes remarked that he should have been a girl. Billy was outraged when this happened, declaring loudly that he was indeed a boy, and never understood why everybody always laughed.

The day Billy left home he was with his mother and Bede walking down Allen Street when his mother abruptly stopped. Billy looked up and saw that her face had lost its vibrance, that it wore the same expression as when she was frightened on a moonless night. He turned to follow her line of vision and saw a crowd of people standing outside their gate: above the heads of Eva, Arthur and their neighbours he saw a tall man, at least two heads taller than the rest. His mother continued to stand there, but Eva saw her and shouted her name. Bede ran off toward the crowd: Billy looked up into his mother's face and cried, 'Mum!' After some moments she seemed to remember him. 'Come on, Billy,' she said, walking forward, and Billy began to cry because it was the first time she had called him by his proper name instead of Tom.

Inside the kitchen everyone talked loudly, but the tall stranger sat in the corner without sound. Everyone seemed to know that this man was his father, returned to earth from wherever he had been. Ethel hovered by his chair, staring; his mother sat next to the man, twisting her gloves. Billy did not like the look of him: his hair was red and too alarming, his hands were cruel as if they had broken apart too many small birds. Only the family cat Blackie was immune from the excitement, obliviously sleeping in his favourite place inside the recently vacated stove. Eva usually shooed him out, scolding Saph for her unhygienic housekeeping habits, but even she had forgotten Blackie in the commotion. Her plump face was flushed and greasy; she gave an uncharacteristic nervous laugh. All the children had been allowed out of school early, for it wasn't every day that a father returned fully standing from the dead. Wherever the man had been in the three years since the war he wasn't saying, and was clearly displeased about everyone making such a fuss. Billy continued to look him over, at his thin mouth and eyebrows which stuck out from his head. Billy supposed he was wearing clothes that somebody else had given him, for his shirt seemed too small, his heavy boots too big. After some time, the man's glance settled on Billy, who met his eyes and refused to look away. The two of them stared at each other in silence, until Mary noticed, nudged Billy and said, 'Don't stare!' But he did stare, he stared at him without blinking, he stared at his eyes, at his nose, at his whole face.

'Come here, love,' he heard his mother say through his help-lessness. 'Come over here and meet your dad.' For the first time, the muscles of his body did not respond to his mother's command as if inevitably, he saw that it was in his body's power to resist. He stood staring at his father, breathing hard.

'Billy,' she said again, and he began to cry.

'A sook, eh?' said his father. 'Saph, you've turned this one into a sook.' The stranger looked at Billy impassively, taking a tin of tobacco from his pocket with care. He stuck a cigarette paper to the edge of his lips; Billy stood weeping, ashamed. His mother made no move to comfort him, but Mary kept her warm hand on his head.

'He'll be five on Thursday,' Saph Hayes said to her husband. She stood up and walked across to Billy; bending down, she talked carefully into his face. He understood that she was trying to convey some urgent message, that she wished him to respond in an unknown but appropriate way.

'What about your dad coming home for your birthday! How about that for a whacko present, Billy Hayes!' Her smile seemed to him fixed too intently, he recognized through his sobs a false note. He broke free and ran from the room swearing vengeance, and felt betrayal for the first time as he ran.

It was clear that the man who was his father was staying, indeed that he was sharing Saph Hayes's bed. The days of them all piling into her bed on Sunday morning were over, for they were all too scared of their father to want to try. Billy remembered when they had all squashed up against pillows, how they would take turns in telling a continuous story, and when it came to his bit, he never knew what to say next. All at once this life was finished, but it was not yet clear what kind of life would come next.

It seemed to Billy that his mother had grown even smaller, as if some vital extravagance had been reined in. She still swung from the occasional lamp-post, but checked now to see if her husband was looking. She still whistled and had her attacks of the giggles, but the giggling fits could be brought to a halt quickly by a loud word from Jack Hayes. He was always watching, asking Saph where she was going, or where she'd been. At first she answered with her usual flash of daring. 'I'm going to see a man about a dog', or 'I've been to see Peter Gillespie.' Peter Gillespie was the family code for Mind Your Own Business and his name was invoked if they didn't want to say where they'd been. But soon she began to give truthful accounts of her whereabouts, to inform him of her movements as if to reassure a child.

Jack Hayes was a taciturn fellow, whose character was understood to have been irrevocably altered by the Great War. In his youth he had been a fine football player, and enjoyed a drink and a sing-along like any other young man. He was a builder by trade and once had many mates, but now he repulsed every offer to share a beer. He carried some private burden, as if the very act of talking were more than he could bear.

His presence in the house soon let in a heaviness, which each of the children felt as the difference between night and day. Blackness had come into the house now, curtains had been drawn to keep out the radiance of light. Every small thing was suddenly difficult, so that a missed tram took on the proportions of catastrophe, a broken handle became the last straw. Jack Hayes needed life to be continually patterned and predictable; the smallest change caused him unbearable distress. He constantly expected disaster, for everything to always go wrong, so that a trip to Bondi Beach became a battle plan instead of a holiday and the days of them all piling into a tram whenever they felt like it were irretrievably gone.

Very quickly the children learnt to tell if their father was home the moment they walked into the house, because his presence was so overwhelming. On the rare occasions when he wasn't it seemed like a holiday and they ran through the house at full and terrible speeds, making as much noise as they dared.

But his anxiety soon began to infect them too, so that they no longer lived in such a haphazard, unselfconscious way. Without any of them noticing their new life had arrived, it was suddenly clear that happiness was only for the stupid, and that life was a long course through ambush and pain.

Billy moved around his father at a distance, careful never to be alone with him in any room. He did not know why his father picked on him particularly, only that he did. Although Billy feared and disliked him, he also had a secret longing for his attention and spent many moments day-dreaming of the day when his father suddenly discovered he loved him. Yet Billy always seemed to do precisely the wrong thing in his father's presence, fatally drawn to making the most disastrous mistakes.

One morning he was drawing with some pencils in the room he shared with his brothers when he poked a pencil tentatively in his ear. The lead was cold and dangerous, and touched something which made him squirm. It felt exquisitely tender and ticklish and Billy pushed the pencil further in; it made him want to cough, to scratch the inner lining of his ear, to giggle, all at the same time.

He slowly took his hand away from the pencil, testing to see if it would fall out. It stayed! He moved his head slightly and the pencil swayed; he shook his head more vigorously, and the pencil swung to and fro. Leaning over carefully, Billy took another pencil and stuck it in his other earhole. He took his hand down and swung his head; the pencils swung softly in the air. He stood up and still they stayed, resting against that delicious thing inside his own head. It felt forbidden, brave: he stood at the window hoping someone might see him.

But it was his brother Cecil who saw him and snuck up from

behind, swinging his hands down hard on either side of Billy's head. Billy cried out as he felt the points snap off, the little broken leads travelling and travelling, falling round and round the coiled piping of his head.

He screamed and chased his brother, who ran away laughing, Billy running after him, the lead jiggling in his ears. 'Mum!' Billy screamed, heading for the kitchen, where he saw his mother standing at the stove and his father reading a newspaper at the kitchen table.

Billy stopped dead in his tracks and looked at his father, but the lead in his ears felt more urgent. He raced toward his mother, who told him to calm down, and who extracted the story before taking him up the road to the doctor who extracted the lead.

'He's got less brains than a rocking-horse,' his father said as they left, and Billy hung his silly head in shame.

As he grew older Billy began to hate the looks his father gave him, the way he did not attempt the semblance of a smile. His father clearly did not feel compelled to even pretend to like him, his conscience did not smite him in the least. It was true that Jack Hayes looked upon Billy with a hard eye, his distaste clear for everyone to see. He goaded and poked fun at every opportunity and took pleasure in seeing how long it would take to make Billy cry. He did not pick on the other children so consistently but mostly ignored them or shouted if they got in his way.

Billy was the perfect target, being completely incapable of defending himself, standing rooted to the spot with an embarrassed duck of his head, his eyes filling with tears despite himself. Sometimes he managed to leave the room, and once muttered daringly under his breath, 'Shut up!'

'What did you say?' his father bellowed, and Billy kept his eyes on the ground.

'Answer me!' his father shouted, but Billy did not lift his head. He realized the room had grown quiet, that Cec had stopped the shuffle of his cards, his mother the stirring of a pot. He felt he should say something but did not know what. 'Nothing,' he said by way of an offering. 'I didn't say anything.'

'He didn't say anything,' Jack Hayes repeated. 'He never does, does he, Cec?'

Billy waited, not daring to look at his brother.

'Never,' Cecil said with a nervous laugh.

He heard his mother moving, but willed her not to step toward him.

'Get the plates out, will you, Mary?' she said, her voice tense. All at once there was sound again, the movement of chairs, of feet. He heard his father coming towards him.

'Next time you don't say anything make sure I don't hear it,' he said. 'Now get out!'

All his life Billy Hayes never knew his father believed him to be a bastard, the product of Saph's wartime dalliance and most certainly not his own child. Jack Hayes could not see that of all his children Billy looked most like him, nor could he see Sapphire Hayes's honourable heart. Saph Hayes herself found it impossible to believe her husband could even entertain the idea: she, Saph Hayes, who he had married as a girl of sixteen! She found it so ridiculous she mistakenly ignored the whole issue completely. Once when Jack Hayes accused her in words she found her ears suddenly hard of hearing. She could not even begin to protest her innocence, to explain how she had found out she was pregnant the very week after he had left for the war. She could not believe he could even think such a thing, let alone defend herself: she stood at her mirror dumbfounded, then opened the bedroom door and walked out.

Saph Hayes continued to make excuses for her husband: it was the war, it was his 'nerves', he needed love. Of course she could not acknowledge Jack Hayes as he truly was, for to do so would mean admitting her life had gone wrong, that she had chosen the wrong man. She could not afford to open the floodgates to her own disappointments, her failures, her own pain. Instead she turned her attention to the children, focusing what was left of her hopes on them. She told herself she was trying to compensate for their father, but in truth she was giving herself comfort too. Most of all she tried to comfort Billy, accompanying him as often as she could on private walks, just the two of them, down Allen Street into Edward Lane and to the water at the end of Glebe Point Road. They always took these walks at odd moments, when Jack Hayes was sleeping, or Ethel was doing the beans for tea. 'Tom and I are just popping out for half an hour,' she'd say to Ethel. 'Where to?' Ethel asked and Saph would say, 'Curiosity killed the cat.' They never made these excursions in front of the others, when visitors were there or if Jack Hayes was awake. Billy understood that these walks were somehow clandestine, which made them thrilling as escape. He'd take his mother's hand excitedly, but let it fall as soon as they shut the fence and turned into the road.

The water always surprised them, appearing unexpectedly at the end of the street. You couldn't see it until you were almost upon it but when you did, it looked implausible in the middle of so many roads. The water was alive with working men; men in singlets who sometimes waved to them or else ignored them, being intent upon their daily chores. Tugs pulled barges piled high with logs into the waters of Rozelle Bay; they moved low in the water, the wood dark with wet. The water itself had its own destination, travelling to Pyrmont, to Balmain, to meet other waters in the huge mouth of Sydney Harbour.

Billy and Saph sat by its workings, sometimes not even talking, picking grass and chewing the ends of weeds. Knotted figs lived in the soil all around them, their roots engaged in vast subterranean toil. Often Saph whistled, or told him stories of her childhood, of her kind father who owned hansom cabs and of an old Sydney with nothing but horses. Once she told him that people always took you at your own estimation, so you might as well think highly of your own self. 'Don't forget there's nothing you can't do,' she finished firmly. She said this because she wished to build up Billy's confidence, and because she feared for his vulnerability, the curious way he had of appearing peeled to the world, as if there were nothing to keep his whole self from showing. She did not know how he might grow the necessary skin to save himself, how best to advise him against such dangerous innocence. 'You're an open book, Tom,' she said as kindly as she could. 'It wouldn't hurt to close the covers once in a while.' Billy looked at her as if he did not quite know what she meant: she patted his hand and pointed out a flock of Sydney cockatoos passing overhead in a great sweep across the sky.

In all these talks Saph Hayes never once directly mentioned Billy's father. The closest she came was one evening walking back when she declared that friends were all very well, but when it came to the crunch, families were the only thing which counted. Billy took this to mean that one day even his father might be there for him, one day even Jack Hayes might stand up for him when it came to the crunch.

Billy began to spend more time on his own, walking. When he was alone he fell naturally into a state of day-dream so that anyone coming upon him would find him with a look of absorption on his face, his eyes all but blind to the visible world. His mouth might be smiling at some internal happiness; he would have to be called again and again before he could hear his own name.

But when he was not alone he was a nervous boy, tense, who perpetually looked as if he were about to turn and run. When he was with other people he developed an awkward physical presence, which did not make him comfortable to be with: he had a kind of nervous over-alertness, an intensity in the blaze of his eyes. He watched other people too closely, sitting with a strained attentiveness, one knee bobbing up and down. He could not wait to get away and could not hide it; people were sometimes relieved to see him go.

Billy was the family loner, always missing, the one who had to be chased home for tea. Alone, he climbed fig trees, balanced on fences; he walked the streets of Glebe, night and day. His body grew quickly and he could run fast, faster than anyone, he was always the one who could climb the tallest tree. When he walked Billy felt the muscles in his calves moving, the coil of energy in the balls of his feet. His body was this great mass of potential, a buoyant collection of nerves. When he walked fast he felt a quick excitement, and had to raise his hands high above his head for relief. He felt he had too much excitement for his own body, and had to keep moving to survive. Some part of him was always in motion, even standing still he could not stop himself from clenching and unclenching his fists.

Billy roamed the streets of his suburb, past his school and into Forest Lodge; once he ran the length of the football oval twenty-seven times. He set himself physical tests: to do a circuit of Glebe without stopping once, for example, or to run flat out into the wall behind the Town Hall without putting up his hands. He succeeded in running into the wall, only narrowly missing breaking his nose. When his nose bled, he was victorious, for he knew he had won by the singular force of his will.

Billy left the house each morning before the others, meeting up with them outside the school gates. After school he sometimes went with Bede or Cec up to Broadway, or played a game of football at the back of the Church Hall. He loved his brothers, but they were always fighting, for Cec tended to echo their father and make fun of him, and Bede always felt obliged to go along with Cec. Billy lacked entirely the ability to treat anything lightly and would get so flustered it was a delight to watch: Cec loved to see Billy do his block. Sometimes when they were late home of an evening, for example, Cec pushed Billy into the water off Glebe Point to give them a good excuse for being late. 'Billy fell in again,' he'd say to their mother. 'I didn't! Cec pushed me!' Billy cried. He grew red in the face at such an unfair accusation but lacked the nous required for revenge and never once paid Cecil back by pushing him in.

But he did grow wary of walking with Cec too near the water, even though Cec always promised not to push him in. 'Promise?' Billy asked every time and every time Cec promised, then pushed him in. His brothers stood on the bank laughing, while Billy floundered, always surprised. Eventually he learnt to avoid Cecil, who soon couldn't catch him anyway because he ran so fast.

Of all his siblings, Billy remained closest to Mary, who was sweet natured and slow. She moved heavily through the air like a somnambulist, admiring Billy's speed because it was so unlike her own.

One dusk Billy left the yard at Allen Street, even though his mother had asked him to stay inside. He was always going missing in the evening, sneaking out the front gate just as she was about to serve tea. He knew it was teatime and his mother would be angry, but the sky was mauve and teetering, hovering on the cusp of night and day. Anything seemed possible, as if some great meaning were about to be revealed. At such moments a boy could believe in his own earthly powers, in the ability of his will to transform the whole world. His sole ambition was to escape and he walked fast, passing lanes and alleys before turning into the street with the old Chinese joss-house, which he had passed innumerable times but until now had never before cared to see.

As he passed that evening Billy turned his head to look in. Years later, he often wondered what would have happened if he had gone down another street, or passed half an hour earlier, or simply not turned his head at all. For what he saw at five past six on a chilly night outside the joss-house were streams of silk flowing in the air like liquid, and a pyramid of human bodies stacked elegantly against the twilight sky. The bodies were still, magnificent, he did not hear a single breath or a cry. He could not see the eyes of the people, so that their faces were dreamlike and obscured. The silk undulated in the air around them; people standing below did not talk or clap. The whole pyramid had the force of a giant, an enormous pulsating beast with intelligence, stomach and heart. It swayed in the air as he watched it, a creation of man and yet not man. It was the logical beauty which struck him, the constellation of bodies arranged by perfect laws of balance and weight. As he watched, bodies fell or rolled to earth silently: the boy at the very peak dived head first into the soil. He picked himself up and walked straight across to Billy; when he reached him he held out his hand. Billy Hayes took the hand which was offered him, the flesh was cool; he could not quite make out the features of the boy's face. Always when he later came to recall this moment, it appeared visionary and weird in the extreme. In his mind's eye he still saw that twilight's breathing pyramid, the bodies falling like leaves from the strangest of trees.

Homeland

Perhaps once in a lifetime, one human heart meets another and recognizes its own beat. Billy Hayes's heart knew Reginald Tsang's without instructions, and from the moment they met they were friends. It was the kind of friendship born out of knowledge of each other, rather than friendship born out of difference. Instinctively they knew each other's wounds and boundaries, and right from the beginning it carried the hallmarks of a lifelong attachment, being capable of overlooking transgressions but also of indulging the personality's worst traits.

Reginald Tsang was a tumbler, the occasional top man for the Hai-long Troupe of Chinese Entertainers, Pastimes of the Orient, Head and Hand Balancers. He was twelve years old, a year older than Billy, small boned, remarkably agile. His body appeared to have no muscles; skin covered his bones as if there were nothing between skin and bone but his blood. Yet he was strong and could run fast, and to Billy he seemed like a spirit boy who conjured himself up and disappeared in a flash. His face was wide with high cheek-bones, so that he might be taken for a Red Indian or Tibetan monk. He lived with his acrobatic family in a street not far from Billy's; his mother and father came from a village in China, but Reg had been born in a flat above Darlinghurst Road.

He was taught by the Christian Brothers at their school in Forest Lodge. 'We're Catholics,' he said in explanation, as if Billy might think the Chinese were heathens and worshipped the family dog. He invited Billy to meet him again outside the joss-house, where the Hai-long Troupe practised on the lawns every Thursday evening around six. Billy did not ask permission, but snuck out with Mary, who insisted on coming after she had seen him walking out the front gate.

This time, Billy walked straight through the lion gates at the joss-house entrance, outpacing his sister in his eagerness to watch. But they were early and there was no human pyramid, just a lot of people talking loudly outside on the lawn. They sat on chairs smoking, drinking tea and apparently engaged in strenuous verbal fights. Mary looked ill at ease and followed him closely: Billy searched for his new friend, Reg Tsang. He could not see him and felt anxious, for the Chinese looked at him without smiling, with unwelcoming eyes and clear distrust as to his motives. It appeared no one spoke English; he and Mary stood about uselessly, stranded in a cacophany of sounds. Billy could not imagine that these sounds could actually carry meaning; it seemed impossible that they could be anything more than noise. To escape the violence of tongues around him, he darted away from his sister, and passed through the open doors of the joss-house.

It was dark inside, there was a sickly sweet smell he could not identify but also the smell of rotting oranges, decaying in bowls throughout the room. Above his head giant coils of burning matter swayed from the ceiling, impossibly large. Smoke moved, obscuring his vision; he could make out leering masks, photographs of the dead. Hundreds of red tickets marked with black Chinese writing were pasted on one wall; long sticks were burning, giving off a pungent stink. The room was close against him; a statue of a large-faced man squatted at an altar down the far end of the room. The whole place was dank and ancient, a fetid crypt, beyond time. Billy thought if he touched the walls they would be damp with fluid, that dead bodies lay beneath stones at his feet. He recognized something archaic and wordless, there was fear and comfort in the room at once.

'Billy,' a voice said behind him and he turned. Reginald Tsang was standing in the doorway, his thin arms resting loosely at his sides.

'Would you like to send a prayer?' he asked, moving forward. 'You know, just like you do at St Ursula's.' He picked something up from the bench next to Billy, and placed it in Billy's hand. It was one of those long sticks which were burning, this one unlit with its powder coming off on his fingers. 'Light it,' advised his new friend. 'Go on, put it over there.'

Billy moved uncertainly toward the squatting statue, going against the teachings of his church. He was about to worship at a craven image, to place an offering at the feet of some foreign god. 'Now think of your grandfather or someone who's dead,' encouraged Reginald. 'Go on!'

Billy wasn't sure if he was supposed to pray out loud, or indeed if any prayer of his would be heard at all since he wasn't Chinese. He couldn't think quickly enough who to pray for, so he plunged the stick in a hole and said under his breath. '*For Mum.*'

'Come on!' said Reg, touching his shoulder. 'I think we're about to start.' Billy followed, his hands sweating, for as soon as he had said the words '*For Mum*' he wondered if he had put a curse on her, seeing she was not dead but most certainly alive. He was thinking this as he was led to his destiny, he was thinking of Sapphire Hayes, his living mum.

The troupe had gathered on the lawn, stretching and pulling legs and hands. Mary joined Billy as he sat at a far corner, his arms wrapped round his knees. He heard Mary talking, but his entire concentration was focused; his eyes, his ears, his whole self was focused on one thing: the small figure of Reginald Tsang, occasional top man, the flyer for Hai-long. Reginald's body was elastic, fluid as the silk bandages that writhed in the air. He rolled and tumbled, he bent backwards, he walked for whole minutes on his feet and his hands as if born with no spine. The larger men threw him about as though he were burning, passing him rapidly from hand to hand. When the pyramid finally formed, Reginald Tsang stood at its crest, the cage of bones in his chest visible, his eyes fixed on some distant point in the sky.

Later, when he had descended to earth and walked across to join them, Billy had trouble remembering that Reg was a human boy. Billy was suddenly tongue-tied: his brain empty, he could think of nothing intelligible to say. 'How'd you learn to do that?' asked Mary, saving him. 'Easy,' Reg Tsang replied. 'Come on, Billy, I'll show you.' And so it was that Billy arrived at his natural destination, and his body met for the first time its homeland.

From that evening, Billy Hayes's body became his personal secret, private knowledge over which he had total control. His body seemed capable of anything: it could balance on ropes and flip itself backwards, it could move without appearing to need the support of the ground. He was small and well proportioned yet powerfully built, so that he could easily catch Mary when she jumped from the veranda and pass her without grief to the grass.

He was not surprised to discover his body's abilities, for it felt like his sleeping body had woken up. In physical action Billy was his own true self, his whole being was free and realized, he was the Billy Hayes he had always sensed that he was. He was his pure self, unencumbered, he saw now he had lived rootbound: in motion he burst from the pot. Only when his body stopped moving and he took up more regular action did he return to his old self, laden and bound. Because he wished to feel continually released, he spent all his spare time practising, both on his own and as often as he could with Reg. Suddenly tumbling was all he could think of: his own body at one with the air!

Reg Tsang had exaggerated when he said tumbling was easy, for he had been doing it since he balanced as a baby in the hollow of his father's hand. It took more than a body to make a great tumbler, it took heart and a certain kind of nerve. Billy saw quickly that a pyramid was made up of working bodies, that a double somersault was more than a lucky roll through the air.

Reg's father, Low, spoke only minimal English; it was his son Reg who was the troupe's conduit to the outside world. Often when Low Tsang explained something to Billy with Reg translating, his words accidentally formed beautiful poems: 'An acrobat has no different eyes from any other man,' he said through Reg once, but Billy could not understand. 'What can a man see when he is falling and whirling?' Low Tsang continued, after Billy asked for further explanations. 'He cannot use his eyes, he must feel in his heart how long he must keep turning.'

Billy tumbled before school, he tumbled at lunchtime, in the afternoons he practised the world's most eloquent forward roll. He had a neat style, with a debonair flourish; he never looked sweaty or dishevelled. His tumbling had a natural grace: when he rolled neatly in the air, his body was all of a piece, there were no longer discernible individual parts. He learnt there was a right way of falling, a right way of rolling, that a body could be taught to absorb only the slightest of shocks.

His brother Bede and sisters took to watching him; Ethel had left school now and often brought along her friends. Once Cecil came with a bunch of his tough mates: Cec laughed and advised Billy to quit while he was ahead. One evening Billy and Reg gave an impromptu performance on the lawn outside the joss-house;

the ground was soft, the grass springy, they worked without using mats. Billy always tumbled in an old pair of shorts and a singlet but pestered his mother continually for a pair of white leggings and some tumbler's pumps.

On the afternoon Saph Hayes finally bought them, Billy ran to his bedroom to try them on. The white pumps looked pristine and professional; he stood admiring himself in the glass.

'What a ponce!' jeered his father behind him. 'Just look at this sight for sore eyes!'

It was too late to close the door: his father's tall body blocked Billy's escape. He continued to stare at his pumps in the mirror while his father stood there and smirked.

'They're beautiful, Tom,' said his mother, pushing past him. 'I knew they'd be just the right size.'

His father snorted. 'Who do you think he is? Cinderella? He looks like a bloody ponce!'

Billy Hayes did not look at his father: he never, ever looked him in the eye. He stared in the mirror and he thought, *The day will come when I will show you*. He did not know when this day might be, but knew he would not fail to recognize it when it came.

Most afternoons after practice, Billy and Reg met Saph Hayes at the cake shop. If it was Friday, Uncle Arthur baked Sydney's most glorious custard tarts.

'One, and one more only,' said his mother. 'Honestly, I don't know how you boys don't make yourselves sick.'

Uncle Arthur winked because he had already slipped them another; they stood watching as he laid his cigarette on the ash-tray and took a tray from the oven. Sometimes he let them serve, but Billy was not good at subtractions, no matter how many times Saph or Arthur told him to start with the money he had taken and add up from there.

'Look, Tom, if something costs twopence and someone gives you a shilling, how much do you give back?' But Billy was hope-less: because he feared the very idea of numbers, his mind pan-icked before he even began. Mostly, he served and Reg handled the money. 'We Chinese understand the value of cash,' Reg said, like a grown man.

The shop had glass counters, polished daily by Saph or Mrs

Munroe. Resting on doilies behind the glass were jam rolls and sponges, butter cakes and lamingtons. In the front window there were birthday cakes and wedding cakes, a collection of silver-painted wishbones and horseshoes, for luck. The shop always smelt delicious, and there were exquisite moments when Billy's mother introduced him to her customers.

'This is my son, Billy Hayes,' she said proudly. 'He's going to be famous one day.' Saph Hayes would tell them of his extraordinary acrobatic abilities, how he had flair and unusual talents you found once in a blue moon. Billy would stand with his eyes on the ground, his heart bursting, but he would not smile or look in the least pleased on the outside because Reg was there. He did not know that all his pleasure was on his face, blazing for everyone to see.

Saph and Rose Munroe were the best of friends; they would often go to Mrs Munroe's on the way home for a cup of tea. Billy was at the shop one afternoon without Reg, waiting to walk home with his mum. 'I'm dying for a cuppa,' said his mother. 'I've been run off my feet all day.' She was locking up the shop for Arthur, who had gone home early after a five o'clock start. Mrs Munroe stood on the footpath waiting, looking with intent at the sky.

'Oh, look at the sunset, Saph! Just stop a minute, will you, and have a look!'

Saph Hayes did not even turn her head. 'Bugger the sunset,' she said as she checked the lock. 'All I want's a ruddy cup of tea.'

It entered straight into the Hayes family lexicon: *Bugger the sunset* became a general expression for annoyance, dismissal, surprise. Its uses were many but found in only one dictionary, the unwritten one belonging to the Hayes family of Allen Street, Glebe.

Swallowing a Cloud

Cecil worked with their father now on building sites, cycling all the way to Bondi to build flats. Work was hard to get so they took any jobs they could come by. Cec took after Jack Hayes in personality, practising the kind of humour Billy found cruel. They'd go off together on their bikes in the early morning, and it seemed to Billy the whole house dropped its shoulders in relief.

Ethel and Mary made hats at the milliner's shop on Broadway, until Mary got laid off and Ethel felt she had no alternative but to leave too. Ellen had been laid off six weeks before at the biscuit factory, so the three of them sat around the house all day talking and drinking endless cups of tea. Times were so hard that men began to leave their families to go wandering, to find work in the country or some other luckier place. No one yet said the word 'Depression', they merely made stew with vegetables instead of rabbit, and later learnt to stand in line to get tickets in exchange for half a pound of tea.

Not even the fame of Arthur's custard tarts could rescue Arthur and Eva's cake shop. Custom dropped off and so to save Arthur the trouble, Saph placed her hand on his arm and said, 'Well, Art, there's not much for me to do here. I think I'll have a picnic tomorrow instead of coming in.' He nodded his head and said, 'Righto', while Saph busied herself collecting her things.

As long as she could, Saph Hayes kept up her Sunday lunches, the only day the whole family sat around the table at the same time. They ate rabbit or a kind of meat loaf, made these days with the smallest scrap of fatty mince, filled out with stale bread and an egg. Saph Hayes was an indifferent cook and only created a fine meal by accident. Yet on Sundays round the table they all enjoyed themselves, eating too fast and all talking at once. Jack Hayes rarely attended, but when he did the table grew silent, and everyone rose from their chairs the minute they finished dessert.

Jack Hayes, at six foot two, was disappointed with the physical growth of his family, for not one of his children took after him.

They all took after the Slys, Saph's side of the family; none of them, not even the boys, grew taller than five foot eight. 'A pack of bloody tiddlers!' he said with disgust. 'The whole damn lot of you, a pack of bloody girls!'

Each of the children, without exception, had also inherited Sapphire Hayes's infamous nose. But it was a nose with a hidden agenda, cleverly clothing itself with respectability in youth before triumphantly planting its flag upon the summit of the Hayes face in middle age. As none of the Hayes children was yet twenty, the Hayes nose merely looked a trifle large: each of them lived happily in youth's innocence, unaware of their own nose's plot.

After Sunday lunch, the stove vacated, Blackie the ageing cat would crawl into his favourite place inside the oven walls. Sometimes he would crawl in as soon as Saph took a dish from the oven, lying inside with his eyes firmly shut. 'It must be a hundred degrees in there,' Eth said as she laid the table. 'Look at him, he's panting as if he's in hell.' And indeed Blackie emerged from these rests swaying, lying floppily on the floor, his tongue out. 'He's mad, that cat,' Eva said if she saw him, 'and you're mad, Saph, to let him do it.'

One Sunday the kitchen smelt delicious. 'What's cooking?' Billy asked, and Saph Hayes stopped. 'Nothing, I'm just warming the oven,' she said, looking at Billy with a puzzled face. They both realized what had happened in the same instant: they rushed to the stove and opened the door. Inside was Blackie, cooked to perfection, his ears crisp, slightly curled. Saph ran from the room to vomit, but Billy stood there and stared. The cat did not look unhappy, he looked like some ancient clay figure. Blackie had chosen his own way, an old cat, in his chosen place.

When the family recovered, the story was taken up and embellished, so that before long the very mention of Blackie's name could send Saph Hayes into fits. The incident spawned an entire crop of Blackie jokes, centred mainly on the prophetic appropriateness of his name. 'Oh dear, done to a crisp he was,' Saph would say, giggling. 'Poor Blackie, what a way to go.' Mary thought it was too awful to think about, but after a while her mother's giggle inevitably caught her too. Eva was the only one who did not find it funny, she clicked her tongue and never laughed once. Eva thought Saph's whole house could do with a going-over with a decent cloth and a bottle of disinfectant; she privately wondered if the oven itself shouldn't be thrown out and replaced.

The house at Allen Street was constantly busy, as the six children and their friends came and went. Bede and Billy were the only ones left at school now, but neither could be called scholars. They went to school all right, but only because it was expected; Bede was to leave at the end of the year as soon as he turned fifteen. Billy and Bede were not close, yet they managed not to fight over the twopence Ellen's sweetheart paid them for acting as lookouts while he clumsily embraced her behind the church. Ellen was a quiet girl like Mary, with a pretty head of hair and neat white teeth. If Jack Hayes had known, there would have been all hell to pay, for he was ridiculously strict with the girls. He clearly regarded them as his possession, and would have kept them under lock and key if he was able.

As work fell off, Jack Hayes's moods grew blacker. He picked on his wife and children constantly and began drinking beer they could ill afford. Saph stacked the bottles at the back door carefully, throwing an old cloth over them lest anybody care to count. Jack Hayes put on a song and dance if Saph was out too long shopping, or if Bede asked for a new set of pencils. He began to imagine that Saph was out seeing fellows, so that he'd be on to her as soon as she stepped in the door.

'And how was Mrs Munroe?' he asked sarcastically, as if his own wife took him for a fool. He clearly believed he knew what she was up to, knowing women and in particular knowing his own wife. He had often seen Saph smile without regard for the consequences at any chap who tipped his hat to her in the street. She clearly seemed to find her own brother-in-law captivating, and Jack Hayes began walking past rooms where Saph sat having a cup of tea with Arthur, passing the door so often she soon learnt to get up. He began to check her shopping list too, and to rummage furtively amongst the contents of her handbag.

Saph responded to this querulous behaviour by ignoring it, as was her usual way. For as long as she could Saph Hayes went about her daily business, running the house and popping into Mrs Munroe's for a chat. She was a familiar figure around the streets of Glebe, well liked. 'I don't know how you put up with him, Saph,' Rose Munroe said at her kitchen table. 'He'd drive me round the bend.' But Sapphire Hayes was proud, and whoever heard of whingeing changing anything? 'Oh, he's all right,' she responded brusquely, changing the subject by asking Rose how her daughter Beryl's wedding dress was coming along. She enjoyed her cups of tea at Rose's kitchen table but did not like the conversation to get too personal.

One afternoon when Saph got home from having a cup of tea at Rose's, she saw Jack Hayes building a fire. She wondered what he was up to, and walked quickly up the side path to the backyard. Her husband was standing over an old kerosene tin, pushing still smoking ashes around with a stick.

'Burning off?' she asked, standing next to him, peering into the tin to see if she could make out its contents.

'Yes,' he replied without further explanation, so Saph shrugged her shoulders and went inside.

It was only that evening when she opened her wardrobe that she found not one dress left. Jack Hayes had burnt every one of them, the whole bloody lot!

At almost thirteen, Billy Hayes began to think he might be handsome. It happened when he realized for the first time that girls were looking at him in the street, and when the prettiest girl in the class, Elsie Peters, unexpectedly passed him a love note. He did not know yet that he was not classically handsome, for his face was too irregularly shaped and featured the infamous Hayes nose. Rather he had the kind of face which made you want to look at how it was put together, and it took a lot of looking to realize it wasn't perfect. It was not his unusual green eyes or his straight white teeth which made girls look twice at Billy: the first thing which struck anyone about his face was its liveliness, the way every feature of his face was fully working. He looked as if his eyes could not be more open, as if his ears wished to catch every sound. This made his face oddly compelling, the kind of face you wished to know.

All at once Billy began taking great pains over his appearance, standing in front of the bathroom mirror to make sure his hair went in the waves he wanted it to go. He admired his hair particularly, and stood for hours brushing it this way and that. He had seen the Hai-long Troupe applying performance make-up, and wondered what his own face would look like made up for a show. Occasionally he caught in his features a glimpse of his father, but stared it down until his own face was reclaimed. He hated it when people said he looked like Jack Hayes, for to Billy his father's face was indivisible from his personality. His cruelty seemed to have broken the bounds of the internal, and seeped into the outward expression of his face. Billy could not imagine what had possessed his mother to marry Jack Hayes in the first place, and could certainly not believe his father's lip might once have turned up in handsome glee.

Billy was pleased to discover that girls looked at *him*, though, that he, Billy Hayes, warranted a second glance in the street. He and Reg walked up Glebe Point Road, turning left into Broadway, admiring girls all the way up George Street and into town. Billy felt that he looked older than Reg, who was, at any rate, Chinese.

'Won't you have to marry a Chinese girl?' asked Billy, imagining that this would leave the pickings to him.

'I'll marry when I fall in love,' replied Reg. 'An Eskimo, an African, a Chinese.'

Billy did not believe this, for he had never known a people so tightly bound. It seemed to him that the Tsangs had imported China with them, that Chinese soil would still be found between the toes of their feet. They weren't Australian in the slightest, the entire continent of Australia had not impressed upon them the tiniest of dents. When he went to lunch at the Tsangs' Billy left Australia and journeyed to a village near Canton, where he sat at a table swallowing clouds. Reg told him that the steamed dumplings were called *wuntun*, which meant 'swallowing a cloud'. Billy watched the *wuntuns* floating in clear soup; clouds on the surface of the sky. Old relatives sat about in high-necked pyjamas, shouting fiercely at each other while Billy waited for Reg to translate. It seemed to Billy there was always some emergency, a catastrophe about to break over their heads. 'That's just the way we talk,' explained Reg. 'Chinese always think you're talking about them if you talk softly.'

Reg's old grandmother, who had recently come from China, smiled vaguely at Billy, although it was clear she did not fully understand his existence. He appeared to be so far beyond what she knew represented a boy that it seemed to Billy she could barely see him. But Reg's two sisters were certainly fully aware of him, as he was of them: to him they were mysterious and beautiful, even though they spoke Australian, like Reg. Lily, the elder, had a languid sensuality, her thin body moved through air with a delirious sway. Billy always engineered to sit next to her, to brush against her thigh so he might feel the heat of her blood.

He sometimes lay in bed at night and thought of Lily, the way she had once told him a secret and her soft mouth had accidentally brushed against his ear. He could no longer recall the secret but he could still feel the slide of her lips and smell her breath, which was strangely sweet, as if she ate nothing but clouds.

Billy and Reg walked all over Sydney, down George Street and into the Rocks, down to the Harbour, where the two halves of the arch of the bridge slowly grew closer. They walked through the Domain and lay on the grass in the Botanical Gardens, thick beneath them like a great field of down. They followed the road up to King's Cross, where women would shoot you for a quid, and went over the hill down into Rushcutter's Bay. But mostly they walked the streets of Glebe, their own pocket, wedged between water and Broadway. They walked to Glebe Point, where the rich people lived, down Talfourd Lane, where the houses lay, block to block. They were from the Glebe, their feet knew it. They were tracing a map, declaring their own shape; two boys, testing edges.

Both Hands out to God

Billy went to every Hai-long performance he was able: to the National in the city, to the Olympia at Bondi Junction, to the Australian just behind Newtown Station. Even if the people of Sydney had less money in their pockets they still managed to put some aside for a show. The Hai-long Troupe shared the bill with dancers and comedians, with Australia's most famous radio stars. Once, Billy watched as the famous comedian Roy 'Mo' Rene played cards only moments before the curtain went up at the National, nonchalantly laying the cards aside before strolling casually on stage.

Reg was top mounter for most of the Hai-long performances but was not allowed to work during the week because of school. Lily and Anona worked full time as winskas, hanging off the sides of the pyramid. They also shared an act with their mother, a Chinese ballet which involved dancing with silk cloth round the stage. The three of them turned silk into water; it rippled and flowed as they ran. Later, Lily was raised to the roof by her father and uncle, who stood on each side of her, a careless hand placed lightly on each thigh.

Billy was allowed to enter by the stage door and watch the show from the wings, as long as he did not get in the way of the set men. They moved props with alarming speed and precision, knowing exactly how to turn a large set around quickly without damage. Billy had once seen a piano stuck in a stairwell for three weeks because of inexpert handling, so he admired their skill. He flattened himself against walls as they moved about him; every show was a flurry of curses and jokes. He was amazed that dancing girls on the stage shouted rude messages to friends in the wings: if Billy had once believed that the audience saw everything, he realized now he had been wrong. The cast had their own private jokes and means of keeping going too, and found ways to amuse themselves as much as the audience.

Billy loved it the moment he stepped through the stage door:

he loved the dressing-rooms with their mousetraps and dirty stockings, he loved the slovenly dresser who stood with a cigarette in her mouth as the lead dancer handed over her clothes. She hooked up the backs of dresses, straightened shoulders and patted bottoms, all the while dragging on a burning cigarette. He loved how the girls took off their clothes with abandon, unbuttoning as they were running from the stage, hardly waiting till they reached the dressing-room to fling aside a lacy top. He saw stockinged legs and garters, the brassièred bosoms of beautiful girls. They hardly seemed to notice his existence, or if they did they smiled, rumpled his hair and said. 'How's it going, gorgeous?'

But Billy didn't love it for the girls only, although their dream forms returned frequently to his bed. He loved it for the movement, for the charge of it, for the dream that he might one day move too. He certainly wanted to astonish someone, to show the world who he truly was.

When Reg told him about the Talent Quest, he simply asked, 'Where? What time?'

'Glebe Town Hall, Saturday fortnight,' Reg replied. 'I think we should do a double act.'

Straight away Billy felt the rush of possibility. Although he was frightened, it seemed the only thing: his first public performance as a tumbler!

There wasn't much time to practise; they devised an act they hoped would prove simple and yet daring. First, Billy balanced Reg in the air above him, their arms straight, hand to hand.

'We'll get the best line if we both stretch out to the fullest, Dad says. I'll point my toes in the air, you reach up as high as you can.'

Low Tsang sat cross-legged on the ground advising them, while Reg translated as he worked. Through Reg, Low Tsang told Billy to push himself straight up to the clouds, as if reaching both hands out to God. 'Your back will arch beautifully. And reach your right leg out behind you – point your toe as far as it will go.'

Their bodies formed a single line vertical to the horizon: Billy arched his neck to look up into Reg's face. He imagined they appeared strong yet graceful, two bodies elegantly striving.

Next, they engineered somersaults, with the aid of a borrowed trampoline. The trampoline added impossible daring, catapulting them high into air. They rolled and turned themselves over, they went free-wheeling absurdly into sky. Billy's legs felt shapely and powerful; an acute happiness shot out of the furthest reaches of his toes. He and Reg jumped to the ground, finishing beautifully. Low Tsang smiled and said, in English, 'Better. Again.'

For their finale, they could not agree on anything, which surprised them both, for it was the first time they had disagreed. Reg wished Billy to balance him atop a pole using his chin, but Billy wanted action, and speed. They tried compromises which did not prove promising; they tried Reg's idea of pole-balancing, but it did not quite come off. 'I need to do something while I'm up there. You know, play a flute or a violin.' But since Reg could play neither, he agreed to give up the idea.

'I know!' cried Billy. 'Let's try that trick we saw at the Majestic.' So they tried the spinning trick they had seen performed by Andrews and Lyttleton, with Reg spinning on his stomach on Billy's bent back. After each spin, Billy swung Reg's body off and around like a rope, then swung him on to his back again. At first they could not quite get the hang of it, with Reg falling off, again and again. But then they began to work in perfect unison, to gain co-ordination and speed. They were bewilderingly fast, one giant oiled muscle, working tumbling hand to tumbling hand.

Jack Hayes was sitting on the veranda, apparently drunk, when Billy came home. 'Where's Who-Flung-Dung?' he called as Billy passed. 'Bugger off,' Billy muttered, under his breath.

'A bloody coolie,' Jack Hayes continued, 'his boyfriend's a bloody Chink.' Billy was glad Reg had not come home with him, that he had turned off before number 61. For four years, Billy had successfully kept Reg Tsang from his father, and had no plans to do otherwise.

'How was practice?' asked his mother, and Billy told her all he knew. She still listened as if you were telling her the world's greatest secret; she still looked at you as if you were divine.

Reg's eldest sister, Lily, came on Sunday to watch them. Their father wasn't there, so she lit a cigarette. Billy worked hard at gaining her admiration, even though she was seventeen years old and must regard him as a boy. Nevertheless he wanted her to look at him using all the powers of her eyes. Lily's hair hung like a shiny cap around her face, cigarette smoke weaved about her head. Billy and Reg went through the act with precision, but Billy was conscious of Lily Tsang the whole time. They worked fast, fuelled by confidence: when they finished, Lily stubbed out yet another cigarette, and clapped.

'Good, Reg, only *smile* more. Finish smiling, like Billy does.' Reg blew air from his mouth in exasperation, threw a towel round his neck and sat down.

'Girls need to smile, Lily. I don't,' he said, wiping his face. 'Anyway Hayes is only smiling because he's showing off.'

Billy blushed, and kicked him. 'Speak for yourself, Tsang! I've never seen such a show-off as you!' He lay back on the grass till the blood left his face: he hated to blush, he felt so foolish.

'What colour's red?' Reg teased, and Billy wished himself dead. Reg is such an idiot, he thought to himself; he was such a bloody idiot, Billy wondered why Reg Tsang was his best friend at all. He sat up and glared at Reg, who did not see, having wrapped the towel completely round his head.

Lily smiled at Billy. 'We'd better get home,' she said, standing up. 'A-Ting's coming for tea.' Reg dropped the towel and picked up the end of the trampoline; he stood there, waiting for Billy to take the other end.

Finally Billy stood up too and helped Reg move the trampoline over to the joss-house, where they leant it on its side and covered it with a tarpaulin. When they had finished, Lily asked Billy if he wanted to come home with them for tea. He said he would but was careful to address only Lily, and not look at that idiot once.

The Tsangs had a small red shrine in one corner of their lounge-room in which joss-sticks constantly burnt. Mrs Tsang left offerings to household gods there, jars of eternal bamboo, oranges; once, Billy had seen a whole cooked chicken. Whenever he entered the room he looked at the shrine with interest, never knowing what he might see.

Mrs Tsang kept everything, she threw nothing away. The Tsangs' backyard was littered with what Billy regarded as garbage: rusted bicycles beyond repair, cracked chamber-pots, items of furniture riddled with woodworm. It was as if the Tsangs were preparing for some world-wide disaster, when Sydney broke down and street lamps no longer worked, when Glebe was reduced to rubble. It seemed to Billy that the Tsangs had plans to rebuild from scratch, so that they never knew when the odd piece of wood or a broken bicycle spoke might come in handy.

The Tsangs ate quickly and noisily around a circular table, resting their bowls against their lower lips and shovelling in large amounts of food. At first this struck Billy as bad manners, for his mother was always telling him not to bolt his dinner. But he was deft himself now, and believed it to be the best way of eating. It stripped mealtimes of ornament, you sat down in order to get food into your mouth.

He shovelled food now with chopsticks, watching Lily over the rim of his bowl. She ate rice and looked back at him: he thought he heard the sound of chopsticks hitting her small curved teeth. Her wrists were frail, unbelievably thin; he imagined that if he tried to enclose one, his thumb and index finger would form nothing but a circle of air.

A-Ting proved to be the oldest woman Billy had ever seen, a cracked statue who ate as if human. She sat next to Lily and looked at Billy through small black marbles; folds of skin covered what he presumed to be her eyes. Lily next to her appeared new born, tender, alive. Together they represented both ends of the cycle, but to Billy, Lily Tsang's body alone ran with blood.

The boys discussed how the act was going; Lily was enthusiastic and pronounced it great. 'They'll win for sure,' she said with certainty.

'Shut up, Lily,' Reg protested. 'You'll bring us bad luck.' Reg was superstitious, much to Billy's amusement; he believed in omens and signs. He advised Billy to move his bed away from his bedroom doorway, for example, because it was bad *fung shui* for a door to open straight on to a bed.

'Why?' Billy asked, and Reg sighed as if Billy were stupid. 'Because ghosts have an easier passage. You must make it harder for them to walk around.'

'You're worse than my mother,' Billy replied, but afterwards he moved his bed, just in case.

When they finished eating, Reg stood up. 'I'll walk you home.'

Billy immediately thought of his father, and stood too. 'Oh, it's OK. Really.'

Reg shrugged his shoulders and sat down again; Lily lowered her eyes.

'See you tomorrow, then,' Billy called from the doorway, but Reg was already talking Chinese to A-Ting. He seemed to Billy already a different person, someone who dwelt in a place where Billy could never travel.

Outside in the street Billy lowered his shoulders, feeling the tension leave his body at once. Always when he was with other people his body knotted, becoming over-alert, tightly wound. He never relaxed, not even with the Tsangs. Other people to Billy Hayes always induced a kind of physical strain. Only when he was in motion did Billy feel any sense of relief, and sometimes when he was alone with Reg. Then, his body surprised him: he would realize that his muscles felt comfortable, and were not tensed as though he was about to run. Billy liked this feeling, and liked Reg for it, although how he might tell Reg he could not begin to say.

He walked home, once again quietly breathing, and was at the top of the street under a street lamp when Lily Tsang called his name. She called softly, as if from a long distance: he took a while to understand that her voice was not in his own head.

Billy turned around and watched as she came toward him. She was alone, moving quickly; moving as only Lily Tsang could. He waited for her to reach him; part of him had expected her coming, and had been ready for it all this time.

The day of the Talent Quest Billy Hayes woke nervous, convinced. He was still young enough to believe in his talent to astonish, to turn eyes to look hard upon himself. He got up and left the house early, before the day had realized it was day. He walked fast down to the water and threw small stones as far as they could go. He liked morning, its shivering potential, its sense of movement and possible escape. A fifteen-year-old boy might rejoice in early morning, feeling himself to rival the dawn. Billy picked up a stone and made a bet with himself: if the stone got as far as a certain point in the water, they would win; if it did not, they would lose.

He reached his arm back and threw the stone as hard as he

could, using his body's whole strength. It raced past the point, and flew far, far beyond, rushing, it seemed to him, toward victory.

At six o'clock he was in his room dressing when his father came and stood at the door. Billy pretended he hadn't seen him and continued to pull on his pumps, bending down to do up the strap. He was sitting on his bed but even from that distance he smelt alcohol, the unmistakable mix of certain chemicals in the human gut.

Billy fiddled with his shoes for as long as possible before he was forced to lift his head. His father's tall figure leant against the door frame; a cigarette hung from his lip.

'You really think you're something special, don't you?' he began, while Billy calmly continued to comb his hair. He willed himself to hold his hand steady, to think of that moment when he would suddenly be made graceful, indistinguishable from the earth's air. If he could only pass beyond this danger he knew he would find himself safe; holding the comb carefully, Billy drew a neat split in his hair, revealing the white flesh beneath.

'If you could only see yourself,' Jack Hayes sneered. 'You look like a fucking girl.'

Billy walked to the cupboard and got out his bags, as he moved he felt the arch of his spine. The breath rushed within his lungs; he felt the full reach of his legs. It seemed to him that his stride was huge, that a great energy surged up from his feet.

'Think you're going to meet your boyfriend, do you?' Jack Hayes said, and something in his voice made Billy turn his head and look into his father's eyes for the first time. All at once Billy saw his intention and it was suddenly vital that he succeed in passing through that door. He rushed forward, but his father's body stopped him, his father's great fist came down upon him, knocking him straight off his feet.

Billy Hayes immediately stood up again and charged a second time: once again his father stopped him, once again he found himself on the floor. His eyes filled with tears, but he got up, propelled by an act of his will.

'You bastard!' Billy roared as he put his head down and rammed Jack Hayes hard in the chest.

From somewhere in the house Billy Hayes heard a cry and it was this cry he was to remember from the night he did not make it to the Talent Quest, this cry above all he did not forget.

A Big Life

Billy had never had a proper girlfriend, only crushes on girls from afar. All of a sudden there was Lily Tsang, who knew exactly what he must do. If Billy had once imagined a Chinese girl was like a flower he soon found out he was wrong: Lily Tsang was meat and bones, all right, more substantial than any flower Billy might name. Her thin wrists had a certain dedication, her black eyes a certain aim. She was two years older than Billy, and knew all about boys. For ever after it seemed to him that he had simply lain back in Lily Tsang's arms, confident she knew the way.

She was a mature, confident sort of girl but mercifully also a chatterbox. Lily never noticed Billy's clumsy silences, being so busy talking herself. Lily Tsang told him all sorts of unrelated things, everything came out in a jumble, about a great-uncle who took fireworks to the gold fields of Victoria, her old boyfriends, how the Chinese believed there were certain days all ghosts were released from hell.

Billy did not ask her if she had talked about him to Reg, for he had certainly not said anything himself. What was there to say anyway, Billy thought – that he had kissed his forward elder sister once or twice?

One afternoon, some weeks after Lily had followed Billy home, he and Lily arranged to meet behind the church in Glebe. All the young people of Glebe went there if they wanted to be alone: it was hidden from the street and you could stay there for hours, kissing and holding hands. They had already met there twice before and kissed without doing anything further.

Billy was pleased to see that no one else was around, and leant back against a sun-warmed wall. Lily kicked a few stones away then sat down too, holding Billy's hand and chattering on about her first boyfriend, a Hungarian dancer she had met doing a show at the Olympia.

'We spent the whole time trying to stop Dad finding out,' she said, 'but I think Mum knew.'

Billy was silent and wondered if he should add a reminiscence of his own, about some old girlfriend who had sadly moved away. He began inventing a story in his head at once, even imagining the tender words this dear girl had written to him on a postcard.

Suddenly Lily stopped talking and lifted his hand to her breast: it was the first time he had felt a girl's bosom. All at once his hand grew heavy, yet he found himself unable to move it. He felt she must find the weight unbearable, his own dumb and senseless hand pressing down against all her lightness. His palms began to sweat, he could not feel anything except his own failure, his inability to know what to do next. Right at that moment Lily gently released his hand, and raised it to the side of her face. 'You're a funny boy,' she said, not without kindness. 'You don't have to if you don't want to.'

He was supposed to say that! He was the boy, the one supposed to plead, the one supposed to woo girls with kindness. He leant forward and kissed Lily Tsang hard on the lips: the soft flesh of them pressed flat beneath his own. He moved his hand back to her hard little breast and felt the warmth of her beneath his open palm.

Suddenly it was all right, his body came alive, he felt all his senses, every working detail within his own self. Billy Hayes discovered he had known the way all along, even though his body had never before travelled in that direction.

He entered into an erotic daze. At school he sat at his desk and thought of Lily, her personal landscape, the way her gums showed slightly when she laughed. Once he lay for hours with her under a blanket on the grass in Wentworth Park and had the sensation of being immersed, of floating endlessly on his own pleasure. When he stood up he was a drowning man brought to the surface, and all he wanted was to plunge to the bottom once again. He was tracing the shape of her, his original woman, learning the secret lines of Lily Tsang.

She seemed to want him too, although he could not fully believe it, and part of him expected her to walk away at any time. She told him she liked his face. 'You look so hopeful,' she said and afterward he inspected himself for a long time in the mirror, trying to see exactly what she meant.

One Saturday evening when the Hai-long Troupe had a booking at the Australian, Lily feigned a sudden sickness and stayed home. Billy arrived at the door half an hour later by prearrangement and they walked quickly to Lily's room and closed the door. Inside this room they completed their journey, their bodies leading them forward. Billy held Lily Tsang, her slender bones, her breath of clouds, and dared not move for all the happiness inside him.

The following Thursday Billy walked through the lion gates to see Reg. He saw him talking to Low Tsang in a far corner; Billy whistled, and Reg looked up. But instead of waving as he normally did, Reg turned straight back to his father.

'Hello,' said Billy as he came closer, but Reg still did not respond. 'Cat got your tongue?' Billy asked as he sat down.

'Lily's over there,' Reg said. 'You came to see her, didn't you?'

Billy blushed and looked away. 'I came to see *you*, fishface.' Low Tsang smiled at Billy, repeating the word. 'Fishface,' he said. 'Very good.'

Billy smiled; Reg did too, before he caught himself and rearranged his features.

'Don't smile, will you?' Billy goaded. 'Don't smile, you might crack your stupid old fishface.'

'Fishface!' Low Tsang cried loudly, breaking into a high laugh. 'Fishface!' he cried happily, and both boys began to laugh with him.

The Tivoli was Billy's favourite theatre until the Depression finally closed it down. It was a small theatre, you could hear everything, no seat was ever far from the stage. The Tiv had all the imported acts: from London, from Spain, from New York. There were comedy acts, there were contortionists, there were piano players and men who could break free of chains. Long Tack Sam did illusions, swinging beautiful Chinese girls by their pigtails or putting needles in his mouth together with cotton threads. He drank a glass of water, put the glass down and pulled the needles out, all threaded. Billy couldn't work out how he did it, but Reg said he'd seen Long Tack putting the needles in his mouth already threaded. Billy thought it was an astonishing feat all the same, drinking a glass of water with your mouth full of threaded needles.

Billy watched all the acts with fascination but sometimes turned in his seat to look back at the crowd. It seemed to him a remarkable thing to be able to conjure up wonder with your bare hands, and he began to wish that one day he might do it too.

Billy went often to the Glebe Town Hall after the Tiv closed, usually with Lily and Reg. He sat between them, conscious of balance, careful not to tilt to one side. He did not wish to offend either of them but sensed there was some struggle going on as both tried to claim him as their own. And yet Lily's physical presence always disarmed him, and he sometimes found himself overcompensating by ignoring her altogether, precisely because he was conscious of her breathing lungs so close beside him.

But Reg always ignored Lily, talking only to Billy, bringing his attention to things he thought Billy should know. He told Billy that the Town Hall had a dead stage, for example, in that the stage floor had no bounce. 'It'd be hopeless for tumbling,' he said in a loud whisper. 'I'm glad we never did that Talent Quest. Just listen to the falls!' Billy did not like to think of the night of the Talent Quest so he concentrated on watching the floor, listening for hard falls: Reg was right, even with mats you could hear them.

If Reg ignored Lily, she ignored him back, staring at some point past his head. 'He's just a boy,' she said to Billy once, as if he wasn't too, and a full year younger than Reg. He supposed he had told a kind of white lie to Lily, in letting her go on believing he was the same age as Reg. It wasn't as if he ever told lies deliberately: Billy only invented stories to save himself, or to appear more interesting than he felt he actually was. He believed he could not stand alone without embellishment, for he did not trust anyone to like him unadorned. He hated being at school when Lily had already left, and did everything to avoid letting her see him leaving the school gate. He hoped like anything she and Reg would not compare notes, so she would find out accidentally that he was really only fifteen.

After the show the three of them often walked down to Pyrmont, where great ships lay tethered like beasts. Their enormous hulls rose up from the water, bound for Shanghai, London and

New York. They were symbols of possibilities, of the future; the three of them watched the ships for hours, making plans.

'I'll sail on the *Queen Mary* when she's finished,' announced Lily. 'I'll go right up the Bund, into Shanghai.'

Reg thought he would go to New York, to see the Statue of Liberty and the Empire State. 'Where would you like to go, Billy?'

'Nowhere,' Billy answered, picking up a bottle top. 'Oh, anywhere, I guess.'

He dared not confess the enormity of his ambitions, how large his plans really were. Anyone could have an ordinary life, but Billy Hayes wanted an extraordinary one, to go everywhere and do everything. He wanted to run away and start his big life at once but would bide his time until his moment came.

In March the Sydney Harbour Bridge was opened and, like a lot of other people, the Hayes family could get no closer than Walsh Bay, despite leaving the house at 6.30 in the morning. The streets were swarming, for the whole of Sydney had turned out. Trams were impossible to squeeze on to; motor cars stalled in the streets. Saph and the children ended up walking all the way to the Quay, where they decided to catch the world's most overloaded ferry across to the other side first. The ferry listed dangerously, as all the passengers moved to the bridge side to have a look. The ferrymen blew whistles and shouted at everyone to move away; one side of the boat grazed the water, until women panicked and fled.

Suddenly the bridge was high above them, its stone pylons stacked against the sky. 'It's the biggest bridge in the whole world!' Bede declared, but Cec said he was wrong, it was the longest. 'You're all wrong,' put in Billy. 'It's the world's longest *single span* bridge.'

'Oh, put a sock in it, you boys,' said their mother. 'It's magnificent, whatever it is.' And it was: the Sydney Harbour Bridge was extraordinary, its steel arch blooming in the sky. Billy raised his head and screwed his eyes up: plain men had built it, block upon extraordinary block.

Because they could only get as close as a pier at Walsh Bay, the family did not see the rebel from the New Guard swoop down on his horse to cut the ribbon with his sword, beating the official dignitary waiting with his jewelled scissors. But Saph Hayes swore she heard a roar at the appropriate moment, and stuck to her story the rest of her life: she was a witness to history and proud of it, even if the main thing she remembered about that day was that the man standing next to her was decidedly whiffy, and she'd spent the best part of four hours trying to breathe in through her mouth instead of her nose.

Billy remembered the opening of the Sydney Harbour Bridge for another reason, for some months after this his old life came to an end. In his mind, the two events became jumbled, so that years later he often dreamt of sailing out of Sydney Harbour amid jubilation, on a blue day with many people waving.

On the day of the bridge opening, Saph and the children got home about ten, to find the house in darkness. 'Jack?' Saph called, but there was no reply. Jack Hayes rarely went out by himself, night or day, but Saph checked every room just in case. There was no note, or evidence of drinking, but neither was there evidence of her husband.

'Maybe he went after all,' suggested Mary, but Saph thought this unlikely. 'What a lot of hoo-ha over a bloody bridge,' Jack Hayes had said only the night before while she was making sandwiches. Saph busied herself getting tea, but no one was particularly hungry. Cecil was only home five minutes before he went out without so much as a thank you. 'Cec!' Saph called as he slammed the front door. She sighed and said, 'You've got to have the patience of Job.'

Within an hour everyone was asleep except for Cec and Jack, who were still out, and Saph, who lay awake, waiting. She knew there was something up, but she could not quite put her finger on what it was.

Billy was practising full twisters on the lawn with Reg, perfect back somersaults with a full twist. He could do them with ease, one after another; Reg bet him he couldn't do fifty full twisters in a row. Reg stopped counting when Billy reached seventy-two. 'That's enough!' he shouted. 'You win!'

Billy's muscles ached with the effort, but he could have gone on to reach one hundred. When he stopped, Reg asked Billy if he knew who the lady was, standing at the lion gates watching.

'Never seen her before,' Billy said. 'She's not from round here, though.' The woman had a fox fur settled around her shoulders, she looked rich and haughty. The two boys stopped to watch her; she did not acknowledge them but turned her head and beckoned someone they could not see. A man appeared and stood next to her, dressed in a bright white suit.

'Jings,' Reg said, 'look at that.' Billy thought the man looked dashing, his suit gave off its own light. The boys stared until Billy decided to resume his practice: he did neck rolls and twisters, round off flip-flaps and more full twisters. His body worked hard and obeyed him; he performed for the lady with the fox fur and the man in the white suit, he performed as if in Carnegie Hall. Billy flew and rolled, feeling in his heart how long he must keep turning. After each roll, he finished as if amidst thunderous applause, bowing to an imaginary crowd. Reg did not join in but watched Billy, sitting cross-legged before him on the ground.

When Billy finally stopped he looked toward the lion gates: the man and the woman had gone, there was no one watching from the gates at all.

A few days later, Billy came home from school and found his mother crying. He had never seen her cry before, and was alarmed. Her infamous nose was red and swollen: she looked more than ever as if she were wearing a false nose.

'What's wrong, Mum?' he asked, dropping his bag.

'Don't bother her,' said Eth, who always liked a good crisis.

'Are you all right?' he persisted, moving closer and patting her tentatively on the shoulder. As he did this, she began to cry harder. Billy drew back his hand in fright.

'She's all right, Billy,' Ethel said loudly. 'Can't you see I'm taking care of her?' Billy looked uncertainly at his weeping mother, shrugged and walked to his room.

When he opened his bedroom door he saw an old suitcase lying on top of his bed, his tumbling pumps neatly placed beside it. He walked over to the suitcase and opened the lid; inside were all his clothes. His body began to tremble and he sat down on the bed, placing his head on his knees as he had been taught when in danger of fainting. He heard sounds very clearly, the chirping of birds, the sound of a motor, far off. He saw everything in his room with the utmost precision, as if all the colours and lines of the furniture, the bedspread, the curtains had been redefined and newly drawn. He knew that disaster had come and that he was living it, that his life had been moving inexorably toward this one point.

Billy stood up and went to the doorway. He looked at his room, every item in it, before closing the door and going back to the kitchen table to comfort his mum.

Saph Hayes came to Pyrmont to see him off, along with Auntie Eva and Uncle Arthur, Mary, Ethel and Ellen and every single member of the Tsang family. Billy viewed everyone as if from a great distance: some vital part of himself had temporarily shut down, so that he felt oddly removed from them, as though they were merely acquaintances he had not met for some time. He saw that his mother looked small and somehow diminished, that her lip trembled and her nose was red from crying, her face made ugly by some great internal effort. The Tsangs appeared to him in all their strangeness, and he momentarily wondered how he could have become close to a people so different from himself. He noticed again their Chineseness, their alien faces, their foreign souls so far removed from his own.

The *Kitano Maru* was as large as the Harbour Bridge, its decks as wide as George Street. Reg wanted to explore further, asking Billy to come with him, but Billy said he would have plenty of time to look later. Everyone came into his cabin and marvelled at the portholes; Ethel tested his bed and pronounced it too hard. Lily hung back, crumpling a handkerchief. Billy observed that she had been crying too. He could not look at her and turned his head away, all his love locked up inside him.

Afterwards, when the whistle had blown and the cabin boys had cleared everyone from the ship, Billy Hayes stood on the deck looking down on his family and friends. The man in the white suit stood on one side of him, the lady with the fox fur stood on the other. They had given Saph Hayes their word they would take good care of him: she could do nothing more since Jack Hayes had already signed the contract and received an advance of twenty-five pounds. If there had a been a moment when Billy Hayes might have resisted, he had chosen not to, for here at last was his longed-for escape in disguise. Mr Vernon Rome and Miss Connie Connor would assume responsibility for taking him to London, and feed and clothe him; they promised Saph they would treat him as if he were their own son.

Billy Hayes stood on the deck and escape did not feel as he had dreamt it. He thought he might die as he stood there, that his heart might stop beating from grief. As the ship moved away, a single sound broke involuntarily from his lips. The man and woman on either side of him left him. Billy Hayes bent his head back and wept.

It seemed to take hours for the ship to reach Sydney Harbour, to move slowly through the waters of Darling Harbour, away from Glebe Point where he had sat with his mother, away from Rozelle Bay. It moved slowly through the water, rounded Dawes Point and came up under the Sydney Harbour Bridge. Billy walked to the furthermost point, at the prow, and looked up. The ship passed under the bridge as if in slow motion, he could see the bolts and steel girders, its full belly. Coming out, the *Kitano Maru* emerged into Sydney Harbour proper: he saw the peaks of cathedrals, the grass of the Botanical Gardens, Circular Quay, all the ferries. A southerly buster was blowing straight into his face, his eyes streamed with tears in the wind. Billy turned away from the city and looked across to North Head, where he saw the quarantine station, just like he did every time he caught the ferry to Manly. But this time he was not going past the Heads, he was sailing right through them, into the waters of the world. The sea began to swell as the *Kitano Maru* entered the Heads; the huge ship began to delicately roll. Billy watched the surf crashing at the base of the great stone cliffs; the sky was streaked purple, blue and grey. As the ship sailed through the Heads, he looked to the horizon, seeing nothing: in panic he turned his head back but found he could no longer see Sydney. It was then that he realized Auntie Eva had pressed something into his hand and that he still held it: he opened his palm to find a carefully folded ten pound note.

William Sly Hayes turned to the wide expanse of the horizon.

He was fifteen years old, a tumbler, a frightened boy leaving his entire known world.

PART 2

Over Seas

Lost at Sea

Miss Connie Connor was a woman who had just turned twenty-five and a man had told her yesterday that twenty-five was a dangerous age for a woman. She had asked him why, and why this applied only to women, but he had merely smiled and said she would find out soon enough. Most certainly Miss Connie Connor felt dangerous but she had felt dangerous every year of her life. She prided herself on living adventurously, even if at twenty-five she already knew the price of adventure was sometimes impossibly high. It was nerve that had rescued the former Gladys Wilson from a life like her mother's, sealed up with a boring husband in a semi-detached in Liverpool and never a trip to London in her life, but also nerve that brought Miss Connie Connor to a cheerless rented room in Brixton, its single bed empty most nights. At twenty-five she already knew that it might all come to nothing, yet what kept her going was that it also might not. She was still willing to take a risk and live dangerously, to dream a life vivid and free. Miss Connie Connor had already seen Africa, the great pyramids of the Nile; she had been to New York and Rome, and once witnessed the King of Spain pick a thread of chicken from his teeth with a match. She might not have a house and a husband like her mother, nor money beyond her next pay, but what she had was all right. She sucked on her cigarette and leant over the ship's railing, turning her face to the moon. She was sailing on sweet currents which were eventually bound for China and the Arabian Sea. Miss Connie Connor was a million miles from Kirkby, Liverpool, and if she died right now at least she could say she had tried.

In his bunk, Mr Vernon Rome was counting his money. He had his English pounds carefully tied with a ribbon, his Japanese notes still folded down the back of one shoe. He was a handsome, rather heavy-set man of twenty-six, with an accent which swam between

London and Hollywood. Actually he was Australian but had learnt to hide it after years of living in London.

Vernon Rome was well known in certain quarters as a ladies' man and, three days out of Sydney, he had already sussed out where to strike. That bosomy young mother was a goer, he was sure of it: no husband for twelve bloody weeks! Vernon Rome had left three wives and seven children but swore that he'd married for the last time. He believed women always started out nice as pie and then turned on you, showering you with impossible demands. Recently he had decided to leave them at the nice as pie stage, and make do on his own from now on.

But if women were Vernon Rome's passion, tumbling was his truest love. Even Connie had not understood this, and he'd have sworn she was a woman with more sense. Bringing the boy into the act had been a stroke of genius, even if he did say so himself.

He got up from the bed and carefully hid his money. Before going out the door Vernon Rome looked in the mirror. Satisfied, he left the room.

Billy had not long found his sea legs. He learnt to roll with the ship, ride it like he rode a wave, to treat the wood beneath his feet as kindly. He had explored the ship in great detail, from the engine room where he was supposedly not allowed to the crews' kitchen where the Japanese crewmen ate live creatures and thin translucent noodles. They somehow caught fish and laid them cooked on newspaper, eating the heads and eyes. He sat at their tables in speechless agreement; they fed him small morsels as if he were some breed of dog. The sounds of their language swelled about his head; he rocked on their words, lost at sea.

Billy walked the wooden decks following the cabin crew; he stood in the Captain's cabin following maps. He saw tide drifts and monsoon colours; the outlines of great lands. He saw the arbitrary line which divided the world neatly into hemispheres, and the lines of his own country whose shape he knew by heart. In his head he recited the names of the great New South Wales rivers, the Richmond, Clarence and Macleay; at night when he closed his eyes he saw the flat dun colours of the bush outside Hornsby, paper barks peeling in the sun. He watched other boys attended by their fathers, families playing croquet on deck. He wore his white tumbling pumps at all times, together with a new striped blazer he had found at the bottom of his bag. He walked the decks as if he were used to it, his hand in his left pocket, clenching and unclenching his fist.

Mr Rome and Miss Connor sat with him every night at dinner, and Mr Rome told him all about their variety act. But Billy could not raise his eyes long enough to look clearly at them, and for the first week he had only the merest recollection of their faces. He was never hungry and waited only for dinner to be over, every muscle in his body straining to attention. He began to fear dinnertime long before the dinner bell rang, so that by the time it sounded he was already in a state of nervous alert. Each night he sat at the table in temporary blindness, too panicked to look up.

Nevertheless by the second week Billy had the impression Miss Connor was beautiful, forever smoking her long cigarettes and looking away. He sometimes raised his eyes long enough to notice that she wore long silky dresses which revealed the outline of her figure, a little dead fox hung apparently permanently round her neck. Its mouth was shut in a malicious grin, its eyes were dim yet conniving.

Billy's waking life aboard the *Kitano Maru* had an unreality, for he could not yet believe where he was. It was as if he were living out some other boy's life and his true self still walked the streets of Glebe. He did not think of his sisters or his mother; he did not think of Lily or his best friend, Reginald Tsang. His body seemed to have reverted to its biological existence, in that it slept, it ate, it produced waste. He got up and walked as if normal, his muscles and bones kept him straight. If he lived beyond biology, it was in the private small moments of dawn: the light rose up and relieved him, throwing frail glory about his head. Half asleep, he imagined a great wave of pure sunlight real as matter, thrown through the window in a perfect arc. He opened his eyes to the morning, reclaiming himself and the world; he lay for long moments quietly breathing, safe in his own skin, at rest. Inexplicably at such moments he also divined his own terror; he shut his eyes hard against grief.

Mr Rome banged on Billy's door one morning before Billy had risen from bed. 'Just a second,' he called, pushing the covers aside and making sure the fly on his pyjama pants was properly closed. 'Yes?' he inquired, standing at the cabin door furtively, looking out at Mr Rome through the narrowest of gaps.

'Well, open the bloody door, lad,' boomed Mr Rome, pushing past him. 'I won't bite.' The two young men with whom Billy shared the room rolled in their beds: the older one, Digger, lifted his head and peered at Mr Rome. 'Listen, mate, this might be a third-class cabin, but it doesn't mean you can come banging in any time you damn well like.'

'Oh yes I can,' declared Mr Rome. 'I am this young man's legal guardian.' Digger looked at Billy and shook his dishevelled head. 'Better you than me, mate. Now bugger off!' he said to Mr Rome.

Mr Rome ignored him, instructing Billy to get dressed for practice and to meet him on the upper deck in ten minutes. 'Ten minutes, Billy,' he warned, stepping outside. 'Sharp.'

The upper deck was wide and empty, the boards already warm from the sun. Mr Rome had mapped out a practice space near two large funnels, next to a wooden container and the ship's sirens. Billy saw Miss Connor dressed in a green silk bra and frilled shorts, stretching a long limb behind her. Her blonde hair was set on her head in a myriad of shiny ripples, she wore on her eyelashes a curled row of false hair. She smiled at Billy and lifted her leg up sideways to touch her chin with her toes, stretching both arms up above her. Her foot was encased in a pale pink satin slipper, and rested at the point of her chin; the leg appeared to belong to somebody else, so improbable was the angle from her body. Billy had seen contortionists before but had never known one as unlikely as Miss Connie Connor. As he watched, she gently lowered her leg and began to walk on her hands, bending her body back up over her head until her feet rested against each side of her lovely white face. Framed by her own feet, she walked the deck on her hands, smiling prettily between pink slippers.

Billy leant against the railing, waiting for further instructions. Mr Rome laid out the practice mat and achieved a few creaky somersaults before beckoning Billy to join him. He whistled to Miss Connor, who responded with a bark. She unwound herself back to human dimensions and retrieved a crushed cigarette and a small box of matches tucked up inside the elastic leg of her pants.

'Don't whistle at me, Vernon,' she said when she joined them. 'I have got a name.'

Vernon Rome looked at Billy and raised his eyebrows. 'Yes, Miss Connor,' he said without looking at her. 'Can we start now, please?'

She cast her eyes over the horizon, resting an elbow on the edge of the rail. Her mouth was crimson and turned down slightly at the edges, her nails were long and painted red. She had a wonderful ability to remove herself from any situation, so that she stood at the rail as if alone: she did not acknowledge Vernon Rome's presence and might have been contemplating maths.

'Connie!' called Mr Rome, snapping his fingers in front of her face. 'Are you home?'

She idly turned her head, brushing away his hand. 'Well?' she said. 'Get on with it!'

Vernon Rome looked at her and rolled his eyes in exasperation. 'Here's how I see it,' he said like a criminal. 'We'll work the kid into a Risley act and bring in the trampoline as well.'

'What'll the trampoline do?' Connie Connor asked, smiling sweetly, but Vernon Rome ignored her and went on. 'We'll have to get new costumes. I thought something Russian, with boots and waistcoats and the like.'

Connie Connor did not say anything but looked at Billy and winked. He blushed and moved his lips oddly in embarrassment, compressing and twisting them about. His head felt hot and swollen; he hoped he would not have to speak. He felt he would say something stupid, or that no words would come out at all. He knew himself to be impossibly young, an impostor, a boy from Glebe who knew nothing of professional acts. In panic he wondered when they would realize this, when they would see he had no ideas of his own: his saliva dried up and his hands sweated, he had not heard anything Mr Rome had to say. He looked up at Mr Rome and Miss Connor in a frenzy, trying to quell the frantic movements of his mind. He thought only of the safety of his cabin, the four sides of his known bed. He turned, muttering, 'Excuse me', and ran down the length of the deck.

'Hey!' he heard Mr Rome calling, but Billy Hayes kept running, he ran until he reached cabin 36C.

He stayed inside all morning, pretending to be asleep when Mr

Rome knocked. He lay under the covers waiting for Mr Rome to go away, then sat up in bed and played cards. About midday he heard the key turn, and scrambled quickly under the bedclothes. He rolled to the wall, his eyes closed, and heard the voices of Digger and Mr Rome.

'He's OK,' whispered Digger. 'See, he's asleep.' Billy felt Mr Romes's warm breath at his ear, the pull of the sheets as he leant across the bed. Billy's eyelids fluttered and he deepened his breathing, making as much noise as he could breathing out.

'Must be seasick,' Mr Rome said quietly. 'We'd better get the doctor to have a look.'

Billy lay quietly and waited for them to leave; when he heard the door close he turned around. Digger was sitting on the other bed watching him. He smiled when he saw Billy's face.

'I can tell a shyster when I see one,' he said gently. 'Now come on, mate. What's up?'

Billy looked at him and shrugged his shoulders. 'Nothing,' he said. He wanted to tell Digger Crew everything, how his own father had shipped him off for twenty-five pounds, but he feared if he opened his mouth he would not survive the virulence of the deluge, so he lay there and did not say a word.

Digger got up and sat next to Billy. 'Want to play cards?' he asked, dealing out.

After dinner, he heard Miss Connor call him. 'Are you decent?' she asked through the door. Billy got up and let her in, returning to bed and pulling up the covers.

'How're you feeling?' she asked, not waiting for an answer. 'Here, I bought you some butterscotch.' She tossed a packet on the bed and began to walk around the room, lifting things up and inspecting them.

'I'm always fascinated by boys' rooms. I didn't have any brothers, you know.' She picked up Digger's shaving brush, rubbing it gently in the nape of her neck.

'I've got a sister, Grace. She's got four boys, and another one on the way. God forbid that she should have a girl – her boys are savages, they'd kill it.'

Billy sat stiffly in his bed watching her, his hands neatly placed at his sides. Miss Connor appeared to take up more space than three young men combined, with her bright hair and double-jointed body. She commanded more air than most humans, the full use of oxygen and light. Her voice was low and charged with authority; she moved through the room, talking loudly.

'You can call me Connie,' she said with her back to him, bending down to look shamelessly through cupboards. She turned around holding a bottle of Digger's cologne, which she proceeded to open and slap on her wrists.

'Vernon's all right,' she said unexpectedly, 'he's just a fool, that's all.' She sat on a chair and lit a cigarette, blowing smoke absent-mindedly at the ceiling. The ever present fox lay strangled down one shoulder, its paws pointing mournfully at the carpet.

'I was in love with him once,' she said matter-of-factly, 'but I used to leave thistles out for Father Christmas once too.' She laughed. 'You grow up, don't you?'

Billy smiled wondering what she would say next: he had never heard such clever conversation. He watched her in fascination, the whole pale lot of her, here, in cabin 36C. He hoped that Digger would come in and see her, sitting in the chair and talking only to him.

He listened to the shape of her accent, the odd way her words fell about. He understood the words but not their delivery, rendered different by Miss Connor's Liverpudlian tongue. It was clear she was speaking English, but an English unknown to him. He listened with rapt attention, while she talked about Cossack shirts and boots.

'You can help me shop in Alexandria,' she continued. 'You'll come in handy fighting off men.'

She stubbed out her cigarette and stood up, rearranging the fox in the mirror.

'I'll see you in the morning, then, my love. Nine o'clock on the top deck. OK?' She left the room without waiting for an answer: the room smelt of cologne and smoke.

At five to nine Billy made a decision: he dressed quickly and ran up the stairs. He saw Miss Connor and Mr Rome on the tumbling felt as he rounded the corner: Miss Connor was astride Mr Rome's back. She was balancing on her hands from his shoulders, pointing her slippers to God. The satin was worn and discoloured;

their soles carried marks from the floor. Around her left calf was a bandage, and he knew that tucked up the leg of her green frilled pants would be a box of matches and three crumpled cigarettes. Billy saw that Mr Vernon Rome was a bit too heavy for a tumbler, and that his skin was shiny in the heat: nevertheless Billy Hayes moved towards him, his tumbler's pumps embracing his feet.

Vernon Rome looked up at him and nodded, and it seemed to Billy that in this nod was a welcome he was only now ready to receive.

Reckless and Willing

It was a rainy morning toward the end of his third week at sea when Billy dared to lift his head. The sea moved endlessly around him, the sky was wide and emptied of birds. He suddenly realized he was free of both the past and the future, for he certainly had no immediate means of reclaiming his past, and no idea of what his future might hold. For the first time he felt the nudge of curiosity, the tentative butt of courage. It occurred to him that he was moving irretrievably forward, caught up in something unknown. For one brief moment Billy Hayes was not frightened and leant against the rail, this new feeling bringing him a strange comfort.

Every morning at breakfast he sat next to Digger, who did not fail to eat three bowls of porridge heaped with sugar followed by at least six slices of thickly buttered toast. 'Don't mind if I do,' Digger said every day to their table waiter, Akiko, who now offered him another rack of toast as a matter of course. Digger Crew's appetite soon became famous and Akiko arranged for all the other waiters to take it in turns to serve him. They stood about the table watching Digger warily, as if contemplating the dynamics of ingestion. Some giggled helplessly, showing their teeth, forgetting other tables and calls for hot milk. Yet Digger never exploded or disgraced himself in public, he continued to plough through his meals with aplomb. Dick Sergeant, the other young man who shared their cabin and table, often pushed unfinished plates toward him. 'Think of it as scraps for the dog,' Dick said to Billy, and Digger was known as Digger Dog or plain Dog from then on.

Digger Dog Crew was even smaller than Billy; it seemed unlikely that his internal organs could take the strain. But they did, for he moved about happily, always looking forward to lunch. He was nineteen years old, with a boxer's pug face, and heavy eyebrows planted low on his forehead. His eyebrows gave him a glowering look, so that he appeared obscurely threatening but also slow witted. He looked like a crook, an ex-member of a razor gang, hardly helped by his favouring of loud suits and expensive hats. He wore his hats at a rakish angle, pulled low to cover one eye: smoke curled up from a Capstan cigarette perpetually burning between his lips. He talked without removing his cigarette: it bobbed up and down on his lip. Digger Dog walked the decks with a swagger, raising his hat regularly, bowing exaggeratedly to women. He didn't know he looked rather foolish: a burglar saved by the Salvos, a small man trying to appear grown. For Dog Crew was oblivious to the effect his appearance had on the world, thinking young women who fled at the sight of him were merely shy. It was many years before he learnt that he was trapped by his own face, that the congregation of his own genes had conspired against him. That he should also possess a heart perilously sentimental was as yet only a minor problem: for the moment, aboard the *Kitano Maru*, Digger Dog had the full confidence of his nineteen-year-old self, anticipating the unfurling of the future.

After breakfast, Digger Dog immediately drew a Capstan from his cigarette case and offered one to Billy. The second week out, Billy had accepted and now smoked Dog's cigarettes freely. He rested back in his chair like Dog did, his hand folding the cigarette the same way. Billy drew the smoke deep into his lungs, breathing out carefully through his nostrils. He felt the rise of blood to his head, a great rush of air shooting upwards. Sometimes on the first drag of smoke into his lungs he felt so dizzy he had to hold on to something, placing his cigarette in the ashtray in order to grip the arm of his chair.

While the dining-room cleared and the second sitting began, Digger Dog and Billy continued to sit and smoke. Dog was in love with a married woman who cast him nervous glances, which Dog interpreted as longing. She came in with her husband, an officious-looking fellow who obviously considered himself important, and sat with him at a table adjacent to theirs.

'I'll leave you to it,' said Dick, who had made it plain to Dog he thought the whole thing ridiculous. Dick raised his brows at Billy in contemptuous alliance, but Billy chose to ignore him and stay on.

'She's really beautiful,' Dog said to Billy in a loud voice, so loud

Billy feared the husband might hear. 'I'll tell you, mate, I've never seen such a looker.' To Billy she appeared a rather ordinary young woman, a trifle heavy, with nascent jowls. But Billy already knew that Dog fell in love regularly, appearing to love the state of love rather than love's object. He was easily the wettest young man Billy had ever met: he cried at the drop of a hat. Digger confessed that he had been sacked from his job as a hospital wardsman because he stood about too much weeping. He was leaving Australia because his heart was broken, but who by it was hard to tell. It might have been by Dorothy, who had lips like Mary Astor, or by Jessie, whose breasts were white and alive in Digger's hands. It was clear that if Digger Dog's criminal face did not bar him altogether from being considered by a woman (and it frequently did), then his softness and complete attention often won her.

Dog had taken Billy up as a kind of protégé, viewing him as a rescued orphan, with himself in the role of rescuer. 'That bastard Rome's working you too hard,' he said now, stubbing out his cigarette. 'You should get a proper deal, laying out wages and conditions.' Dog was a union man; he intended to act as Billy's personal shop steward. He talked, keeping his eye all the while on the married woman, who shifted uncomfortably in her seat. 'Do you want me to talk to him?' he asked Billy, suddenly turning around to face him.

'Oh, no,' Billy said quickly, 'it's all right. Really.' He did not want to cause trouble, for as far as he could tell, Vernon Rome and Connie Connor were his only protection. How could he possibly make his own way back to Australia? Without money, without sense? 'Please don't,' he said to Digger, in a voice more desperate than he had intended. Digger's awful eyebrows burrowed further down his forehead; he moved his upper body closer to Billy's. 'Don't worry, mate, I'd never do anything to hurt you. You know that, don't you?'

Billy looked at Dog's animate eyebrows, moving expressively about his forehead. Dog glared at him intently. 'I'll look after you,' he said, patting Billy's hand gently. Billy hoped Digger Dog Crew would not cry: he smiled hopefully at Digger, who reassuringly smiled back.

The first time the ship docked, in Manila Harbour at sunrise, Billy stood alone on the deck. The unexplored city lay below him: he immediately felt the difference of the air. All at once he could not wait to go ashore, for his feet to touch uncharted ground. Digger Dog came up and stood beside him; Billy was grateful that he did not speak as the great ship was tethered.

Only as the gangplank was lowered into place did Digger turn his head. 'Ready?' he asked, suddenly smiling.

Dog Crew proved great to go ashore with; he was reckless and willing, his pugnacious face somehow granting them protection. Once on the ground he seemed to know who to ignore and who to speak to, and found them a reliable guide within moments. He moved his small thug's body deftly through the rabble; Billy followed, anxiously keeping an eye on Dog's head. By the time Billy reached him, Dog had already employed the services of a twelve-year-old boy called Jesus, who promised to show them the vitals of his home town.

'The vitals?' inquired Billy and Jesus grinned. 'The heart, sir! The belly! All!' He walked off briskly, followed by Digger Dog, who stood exactly at the same height. Billy smiled, moving fast to catch up.

Billy walked the streets of Manila with his head up, his eyes trained on the skies of the world. Dawn cracked all around him: colours, smells, sounds. Live things swelled in the soft air, unfurling themselves for the day. The burst of green tree, vine, grass hit his eyes with a tenderness, everything looked unbearably new, fresh born. The air against his skin was wistful, warm like the clean breath of a child. He heard the small cries of birds and cats, the creak of wooden shutters being opened, the chink of windchimes. Every sound came to him with clarity, every colour, every smell. He smelt incense, rotting garbage, the high sweet stink of Asia, the freshness of dawn. He walked quickly, all the time smiling, moved by a quick joy. It seemed to him he was filling his eyes with the houses and grounds and colours and skies of the world.

Every day Billy kept tumbling. He practised alone on the top deck, hours before Connie or Vernon were up, he tumbled in the evenings when the sky was filled with stars. At those moments when a terrible pain came to strike him he climbed the stairs to move through the air, and once again tumbling lifted him up. All his memories were stored in his muscles, all his knowledge, all his love; only in motion did he knit himself together, only in motion was he once again healed.

As it grew hotter, Billy took to working without a shirt, wearing only a pair of black shorts, comfortably cut for tumbling. The sun was hot on his back; he carried a towel to wipe the sweat from his neck. He was trying to teach himself to roll completely loosely, to wave his body as easily as you might wave a hand. He practised letting his muscles grow lax and viewing air as if it held the safe properties of water. He felt the shuffle of air against his skin, its hasty rearrangement to make way for him. It occurred to him that what he was really doing was seeing how much he could get away with, testing how long his body could break the rules of gravity without the air knowing.

Akiko from the dining-room sometimes came to watch him working, standing well away under the shade of the steel roof. Billy sensed him standing there, or else caught a sudden glimpse of movement as he turned in the sky. After a while Akiko got sick of standing and squatted on his haunches, clasping his brown hands in front of his face. He rarely spoke to Billy but nodded his head when Billy acknowledged him, giving a barely noticeable smile. He had endless patience, and always stayed until Billy had finished. Akiko's English was minimal, consisting mainly of the names of foods on menus. His face was broad and expressionless, his eyes oddly slow moving. He never once gave Billy a word of encouragement, or seemed interested in Billy's experiments in the least, yet Billy always missed him when he wasn't there, and felt the absence of his watchful eyes.

A nine o'clock every morning, all three began the day's tumbling. Billy saw Vernon's head emerge first up the stairs, followed by his broad shoulders. He began undressing before he reached the top, pulling his jumper carefully over his head so as not to spoil his *coiffure*. He wore an odd black garment to work in, like a swimming-costume, high waisted with straps over his shoulders. Before starting work, he always checked his hair and his costume, facing the sun as if it were his own personal mirror.

Although Vernon Rome carried too much weight, his height somehow allowed him to get away with it, for he appeared well conditioned rather than fat. He was tall for a tumbler, but the big surprise to Billy was that Vernon Rome could actually tumble. He could do somersaults and hand springs and cartwheels, he could do wonderful comedy tumbles and was a lovely, bouncy faller who looked good when he fell. Billy saw that Vernon Rome did not seem to mind making a fool of himself; he fell about all over the place and it worked. For the first time, Billy recognized in Vernon's eyes the gleam of ambition. He was prepared to try anything as long as it looked good, he had high standards, both for himself and for Connie and Billy, and absolute control of his body and the air.

It was Connie Connor who lacked concentration. She wasn't lazy but she was dreamy, lost for long moments in private plans. Her grey eyes often grew remote and unfocused, as if in preparation for sleep. At such moments she also lost the faculty of hearing: Vernon had to call her half a dozen times before she heard him. Sometimes Billy watched her face, wondering what she was thinking.

When she was attentive, Connie's body was more than capable of obliging, if only she cared to instruct it. She had a contortionist's weird abilities, double-jointed limbs which broke all the rules of anatomy and removed their owner beyond the realm of the norm. Her legs, for example, appeared to have a life independent of the rest of her, and roamed as if of their own free will. Billy came to view them as separate, animate creatures and half expected to see Connie's legs march off without her, kicking with delight at escape. She utilized them as much as she was able, using a legmania routine which she'd pinched from Snakehips Johnson. She occasionally struggled up the stairs with her large gramophone, on which she played Indian music, and weaved about, her legs moving in unexpected directions.

Connie could also tumble but she was merely competent and clearly not interested in learning to do double somersaults or even round off flip-flap full double-twisting somersaults like Billy was. She consented to watch him practise doubles, but was not particularly thrilled to see him almost attain them. It was Vernon Rome who kept him going, who watched him keenly, talking all the time.

'A professional tumbler's got to build showmanship,' he said to Billy with an unmistakable eagerness. 'When a professional comes out of a somersault he presents himself to the audience. You're not a bloody gymnast who has to finish at attention with your fingers pointed to get marks!'

Billy wasn't sure what showmanship was exactly, other than a different word for showing off. But he liked the sound of it, its confident ring, the way the word suggested wit and polish. Showmanship was obviously what Vernon Rome had, a self-confident quality that imbued his very posture. He held himself as if he were already famous, expecting calls for autographs and the flashing of lights. He had a way of holding his hand across his face, which caused people to stare to see what he was hiding. Billy saw that he commanded attention: he stepped into a room and people noticed him, which seemed only what Vernon Rome had come to expect.

Vernon told Billy that if he seriously wanted to be a good tumbler he would need the following: nerve, strength, balance and co-ordination.

'And all those things aren't worth a pinch of salt unless you're prepared to do a lot of hard, dedicated training. This stuff about tumbling being in the blood is all crap. I'll tell you what makes a tumbler – practice, practice, practice.' He looked at Billy. 'It's easy to impress the josses, Billy, they're just as thrilled by a straight-back somersault as a double-twister and half of 'em wouldn't know the difference. It's going to be up to you to work hard.'

He smiled at Billy, pointing his finger. 'You're all right. You've got a good, neat style, but I've yet to see what you're made of. I'll reserve my judgement till I see the whites of your eyes.'

Vernon raised his finger and placed it in the centre of Billy's forehead. With his other hand, he pulled his thumb back, pretending to shoot. 'And now you can roll the felt up,' he said to Billy, walking away.

Connie wanted to know if Vernon had been going on at him, spouting garbage about Tumbling As Great Art.

'Well, he said something about dedication – ' Billy said, but before he could say anything more Connie interrupted him.

'He thinks he's an Artiste. My God, he hasn't got a sensitive nerve in his body!' She was taking off her make-up in front of the mirror, slapping cream on her skin in great arcs. Billy sat behind her on the bed, watching closely.

'Just what did he say, exactly?' she asked, putting down the jar of cream. Billy began to tell her, but she immediately talked over him.

'He's a fool, Billy, don't listen to him, he'll fill your head with romantic nonsense. If I'd listened to Vernon, we'd be broke by now.' She took a breath. but only so she could continue. 'He'd rather starve till he's perfect – do you know he once turned down a job because he couldn't get a few adagio steps quite right? Hell, he could have faked it, but not Vernon, oh no.'

Two pink spots had appeared on both cheeks, now visible as she wiped the cream off. Her eyes looked bright and too intense, their dark pupils overly large. Her yellow hair was pushed back behind her ears, which looked endearingly big in the light. Billy was embarrassed and lowered his head, inspecting his fingernails for dirt.

After a while he heard Connie rise from the chair and judged it safe to lift his eyes. She was walking away from him, unhooking the back of her bra. Because she had her back to him, Billy saw nothing, but in his head he clearly saw the tremble and sway of the front.

Before long, crowds began to gather to watch them practising. Word had got around that there was a variety act on aboard and if you got there early enough you'd get a seat. Girls sat along the rails holding on tightly; children sat where they could on the steps. Groups of old ladies took to bringing up deck-chairs, until one of the cabin crew found out and declared it forbidden on that part of the deck.

Vernon was in his element with an audience, and as it was only practice, he did not seem to feel the pressure of perfection. He clearly loved being the director and ordered Billy and Connie about shamelessly, with Connie pretending to bark like a dog and the crowd laughing at their fights. Connie had a sense of the ridiculous and pulled faces when Vernon's back was turned: sometimes she'd be standing perfectly upright one minute and he'd turn around to find her body inside out. Billy couldn't help laughing too, although Vernon gave him warning looks. Digger

Dog looked on proudly from under the roof, telling whoever he could that Billy was a good mate of his.

Vernon had trained with Arab tumblers and consequently knew some beautiful Arab turns. He was trying a routine where Billy balanced in Vernon's cupped hands, then jumped with the aid of propulsion, turning a somersault before landing neatly back on Vernon's shoulders. It was a difficult routine, requiring a certain skill, particularly on Vernon's part: he had to make sure that his shoulders were in exactly the right place, dead centre of Billy's down-coming body, absorbing the shock as he landed. As bearer, it was Vernon who actually did all the balancing, yet it was Billy who won the applause. To the audience his somersault looked like the hard part; they even clapped indulgently when he landed with his feet in Vernon's ears.

'It's all right, lad, try again,' Vernon said without irritation, holding out his cupped hands one more time. 'I've had many more years' practice than you.' So Billy would try again and again, willing his body to obey him. He felt brave and alive and full of ambition and dreamt every night of landing perfectly on Vernon Rome's waiting shoulders.

Birth Day

He didn't mean to tell anyone it was his birthday, but somehow it slipped out. Digger had suggested staying aboard to play cards instead of wandering around Alexandria for another day while the ship loaded up, but Billy's face betrayed him, for soon his secret was out. Before Billy could stop him, Digger had informed Dick and Connie and Vernon, and they all gathered at a table over tea. Billy was told to make himself scarce; he got up, trying not to grin. He felt a shameful burst of excitement, as if he were turning six instead of sixteen. As he left the room he could not resist one last look back: all of them around a table, because of him!

He was lying on his bed trying to look relaxed when Digger came in, his criminal face perilously serious. He handed Billy a white calling-card: Billy saw for the first time Connie's rich, flamboyant flourish. In ink, it read:

Your presence is kindly requested
at the Royal Alexandria Yacht Club
6 p.m.
RSVP   DRESS: FORMAL

Billy hung his head and kept his eyes on the card, not looking at Digger Dog once.

'OK. I'll come,' he said in a dry voice, all the time his eyes on the card.

Only when Dog had left the room did he leap from the bed and walk quickly up and down, his legs taking great long strides, his fingers flexing and unflexing ceaselessly.

Billy had to borrow a dinner-suit from Dick Sergeant, but it was too big and they had to use pins. From the front you could hardly notice; from the back the pants did not hang well. But to Billy this hardly mattered: he kept staring at himself in the mirror, for it seemed to him he was a completely different boy. He appeared carelessly handsome, a young man of charm and ease. He stood tall and pulled back his shoulders, carefully combing his hair this way and that. He smiled at himself when Dick wasn't looking: there was no trace of his old nervous self.

He was the first dressed and strolled on to the deck while he waited for the others to finish. It was not quite dark and the city of Alexandria was spread before him. The sky above the ancient city appeared boundless, bigger than any sky he had seen. It was wiped with violent pinks and oranges; the pale blue of evening rose slowly with the Egyptian moon. Because there were no hills around the city, Billy had the impression he could see everything he might wish to see. He saw the outline of mosques, their curly domes and spirals, the flat roofs of houses and a thousand palm trees. He heard the sound of trams and car horns, the voices of men rise in chant. From the deck he saw Arabs dressed in white robes and turbans, the narrow alleys and bazaars of the old city and, directly below the boat, groups of children. They were selling something he could not make out. One of them saw him and began a plaintive cry of 'Monsieur! Monsieur!' The boy held up a basket: in the fading light it looked empty. Just as he was planning to get away from the boy's ceaseless cry Billy heard the voices of Digger and Dick Sergeant coming up behind him.

'Ah, the birthday boy,' Digger said, patting him on the shoulder. 'Righto. Let's go!' They moved off in the direction of Connie's room, where there was ice and liquor waiting to begin the first toast.

It was Vernon, of course, who got them into the Royal Alexandria Yacht Club; he knew someone who knew someone who was at the bar when they got there waiting to sign them in. 'Thank God,' said Connie to Billy *sotto voce* as the man came up to greet them. 'I thought Vernon might have outwitted himself this time.' Billy did not fully understand what Connie meant by this remark, knowing only that it related to her lack of confidence in Vernon. Billy himself considered Vernon to be unimpeachable, an outstanding man among lesser men. He looked over now at Vernon as he talked to his friend: he appeared elegant, poised. One hand was across his face in that particular way he had, the other was draped loosely in his pocket. Vernon's suit was well cut, his hair perfectly combed, his face well tanned from mornings in the sun at practice. Billy thought he carried himself exceptionally well: clearly the man he was speaking with also regarded him as important. The man was a squat Continental-looking fellow, swarthy, with a neatly clipped moustache. When Vernon began introductions, Billy quickly stepped behind Connie.

'And let me introduce our guest of honour, Mr William Hayes. Monsieur Aristotle Stomadio.'

He was forced to step forward, blushing furiously, and shake the short gentleman's hand. 'How do you do?' he said, without realizing he was going to say it, hearing somewhere the instructive voice of his mother. 'Pleased to meet you,' he added daringly, but the man already had his eyes fixed on Miss Connie Connor.

'Enchanté,' Connie said to Mr Stomadio, making a kind of curtsy. Billy looked at her in surprise.

Mr Stomadio was dressed in a dinner-jacket too, and took from his pocket a white handkerchief and began to dab daintily at his forehead. Turning to Vernon, he asked if the group would prefer perhaps to take a drink on the veranda.

'It is a pleasant night, is it not?' Mr Stomadio held out his arm; Connie took it. Digger, looking more than ever as if he were about to commit a crime, shrugged his shoulders and said, 'I'm easy.'

The little group followed Mr Stomadio and Connie, with Billy at the rear. Beautiful women sat alone or together with men, in clusters around the room; waiters carried silver trays and moved soundlessly. Billy had never seen such a magnificent room, cast over with warm, golden light. There were dark paintings on the walls, lamps with velvet tassels and, on the floor, enormous oriental carpets. French windows opened on to a wide stone veranda; beyond that there were cut lawns, green and seemingly endless. As Billy walked through the room he felt his limbs begin to stiffen, his walk grow unnatural and ungainly. He was convinced all eyes were upon him and knew his lips had curled up into a kind of embarrassed smirk. For one dreadful moment he did not think he would make it across the room but kept his head down until the ordeal was over, until he was out of the room, and breathing.

On the veranda, the group was already settling into wicker chairs strewn with mirrored cushions. Before Billy could collect himself, a waiter appeared next to Mr Stomadio, who asked what everyone would like to drink. Billy's mind was blank, he could think of nothing: to his horror, Mr Stomadio turned directly to him.

'First, the guest of honour!' Billy felt himself growing hot and sensed the flare of colour. Panicked, he could think of no drink known to man: it seemed that everyone was looking at him, that every one of them thought him an unsophisticated fool.

'Why not a bottle of champagne?' he heard Vernon say. 'It's not every day you turn sixteen.' Billy looked at him gratefully, but Vernon refused to meet his eye; he was too practised to acknowledge he had saved him.

When the champagne arrived, Connie declared it delicious; they toasted him and Billy smiled at last. Digger readily admitted he had never before tasted champagne: Mr Stomadio proclaimed himself shocked. Neither had Billy but he would never confess: he tried to give the impression he might have tasted finer.

After supper, Mr Stomadio announced, they would go to the Mohammed Ali Club, where they would meet 'rich cosmopolitans'. Billy still had no clear idea who Mr Stomadio was, only that he had declared himself a true Alexandrian Greek. He seemed to know everyone, raising his hand constantly to passing guests throughout the course of the meal. Billy ate food he had never before heard of, and might well have been eating produce grown on the moon. Plates were set before him laid out with unknown organs, arranged prettily under the palest of sauces.

Digger certainly tucked in with his usual relish, unembarrassed by his stomach's potential. He ate the tender hind legs of small creatures, the hearts of vegetables, the breasts of wild, unnamed birds. He clearly did not feel the least intimidated by his new companions like Billy did, nor deterred by the fact that he did not know what he was eating: it was obviously all food to him, and delicious. Mr Stomadio looked at him warily, for he was sitting next to Dog and perhaps feared for his dinner, but Dog was using his best going-out behaviour and did not request a taste from anyone else's plate. It occurred to Billy that Digger Dog Crew did not even realize that the food was unusual, or that the whole evening was in any way different to an evening around his mother's kitchen table in Five Dock, Sydney. Billy envied Digger this unselfconsciousness, his oblivious ease. He himself had his eye on Mr Stomadio, who he felt had not properly seen him, for he wished Mr Stomadio to notice that he was an exceptional and outstanding boy.

The Mohammed Ali Club was crowded; a jazz band played in one corner. The musicians were American Negroes, as was the female singer: Billy saw her as soon as they came in, her blowzy grace, her sulky voice delivered in indolent phrases. He had never seen such a place except in American movies; it was a kind of supper club, with tables and a small dance floor. Mr Stomadio again led the way: they sat down and he ordered them all cocktails.

'Oh, not for me,' Connie protested.

'She'll be on her ear,' added Digger, winking suggestively at Vernon.

Mr Stomadio insisted and the drinks arrived; Billy took tentative sips. He looked around the room, which was dimly lit, finding everyone interesting.

'Here people converse in a variety of tongues,' Mr Stomadio explained as if he had divined what Billy was thinking. 'They are all citizens of since-lost kingdoms and the almost forgotten principalities of friendlier days.' He gazed around the room with a sad expression, as if imagining vanquished glories. Billy looked too, for signs of loss, but could only see brightness and light.

Billy danced with Connie, who as usual cleared a space, performing a kind of jazz dance. He tried to keep up, but her skills were beyond him: he stood back and clapped with the rest. Digger Dog was smitten by a dark-eyed Egyptian girl who spoke no English, but that did not seem to bother him: he kept asking her to dance and she kept accepting, so he clearly thought he was in with a chance. He raised his eyebrows suggestively over her shoulder: Billy had to turn his head away to laugh.

Billy drank and smoked, moving to the music, entranced by the limbs of the singer. She appeared to move in a completely new way, compelled by her body's private laws. She wore a dress of blue silk, which stayed close to her body, clinging to her ribs where she sweated. Billy did not yet know that he was drunk, and the words of her songs seemed to proclaim meaning not before spoken. He watched her steadily, a drink continually in his hand, turning away only when she left the stage between sets. When she was not there, the stage seemed empty, even though the jazz band continued playing.

With the woman gone, Billy was bored; his eyes had nothing to look at. He cast a desultory glance over the floor, seeing Connie dancing with Mr Stomadio, Digger Dog with his Egyptian princess. It was not until he tried to stand up and knocked a chair over in doing so that Billy found out how drunk he was, and that the toilets were a long way away. Nevertheless, he made his way across the room, weaving and bumping into tables.

Billy put his hand out to the first door he came to, opened it and walked in; what he saw immediately was Vernon Rome's white bum, his pants down around his ankles. Billy focused for a long time before he understood he wasn't in the men's room, and that Vernon wore around his well-combed head a garland of brown curling feet belonging to the jazz singer. She was lying on a table and Billy saw the gleam of her blue dress before he realized that Connie had come in behind him. As soon as he noticed this, she was gone.

Secret World

The rest of the journey passed in a series of disgruntled days and nights, with Connie not speaking to Vernon and Vernon growing more and more annoyed with Connie. Billy moved between them like an envoy, used by both as a conduit. He carried messages and translated sign language, he acted as interpreter and as guide. He found himself saying, '*What Vernon means is*', as if Vernon could not say it himself. Connie either misunderstood anything Vernon said, or else Vernon did not speak in the manner to which she was accustomed. Practice sessions became unbearable, with Connie not listening to Vernon and Vernon shouting at Connie until she picked up her things and left, retiring to the privacy of her room. She never cried but grew still and quiet, withdrawn to some interior place. Billy thought she had a certain dignity, as if she had chosen contemplation above the meaningless speech of men. When she did speak, her voice was softer and more subdued, as though she had not used it for some time. She would say to Vernon, '*I don't understand*', and Vernon would have to explain some move all over again: she appeared sincere, genuinely puzzled, yet Billy could see as she listened that she was still not concentrating properly. She had trouble looking at Vernon as well, her eyes glanced off him as from too bright a light.

Billy took to eating all his meals with Digger Dog now that Vernon and Connie no longer ate together in the evenings. Connie sat at a table with an elderly couple who were on their way to Edinburgh to see their first grandchild: she looked kindly upon every one of their photographs. Vernon occasionally joined Billy at his table but mostly offered himself around like a kind of cake. He had begun a romance with a pretty young woman travelling without her husband, a bosomy mother whose little girl was always being sent elsewhere; he did not sit brazenly at her table but could sometimes be seen in the lounge afterwards having a drink with the woman and her companions. Dog and Dick Sergeant thought Vernon's conquests remarkable, and had long discussions about what it was exactly that made some men attractive to women.

'It's the eyes,' said Digger. 'All women love to be looked at closely.'

'Bullshit, Dog,' said Dick Sergeant. 'If you looked closely, they'd think you were sizing them up to rob them.'

Dog seemed hurt, but Dick affectionately knocked his arm and before long he was smiling.

'I know what it is,' said Dick, leaning forward. 'Girls always fall for you if it looks like you don't care. I tried it once and this girl was all over me like a rash.'

Billy glanced over at Vernon and his new girl, who certainly appeared to have fallen for Vernon. He didn't think Dick's theory had worked with Connie, though; she had never been the same since presented with evidence that Vernon did not care for her on a full-mooned night in Alexandria.

As the *Kitano Maru* drew closer to England, Billy sensed a mounting of tension. An outbreak of excitement raced through the passengers, passed along like news or infection. Something held low suddenly rose up, broken free of its hidden moorings. People talked louder, their movements were quicker; impatience made itself known.

When Billy thought of England he thought of Shakespeare and the King but could not imagine the insides of houses. He could not even imagine a street where he might live, a room, with four walls and a ceiling. Whenever he imagined a house he saw the walls of his bedroom at 61 Allen Street, the couch grass which ran off the back veranda. He wanted to tell his mother of all he had seen and how he was about to see England. He missed her with a painful longing, a feeling that ran beneath the course of his days as unseen but certain as his own blood. She was that part of himself beyond words or explanations, yet he was aware that this feeling did not make him want to go back: he saw himself as being on a kind of mission, both for himself and for his mother, and knew the only possible direction he could travel in was forward.

The night before the ship docked in Southampton, there were

celebrations in every room. Billy had come to see that alcohol played certain tricks on him, and chose to stay away from all the farewell parties. At supper everyone wore silly hats and blew whistles, exploding balloons in the air. The waiters joined in too, singing Japanese fishermen's songs, and even Akiko sang a long mournful ballad. Akiko had bowed to Billy formally and said goodbye, pressing a small polished stone into his hand. 'For luck,' he said, walking quickly away, too quickly for Billy to properly thank him.

After supper, Billy strolled along the decks, passing his hand over surfaces. He felt a kind of melancholy that the trip was ending but also a quick impatience that it end at once. He didn't know how he was going to get through the next twelve hours, let alone how he might grow calm enough to sleep. He began to walk fast, to kick the edges of stairs and rails. He knew his mother would say he had ants in his pants, or that loose ends were better tied up. It was true, he was at a loose end and could think of no way of tying himself up.

He went down to his cabin but before he reached it he heard noise coming from inside: Digger and Dick Sergeant were obviously enjoying themselves, there was music, and singing. Billy didn't bother opening the door and continued his rounds of the decks; cabin doors were left ajar and he looked inside shamelessly, but no one seemed to mind. 'There's a tumbler!' someone called: he turned and gave a shy wave. He was walking past Connie's cabin with his head down when he heard her call, 'Hey, gorgeous! Like a drink?'

He retraced his steps and stood at the door. Connie was sitting with her back to the mirror, her wild legs propped up on the bed, crossed at the ankle. The little fox around her neck had its nose in her glass, which she hadn't noticed till Billy looked in its direction.

'Hey, get out of there!' she scolded, slapping the fox on the nose. 'That's my drink!' She lifted the fox head out of her glass and rearranged it over her shoulders.

Billy stepped tentatively inside and sat at the far end of the bed. If Connie was drunk, he did not want to know: he had had enough of alcohol and its consequences. She offered him a drink and he politely refused, remaining tight and enclosed in his corner.

'You don't mind if I do?' she asked, standing up, her pretty hair falling in one eye. She looked young and undamaged, more fragile than he had seen her, as though she had been freshly peeled. He followed with his eyes as she moved across to the cupboard where she kept liquor bottles and a set of crystal glasses. She picked a glass up and held it to the light, closing one eye as she did so.

'I bought these in Shanghai,' she said, 'although I think they're imported from Paris. Beautiful, aren't they?'

Indeed they were, hand-blown, very fine, as if meant for the personal use of angels. Billy hoped she wouldn't drop it, but Connie replaced the glass carefully, ministering tenderly to the crystal. She then poured herself a drink in her usual glass, pinched from the upstairs lounge.

'Have you had a good trip?' she inquired, unexpectedly, appearing genuinely interested in his reply.

To such questions Billy never knew what to say; he shrugged his shoulders and noncommittally nodded his head. 'OK, I guess.'

She continued to look at him as though seeing him for the first time: she looked in his eyes, at his hair, at his feet. He began to grow uncomfortable under such appraisal, and crossed his legs for something to do.

'Are you lonely?' she asked, sitting down again, looking intently into his eyes. Billy moved his own eyes to the floor: he had no words for telling his feelings, which lived beyond the reach of his tongue. He did not know how to tell how his heart raced at memories, how he lay in bed at night, burning.

She took a sip of her drink and looked at the ceiling. 'I'm never lonely,' she said in a far-away voice. 'I have this whole secret world in my head. I can think about one tiny thing for hours.' She balanced her drink on the arm of her chair and from her pocket took a cigarette and a box of matches. Billy watched, keeping very still, imagining he was about to hear something important. He recognized that some vital membrane between Connie and the outside world had momentarily broken, and that he was witnessing a private unveiling. He began to listen with a kind of honour, using all his powers of hearing.

Connie sat smoking her cigarette, continuing to stare at the ceiling. She appeared to be thinking about something significant; her forehead was creased, her brows bent. When she finally spoke, her voice shocked the silence, although she spoke of ordinary things, soft and low.

'Do you think it's strange never to be bored by your own company? I never am, not ever.' Billy didn't think this required an answer: he waited for her to go on.

'You know, sometimes I get so excited, just thinking about nothing much. It feels like I'm on the verge of some great thing, like I'm about to get some wonderful secret reward.' Her pale face was charged with brightness; her blonde hair shimmered in the light. Turning her eyes from the ceiling, she looked toward Billy again.

'And I'll tell you another secret. I'm always thinking and dreaming and planning – I still think I'm going to live this astonishing life.' Billy smiled at her by way of recognition: she smiled back guilelessly, her face clean of everything corrupt. She took another sip from her drink, then seemed to think better of it and drained the glass, stood up and returned to the cupboard. All of a sudden, she spun round to face him.

'Now you tell me something, Billy. You're a man, you should know what other men think.' A man! Billy swallowed, frightened of the question to come, wondering in advance how he could possibly know the answer.

'Vernon Rome,' she said, and his heart dropped: he did not want to breach any loyalties. 'That man has slept here, over my heart. He lay right here, breathing.' She placed a long hand against her breast, as if her heart were suddenly in need of protection.

'I want to ask if he knows who I am. Or if he even sees me. Sometimes I think the only real thing to Vernon is Vernon and everyone else is a ghost.' She returned to her seat and spoke more softly now, her voice sounding puzzled and vague.

'I want to know if he knows me at all, if I've pressed my shape on him in any way. Sometimes I want to shout at him, "Do you see my heart, Vernon? Do you hear the unique way it beats?"'

She took another drink and Billy sat very still, conscious of his own breathing.

'Oh, perhaps it's my fault that I didn't speak louder, maybe I didn't make myself real. I only know that I've passed over Vernon and it's like I never existed.'

Billy realized with relief that he would not have to speak and leant back against the wall, the muscles of his body relaxing. He didn't know how Vernon Rome saw Connie Connor, or for that matter how Vernon saw him, although he recognized some kind of truth in Connie's description. Billy saw that Vernon had left some mark upon Connie, and also that Vernon might never know it.

He looked at Connie, whose mood had suddenly changed; she was energetically sweeping clothes from the top of her gramophone. 'Music!' she cried. 'I'll play something especially for you, my love.' To his surprise she picked 'Annie Laurie', which she knew by heart. When he left the room, she was singing softly with her eyes closed. He did not think for a moment Vernon Rome had broken her for good: he thought the bright secret world in her head would save her.

Billy finally fell asleep as the sky began to lighten and objects around the room were slowly pushing their shape into the dawn. His dreams were dense and complicated, full of messages and urgent plots. He was back at his old school in Glebe, come back to live his life over again. Only this time he was conscious that he would live it better, that he would try as he had never tried before. He was sixteen years old but back with the first formers, beginning from the bottom up. He had never before given school his full concentration and knew that this time he must: he felt an intense, critical pressure, his whole life depended on his success. At his dream school Billy studied and studied, never going out or rolling through the air; he had to collect a specific number of points and counted these points a thousand times a day. As he emerged from sleep he was still trying to work out if he had enough: it was only when he was fully awake that he remembered he was in England.

PART 3
England

Capturing Grace

When they got off the train at Victoria Station, Digger Dog Crew burst into tears. It was most alarming to see his boxer's face weep, his thin mouth pulled about so: Billy lay a hand tentatively on his shoulder, patting Digger to his mother's beat. 'There, there,' he crooned, looking past Digger's shoulder, wishing he could comfort Digger with the whole of himself instead of reserving a part for his own embarrassment. Billy raised his shoulder at Vernon as if he didn't know what to make of Digger but he hated himself for betraying his tender-hearted friend.

Dick Sergeant finally let his bags drop and said in a harsh voice, 'Now, come on, Dog. Enough's enough.' Vernon was looking impatient, as if about to move off; Connie was peering into a small gold mirror, patting her hair and reapplying lipstick. Their little group was the last to remain, on the very far end of the platform.

Digger took a handkerchief from his pocket and began to wipe his eyes. 'I'm sorry, mate,' he said to Billy, 'I just hate saying goodbye.' Billy smiled at him, giving him an extra heavy pat. 'It's not goodbye, Dog. We'll see each other again.'

'Jesus Christ,' said Vernon Rome, 'you'd think it was his last night on earth!'

Digger Dog looked at Vernon, drawing himself up to his full height, which wasn't much. 'Listen, Rome, you wouldn't know what friendship was, so I'd shut your bloody trap if I were you.' He turned back to Billy and handed him an envelope: inside was his address.

'Now don't let that bastard bully you. Just get on a bus and come to me right away. Promise?'

Billy nodded his head, but Vernon was already walking off, carrying his own bags and Billy's too. Billy tried to get away from Digger, who now held his left arm in a terrible grip. He could hear Digger's voice going on at him but he was watching Vernon and Connie as they moved further and further away. When at last he pulled free, they had already reached the far end of the platform and were handing their tickets to the man at the gate. As Billy ran toward them he was in a panic about not having his own ticket, and did not stop running until he saw Vernon nonchalantly holding it: the ticket collector did not even lift his head as he waved Billy through. Billy later came to regard this moment as his true arrival: he was wrenched and dishevelled from leaving, but straight away his betraying heart soared.

As they emerged from the station, Billy looked at the sky. He could not see the sun so that light seemed to come from the sky itself, a diffuse yet steady light like a glow. Billy looked with his own careful light upon England; upon its buildings, its people, its dark, shiny cars and buses edging slowly along its streets. Yet it was the sight of his own two feet on a pavement littered with tickets, wrappers and gobs of phlegm which struck him, reminding him of other places they had already traced. He looked at his feet and knew they carried the shape of land they had travelled, that memory was made of blood and nerves. At that moment he happened to look up and see the skin on the back of an old woman's hand, fine and translucent like the thin sinewy film attached to certain cuts of meat. The filmy skin was unmottled and very white: Billy saw the trace of veins beneath it. The woman's hand rested on the knob of a stick, her back arched like the crest of a wave. She passed Billy, a whole continent of human memory; he stood and watched until she was out of sight.

He picked up his bags and hurried after Connie and Vernon. Moving quickly, he pushed his way through the crowd.

Outside the station they stood in a taxi queue, Billy admiring the large black cabs. It wasn't until it was their turn and Connie began to give the driver directions that it became clear she thought Billy was coming with her.

'But I thought he was staying with me,' said Vernon, and Billy sat down on a suitcase, preparing for a long debate.

'You'd never feed him,' protested Connie, opening the door of the cab.

'And I won't get *my* grub if you don't hurry up,' said the taxi driver, his arm resting on the window. Billy smiled, enjoying the parry; the taxi driver winked at him and tipped his cap. People in the queue behind them were making impatient noises, clucking their tongues and muttering. Billy thought it might turn into a stalemate, but Connie stepped into the cab and held the door.

'Well, are you coming?' she asked and Billy's heart stopped. He hovered between them as if in the air, conscious of making the right movements. He did not wish to decide and offend either one: he wished to disappear or split himself in two.

'Oh, never mind,' Connie said crossly, slamming the door. 'You two can play boys together.' She sat back in the seat and the cab moved away. Vernon put up his hand. As the next cab arrived, he opened the door, throwing in their suitcases carelessly.

'Women,' he said conspiratorially as Billy climbed in, 'don't you love 'em?'

Vernon's home turned out to be a room in a boarding-house in a place called Herne Hill, but a different room to the one he had left before he went to Australia. When the taxi pulled up, it was getting dark and Billy stared dubiously at the blue door with its brightly polished knocker and the leafless tree in the front garden.

While Vernon knocked on the door, Billy inspected the garden. Because it was autumn, all the plants looked tired, their vivacity spent. Billy turned around when he heard the door open and was unsurprised to see a smiling woman.

'Vernon Rome, you cheeky villain! Come in, don't just stand there!' And so Billy walked through the door and met Mrs Min Campbell and his new home at Croxted Road, Herne Hill. He did not know what to expect and kept his eyes wide open, as if looking hard might afford him some protection.

He was shocked that Vernon Rome did not have his own house or even a permanent room of his own, a place where he might open a drawer and find all the usual accumulated debris of life: odd socks, old letters, fallen buttons which would never get sewn on. Vernon's life was clearly haphazard; odd socks did not get the chance to accrue.

Mrs Campbell led them in through a narrow hallway, past doors with crooked handwritten numbers which opened off it. She stopped at a room where the cupboards were empty, waiting to adopt an identity.

'Haven't you got another room further away from the bathroom, Min?' Vernon pleaded. 'What about that back one overlooking the garden?'

Mrs Campbell stood with the keys in her hand, a neat round woman, slightly prim. Her face was large and unoccupied; she had the peculiarly naked-looking skin Billy had already noticed on certain English people, as though she had just been pulled, blinking, from beneath a rock. Billy had never seen skin so pink and unlived in, as if it had never seen daylight.

She fixed Vernon with her clear blue eyes. 'There's a nice young girl living there, Vernon Rome, and I won't have you causing her any trouble.' Billy could tell by the way she smiled at Vernon that this warning was made in good faith: Min Campbell clearly had a soft spot for him which Billy knew Vernon would exploit. She pulled the door closed and walked back along the hallway, rattling her giant ring of keys.

'Nine months away and not even a postcard! And now you turn up without so much as a never-you-mind, bringing a boy as well!' Billy followed, keeping at a distance, wondering which room would be his. Mrs Campbell led them up another flight of stairs before finally stopping by the door at the top.

'Right, this is it. And there'll be no ifs or buts.' She swung open the door and Vernon walked in: Billy hovered, unsure, by the entrance. Mrs Campbell looked at him, clasping her keys. 'Now what about you, young man?'

He heard Vernon's voice coming from the cupboard. 'Can't you give him the room in the attic?' Billy moved nervously from foot to foot, clasping the bag his mother had packed for him.

'Oh, come inside, you nincompoop,' said Vernon, reaching round the door and grabbing his wrist. 'He'll learn, Min,' he added when Billy was inside.

The first night he lay awake in the strange half-light of the moon and the electric light coming from the hallway. There were lace curtains on the window which made shapes against the wall, merging with the tiny faded flowers of the wallpaper. Right next to his bed was an enormous oak cupboard which he kept catching out of the corner of his sleepless eye and mistaking for a murderer. Billy listened to Vernon's snoring at the other side of the room: a harsh growl which sounded like animals. The ceiling appeared to him unnaturally high; he did not know why it was scorched around the edges as it from fire. He lay in bed trying to make out all the other furniture in the room, which either looked too large, like the cupboard, or too small, like the frail blue chair which Vernon had used as a footstool to tie up his shoelaces. The wood of the chair legs seemed frail as a twig, the blue velvet cushion too insubstantial for Vernon's big foot. Billy did not know how he and Vernon would fit for long in such a place, how their two bodies would divide air and light. He heard again the snarl from Vernon's throat and turned his head, covering his ears with the pillow. He felt very far away and not brave at all and would have given anything to hear his mother's whistle.

The next morning, Billy got up the moment he opened his eyes. He went to the window and pulled aside the lace curtains, looking out upon a new world. Their room overlooked gardens and backyards; there were walls built of small dark bricks, made from a clay or sand unknown in Australia. The sky was hardly sky at all, being low and muted, strangely bleached. He was struck by how small everything was in England, how like a world in miniature it appeared. Flowers were small and brightly coloured like the flowers in children's books, clouds were hardly clouds at all. In the garden directly below the window he could clearly see a timid path of green grass, much greener and finer than anything he had seen in Sydney. He thought of the tough, muscular grass of his own backyard, with names like buffalo and couch. Billy turned from the window and pulled on his clothes, which lay on the floor where he had stepped from them. Treading softly, he walked past Vernon, who lay sleeping, his mouth gently open. Billy opened the door and ran down the stairs, then let himself out the front door.

In the street he walked quickly, his hands in his pockets, clenching and unclenching his fists. It was early and the street was empty, the houses still emerging from sleep. He saw now that his house was part of a row of houses exactly the same, with small front yards and large windows like eyes looking on to the street. They stared bulbously out at him as he made his way down the road, walking fast, feeling the muscles of his feet. The air rushed about his face, slightly damp, prefiguring the cold. Around him were the colours of autumn; crunchy leaves were strewn in the gutter.

When he got to the end of the road he saw a row of shops, small too, with a myriad of small painted signs. Across from the shops was a beautiful park, shut up behind iron gates. The fence around the park was designed like a row of spears, held together by scrolls of iron. Billy looked at the pointed ends of the spears, on guard in the morning air, and then he turned and ran all the way back to his very own house in England, where he found that no one else was up.

That first day Vernon kindly took him to the city, where he pointed out monuments and palaces. Billy sat politely on the bus listening, but all the time he was really waiting for his new life to emerge. None the less, he noted the shape of the city, its river; he saw a boy kick hard at a pigeon, the wash of cloud over the sun. His inner eye was recording everything, the shape of faces, shadows, an expression under a grey hat. He felt his whole self to be straining forward, as if trying to reach his own future. He heard Vernon telling him that they would have to be up early in the morning to be at a photo session at Charing Cross Road.

The next day Billy woke far too early but decided to get up anyway. With his fingers he felt for the coin for the hot water he had carefully placed by his bed the night before. In the half-light he found it, then crept out of the room and down the corridor to the bathroom where he could have his bath without worrying if anyone was going to knock.

The photographer's studio was up a flight of rickety stairs; there was an expensive sign on the door completely out of character with its surroundings. *Bobby Bega Studios*, it read. Vernon did not even bother knocking. 'You there, Bob?' he called, barging in. 'The man's a genius,' he added, to Billy. Inside was a large room, with wooden floors and a row of windows overlooking the street. The room was strewn with drop-cloths, both plain and painted. Bobby Bega came toward them. 'Where's the goddess?' he asked. He was a plain-faced man and did not look like a genius to Billy.

'She's busy thinking of new ways to murder me,' said Vernon. 'She'll turn up.' He glanced around the studio, his handsome face suddenly earnest. 'We want something really great, Bobby, something outstanding to go with the new act.'

Bobby Bega smiled at him. 'You all do,' he said not unkindly, his gaze turning to Billy.

'Oh, this is Billy Hayes, the kid I was telling you about. It's a great act, Bobby, I've got a feeling about this one.'

Bobby Bega shook Billy's hand. 'You're a brave man,' he said.

Connie was late as usual. When she finally burst through the door, a great smile broke out on Billy's face, so familiar did she look among the strange. 'Hello, my love,' she said as she passed him, and he tried to pull his smile in, for it threatened to take over his face.

'Thanks for coming,' Vernon said sweetly.

'Oh, shut up,' she replied and went to change. 'Hi, Bobby,' she called from the changeroom, a fragile contraption of wire and old sheets.

Because Connie was late, Vernon and Bobby had already chosen the backdrop: a cloth depicting a sea wall, a little bay, and across the bay Italian-looking stone houses. The huge painted sky reminded Billy of a Sydney summer sky, vast and cloudless. Billy stood before it, his feet touching the pretend stone wall.

'Wake up, Australia,' he heard Vernon call; he turned in surprise, for it was an expression his mother sometimes used. Vernon was standing next to Connie, both of them now dressed as if for a show. Vernon wore a pair of white pants drawn in with elastic at the calf, where they appeared to blossom; below these, white stockings and clean white tumbling pumps, and on top a fresh white cardigan cut in a clean V shape at the neck. With his tanned skin and dark hair he looked handsome as the finest Italian; standing next to Connie, he looked exactly right. Connie's beauty was as luminous as Vernon's was dark; she shone and rippled in her own light. She wore silk shorts which swung about her thighs and a midriff top which clustered in the front in a frothy bow. Billy looked down at his own white leggings and tumbler's pumps and suddenly they looked all wrong.

'Let's get on with it,' said Bobby, slapping Connie lightly on the bottom.

'That's mine, not yours,' Connie said tartly, moving his hand away.

'One of these days . . .' said Bobby Bega with mock tragedy, holding his hand theatrically against his brow.

He moved Connie to the centre of the drop-cloth so that she stood incongruously against the wall, a frail light thrown against the rocks.

'Now do some of that weird stuff,' Bobby Bega instructed and Connie immediately raised her leg. She brought it up against her face in her strange, convoluted fashion, which went completely against the natural laws of the body. Instead of one leg pointing straight out, it bent at the knee, the calf curling back toward her face, so that her foot ended up daintily pointed beneath her chin. It seemed to Billy to involve some dislocation of her hip-joint, so oddly was the leg turned around. Bobby Bega then asked Billy and Vernon to stand on each side of her, while she raised her arms in the air in two points.

'Look amazed,' Bobby Bega ordered and Vernon immediately adopted an exaggerated posture of wonder, scratching his chin and screwing up his brow.

'Ham,' said Connie out of the side of her mouth, which was fixed in a permanent smile. She was motionless, strange and upright. Billy turned to her, bemused under artificial light.

Bobby Bega then asked Connie to bend over backwards and walk on her hands while Billy tumbled over her and Vernon stood behind. Billy had not expected that they would tumble for photographs; he paused too long, looking around for a tumbling felt.

'It's going to be floorboards all the way, kid. Hop to it,' said Vernon. So he did, he rolled and tumbled, he folded up his knees neatly as he turned. It was the first time he had tumbled since he left the ship and his body unfurled with relief. All his muscles shook themselves out gladly; he felt loose again in his own skin.

Bobby Bege might not have a tumbling mat but, surprisingly, he did have an old trampoline. They dragged that over too and did more somersaults; the flash of Bobby's camera hit Billy's turning eyes.

Finally, Bobby Bega wanted some formal shots and he waited while they wiped their faces and rearranged their hair. When they were ready, he placed them in front of the little painted bay, the three of them, all in a row. They stood sideways, their heads turned to the camera, their hands hanging loose at their sides. Billy stood first in line, being the smallest, then Connie and next to her, Vernon.

Billy knew himself to be part of something, a member of a secret race. He stared firmly into the lens, addressing it with the full force of himself. He thought it could not fail to capture grace, and that such grace would be visible even as far away as Australia.

The Wallabies

Years later, when he thought of that first autumn and the time which followed, Billy Hayes remembered only lightness. Memory weeded out for him all his sorrow, all his doubt, so that afterwards he always came to recall himself sitting in the Express Dairy café in Charing Cross Road, smoking cigarettes and laughing. It was in the Express Dairy that Billy learnt he was to be included in the 1934 Royal Command Performance for King George V and Queen Mary at the London Palladium, and it was over Express Dairy coffee that his heart grew light and he asked Miss Bubbles Drake to marry him.

But on his first visit there, alone, Billy ate rock-cakes and wrote postcards to his friend Reg Tsang and to his mother, Sapphire Hayes. He did not write to Lily because he did not know exactly what it was he wanted to say. He knew only that he could not stand the thought of Lily Tsang with anyone but himself, but also that he had no right to claim this. He felt himself to be stranded with his love: she was there and he was here, and for the moment any clarity seemed beyond him.

The postcards Billy was using were Bobby Bega's photographs, which had been turned into handsome, stiff-backed cards, with their new name printed underneath:

THE WALLABIES
Sensational & Comedy
Trampolinists & Whirlwind Tumblers

Billy scattered the cards around the table, hoping someone would notice. He picked up a card with a montage of twelve photographs. The tiny frames held within them somersaults in mid-turn, trampoline bounces and handstands; they showed Connie in absurd poses and Vernon in silly falls. Billy unscrewed the new pot of ink he had purchased and dipped the nib of his pen. Careful not to make a blob, he wrote on the back: *Best wishes to my pal Reg, from Billy.*

He didn't know which card to choose for his mother; he considered for a long time before picking out the photograph of the three of them looking into the camera, an unseen light illuminating them from behind. He picked up his pen again and lowered it into the ink. After letting the excess ink flow off, he wrote: *To Mother, May we all be togeather again. God bless you, Billy.*

He laid down his pen and blew on the words, very hard, until they were dry. He wasn't sure how to spell 'togeather.'

All his life Billy Hayes remembered his first professional performance at the Finsbury Park Empire, for it seemed to him that no subsequent performance was ever like it. Never again would the faces of the audience blaze so whitely under limelight nor the white-blue light of the carbons look so alive. Everything that night in November seemed to Billy to be cast in a lucid light; every gesture seemed to him the right one.

'How do you feel?' Vernon asked before they went on, but Billy found he could not reply. He imagined he felt the pump of his blood, his eager nerves, ready to fly. As he stood there he swore that he would remember everything, every sound, every sight. When he ran on to the stage he looked straight into the limelight, and it seemed to Billy his moment had arrived.

The Wallabies worked constantly after that first night, in London and in the south; in Hull, Newcastle and Manchester. Straight away Billy became adept at catching trains, at eating at midnight, at all sorts of new and unexpected skills. He discovered, for example, that he had the odd knack of packing bags well, so that he could fit in remarkable amounts: Connie often asked him to come over early to pack hers, seeing he was much better at it than she was.

He took to this new life as though he were born to it, as if he had not spent his first fifteen years in the one house. He liked immediately being part of a sprawling network of people, knowing all the faces changing trains at Crewe on Sundays.

He wrote to his mother, taking care to list his achievements, but all at once his life in Australia seemed a long way back in time.

The busyness of his present life cast the old into a series of still photographs; motionless, ancient. In his letters Billy tried to describe his new life as best he could but soon realized that the only way Saph Hayes could know him now would be for her to see the whole of him, the shape of his days, and he had no immediate means of bringing this about.

In all his letters, Billy never once mentioned his father. Sometimes when he lay sleepless in his bed at night he thought of Jack Hayes, and hatred rose like a physical sensation. Occasionally he was forced to get up from the bed and walk quickly around the room, for this was the only way he could find physical relief. He dreamt of revenge, of personal vengeance, he dreamt of a day still to come.

But mostly Billy revelled in the freedom distance had unexpectedly granted, which meant his father's black life could no longer touch him. He lived unburdened, light on his feet, and found he could safely remember his mother's giggling fits, and make Connie laugh by telling her the story of how his mother had once cooked a cat. He was free to reinvent himself, to tell the story of himself in any way he liked. And because Billy felt he did not truly belong in England, nor fully believed his exile was in any way permanent, he revelled in a kind of frivolous detachment, as if he were on some permanent holiday. If Billy could not quite see the future he would concentrate on the present, which was light and effortless and seemed long.

Every day he found out another surprising fact about Connie or Vernon, so that soon he could even imagine them having parents. He found out, for example, that Vernon was Australian, born in Melbourne in the suburb of Box Hill. Billy privately thought that this accounted for Vernon's sentimental choice of name for their act but he later learnt they had previously been called the Bohemians and the Arab Twins.

Another time, several children knocked at the door and they all turned out to be Vernon's. 'All of them?' Billy asked and Vernon nodded his head, looking pleased with himself. Billy did not quite believe it till the oldest child, a scraggly boy, walked up to Billy and asked if he'd like to play soccer. He handed Billy a soccer ball and headed for the door. 'Come on, Dad!' he called to Vernon.

Billy looked at Vernon with completely new eyes: seven children, Billy counted.

Later, when their mothers came to pick them up, Vernon skulked about in the bedroom. Billy watched from the drawing-room window as the children dawdled or dashed to their mothers: the thin blonde woman, who was the mother of the tall scraggly boy; the greying redhead who, unbeknown to Billy, had once threatened to chop off Vernon Rome's faithless penis. A young woman who reminded him of Connie stood alone, well away from the other two.

Billy wondered how they kept track of Vernon's movements, how they had organized their children to visit Vernon on the rare occasion he was actually home. Billy was fairly sure Vernon did not contribute money regularly: he was bad enough at parting with Billy's half a crown pocket money each week.

As he watched them leave Billy caught himself thinking badly of Vernon. He couldn't imagine anyone allowing his own children to walk away, to live their lives so far from his eyes. He promised himself that if he ever had children, they would grow up within easy reach of his arms.

He began to have his favourite theatres, his favourite landladies, his favourite digs. He was fond of Mr Sharpe of Birmingham and his big house on the corner of Bristol Road because he had once heard Mr Sharpe answering the door to a young secretary inquiring about a room. 'Oh,' Mr Sharpe told her gently, 'I don't take ordinary people.' Billy knew then that he was in the business, he was a pro, a working artist whose material was air. His work was his own body, the vehicle through which he apprehended the world: his brain and his body soon seemed to him indivisible, all part of the same working muscle.

He slept late every morning wherever he was, except Mondays in a new town when he got up early to go to the theatre for a band-call, and to get the running order of the acts from the stage manager. He had his own agent, or rather the Wallabies did, a poker-faced man by the name of Frank Hurley who kept a pencil permanently tucked behind one ear and who acted as their sole representative. Billy now proudly carried in his wallet a date book marked with all the dates he was working that year.

He began to know the towns where Connie had to have her midriff covered, where the Watch Committee was particularly vigilant on Monday nights vetting new shows. He got used to eating his breakfast at midday, to the burn of his nerves after performance. Often after a show he would walk the streets of some new town, through its centre, its suburbs, to its very edge. In this way England unfolded itself to him, a drawing slowly gathering shape and dimension under his hand. He began to recognize main streets and the lives lived out on them, to hear meaning beneath pauses as well as words. These small towns at night were never lonely, the starry sky felt close and snug. Billy walked past houses and thought of the warm mingling of breaths in sleep, the slow bake of bodies sharing beds. He walked but he was never tired: at certain moments his head felt clear, and holy.

One Saturday night after the second and final house at the Palace in Newcastle, the front-of-house manager came around to their dressing-room with their pay. He was an affable fellow and Billy liked him: he made a small speech thanking them for their performances, adding that he looked forward to working with the Wallabies again. He then ceremoniously took out his wallet and handed Vernon a prearranged sum of cash.

'A pleasure,' said Vernon, folding the notes carefully before shaking the manager by the hand. 'You know where to find us. We'd be happy to work at the Palace any time it suits you.'

The manager smiled and shook hands with Billy and Connie, then excused himself to continue his rounds of the dressing-rooms. Connie waited until he had closed the door before sticking out her hand.

'Come on, Vernon, hand it over. I don't know why all managers automatically hand money to the man.' She walked over to him and poked him with her outstretched fingers.

'Hang on!' he said crossly. 'I haven't taken out Frank's ten per cent yet!' Vernon always made sure their manager got his money quickly so that he would continue to look kindly upon the Wallabies and keep the bookings and contracts coming.

Connie waited until Vernon finished his mathematics, her hand out all the while. When he handed her some notes, she tucked them under the elastic of her pants, then turned away to finish taking off her make-up.

'Can I have some?' asked Billy and the words were out even before he knew he was going to say them.

Connie lowered her face-cloth and Vernon stood motionless: Billy swallowed hard. It was only after he heard Connie laugh that he knew it was going to be all right, that Vernon would look upon his request as endearingly cheeky rather than as mutinous revolt.

Vernon walked over to him and ruffled his hair: Billy pulled away from his hand. 'Listen, lad. You get your keep and your clothing. I only throw in the half a crown a week because I like you. There's no other reason, you know.'

Billy stood up before Vernon could continue. He did not wish to hear the terms of this contract, the exact conditions under which his father had got rid of him. It was enough to Billy to know that he had done it: he did not need to hear the contractual proof.

When they got home late on Sunday night, Min Campbell had laid their mail in a neat pile on the hallstand. Billy recognized his mother's careful crabbed hand as soon as he saw the envelope. 'For you,' said Vernon, handing the letter over, not raising his eyes from the pile. Vernon continued to stand and sort through the letters. Billy put the envelope in his pocket and turned to go. 'I'll be up in a minute,' Vernon called and Billy cursed him, wishing fiercely that he could be left alone. He did not want to read his first letter while Vernon was there, nor did he want to read it in haste before he arrived: he wanted to read his first letter slowly, and in private, to look carefully upon every word.

Billy was unpacking his bag when Vernon opened the door, whistling and looking pleased. 'Another fan letter,' he said loudly. 'I'll need sticks to fight them off.'

Billy did not smile as he usually did. 'Sh,' he said. 'Old Thompson will complain.'

'To hell with old Thompson. Who cares what the old bastard thinks?'

Billy did not bother answering: Vernon was not to be tamed. He began to read the fan letter aloud to Billy, who pretended to listen for peace. As expected, old Thompson began to knock on the wall, loudly, using his drumming stick.

'It *is* 1.30,' said Billy.

'No!' exclaimed Vernon, his hands up in mock surprise.

Billy finished the last of his unpacking and picked up his towel from the hook.

'I'm going to the bathroom,' he said to Vernon.

'At 1.30?' Vernon asked, but Billy was already shutting the door.

In the bathroom he sat on the edge of the bath. The room was cold and the rim of the porcelain felt icy through the seat of his trousers. He stood up and folded his towel into a cushion; sitting down again, he took out the letter.

He inspected the stamp and then the postmark, which he saw came from Newtown and not Glebe. His mother always claimed not to be much of a scholar and was embarrassed about her poor penmanship. Consequently she addressed envelopes carefully like a child might, always writing her sender's name and address conscientiously on the back. It was when Billy saw the address that he became alarmed, for it did not say 61 Allen Street: it named a street in Newtown he had never heard of and where he and his mother had certainly never lived. He ripped the envelope open and released the letter: it was a short one, dated some months previously: he tried to read slowly and not bolt.

Dear Billy, it read, *What a red letter day it was when we got your letter and found out you were all right! I can picture you now in that nice big house and know youre being looked after. From the sounds of it Mrs Campbells a good woman and Mr Rome and Miss Connor are decent people. By the time you get this I will be set up in my spanking new flat off Station Street, just the girls and me. We move tomorrow and seeing how long the mails take I thought I should get this off quick smart. I know youll be surprised but I left your father. When I went home that day after seeing you off on the ship I just could'nt stand to look at him a minute longer and went to stay with Rose Munroe that same night. Eva's wild at me I can tell you but Art's a pet and giving me a few days at the shop. The boys will get over it (but I don't know about Ellen – how did she get to be Miss High and Mighty?) I say a prayer for you every day love and we are all saving up for your fare home. We've got your photograph up at the shop Art thinks I'll pop my buttons. I tell everyone who comes in that if my son doesnt end up doing something wonderful I'll go hee. Make the best of it while your over there Billy, show those Poms what youve got. Don't forget theres nothing you can't do if you set your mind to it. I see your face on that boat every day it will never go out of my heart. Love Mum.*

She had finally left him! Billy leapt up and did a few triumphant laps around the bathroom, before sitting down to read the letter once again. He laughed out loud to read her expression *I'll go hee*, for he had quite forgotten it. In the Hayes family dictionary it meant Saph Hayes would go crazy, or eat her hat, if Billy didn't do something wonderful.

She had left him! He could hardly believe it and had to stand up again out of excitement. And then he realized that Saph Hayes was saving up for his ticket home and guilt struck him hard as he stood. Billy Hayes did not want a return ticket to Australia. He did not want to go home, not now.

Youth and Beauty

That year the Wallabies worked constantly, sharing bills with famous radio stars, sopranos and talking dogs. Even though there were hunger marches by unemployed men and more theatres being turned into cinemas every day, people still treated themselves to cheap seats for a show. 'They always will,' said Vernon, 'even if it's their last bob.' When the Wallabies began to get regular bookings with Moss Empires, the largest theatre circuit in the country, Vernon declared them set for life. 'It's going to be roses all the way, baby,' he crooned to Connie, sneaking up on her from behind and wrapping two arms round her waist. Of course Connie rebuked him, but not before winking at Billy.

Connie and Vernon's relationship was still a see-saw, but Billy had learnt to recognize its motions. He could anticipate disaster and introduce diversionary tactics, which sometimes worked and sometimes not. When Connie began an affair with a hypnotist, Billy was puzzled to find that Vernon was jealous. He made cheap cracks about what the hypnotist did while everyone was hypnotized and sent up the hypnotist's fake Eastern European accent.

'He's from Middlesbrough,' Vernon said dismissively.

'And we all know where you come from,' replied Connie. To his surprise Billy learnt Connie shared a British opinion of Australians as a bastard race, as a kind of skewed but flawed version of Englishmen. She knew that Vernon was sensitive to this and had worked hard to lose all trace of his accent. To Billy, Vernon's accent was unremarkable, for Billy knew lots of Australians who worked in the business in England and all of them spoke like Vernon. Yet Connie needled Vernon about being from the colonies whenever she got the chance and Vernon unfailingly took the bait. She never did it to Billy, though, and Billy believed this was because Connie saw he did not mind being an Australian.

Billy himself had a fondness for the hypnotist, whose stage name was Lawrence La Fosse. Billy didn't know his real name, buy everyone called him Larry. He was a short friendly man who always had a smile on his face and looked less like a hypnotist than a butcher. Larry and Connie looked odd together, his shortness making Connie appear taller; Larry walked beside her as if he were some kind of queenly attendant. She slung her arm through his with her usual nonchalance and Larry always looked pleased as punch.

Larry came with them on Sundays when the word got around that the tumblers would be out by the river, near Walton. Billy or Vernon would be in the Express Dairy and someone would pass the word: it seemed to Billy on these Sundays every tumbler in London came to Walton to show off, to practise and to tumble for nothing more than the joy of it. It wasn't a competition exactly, more like a game or a picnic: a boy from the Nine Wonders would do a full-twisting somersault and Billy found that he would have to do a double-twisting somersault next to prove that his tumbling was finer. Sometimes the tumblers made a kind of camp, building a fire and making tea. People spending the day by the river would gradually wander over and soon there would be a large crowd.

But the crowd always stood well back and was silent, unlike audiences in a theatre. It was as if everyone sensed the joy in the task, the rush and flow of bodies giving freely. The air in Walton on those Sundays always seemed sweeter to Billy, the people kinder.

When any of the girl tumblers came forward, the boys always hooted and clapped. There was a young girl named Ida Connolly who could slice the air without pain: Billy loved to watch her, she was economical in everything and wasted no movement or breath. She was the only girl who could do a double-twisting somersault, which was more than some of the boys could so. She worked in an act called Youth and Beauty; Billy was given to understand Ida represented Beauty.

When Connie and Larry came to Walton, Connie always packed a picnic: smoked meats and pickles, cheese and a boiled egg for Billy because he liked them. Vernon never ate with them but always made sure he brought a new girlfriend along so he could flagrantly kiss her in front of Connie. He had only started doing this since she had taken up with Larry, previously he had taken pains to keep his other women away.

After lunch Billy liked to lie with his eyes closed, the grass nestling round his head. Summer in England seemed to him a frail thing, fresh born and wobbly, like a recently struck plant which needed to be closely tended. Billy thought of new plants in his mother's garden whose frail necks needed to be supported by sticks and string until they were capable of standing alone. The light too seemed different in England: Billy lay there, pondering the properties of the sun.

Billy didn't know for how long his contract ran, never having had the courage to ask. When he turned seventeen he considered asking, but spent a long night weighing up his life and concluded that he liked it well enough. For the moment he had no thoughts of returning to Australia, at least not yet, and decided he would stay with the Wallabies until something better came along. Although he missed his mother and his sister Mary and Reg Tsang, and still thought longingly of Lily, he had come to regard himself as being on a kind of adventure. He could not help but feel going home would put an end to this adventure, and had slowly come to believe himself to be in the right place. Besides, Vernon paid him more than a half a crown now, and Connie slipped him fivers every now and then. He also earned extra cash filling in for tumbler friends with injuries, if he wasn't working himself those particular nights. He had some nice clothes too, a Sydney Fischer variety suit especially cut for tumbling, with elastic and a special inner lining so that the jacket dropped beautifully after a somersault instead of bunching up gracelessly under the arms. Sometimes Billy wore this suit in the street; it was cream and he wore with it a dark blue shirt. It seemed to him girls looked at him a certain way.

Occasionally he took a girl out dancing or gave a girl and her mother complimentary tickets to a show, which always impressed them. But he did not meet one single English girl as forward as Lily Tsang. Lily struck him now as highly unusual, with her straightforward manner and clear, purposeful eyes. He remembered the way her thin wrist felt, the surprising hardness of her small pointed breasts.

The first girl Billy took out for any length of time was a waitress named Joan. She lived with her family in Shepherd's Bush and for a while Billy went there regularly for Sunday lunch. But Joan's pale good looks were devoid of vivacity; her house was cold except for one large room the family spent all its time in, rushing out into the freezing air of other rooms as if to far reaches of the Arctic. It was Billy's second English winter and he still imagined the cold as an actual presence lurking outside the window, a malignant force only waiting to get him. His earlobes burnt if he didn't cover them; the moist avenues of his nose froze over like a stream.

Although Joan was kind to him and clearly liked him, she never made suggestions of her own. 'If you like,' was her most common expression and at first Billy longed for her to suggest that they run off to Mexico or at least take a boat and cross the Irish Sea. He would have proposed something himself but for the lacklustre way she had already greeted any of his suggestions. Joan never even proposed a visit to the cinema, much less a walk on Hampstead Heath; she didn't ask anything of him and didn't seem to wish much for herself. Her lack of enthusiasm did not do much to fire Billy's, and he quickly knew their affair would naturally peter out. He remembered with fondness Lily Tsang's erotic ambitions, the way she had lifted his hand so surely that first time to lay it upon her breast. With Joan, Billy achieved a few mildly exciting moments, but her faintness of ardour eventually cooled his own. He could not imagine what moved her, and found her silences depressing rather than intriguing. He didn't need to tell her it was over, since it was he who always contacted her: one day he simply stopped calling. He felt relief but also a kind of sadness, because he knew she had not acted badly.

It was after this that Billy wrote to Lily, a careful letter aimed at gauging her feelings. She replied with a letter written exactly as she talked: all over the place, full of gossip, revealing little. Right at the bottom she wrote that she still thought of him, and signed it *With love from Lily*. He told himself the situation was impossible, and yet part of him could not give up the idea of Lily Tsang.

Vernon was unexpectedly authoritarian about Billy and girls anyway, giving Billy the impression that he had to ask Vernon for permission. He did not like Billy to go out before a performance or to get involved with anyone in the same show. Billy couldn't believe it: Vernon Rome lecturing him about restraint! It seemed to him beyond the bounds of their working arrangements, but Vernon clearly thought that as he was still paying for Billy's keep and clothing he was entitled to regulate other areas of his life.

Billy found this highly annoying but was not angry enough to push the issue toward direct confrontation. Because he didn't feel violently about any one girl, it didn't seem worth pursuing, so he more or less fell in with Vernon's rules. Vernon also had the aggravating habit of vetting Billy's girlfriends, like the worst kind of overly intrusive father. He pronounced Joan dull after the briefest of meetings and made it clear he thought Billy's girls plain. He himself always went for the stylish, real women who had about them a dangerous glow.

Yet the day Frank Hurley told him the Wallabies had been chosen for next year's Royal Command Performance, the first thing Billy wished for was a girl to tell. He would have liked to swing her in the air and drink champagne from her shoe. Instead, the only person he could think of was Digger Dog Crew in Brixton. 'You beauty!' cried Digger, crushing Billy to his chest. 'You little ripper, Billy Hayes!' He had instinctively known that Dog would not let him down but could not help ducking his head so Dog would not see how moved he was. Dog insisted they go out to celebrate, even though he was leaving at four for Liverpool to take up a job on the docks. Grabbing his hat, Dog pushed Billy out the door; they walked down the street, their arms around each other's shoulders.

Although Digger Dog Crew was happy for him, Billy felt it was not the same thing. He would have given anything for a girl of his own to tell, for his own girl to share all his happiness.

The stage director for the Royal Command Performance filled Billy with terror, he was so quick tempered and demanding. He was very good at his job and knew what he wanted; he was a perfectionist who drew out the best. He was meticulous about timing and went through the programme again and again to ensure there wasn't the slightest pause between acts. 'This is variety', he shouted at a tearful soprano, 'not frigging Covent Garden!' He told the singer to cut four minutes from her act; when she told him it was impossible, he told her to change the bloody songs or get out.

To Billy the London Palladium seemed grand and hallowed, its air felt old and trapped, as if it had been circulating for centuries. Yet it did not feel stale but pure and clean, revitalized by its own forces. Although there was noise coming from the stage, everything was strangely muffled, as though the walls contained layers of wadding. While he waited Billy walked on thick carpets, his head back to stare at the domed ceiling. He had the impression of gold leaf and red velvet, of seats deep and well padded. It seemed to him that the whole place had an air of expectation, that the very walls were holding their breath. Billy sat down where he could see the stage, and the Sherman Fisher Palladium Girls who were on it. They were wearing full costume and looked spectacular even though they were not doing anything but waiting: the stage manager was checking some point with the musical director, leaning over the stage to talk to him in the orchestra pit. Groups of girls stood with their hands on their hips or stretched their legs for something to do. Because there were microphones newly installed in the footlights, Billy could hear everything: the stage director arguing with the musical director about playing too fast, the drummer throwing down his sticks in pique.

Billy looked up into the royal box, a gentle curve above the right side of the stage. It looked small but forbidding and terribly close, only feet above the heads of the girls. He tried to imagine the King and Queen sitting there but found he could not. He looked away and walked quickly back toward the stage, through the pass door and into the dressing-room.

The day of the show even the famously cool Vernon Rome awoke nervous. 'Don't do that!' he snapped at Billy, who was lying in bed making a harmless sound with his lips. Billy stopped and then grinned with pleasure. 'How are you feeling?' he asked with glee.

'Oh, go to hell,' said Vernon, getting up and pulling on his dressing-gown. 'I don't want backchat from you.' Billy noticed that when Vernon got nervous or angry, his natural speaking voice miraculously returned: the vowels of Australia sprang up undefeated and Box Hill conquered London. Billy lay in bed smiling, until his own nervousness crept up to shout in his ear.

He immediately got up and stood by the window feeling awful, trying to remember why he did this to himself. He wondered why he could not be that boy in the next yard, greasing the chain of his bike; the boy looked mercifully free of terrible obligations, the sky above his head was blue and clear. That boy probably imagined himself to be unique just like Billy did, yet he did not feel compelled to show his difference to the world. All at once Billy longed to be him, to forget all about this business of casting his own true shadow. He saw other people moving about: hanging out washing, carrying bags of garbage. They all walked around unburdened by what was before them, as if it were an ordinary day like any other. Billy wished to be among them, to lay down his burden and never again force himself to make his mark. In his mind's eye he saw the act go irretrievably wrong, failing badly because he, Billy Hayes, let them down. He suddenly saw the muscles of his body frozen, being unable to walk let alone to fly. He would land badly, he was sure of it, he would drop Connie, he would not be able to send the right messages to his bones.

Standing by the window, he felt his body sinking, his confidence draining away. When the door opened, Vernon was just in time to catch him falling; he held the lace curtain as he went down.

After Mrs Campbell brought him another hot chocolate, Vernon sat on the end of Billy's bed. 'Feeling better?' he asked, giving his foot a quick pat. Billy's nervousness had the effect of banishing Vernon's own fear, which now seemed small and manageable in comparison.

'It's OK, lad, it's happened to me plenty of times. You wouldn't be any good if you didn't get nervous.' Vernon cupped his hands around his knee, calm now, oddly paternal.

'I've got an idea. Instead of going to the theatre, why don't we go out to Walton? We'll have a final run-through there and give ourselves plenty of time to get back. What do you say?'

It sounded like a wonderful idea to Billy. When he stood up he was surprised to find his body held him.

At Walton there was no one much around, for even though it was May it was still chilly. They found a level spot to place the springboard and began at once. They had worked out a special routine for the show. Vernon and Billy spun Connie between them, catching her by one wrist and ankle, spinning around themselves and passing her to each other. They slowly gathered speed but worked with precision, their grip sure and strong. Next they practised throwing Connie into the air, higher and higher, until she was fifteen feet up. Connie swung through space, her back arched gracefully, her arms in balletic line behind her; she knew how to land well and Billy knew how to catch her. It was a question of balance and weight: when Vernon threw her, he appeared to cast nothing heavier than a handkerchief; when Billy caught her, Connie appeared to settle in his arms like cloth.

The springboard was the most difficult feat and their finale. Vernon somersaulted off first, followed by Connie, who landed on his shoulders, and finally Billy, who did a double somersault to land on hers. They practised this again and again, landing perfectly every time.

Afterwards, sitting on the grass, Vernon pronounced himself pleased. 'The josses only get excited if it looks dangerous. What do you think, kid?' He playfully knocked Billy on the head as he stood up. 'I'm off for a pint. Coming?'

When they got to the theatre late that afternoon, Billy felt the excitement and strain as soon as he walked in. The stage-hands were wearing plimsolls to deaden backstage noise, but the stage director was still shouting irritatedly for quiet. 'Bleedin' pansy,' one of them muttered as he passed, carrying under his arm a papier mâché grandfather clock. Billy saw the star of the show, the comic Billy Bennett, coming up the corridor toward them: the stage-hand put down the clock and wiped his hand on the back of his pants. 'Boom-boom,' he said, using the comedian's own line with which he ended his jokes. Billy Bennett shook his hand and managed to smile. 'And boom-boom to you,' he said, walking away. Billy thought he must get sick of people crying 'boom-boom' in his face: if *he* was ever introduced to Mr Bennett he would never say it.

Once they reached their dressing-room, Connie immediately lit a cigarette: Billy saw her hand shake as she lit it. His own nervousness had come back, but with it an exhilarating excitement. As he dressed he thought of Digger Dog listening to the live broadcast in Liverpool; he imagined him sitting boastfully around the wireless with his mates. Billy Hayes thought of his father at home in Sydney, and this thought immediately sent a rush of energy through him, a fierce desire to push his whole self flawlessly through the earth's air.

He sat down, strangely calm, and began to put on his make-up. Looking in the mirror, he saw that his eyes blazed in his face, that they had a sharp, unnatural glitter. He strengthened his eyebrows, drawing one single dark line around the rim of both eyes. He worked quickly but deftly and finished within seconds: the Wallabies weren't on till the second half, and suddenly he found himself stranded in too much time.

'I'm going to have a look,' Billy said and as neither Connie nor Vernon protested, he left the room. Coming up through the corridors behind the stage Billy heard a sudden quiet, an absence of noise which sounded odd: he stopped in his tracks, then heard a drum roll. Ahead he saw some of the girls and members of other acts trying to peer round the curtains; the stage manager pushed everyone away soundlessly. He could hear the sounds of people rising from their seats, coughing and rearranging their clothing, before the National Anthem began and King George V and Queen Mary entered the royal box. He stood with a group of girls to one side of the stage; a girl he didn't know squeezed his hand with excitement. Then the stage manager cleared them completely from the area: Billy followed someone dressed as a genie back down the corridor to the dressing-rooms.

'They're here,' he announced to the room, and Connie turned and said, 'Who?'

Billy and Vernon looked at each other. All three of them burst out laughing, slightly hysterically, in that way which seems impossible to stop. Connie stuffed a face-cloth into her mouth in a vain attempt to gain sobriety: this only made them laugh more. They stopped when they heard the warning buzzer sound in the dressing-room next door: through the wall, they heard a voice say, 'Miss Laye, you're on in five minutes.'

'No turning back now,' said Vernon.

What Billy Hayes remembered most about that night was looking straight into the eyes of the King. He was supposed to be facing the audience but found himself completely level with the royal box: Vernon quivered beneath him, and Connie's bony shoulders held him up. He turned his head and looked through the lights into the eyes of the King of England, which were pale and sad and appeared to be watering. He saw Queen Mary, who was watching Vernon's powerful legs; he saw the lace at her throat, the ladies-in-waiting around her. He knew he was supposed to be looking straight ahead but his eyes kept returning, again and again, to stare into the eyes of the King. It seemed to him he saw every movement, every breath, the pale glitter in an old king's eye. He was aloft in the light, high in the air: he was William Sly Hayes, shining.

The Mechanics of Pride

In the weeks following the Royal Command Performance, Billy felt a curious flatness. A focus was gone, his clear point at which to aim, his days were formless and empty. Of course he had written to his mother straight after the performance, including a copy of the programme, and knew she would find some means of getting it to his father. He felt certain she would make Jack Hayes see with his own eyes how well Billy had done, how he had turned his banishment into a triumph. Yet somehow even the thought of his father seeing his name on a programme for the London Palladium did not bring Billy the elation he expected. Nor did a letter from Digger in Liverpool, telling him how the radio commentator had described Billy as 'the nearest artist to their majesties, looking right into the royal box', give him the satisfaction he might have hoped for. The exultation of that one night had somehow thrown a cold light over all his other days so that none was as brilliant, or alive. Billy could not imagine the next high point, and whatever its shape it seemed a long way off, with long days to pass in between.

He could barely feign interest when Frank Hurley and Vernon sat down to work out some new bill matter, something which would include their recent Royal Command Performance.

'What about "Direct from Their Triumphs at the Palladium," ' suggested Frank, and Vernon asked Billy for his opinion. 'It's OK, I guess,' he answered without enthusiasm: Vernon turned away in exasperation.

'How about "Direct from Their Successful Royal Command Performance," ' Vernon countered, ignoring Billy and giving Frank Hurley his attention.

'Not bad,' said Frank, chewing the end of the pencil he usually kept tucked behind one ear. Billy's glance wandered off and out the window of Frank's office, where the sounds of Charing Cross Road could be heard. He detected the first whiff of summer, a warmth in the air blowing through the open window. He got up and crossed the room; perching himself on the ledge, he looked down upon heads and hats, the arms of children. He noticed that at last people were beginning to appear well dressed again; they seemed well fed once more, hopeful. Just then, Billy's eye tripped on a face. 'I don't believe it!' he cried, standing up. Rushing past Vernon and Frank, he pulled open the door, leaping down the stairs four at a time.

'Reg!' he called when he was in the street, and everyone in the vicinity turned around. Up ahead Reginald Tsang turned around too, yelled and ran fast toward him. Even as their bodies collided Billy could not believe it: Reg Tsang, in London, breathing!

Reg Tsang had come to England with his uncle's acrobatic troupe Yuk Fan Ching, Chinese Wonders. This uncle was from a branch of the family who had gone to America: not long before he had turned up unexpectedly on his sister's doorstep in Glebe, the other six members of his troupe standing in a queue behind him. Reg's mother had jumped back in surprise then recovered herself and stepped forward to quickly rub her cheek against her brother's. She had not seen him for sixteen years and thought he had changed in that he looked more American.

'But what are *you* doing here?' Billy shouted because he couldn't help it, while they still stood clasping each other in the street.

'My uncle needed a replacement,' Reg said, his whole face smiling, 'so I came.' From above their heads they heard a loud whistle. They looked up to see Vernon and Frank Hurley hanging out the window. Their sleeves were rolled up and they wore identical puzzled expressions.

'We'll be right up,' called Billy. With his arm around his best friend's shoulder he walked up the stairs for the second time that day, feeling lighter than the first time he had climbed them.

Billy could not stop his eyes returning again and again to his friend: Reginald Tsang in person in front of him, sipping weak tea in Frank Hurley's office in Charing Cross Road. He could not understand how in a city of millions his glance should alight specifically on the head of his very best friend. Reg Tsang's body was only waiting for Billy's eye to fall upon it; Billy's eye was only waiting to see Reg Tsang. He beamed at Reg and touched his shoulder, to make sure that Reg Tsang from Glebe, Australia, was really there.

Billy saw that Reg had changed from a boy to a young man and knew then that he had changed too. Reg was a mirror he could hold up to himself, who showed him how the bones of his face had risen to the surface, pushing out the boy and taking on the dimensions of the man. He saw that Reg had grown into his own skin, so that he fitted himself better and appeared comfortable wherever he was. He was taller, his jaw firm; he looked more than ever like a handsome Red Indian. He had about him a self-assurance, a confident calm which Billy took to be the poise of experience. He had travelled to England with the troupe via North America, visiting New York, San Francisco and Chicago: to Billy, Reg looked as if his eyes had seen things.

They fell at once into their friendship, there was no awkwardness, no sense of lost time. They had not seen each other for more than two years and yet Billy felt comfortable straight away. Their shared history constructed a bridge beneath them, allowing them to cross with ease. He looked at Reg and then at Vernon: it seemed to Billy his old life had now met the new.

Over the next few days they spent all their time together: Billy plied Reg with questions which came so fast Reg did not have time to finish answering one before Billy asked him another. He did not ask anything dangerous, for he did not know how to speak of difficult things directly. Yet without once speaking openly he and Reg divined their own rules, each knowing where the boundaries lay. Billy wanted to know, for example, if Reg had seen his sisters and brothers, if he had met Mary's new husband, whether Rose Munroe still worked at the Ivy Cake Shop, and what his mother's flat in Newtown was like. His whole life had suddenly come back to him at the sight of Reg Tsang: Reg had handed him back his old self. Reg brought with him the entire lost continent of Australia: all at once Billy could see the streets of Glebe at night, and feel again the grass beneath his feet on the joss-house lawns. The presence of Reg Tsang told him this other world still existed, and he suddenly knew that even as they sat on chairs in a backyard in Herne Hill, London, his favourite sister

Mary was sleeping curled next to her new husband in Marrick-ville, Sydney, her feet tucked perhaps between his bony ankles.

Reg was good at giving Billy information: he had a keen eye and noticed things other people did not. He described Mary's husband in spirited detail so that he came alive to Billy at once. Reg thought that Mary was happy, her face had a certain sheen. He told Billy that his mother seemed happy too: she had taken up dancing, going every Saturday night to a dance with Rose Munroe or one of Billy's sisters. Billy could easily imagine this, his whistling mother unburdened at last. She would remember all the tunes of the dance songs and whistle them in the mornings while she made breakfast; Ellen and Ethel would lie in bed listening, until at last it was time to get up.

He did not ask if Reg had passed 61 Allen Street, where his father must be holed up with his hate. Reg had never met his father anyway, and Billy did not know the words for such a question. A picture came into his head of Jack Hayes festering in a room somewhere, comforting himself with brown bottles of Pilsner. Saph Hayes had not mentioned him for many months and Billy had never asked, just as he could not ask Reg now.

He could not bring himself to mention Lily at all, and yet her presence was constantly between them, an invisible third. Just when Billy thought himself in danger of breaking down, Reg casually brought her name up, in the guise of other news. Because Reg understood the mechanics of pride, he avoided looking at Billy; Billy himself sat carefully in his chair, waiting for Reg to go on. Reg told a story involving his other sister, Anona, and a new girl who had joined the Hai-long Troupe.

'She's only half Chinese, but you'd never know it – she could pass for one of us any day,' Reg said. He bent down to take a biscuit from the tray Mrs Campbell had given them, talking all the while. 'We started looking around as soon as Lily told us she was getting married. The funny thing was, it was Lily who ended up finding her. She's a cousin of her fiancé, I think.'

Reg concentrated on his biscuit, breaking off a bit and crumbling it between his fingers. Because he knew that Billy could not and would not ask for elaboration, he conveyed all that Billy needed to know, as quickly and briefly as possible. He told him that Lily's fiancé was also a tumbler and that they had met when they were on the same bill at the Australian: Vince was a nice bloke, Irish-Chinese, and was kind to Lily, who bossed him about.

Billy heard Reg's voice, but it sounded far away from him. He stared at the cup of tea in his hand and a great wave of sadness broke over his head, a sadness for everything he had lost. He heard Reg's voice but kept looking at his hands, at the small scar on his thumb from the time a glass had once broken in his hand.

With an effort of will he finally raised his head. He tried to tell himself that it was only to be expected, a twenty-year-old girl could not be made to wait for a young man living indefinitely on the far side of the ocean. He told himself that mourning Lily Tsang would be like mourning his old life, which was unrecoverable, gone for good. He could not do that, it was not his way; to Billy regretting the past was like regretting his own self. Only then did he realize that Reg had stopped talking and was watching him with a certain care. Billy saw instantly that Reg might be about to break their unwritten rules, for he seemed to be hesitating over whether to reach over and comfort him.

Billy quickly put down his cup and picked up a biscuit, looking away from Reg and out over the garden. 'I'll send her a card,' he said, taking a bite, believing his voice to sound jaunty. 'At least this Vince is a tumbler,' he added, his mouth full.

The danger had passed and they went on to speak of other things, yet all the while Billy was grieving for Lily Tsang.

Pleasure Beach

It was early in the spring when Reg suggested they take a holiday. The weather was brilliant, and it suddenly seemed the perfect idea. The thought had never occurred to Billy, who had not taken a holiday since he joined the Wallabies. He saw now that he counted the days off between contracts as holidays of a sort, or at least rest days, which he mainly spent lying on his bed day-dreaming or playing cards with Vernon or spending too much money in the Express Dairy café. The idea of a proper holiday immediately gripped him: he remembered the feel of hot sand beneath his towel, the smack of clean waves against his skin. Reg suggested Brighton, but Billy recalled playing the Grand there one bank-holiday weekend and the swell of too many people. Grotesque seagulls had stalked him, large as geese, bullying him for scraps. Besides, the beach was composed of pebbles and the sea had reminded him of nothing as much as a dull kind of lake, without the massive energy he expected from an ocean.

Through a process of elimination they decided on Blackpool, which was rumoured to have waves and pretty girls who liked to go dancing. But when Billy told Vernon, he immediately put up reasons why Billy should not go, ranging from his conduct as a professional to an engagement several weeks away. For the first time Billy found himself willing to argue, to get out his date book to use as ammunition.

'Look, we haven't got anything till the twelfth,' he said confidently. 'That's ten days from now!'

Vernon said that other dates might come in; they might be called by Frank Hurley at the last moment to replace an act.

'Tell him we can't do it,' Billy countered. 'Or you and Connie do it by yourselves.'

Vernon pleaded an artist's dedication, the real pro's willingness to work at any cost.

'I'm going, Vernon,' Billy said, closing the subject, and saw by the look on Vernon's face that he really was.

On the train to Blackpool men carried sides of bacon, to give to their landladies to cook; girls looked at Billy and Reg with open interest, but turned their heads away if Billy or Reg smiled back. Billy sat by a window with the glass pulled down, his face buffeted by the wind. He was as excited as a child and could not stop smiling: he kept turning to Reg and grinning like a fool. Because he was excited, he could not sit still and kept fidgeting, crossing and uncrossing his legs, tucking them up under him on the seat only to put them down again. Reg sat opposite him quietly reading a copy of *The Performer*, looking up every now and then to meet Billy's grin: he smiled and occasionally glanced out the window; Billy saw the flash of light pass over the brown centre of his eyes. Billy frequently kicked him inadvertently, but Reg did not seem to mind, being well used to the agitation of his friend's body. The woman sitting next to Billy was not so understanding: at first she smiled when he apologized for poking her, but her smile grew thin when it became clear he was going to continue like a bucket of worms all the way to Central Station, Blackpool. Quite soon she began to openly frown at him, clicking her tongue dramatically to show her annoyance. Billy couldn't help it: he knew he was irritating her, but pleasure moved in his muscles, making itself known. To relieve her and himself he stood up and made his way to the aisle, treading on several toes along the way. Even though it was early in the season the train was crowded, so that people had to move their knees as if in a row at the cinema.

When he was finally free Billy leant against the wall by a doorway, watching small towns passing. Trees were declaring themselves; the light was clear and every single colour seemed to blaze. It occurred to Billy as he watched that he was no longer comparing; he was not translating what his eye saw into an image of another country inside his head. He suddenly realized that England for him now was simply the place where he lived, as true as any other: he no longer used his old country as his reference map.

This revelation caught him by surprise, for even though he had been away for four years, he had not understood before just how far he had travelled.

He was asleep as the train pulled into Blackpool and perhaps would have stayed that way until Reg had woken him if a child had not screamed in his ear.

'There's the Tower!' the child yelled over and over. 'Mummy, the Tower! Look!'

The whole carriage was looking as the train rounded a wide corner. In the distance Billy saw the great steel construction. A mayor had seen a tower in Paris and wished for one like it by the Irish Sea: it rose up from its flat surroundings, visible from many miles off. As the train drew closer, the suburbs of Blackpool obscured it; rows of terraces, lined up along hills. When the train pulled in, Billy and Reg were first off, jumping to the platform before it had fully stopped.

They raced out of the station and into the streets of Blackpool. Flocks of birds flew in figures of eight above their heads; pigeons perhaps, showing off. As the birds completed their strange circuit, Billy and Reg watched them; they were not concentrating on where they were going but followed their feet, which headed as if they knew toward the water. The Irish Sea stretched out before them. They crossed the promenade and leant over the railing, where the sea crashed against the wall. The air was clean and smelt like fresh oysters recently prised from a rock. Billy and Reg looked at each other. 'Yee-ha!' cried Reginald Tsang to the sky.

At breakfast at the Astor House Private Hotel that first morning they sat at table eight, because Reg said this was a lucky number. A thin, tired-looking woman nibbled on cold toast at the table next to them, wiping her mouth fastidiously after each bite. She said good-morning as they sat down, smiling nervously at her plate the moment she said it.

'You lads been to Blackpool before?' asked a stout woman from the only other occupied table. They admitted they hadn't and the woman launched into a long monologue about the town's attractions. Sitting opposite her was a plump young girl with a mournful expression; she ate a bowl of porridge, her eyes trained on the stout woman.

'And this is my daughter, Shirley,' she added when she had finally finished. 'Say hello, Shirley.' The child said hello with her eyes averted; her mother inspected her closely, reaching across to straighten her collar.

'Had her when I was forty-three. I said to my Stan, "If I ever have a little girl I'm going to call her Shirley." '

Shirley the late child got stuck into her porridge, her swollen legs swinging beneath the table. Her sandal scraped the lino with each swing; one hand lay oddly beached in her lap.

'Mrs Stafford here has left her husband,' the woman said, transferring her attention. 'She's looking for work as a maid.'

The thin woman at the table next to them blushed furiously and continued to look at her plate.

'He beat her,' said the stout woman. 'Blacked her eye Monday last.'

The woman risked a quick look at Billy, who smiled at her and took the opportunity to offer his hand. He introduced himself and Reg just as the proprietor placed before him a plate of bacon, two runny eggs and a thick beef sausage.

'Call me Mavis,' she said in a soft voice. 'I'm from Glasgow.' Billy felt Reg kick him under the table but he was not sure of its meaning. He was saved from responding by the proprietor asking if he wanted tinned peaches or an apple to follow.

'There are a lot of Scots around Blackpool, aren't there, Peter?' announced the stout woman, addressing the proprietor. 'It's quiet in Scotland, so they all come here for a bit of fun. My name's Mrs Cotes, by the way. Shirley and I come here every year from Leeds, don't we, Peter?'

The proprietor, whose name was obviously Peter, nodded his head. 'She dumps poor old Stan on the son.'

Mrs Cotes turned her steely eye upon them. 'And where are you lads from, then?' She had finally got around to asking the question Billy suspected had been her destination all along.

'Africa,' answered Reginald, and Billy turned to him in disbelief. 'We've just finished the hunting season.'

Mrs Cotes peered at them with naked curiosity: Billy could tell she was going to be shameless with her questions. 'You're not Japanese, then?' she asked Reg, who replied that he was born in Siam.

'Have you heard of it?' he asked, warming up, putting down his knife and fork. Billy smiled uncertainly at Mrs Stafford at the next table, whose hands seemed to him wrinkled and old. For some reason he felt sorry for her, sitting tired and worn out in the splendours of the Astor House Private Hotel. Her thin gold wedding band was too large for her finger: it swung on the bone as she rested her hand on the edge of her saucer. Billy heard Reg telling all sorts of lies but was far too earnest to join him: even though he knew he would never again see Mrs Stafford, Mrs Cotes or the fat child Shirley, he could not bring himself to indulge in such sport. He had disliked Mrs Helen Cotes instantly, yet he could not bear to send her up like Reg did. Reg was clearly having great fun with her, though: he now had her asking questions about cannibals. Billy watched his friend sailing dangerously, enjoying himself, not taking it seriously at all: the trouble was, Billy took everything seriously, which was one of the reasons he needed Reg Tsang. Reg showed him that you could poke out your tongue and the sky wouldn't fall down, you could laugh without expecting to pay for it later. He looked over at stout Mrs Cotes who appeared not to know she was being taken for a ride. Billy thought that perhaps jokes were possible after all, but would leave the pulling of them to Reg.

Blackpool lay under a watery sun, its streets full of holidaying families. Babies nodded under sunflower hats, their eyes closed against the morning sun. Grandparents walked their grandchildren, who ran ahead knowing old legs could never keep up. Ahead of Billy and Reg a group of ageing idiots were being steered along the street, their hands linked like children. It seemed to Billy that there was an enormous number of old men and old women, sitting stiffly in chairs facing the sea. There were indeed waves, small eruptions of water which welled up into a series of watery cliffs before falling over themselves on to sand. The sand was greyish and damp looking all the way from the sea wall to the ocean; clumps of donkeys wearing brightly coloured blankets under saddles stood dejectedly upon it. Gypsies tried to cajole passing parents into buying rides for their children, but the donkeys did not seem interested enough, being transfixed by some donkey message in the sand. The water looked cold; children shrieked; young girls squealed when it touched them.

Billy and Reg walked the length of the promenade, where acts were just beginning to be set up again after the winter break. They stopped to look at a fire-eater in a loin-cloth, and at a two-hundred-pound woman. The woman's flesh lived an independent life well away from her bones; her head seemed a million miles from her knees. The flesh quivered with effort as she reached down to shake a small boy's hand. The woman caught Billy's eye as she did so and she smiled at him, pursing her lips as if about to move forward with a kiss. Pushing Reg on, Billy walked off hastily, but not before the crowd saw his panic and laughed.

Reg laughed too, but Billy felt embarrassed, not finding it funny at all. He began to walk a little ahead of Reg, moving fast so that the distance between them slowly grew. He looked at the trams headed for Pleasure Beach, the piers stretching out over the sea and the grey tower, its needle tirelessly pointing. He wore his new round aviator glasses and smoked a cigarette; he had on his new wide-lapel suit. A girl passed and he smiled at her: unexpectedly she smiled back. On the strength of this Billy decided he would like to go dancing; he stopped at a window and waited for Reg to catch up.

At that very moment at 26 Osborne Road, Blackpool, Miss Bubbles Drake was painting her toenails. She was preparing to go to the same dance as Billy Hayes, so in effect she was preparing to meet him.

Christened Olive Jean Drake, she would never be seen by Billy Hayes without her toenails painted, not once. Yet despite her silly nickname and her penchant for toenail polish, Miss Bubbles Drake was a determined young woman. She was determined to leave Blackpool, her mother, her life: she was determined her coming life would be different.

Miss Bubbles Drake's most salient feature was a preternatural self-possession, remarked upon since her earliest childhood. She had the most startlingly level gaze many people had ever encountered, possibly more pronounced because of the dark and gleaming nature of her eyes. Her eyes were large and appeared oddly moist, cast over with a kind of fine sheen. This accident of birth meant Bubbles Drake often disconcerted people without ever opening her mouth, for she did not smile much and her unnerving gaze caused people to think she had looked into their most private selves and found them wanting. Amongst the girls at school this self-possession had turned her into a minor celebrity, a girl clearly capable of a withering remark, even if no one could actually remember what she said when she did speak. Her face spoke for her, giving her a reputation of being more sardonic than she actually was.

Bubbles Drake had very elegant feet with a high dancer's arch and thin, tapered legs with the merest swell of calf. On the dressing-table in front of her she had lined up her two best pairs of shoes while she tried to decide which to wear. Her knees were tucked up beneath her chin and her toes were splayed out over the edge of the stool she was sitting on: every now and then she blew down. She had cut up an old pillowcase of her mother's so that she could wedge bits of cloth between her toes to assist both the painting and the drying.

She raised her eyes from the shoes to look at her face, which a male teacher had once described as challenging. She was not sure what he meant exactly but took it as a compliment, knowing already she had the kind of face men liked. She had dark wavy hair and a short nose, finely made. She believed her eyes were her luckiest feature, being almost black, and heavily lashed; her mouth was pretty too, plump, well shaped. Miss Bubbles Drake was pleased with what she saw in the mirror, as if she had guessed already that she held the superior hand.

Miss Bubbles Drake

The first thing anyone did on entering the Tower Ballroom was look up. The ceiling was covered in gold leaf and sculptured plaster, frescos of angels weaved between enormous chandeliers. The largest of them was twenty feet in diameter; fat crystal drops swung against the gold. Above the stage, words were written in gold lettering: *Bid Me Discourse I Will Enchant Thine Ear*. On the stage itself there was a painted backdrop of the Bay of Naples and in front of this a Wurlitzer organ. Two tiers of gold-leaf-covered balconies ran the entire length of the room. There seemed to be thousands of people dressed in shiny costumes, a thousand bodies moving under gold.

Into this room stepped Billy and Reg, Billy with his head bent right back so that he tripped over the few stairs leading down. He recovered himself and blindly followed Reg, who was headed for the other side of the room. Small circular tables were scattered on a raised platform above the dance floor; each table had a candle in the centre under glass. Reg reached a table where a lone man was sitting and asked if they could sit down.

'I won't stop you,' the man said, turning his back. Reg shrugged and they sat down: Billy immediately took out his cigarettes while Reg looked around for a waiter. When they had their drinks (a pint for Reg and a sherry for Billy), both of them sat back to watch.

Billy inspected the room with interest: girls at tables smiled at him, young couples moved close on the dance floor. He looked up at the ceiling again, at the band in the distance, at the tiered balcony above his head.

And then his eyes passed a table and stopped: he saw a girl different from the others in her remarkable self-possession. Her eyes did not roam ceaselessly in search of compliments or love, they were not over-alert like his own. She was talking to another girl and did not see him but occasionally turned her head to watch the dancers as she talked. When she had her head half turned, Billy saw her short fine nose and the weave of her hair, which fell in a curvy wave. Straight away it struck him that her head contained distinguished and peerless thoughts, kept private only to avoid offending.

Billy Hayes could not have said what it was about Bubbles Drake which compelled him so intensely, only that he felt a recognition. While he knew very well that he had never before set eyes on this young woman, she was also known to him, as if he remembered her from somewhere. And so it was that Billy picked up his glass and walked toward his future, which he recognized as alive before him.

When he later came to recall this moment Billy could never recall exactly what he had said. He must have stood silently before her, so that she eventually turned and looked up at him quizzically.

'Here's trouble,' was what Nettie Turnbull actually said, giving Billy Hayes a good look. 'It'll cost yer,' she continued, digging Bubbles in the ribs and laughing, but Bubbles was staring at Billy without smiling, staring at him so hard it made Nettie nervous.

'Have you two met?' she asked loudly, waving a hand in front of Bubbles Drake's face. When this drew no response, she held out her other hand. 'Nettie Turnbull. How d'you do?'

This attracted Billy's attention. 'Oh, excuse me,' he said, smiling. 'Billy Hayes. And you're . . .'

'Bubbles Drake,' she answered and Billy heard her voice, which sounded exactly like he expected it to sound.

'Would you like to dance?' he asked and she stood up. He touched her skin for the first time.

They left the ballroom as if they had known they would, leaving together without either asking the other where they were going. They walked straight out the door and across the promenade, taking the stone steps down to the beach. The tide was out and couples lay all along the sand, black shapes you couldn't see until you were almost upon them. They walked up under Central Pier and leant against the cool wood; there was only the thinnest sliver of moon casting a poor light.

Bubbles Drake stood with her back against him; his arms came around to mix with her own. Billy's chin rested on the top of her head: he could not see her face but knew that both of them stared at the moon. They still had not spoken, but Billy knew this was all right, that they had divined each other without explanation. It was the oddest sensation, yet instinct had told him all he needed, and he knew he finally held in his arms the right girl. He had never been surer of anything and felt the rush of something freeing and unexpected, a queer skimming sense that his life was about to change.

'So, Billy Hayes,' Miss Bubbles Drake said in a low voice, and instinctively he drew his face closer, 'tell me who you are.'

He did not feel at all the need to speak and listened to her voice in the night, to the sound of water, of cars. He knew himself to be falling without holding on and relished the danger and exhilaration of the fall. He wanted to fall and forgot the ground: he loved only the rush of the moment.

'Let me see,' she said slowly, drawing her words out. 'You're wearing a new suit, very fashionable, so you must have the kind of job where how you look counts. You're not a waiter at some posh London hotel, are you?'

Billy laughed. 'Well, you never know,' she said, leaning her head back against his chest. 'Actually, I think you're an entertainer. You've got a way of holding yourself . . .'

Billy felt the swell of pride, followed by astonishment at her powers of perception. He held tighter to this unsmiling girl, this steady-eyed girl who was about to unmask him.

After a while he finally spoke, and his voice sounded boastful even to him. 'I'm a tumbler,' he said. 'A *professional* tumbler,' he added, making sure she understood the difference.

Bubbles Drake simply said, 'See, I was right. I knew you were an entertainer.' She did not ask any further questions: her ears seemed not to hear the pride in Billy's voice. He did not know why but he wanted her to ask him more questions, to sound impressed like other people. All at once he felt overwhelmingly compelled to arouse her interest, to make this girl understand what tumbling meant to him, and how it had been the vehicle by which he had come to know his own self. Never before in his life had he tried to explain himself to another person: never before had he wished to be so completely understood. Without intending to Billy Hayes stumbled forward, without the right words, trying

126

and failing, over and over. He could not say how it had happened but he found himself trying to explain his whole life, his father's opposition, how the more his father disparaged him, the more Billy wished to succeed.

Suddenly she broke away. 'Thy limbs are burning through the vest which seems to hide them,' she quoted, walking off. 'You haven't asked one single thing about me.'

She led him by the hand to a hotel a few streets from the water; she stood perfectly poised while he signed the register. He signed them in as Mr and Mrs Billy Hayes and his hand trembled at the look of it. She did not speak as he opened the door but held the tail of his coat like a child. When he kissed her he felt the rush of his whole self toward her.

It was only in the light of early morning that Billy turned to her lying beside him, to look carefully over every inch of her face. She was asleep and lay quietly breathing: he wondered if, like himself, she remembered him too. He did not know anything about her, only that his whole life was now changed.

Miss Bubbles Drake proved to be two years older than himself, and had the unlikeliest job he could think of: she worked as an usherette at the Palace Cinema, a theatre which had only recently been converted. She did not look like an usherette to him, for Billy found her glance far too intimidating. Miss Bubbles Drake unexpectedly loved the movies, the cold and perfect face of Miss Greta Garbo, the lashy eyes of Laurence Olivier. She also loved reading and carried library books around with her: Dickens and J. B. Priestley, a copy of *Madame Bovary*, which the librarian had recommended. She knew certain poems off by heart: Billy had never met anyone before who read books willingly and who could quote poetry. It seemed to him that he was immediately outclassed, that Miss Bubbles Drake was far cleverer than himself. He did not know that she had finished school at much the same age as him and that the only time she had met a man who had gone to university she did not open her mouth once except to say hello. Bubbles Drake felt that quoting poetry gave her a certain class, and experience had told her that it also served to impress certain men. Yet she had grown to like the sound of it too, the sure feel of words on her tongue.

The second morning after they met Bubbles offered to sneak Billy into the Palace Cinema for free. They were walking up Church Street: Bubbles was on her way to work and Billy held the lightness of her fingers in his hand. He had a sudden urge to throw her against a wall, so that he could feel the length of her pressed against him and force her eyes to look properly into his. Her beautiful dark eyes had a tendency to wander, to look anywhere but into his own. He had spent one day and two nights with her but still imagined she had not properly seen him. He had noticed too her tendency to smile a secret smile, as if she were thinking some private thought she would never tell him. He did not know if this smile was deliberate, with the specific goal of arousing his curiosity, or whether it was completely unselfconscious. He knew only that he wanted Bubbles Drake to tell him everything, and for her to listen as he explained himself to her. It did not occur to him that he hardly knew her; she already felt like part of his own self.

When he eventually walked back to the Astor House Private Hotel, Billy's eyes had an infected blaze. High emotion had intensified all the colours of his face: he smiled inappropriately, and often. As he pushed open the front door he saw Reg sitting in the lounge and rushed through the room toward him.

'I've met my wife,' he announced, hugging Reg around the shoulders. 'Reg, I've finally met her!'

Reg stood up and looked into his eyes. 'Sit down, you idiot,' he said, pushing him into a chair. 'I'll just get a bucket of cold water.'

Billy smiled and it seemed to him that all his words would not be enough, all the words in the world could not tell how he was feeling.

'She's wonderful,' he began, regardless, 'she's clever and beautiful and funny. She reads books all the time and can quote all this poetry, she even knows one about tumblers. She – '

'Stop!' Reg instructed, holding up his hand, and Billy looked at him in surprise. He realized that he was sitting on the lip of his chair, and sat back, crossing his legs. Reg still had his hand up; at the same moment Reg noticed this too, and sat back in his chair like Billy. There was a small silence until Billy could no longer bear it. 'Well, what do you think of her?' he asked, uncrossing his legs and once again sitting forward.

'I didn't get much of a chance to find out,' Reg said. 'You two had disappeared before I knew it.'

Billy smiled again, at the memory, at the happiness which seemed suddenly his. 'But you met her,' he insisted, 'you must have thought something!'

Reg looked away from him and out the window. Billy waited, anxious to hear his best friend's opinion.

'Look, I don't really know her,' Reg said, turning to Billy, but Billy's face must have telegraphed its disappointment. 'She's very pretty,' Reg added, and Billy grinned.

'What's her real name?' Reg asked after a moment.

'Ah . . . I don't know,' Billy admitted, suddenly embarrassed.

Reg stood up and walked toward the door. 'You'd better find out your wife's name,' he said. 'It might help.'

Of course Billy had to arrange a formal meeting between Bubbles and Reg. He worried all night about where the right place might be, where each of them would feel most comfortable. He considered the Tower Ballroom for afternoon tea but rejected it as too fussy; he thought of a café somewhere but that would probably be too noisy. Finally he settled on Central Pier, in the sunshine and the open air, with the added advantage of his being able to wear his dark glasses, so he might watch them both unobserved. This meeting was important to him: his oldest and dearest friend, and the woman he had chosen above all others. For Billy already knew that Bubbles Drake would be his: he hadn't actually sat down and thought about this but simply knew it. Lily Tsang was at one stroke banished from his head, and the only thing in the world now was that Reg and Bubbles should like each other. When Billy thought about it he could not see how they could fail to, for Reg was the most easygoing, likeable of fellows and Bubbles was such an arresting person.

On the morning of the meeting Billy got up early for a swim. Reg was still sleeping so he snuck out, running into poor Mrs Stafford in the corridor. She was dressed in her nightgown and on her way to the bathroom; she rushed past him in a flurry of embarrassment. He wondered if she had found herself a job yet, a financial life-raft which would allow her to strike a blow for independence. He thought about her as he walked down the stairs, thinking that she would probably scurry sadly back to her husband if she did not find a job soon. He felt sorry for Mrs Stafford and all the other people who did not have love.

On the street he knew that all the girls passing fell a little in love with him, for love had turned him more handsome. He wore only a pair of black swimming trunks; a beach towel was slung over one shoulder. His body was taut, muscled; he felt the shape of his calves as he walked. He seemed to walk effortlessly, with a graceful posture and all his muscles and sinews worked well. Dropping his towel on the sand, he plunged into the water, which was cold and stung his chest. He was a strong swimmer; his hands carved the sea, pulling him forward by his own force. He swam a long way tirelessly, swallowing salt, feeling the water resist him. He pushed hard into the ocean, turning his head to suck air through his mouth. He finally stopped and dived below the surface, opening his eyes to the wavering sea-world. Kicking up, he broke the surface, and saw he was a long way from the shore. Billy trod water, his mouth closed against the sea: he could have swum to Ireland if he had wanted. He was light, empty of pain and would never feel its heaviness again.

Billy saw Bubbles Drake waiting as arranged outside the Metropole, an easy walk to the pier. She wore a calf-length floral dress, buckled at the waist and puffed at the sleeves; a summer hat framed her face. Because she was reading *Madame Bovary*, she did not see them: when she did raise her head she looked straight into Billy's eyes for the first time, with an accuracy which could not have been planned.

'You're late,' she said as he kissed her cheek.

'You're early,' he countered, giving her bum a light thwack. She smiled at him, for in his absence she had obviously discovered that she was in love too. Unbelievably Bubbles Drake was looking into Billy's eyes as if the whole world were in them; he held her hand for the longest time.

'Ahem,' interrupted Reg, and Billy broke Bubbles's gaze and laughed.

'Bubbles, I'd like you to meet my best friend, Reg Tsang. I don't think you were properly introduced.' He stood back, perhaps waiting for them to clasp each other to their bosoms, and was unprepared for Bubbles's mumbled hello.

Reg held out his hand and she politely shook it. 'Pleased to meet you,' he said tentatively. An embarrassed pause suddenly fell on the little group: each sensed the arrival of a significant moment, yet none was equipped to deal with it. They all understood that from now on their lives would be joined in some way, yet they also knew so little about each other that this fact could only serve to embarrass them.

'How 'bout an ice-cream?' said Billy finally. 'Bubbles?' he queried, holding out his arm.

A ridge of clouds was banked up high behind the city, leaving the rest of the sky free. Through the cracks between the wooden planks of the pier Billy saw the glint of water flowing beneath them. Children screamed as they tried to shoot ducks; a merry-go-round played 'Greensleeves'. In the middle of all this they sat in deck-chairs, hired from an ageing dwarf. Bubbles licked at her ice-cream, her curled pink tongue sliding round the edge of it: Billy watched in fascination, forgetting to lick his own so that it dripped on to his hand. It seemed hard to make conversation: Reg was trying, but Bubbles answered too briefly and the conversation did not blossom naturally as it sometimes does from an unpromising start with questions and answers. Bubbles seemed to have no sense of social obligation; she did not ask Reg any questions in return and Billy found himself feeling obliged to explain Reg's history. He sat with a strained alertness, ready to urge them both on.

'Reg's been tumbling since he was a baby. By the time he was two years old he could balance in his father's hand,' he began, hoping to spark some interest. But Bubbles continued to look out to sea, her dark eyes squinting slightly.

'Have you lived in Blackpool long?' Reg asked.

'All my life,' she answered.

'What does your dad do?' Reg inquired.

'He's dead,' she said, noncommittally, crunching into the top of her cone. 'I live with my mother,' she said, and Billy gave a sigh of relief that she had finally offered information unsolicited. Of course he did not know yet that Bubbles and her mother fought all the time, that her mother considered her stubborn and fatally strong-willed like her father.

'I want to be an actress,' Bubbles Drake said out of the blue. 'Do you think you could introduce me to someone?' She turned to Billy and looked at him solemnly, her steady gaze laying down a challenge.

'Sure,' he said, without hesitation. 'Frank Hurley will know someone, I bet.' He was surprised by this ambition but also pleased that Bubbles Drake had plans like he did. He looked over at Reg to see if he had picked up on this too, but Reg did not meet his eyes.

'What do you think of her now?' Billy asked, as soon as they were out of earshot.

'She's not exactly forthcoming, is she?' Reg replied, and Billy dropped his hand from Reg's arm.

'Oh, come on, Billy,' Reg said, 'you couldn't call her the friend-liest girl in the world.'

Billy stopped walking. Reg stopped too, looking back at Billy in exasperation. 'You hardly know her yourself, Hayes,' he continued, crossing the boundary, stamping on every marked line. Outrage sprang up in Billy's chest: Reg Tsang telling him what he did or did not know!

'I know all I need to know about her, Reg,' he said, 'and I don't think it's any of your business.'

He walked past Reg, toward the Tower, moving fast to burn up his fury. 'Don't ask, then, if you don't want an answer!' Reg called and Billy put his head down, walking harder. It was only after he had walked for a long time that he realized he had just had his first fight with Reg Tsang. He stopped walking and looked around, then made his way back to the centre of town, to wait for Bubbles Drake to finish work and save him.

The rest of the holiday Billy spent mostly with Bubbles, feeling guiltier and guiltier about Reg. He could not quite look him in the eye in the mornings as he rushed off to meet her, and found it painful to ask Reg what his plans were for the day. 'Oh, I thought

I might have a look at Pleasure Beach,' Reg might answer, or offer some outing with a group of recently made friends. They did not talk again of Bubbles, or of their fight, but were exaggeratedly polite to each other by way of a peace offering. Once or twice Billy suggested to Bubbles that they include Reg in their plans, but she argued that they should spend as much time as they could getting to know each other. 'I'm sure Reg can look after himself,' she said, holding Billy's hand firmly. Bubbles told him that Reg was not his responsibility anyway, and that her friend Nettie certainly knew how to disappear when a fellow came along.

'Have there been many?' Billy inquired as if it were a casual question: he thought he might die if she gave the wrong reply.

'Oh, one or two,' she answered, laughing. 'I've been out with a few fellows in my time.' He smiled at her, but he did not mean it.

Returning to the Astor House each evening, Billy's head was filled with Bubbles Drake. Every day she told him another long desperate story about her family, full of dramatic flourish. She described her failed, doomed mother in such acute but overwrought detail, for example, that it seemed impossible there could be any other version. Mrs Elsa Drake sprang drunkenly to life, a once beautiful woman grown dangerous and manipulative, reduced to torturing her beautiful daughter for want of any other outlet. 'She killed my father. He hanged himself,' Bubbles said in a low voice, her face moved by her own violent history. Billy saw that she was inexplicably proud of her history: it was hers, she had earned it. She idealized her dead father, whom she described as a saint, alternately bullied and toyed with by her mother until he had the good sense to flee.

'He killed himself *after* he left her?' Billy asked incredulously.

'It's a long story,' she said, smiling mysteriously, holding his head between her warm hands and kissing him.

Bubbles Drake also made him feel his own life was noble and dramatic, and he found himself talking readily about his father, telling her about the night Jack Hayes had stopped him from going to the Talent Quest. Billy had never before spoken so freely: not to Reg, not to Lily. He felt a kind of inner recklessness, as if Bubbles Drake had made his life sharper. It seemed to him that he had met someone whose passions ran unseen beneath the course

His Shining Girl

The holiday confirmed Vernon Rome's worst fears: Billy returned to London, but not all of him came back. He was preoccupied and disgustingly cheerful, taking up his mother's habit of whistling, but unfortunately Billy's whistle was tuneless and quickly drove Vernon to distraction. Vernon would walk into a room and find him whistling, or else Billy would drift off into space during practice, his concentration worse than Connie's.

He suddenly spent all his time writing letters, and a lot of money placing telephone calls to 26 Osborne Road. He became obsessed with finding work on the northern circuits too, which might not take them as far as Blackpool but would place them close enough. One afternoon he paid his first private visit to Frank Hurley to see how the rest of the year was shaping up. But Billy didn't quite know how to raise the subject of Bubbles's acting ambitions: he had in mind that Bubbles herself might do the best job, which would fortuitously require her presence in London.

When Vernon found out about Billy's visit to Frank he was angry. Billy listened to Vernon's tirade, but it was as if Vernon spoke to him from under water, for nothing unpleasant could reach him, only pleasure came to him direct and strong. Of course this infuriated Vernon still further: the mere sight of Billy's happy face inspired in him a wish to strike it. He stormed off instead, punching a fist hard into the palm of his hand.

It was Connie who asked who the girl was, and who listened as he told her all about it. Her own heart might lately have grown still, but she recognized at once the unmistakable signs of excitation in Billy's.

'That bad, huh,' she said when he had finished. He leant forward to her, his face aglow.

'Oh, Connie, you'll love her!' No words were vivid enough to describe Bubbles Drake, no words existed to describe the violence of his emotions. Nevertheless, Billy watched Connie expectantly, feeling she of all people would know what he meant.

But Connie only looked away and lit a cigarette: she appeared to be thinking of something else. 'Connie?' Billy said tentatively, touching her hand.

She smiled a smile which only concerned her mouth. 'I'll just say one thing, Billy. You're very young, and goddesses have a way of turning to clay. Just don't get married yet, OK?'

He was furious with her, and saw clearly for the first time her spoilt charms. Without speaking Billy stood up and walked away, believing he could never forgive such a jealous, ungenerous moment.

All at once it seemed that Bubbles Drake was his only confidante, his safe berth in a hostile world. He was convinced of both Connie's and Vernon's antagonism, and felt a distinct lack of encouragement from Reg. Reg never again said anything overt to Billy about Bubbles, yet Billy knew that even his best friend was not wholeheartedly urging him forward. He wanted the entire world to cheer for them, and could not understand why everyone did not immediately see Bubbles Drake in all her glory like he did. Only people who did not know the true facts saw their match as a wild, incautious lunge at love. Billy alone knew otherwise.

'We'll have to hide it,' Bubbles said to him on the telephone late one night.

'Hide what?' he asked.

'Our happiness, you ninny,' she teased, her voice close to his ear. 'People don't like it when you get away with it. Do you think it's possible everyone else in the world is unhappy except us?'

'Yes,' he answered, grinning.

'I don't. I think there's a secret society of happy people all pretending to be unhappy just in case anyone accuses them of being smug.'

'Smug,' said Billy. 'I like your voice. Say "smug" again.'

She laughed, a low, erotic laugh, at least it sounded erotic to him. Every night now he sat pressed to the telephone, her voice falling into the curl of his ear. It felt shockingly intimate, as though she had penetrated his most private self, and now had free access to the inside. Her voice seemed to be roaming his ear canal, moving through the far reaches of his head. The telephone itself became an erotic object: when he held it he savoured the feel of it in his fingers, the heat which rose from it after he held the receiver for a long time in his hand.

In this way Bubbles Drake came to him, an intimate secret spoken straight into his ear. She came to him, a disembodied voice over a telephone, so that for ever after Billy felt that he had got to know her from the voice up. It was as if he had been given the essence of her first, without the distraction of her body, and because of this he liked to think they had achieved some kind of unsullied communion. He truly believed they had laid themselves bare, confessing everything of importance, and that no misunderstanding would ever bar their way.

To Billy their coming together seemed a spontaneous natural event, some law of motion which could have no other conclusion. He saw that he had been longing to fall in love, and Bubbles obviously had too. She wanted to know all these things, for instance, about London, about show business, about the West End: to Billy it was clear she found the idea of him exciting. If he still sensed a tantalizing distance between them he felt sure he could close it, just as he felt sure he would one day understand her secret smiles. If Bubbles did not seem impressed by his tumbling, it was only because she had not seen him tumble: once she had, he felt sure she would not be able to withhold her admiration.

And so it was nightly over the telephone that Bubbles Drake coloured herself in: Billy saw her at age five, at ten, at fourteen, the only child of a merciless mother.

'Do you know what she said to me when I went out to my first dance? She looked at me, cold as ice, and said, "You're a pretty girl, Bubbles, but I don't think you're as pretty as I was." Can you imagine? I was just about to walk out the door!'

Billy loved to hear her tell these stories, to hear the fierceness in her voice as she told them. He heard Bubbles's will, her determination, her spit, her steady refusal to bow down. He saw her dark unwavering eyes at fifteen, refusing to cry when her mother shouted that she wished she'd got to the doctor's sooner so Bubbles would never have been born.

'The old cow thinks she might have been someone,' Bubbles said scathingly, 'but it's just an excuse. She's always blaming someone else, me or Dad. It's always someone else's fault that she didn't get the life she deserved.'

Billy thought Bubbles's perceptions acute; he admired the way she saw through people. She allowed him to picture a drunken Mrs Elsa Drake twittering like a fool the moment a man walked into the room, still believing herself a fatal beauty.

He saw at once Bubbles as a grave-faced child, the still centre between her battling parents. He supposed that gravity had settled permanently on her face then, a kind of mask beneath which she could keep her true self hidden.

Always after these hypnotic conversations Billy put the phone down and remained completely still for long moments until he had navigated his way back to the room. Afterwards he felt strangely light-headed and it was all he could do to stand up and make his way upstairs.

One night as he sat by the phone telling himself he should get up Billy felt a flash of something oddly like fear. He glimpsed for a moment the magnitude of what he was expecting, how every hope he had was entrusted to a happy ending. Billy stood up and flexed his hands, walking quickly toward the door. He told himself that love was hard, but that he and Bubbles Drake could not fail it.

At last they got a booking with the Broadhead Circuit, which took them to four towns in the north, including Blackpool. Billy rang Bubbles immediately to tell her; she promised to be at the station to meet him. It seemed inconceivable that time would pass until then; Billy kept Vernon awake at nights tossing and turning. Days were not real to him because Bubbles was not in them: time was a stiff wall he pushed against. Billy began to fear that the months apart had been too long, and that Bubbles Drake was not how he had dreamt her.

When the train finally pulled in Blackpool, Bubbles was nowhere to be seen. Billy jumped from the train, moving quickly along the platform, but he had been looking from the window long before the train stopped and knew she was not there. Vernon shouted at him to help with the luggage, but he ignored this, his eyes searching the crowd. Just as he was about to collapse from disappointment he saw her coming through the ticket gates: she was wearing a hat and gloves, her hair was flying. He stood still and waited for her to see him: she gave a small wave before breaking into a run.

They were booked at the Palace, on a bill which included the hypnotist Lawrence La Fosse. Since Connie had broken up with him, he had sent her many letters, written in the language of lost love. She was convinced he had somehow connived his way on to the same programme as the Wallabies with the intention of winning her back. 'That's all I need,' she said to Billy crossly, 'a love-struck hypnotist and you!' Connie had avoided Larry on the train from Newcastle, by refusing to speak when he approached. He finally gave up after several rebuffs and as they left the station, Billy saw Larry trailing sadly behind.

Connie did her best to ignore Bubbles too as they passed in a knot through the exit, but Billy saw that she certainly gave Bubbles the once-over. Billy had never quite recovered his old relationship with Connie and only introduced her to Bubbles now because it was impossible not to. Billy thought he detected a lecherous spark in Vernon's eye, although he was willing to believe that he might be wrong: because he considered Bubbles Drake the most desirable woman in the world, he assumed everyone else did too. When they jumped into a taxi ahead of Vernon and Connie, Billy saw Vernon's eye unmistakably linger on Bubbles's ankle, before Vernon recovered his anger and yelled, 'Where the hell do you think you're going?' Billy ignored him but could not resist looking back as the taxi pulled away, to see Vernon Rome both angry and astonished.

In the taxi Billy looked fully into Bubbles's face for the first time since he had arrived; he felt embarrassment overcome him, an awkwardness that made him immediately turn his face away. He found he did not know what to say, even though he had already said so much. Confronted by Bubbles Drake's physical person again he was struck dumb, and wondered how on earth they would be brave enough to speak again face to face. And yet he felt a rush of relief too, for he had been frightened of having made her up. He turned to her and knew once more that instinct had drawn him to the right face. Her fingers in his were working instruments, powerful and alive.

Bubbles too seemed suddenly shy; her mouth twisted up as he watched into an odd half-smile. She met his eyes, her own eyes guarded, her small face wary and appraising. He thought he remembered her saying her face was a mask, but to him her eyes were two live things, moving and full of will; her whole face was driven by passion. Billy instinctively knew he must reveal himself slowly, disclosing patiently the fact that he was unarmed. For the moment he turned away but continued to hold her hand, trying to convey to her through the flesh of their fingers that she was safe and that love had saved them.

What She Said Wrong

The morning after his arrival Billy woke alone in bed, remembering at once that this was the day when Bubbles Drake would see him on stage for the first time. He immediately pictured her face in the front row and himself smiling down upon her astonishment. Until now she had only known him as a man on two legs: she had not yet witnessed him travelling. He had tried to tell her how all his intelligence was stored in his muscles, how when he was moving through air he was his own true self, but he knew that until she saw it with her own eyes she could not understand this. All the words in the world could not speak like his body: only when Bubbles Drake had witnessed him moving would she see the whole of him, the best part. Her steady eyes would receive this gift, a public act which inexplicably was also the most private.

He jumped out of bed and knocked loudly on the thin wall where he knew Vernon to be sleeping. 'Rise and shine!' he called just to annoy him: he heard Vernon moving. Billy grabbed his dressing-gown and headed for the bathroom, whistling a silly song which was currently popular.

After they got the running order from the stage manager, Alf, Billy slung his coat over his shoulder and headed for the door.

'I'm off to see Bubbles,' he called as he walked down the aisle.

'Oh no you're not,' Vernon replied. Billy stopped but did not turn around.

'Get back here this instant,' Vernon said quietly. Billy recognized that the moment he had been expecting was upon him. He spun round, his mouth dry.

'Vernon, I'm going to meet Bubbles. There's nothing else for me to do here.'

Vernon jumped from the stage and walked quickly toward him. 'Listen, Billy, you'll do what I tell you.'

Billy knew then that there would be no avoiding this, that it must be seen through to its logical end. He felt himself trembling as if in great fear, yet he was angry and ready to slay. He stood perfectly still while he waited for Vernon to reach him: it seemed important to remain standing where he was. As he watched Vernon charging forward he suddenly realized that he was no longer frightened and that Vernon did not yet comprehend his own impotence.

When Vernon reached him he stood so close that Billy saw a nerve jump in his cheek. His breath came quick and loud; he opened his mouth and pointed a finger. At the same instant Billy placed a hand squarely on Vernon's chest, as if to prevent him from passing.

'I've been doing what you've told me since I was fifteen, Vernon. I'm almost twenty now. No more.'

Billy saw the precise moment when Vernon Rome decided not to speak, when he finally understood it was over. Billy saw this moment pass across his face, and new knowledge settle in his eyes. Vernon closed his mouth and gave a curt nod of the head, an unconscious gesture which signified an ending. Turning on his heel, he walked back in the direction from which he came, moving fast, his back straight.

Billy continued to stand in the aisle of the Palace Theatre stalls, not yet ready to believe the argument to be finished. If he had expected a long and strenuous battle, it was already won, bloodlessly, in all of five minutes. He felt oddly stranded, as if he wished for more, to punch Vernon, to shout at him for trying to run his life. Instead there was only this unexpected emptiness, a sense of anticlimax, and Billy understood that his old life was over in a flash.

Billy had arranged to meet Bubbles at Robert's Oyster Rooms, for she had told him about her fondness for jellied eel. He saw her as soon as he walked in, sitting at a table next to an open window. She did not smile as he joined her but cursorily turned up her cheek to be kissed.

'I've finally had it out with Vernon,' he burst out. 'He tried to stop me coming to meet you!' She did not appear to understand the implications of what he was saying. Billy quickly tried to reiterate how Vernon had controlled every aspect of his life, from what time he ate to how much he got paid.

'Oh, I never understood why you put up with it in the first place,' Bubbles said in an offhand way, her eyes roaming the menu. Billy angrily snatched the menu away from her and grabbed her hands within his.

'Bubbles, this is important! The Wallabies have been my whole life!'

'Don't shout,' she hissed, looking quickly around the room. 'Don't you think I know every damn thing about the Wallabies there is to know?' She must have seen a look of pain pass across his face, for she leant forward and her mouth softened.

'Look, I know it's important, sweetheart. Go on, tell me what happened.' He stared at her but he did not trust her interest. 'I'll tell you later,' he said, picking up the menu.

After they had eaten, Billy asked Bubbles if her mother would like a ticket to the show.

'She would, but I'm not taking her.' She looked out the window; her face was unyielding. Something hard and rebellious flashed across it, and Billy moved closer.

'Isn't there one good thing about your mother?' he asked gently, not willing to believe it.

'No,' she answered straight away. 'Isn't there one good thing about your father?'

He sprang back. 'Maybe there was once,' he said, standing up. Billy recalled that lately in his dreams his father had begun to talk to him kindly, listening to him as if he cared for and respected what he had to say. In the morning Billy could never recollect what it was he said to his father exactly nor what his father said to him. He remembered the feeling of being listened to, though, he remembered the feeling of being loved.

Opening the door of the dressing-room, Billy saw Connie's head over the top of her clothes trunk. She didn't see him and continued to sort through a pile of clothes, her eyes screwed up in concentration. She had her hair wrapped in towel and a burning cigarette hanging from one lip: she looked so much her own scatterbrained self that Billy was struck through at the sight of her.

Just then she looked up and saw him: she removed the cigarette from her lips.

'How goes it, Romeo?' she said, cupping one hand as an ashtray. 'Do you think you could pass me that *cendrier*?'

Billy reached over and handed her the chipped saucer which passed as an ashtray: already it held a little mound of lipstick-ringed butts. She tipped the ash from her cupped palm into it, then stood up and gingerly negotiated her way round the clothes trunk.

'You can see we're not top of the bill,' she said, reaching a stool and sitting down. 'How's Blossom?'

He decided she knew very well what Bubbles's name was: he sat down and began to put on his make-up. He was still cross with Connie, but his anger was now mixed with a poignancy: he had picked up the scent of an ending and everything was cast over with loss. They both sat in silence while they worked on their faces; the only sound was Connie scuffling amongst her creams.

'She's a beautiful girl,' Connie said into the silence, a peace offering which Billy chose to accept.

'Isn't she?' he replied, pulling on his costume. He was pleased by Connie's gesture but did not want her to know this and he wished to make clear to her that he was not seeking her approval. He sensed a shift in the balance of power and knew it would be of tactical advantage to keep silent.

The door opened and Vernon came in, already unbuttoning his collar.

'Evening,' he said to them both with a kind of bow: Connie raised her eyebrows in the mirror. Billy resisted an urge to look at Vernon too closely, for he wished to give the impression he did not care for Vernon's opinion.

'Is Bubbles in tonight?' Vernon asked, giving himself a look-over in the full-length mirror behind the door.

'I think so,' Billy replied, although he knew full well that she was.

'Splendid,' Vernon replied, his voice sarcastic, 'we'll do tonight especially for her.' And with that he left the room. Billy did not look at Connie but went on doing up his costume, his hands shaking only a little.

They were second on the bill: before they went on, Billy stood in the wings and scanned the front row, counting the seats till he got to Bubbles. He could see her face clearly: her head was turned up and she was smiling. As they ran on, Billy looked fully into Bubbles Drake's face and it seemed to him to be full of wonder.

She was standing away from the crowd when he came out the stage door. They moved toward each other and he took her hand, then thought better of it and tucked the whole of her under his left arm. She huddled there as they walked off, although the air was warm and rushed about them. The breeze lifted her skirt so that it floated; the air smelt salty and clean.

When he could not bear it any longer he broke the silence. 'Well, what did you think?'

'It was a nice show all round,' she replied, as if she were discussing something totally unrelated to him. 'The singer was marvellous. He – '

'But what did you think of the Wallabies?' he interrupted. 'What did you think of us?' He was actually asking what she thought of him, of his life's work, his career of air. He was conscious that he was holding his breath, that what she answered was of great significance.

'Vernon's a bit on the heavy side, isn't he?' she said, rearranging his arm across her shoulder. 'I thought you and Connie were fine. You know, I saw practically the same act last Christmas, except it was three girls and they did more dancing.'

By the time she had finished, Billy had come to a decision: he would impress Bubbles Drake if it was the last thing he ever did, he would make her see his tumbling was his very self! He dropped his arm and walked ahead of her, so fast she could not keep up.

'Hey, slow down!' she called plaintively, but he did not stop until he reached the sea.

Billy wanted to meet the infamous Mrs Elsa Drake before he left Blackpool, he wanted to see with his own eyes this killer of men.

'You'll be sorry,' Bubbles told him, refusing to arrange a meeting until Billy finally threatened to turn up at 26 Osborne Road himself.

'I don't understand why you want to meet her,' Bubbles said crossly. 'She's not in the least bit interesting. She'll only try to dazzle you with her beauty and tell some boring story about herself.'

'I just want to,' Billy said with what he hoped was a certain force. 'I want to know everything about you.'

At the last minute Bubbles grudgingly told him that her mother would be home the Saturday morning before they left Blackpool. 'She'd be "dilighted" to meet you she said.' Bubbles added that she was only doing it because she didn't want Billy turning up on the doorstep unannounced and finding her mother dishevelled. 'The last time one of my boyfriends came over he brought a jar of brandied cherries. We caught her in the kitchen draining them off so she could get straight to the brandy. You'd better bring chocolates.'

Billy ignored the remark about former boyfriends and told Bubbles he would be there.

On Saturday morning he dressed carefully and left his lodgings early to buy flowers. He selected a beautiful bunch of summer roses, their heads bursting from the stalks. They were the most expensive flowers at the stall and the stall owner wrapped them lavishly.

'For the girlfriend, is it, gov?' the man said with a wink.

'Her mother,' Billy replied, handing over the last of his money.

'You'd be better off with a bottle,' the stall owner advised. Billy wondered, irrationally, if the man knew Mrs Elsa Drake too.

When the taxi pulled up, Billy had a good look at the house before paying the driver and stepping out. It was a terrace in a row of scrappy houses, in need of paint and a good wash. The sea wind had stunted the garden; not even weeds appeared to grow. Looking up, Billy thought he saw a curtain move at a window. If it was Bubbles, she dropped the curtain to come down the stairs. The door opened before he reached it: Bubbles stood there and he smiled.

She ran towards him and kissed him: it was a slow kiss and involved the soft glide of her tongue.

'Hello, sweetheart,' he said, holding her: she leant back a little in his arms.

'Are you ready?' she asked grimly. 'I did warn you. She's

already half blind.' Bubbles led him by the hand through the doorway: he blinked as his eyes lost the light.

In the gloom of the front living-room, Billy could make out a shape. As his eyes cleared, he saw what he took to be a perfectly ordinary woman in a perfectly ordinary house. She was pushing herself up from a chair and moving toward him.

'How do you do, Mr Hayes?' Mrs Elsa Drake said, holding out her ringed hand. 'I'm very pleased to meet you. Very pleased.' She did not seem to him drunk in the least.

Billy shook her hand, which was warm and soft, and felt the ridges of many rings. He looked at her face and he saw with relief that she did not look at all like Bubbles, her hair was dyed black and cut in the style of the twenties, so that it appeared perched on her head like a wig. Beneath a short fringe were thin, pencilled brows; her generous mouth was painted with dark-coloured lipstick. Her eyes were small and blue, ringed with false lashes so that she gave the impression of a rather plump girl. Billy was so busy taking all this in that he forgot to hand over his flowers.

'Oh, excuse me, these are for you,' he said, placing them with a flourish in her plump hands.

'But they're exquisite!' she exclaimed theatrically. 'Darling, run and get me a vase.' She smiled at Bubbles as if she adored her. Bubbles turned away with a look of forebearance.

'Please, sit down,' Elsa Drake said, 'and call me Elsa. I was not born to be somebody's mother.' She smiled in what Billy took to be a friendly gesture: he could not possibly regard it as flirtatious. He noticed that she moved with exaggerated gestures, her chin high, as if she still imagined herself rakishly looked at.

'Have you been in the theatre long?' she asked when Billy was seated.

'Since I was a nipper,' he said, trying to look relaxed. He was not sure where to put his hands and kept moving them from the arm of his chair to his lap and back again.

'A nipper! How quaint!' Bubbles came back into the room, carrying the vase of flowers.

'What's quaint?' she asked.

'Oh, everything about this boy, darling. He's charming!'

Bubbles walked over and perched on the side of his chair. 'You've only known him for five minutes.'

'That's enough. I'm clairvoyant about these things.'

'Drunk more likely,' Bubbles said under her breath.

'I was in the theatre briefly when I was young. Not in your league, of course, but I often wonder what would have been in store for me had I continued . . .'

Bubbles coughed loudly and stood up. 'Would you like some tea?' she asked. Billy nodded. She left the room again, obviously having decided that this was her best tactic, and Billy found himself alone once more with Mrs Drake. He could not quite find the right position for his body, and shifted continually in his chair. He would adopt a pose and suddenly feel himself to be ridiculous, so that he would have to move his limbs and try again.

To distract himself he tried to imagine Elsa Drake young and beautiful: he searched for traces of beauty in the lines of her face, in the shape of her head which perched on her plump neck. But all traces had been kicked over: all he could see was a brightly painted middle-aged woman, roleless, now that her attractions had vanished.

He tried to imagine her saying cruel things to Bubbles, but his imagination failed him here too. He saw only something pleading in her, something hopeful and blind in the way she still thought she was a beauty. The false eyelashes struck him through the heart, the stiff, curled row of hair propping up a droopy fold of skin beneath each brow. Billy guessed that Mrs Elsa Drake had no idea of how other people saw her, and certainly no idea of how she had hurt Bubbles. She seemed to him only pitiful, a child bewildered by some undeserved punishment. He knew this was a betrayal of Bubbles and yet he could not help it. Billy realized she was asking him something; he sat up and said, 'Pardon?'

'Have you been in the Old Country long?' Elsa Drake repeated.

'About four years,' he replied.

'I think it's a shame to live so far from one's family. My mother and I were like that.' She brought two plump forefingers together, raising them in the air like a sign. 'I always wanted a daughter I could be close to, but Bubbles and I have never got along.'

She heaved herself up again, making her way slowly across the room. 'I don't know about you, darling, but eleven o'clock's late enough for me. Join me?' She held up the gin bottle so pleadingly Billy found himself saying yes.

'Bubbles is her father all over again. Heart like an icicle, same as him. Believe me, she'll need years of thawing.' She handed him a large unadorned gin: he would need all morning to drink it.

'She's a little bitch, actually,' Elsa Drake continued: Billy looked at her, shocked. 'Excuse my French, sweetie, but it's true. She's always done exactly what she wants, our Bubbles. She doesn't care who gets in her way. That girl'd run over her own mother if she had to.'

Billy did not know where to look: he had never heard anyone speak so harshly to a stranger about her own child.

'I know she's my daughter, but I have to say it. She's hard. Hard as nails. I'd go back to London and find myself a sweet soft thing if I were you.'

Billy heard the clatter of crockery. He turned to see Bubbles stand frozen for a moment above the tea-tray before she slammed it down and stormed from the room. As he ran after her Billy had an image of Elsa Drake sitting surprised in her lounge chair, as if she could not for the life of her imagine what she had said wrong.

A Function of the Body

When Billy got back to Herne Hill he was more determined than ever to find a way of bringing Bubbles to London. He thought of it all the time, wondering if she would find a job, where they would live, whether he could afford to keep a wife at all. But mostly he just wanted her, blindly and without reason, he wanted to lie beside her so he might heal her sorrow. This need for Bubbles Drake felt like a function of the body, he lived without noticing it but went about instinctively trying to get this need met. He could not have said precisely what it was about Bubbles that elicited this response in him, only that she felt obscurely familiar: he had travelled the world to find her and had recognized her straight away.

Billy also knew it was time to leave the Wallabies, that part of finding Bubbles had to do with leaving his childhood self behind. It seemed to him that he already felt older, as if he were preparing to take on the role of husband. If he stayed with the Wallabies he would always be young Billy. He saw that even though Vernon had granted his independence, the very granting of it revealed their relationship. Billy knew that there could only be further struggles ahead with Vernon, because Vernon would always regard the Wallabies as his creation.

He was thinking about this when Vernon himself walked in from the bathroom, a towel slung around his neck. He was unquestionably a handsome man, if vain, and Billy watched as he picked up a corner of the towel to wipe his eyes, bending his knees slightly so he could see himself better in the dressing-table mirror.

'You're still gorgeous,' Billy said from the blue chair, 'you've still got what it takes, Mr Rome.'

Vernon turned with the comb in his hand and raised his brows slightly. Billy realized that he had no idea of the inner life of Vernon Rome, despite living in the same room with him on and off for four years. All he knew was that Vernon had a genuine passion for both tumbling and women, and that he loved tumbling more. He was always looking over his shoulder when it came to women, as though he expected a better one at any moment. At least this was what Billy had finally surmised about Vernon: he never seemed to fully commit himself because he did not like to slam the door on all the rest.

'What are you gawping at?' Vernon asked, breaking Billy's concentration.

'I'm amazed by your beauty,' he replied, smiling at Vernon in the mirror.

'Smart-arse,' Vernon said, carefully pouring a small amount of hair oil into the palm of his hand. He bought his oil at a special shop in the Burlington Arcade: it cost a fortune, but Vernon would use no other. Once they had been playing a small town in the middle of nowhere when Vernon discovered he had run out of this precious fluid: he had put on such a show it was as if the earth had run out of air.

'Frank says there's a chance of a booking in South Africa,' Vernon said as he rubbed in the oil. 'A couple of months' work, at least.'

Billy's heart leapt: he had always wanted to see Africa! 'When?'

'Don't know. I'm going to see him tomorrow. Want to come?'

Perhaps he could regard the trip as a final send-off, Billy told himself, perhaps Africa might be a fitting end. And then he immediately thought of Bubbles and the long months away from her. He could not leave her at this tender new stage of their relationship, he could not leave Bubbles Drake now.

'No, you go ahead. I've got a few things to do.'

Vernon wiped his hands on the towel. 'There's not much work around at the moment, kid,' he said, whether as a warning or not Billy could not tell. 'The Wallabies have been lucky.'

Billy knew then that Vernon had divined what he had been thinking. He blushed as if caught doing something wrong.

Vernon moved to the cupboard and took a clean shirt from a hanger. 'Cape Town has this great mountain behind it. You stand up there and you think you can see the whole world.' He buttoned his shirt but did not look at Billy. Billy watched him and it seemed to him that Vernon's eyes were full of Africa.

'It's the only country I've seen which reminds me of Australia.

Not the colours so much but the spaces. I went hunting there one time and we didn't see a soul for weeks.'

Billy wanted to ask what he had been hunting but did not out of loyalty to Bubbles. Nevertheless, Africa suddenly sprang alive in his head, a new land on which he had a chance to walk! Despite himself, Billy began to think of what it would be like to smell the air, to see with his own eyes what he had only imagined.

'I might come with you,' he said to Vernon without looking at him. 'To see Frank, I mean.'

Reg came back from Scotland a week after Billy returned. They both had a Saturday off and arranged to meet by the river out at Richmond. Billy was early and strolled through the park, which was full of babies in prams, running children and parents. The sun was out; faint clouds scudded across the sky, propelled by some high unfelt wind. On the ground there was no wind at all; everything was motionless in the sun. The trees to Billy looked heavy with life, the grass beneath his feet enlivened. He sat down on a plump clump of it and spread his fingers in the thick pile. Small yellow flowers belonging to some weed were scattered where he sat; he ruffled a few with his shoe. He was thinking of Bubbles, he was thinking of Africa, he was thinking of how he could have both. When it was time, he got up to meet Reg, at a kiosk by the water.

He saw Reg sitting on a bench outside the door, his head turned gratefully to the sun.

'That's the main way I can tell I'm Australian,' Billy said as he sat down beside him. 'I need the sun.'

Reg opened his eyes and lightly slapped Billy's leg. 'How's my old cobber?'

Billy smiled at him and slapped him back. 'All right. How's yourself?'

'Fair to middling,' he said. 'Glasgow's a dump.'

'I quite like it,' said Billy. 'I like the way people talk.'

Reg stood up and they started walking along the path by the river, which was busy with boats and screaming children.

'Still in love?' Reg asked, slinging an arm round Billy's shoulder.

'Afraid so,' Billy said, 'although it looks like we've got a booking for Africa.'

'Fantastic!' Reg cried. 'I've always wanted to get a booking there! My uncle says it's wonderful – he reckons he saw a Zulu war dance and shot a lion.'

'Yeah, well I'm not sure if I'm going.'

Reg did not respond to this and they continued walking, their rhythm remarkably complementary. Neither had to change his pace; their strides might have been practised.

'Actually I'm thinking of leaving the Wallabies,' Billy said after a moment. 'I think it's the right time to get out.'

'It's a tough time to start a new act,' Reg said. 'Do you have anything set up?'

Billy stopped and turned to Reg. 'I was thinking of asking you,' he said, and waited.

Reg saw immediately that Billy was serious. 'Christ, Billy, I don't know. Theatres are closing all over the place. I'm in an act which gets work.'

Billy surprised himself by not being offended. 'Just think about it,' he said, starting to walk.

A few nights later Billy was speaking to Bubbles on the phone when he tentatively raised the subject of Africa.

'Africa,' she repeated slowly. 'What, you mean now?'

Billy held the receiver tight against his ear. 'The booking's for Christmas,' he said quietly.

There was silence at the end: Billy waited and did not speak into it. He wondered what was going through Bubbles's head, if she would recognize his desire for bright unknown lands. Surely she would recognize that there were private places he must travel, solitary moments he must negotiate alone.

When she finally spoke, he could hardly hear her, and leant forward in the chair as if this would facilitate better hearing. 'Sometimes I wonder about you, Billy,' he heard her say. 'Sometimes I wonder if you've got the courage to leap.'

'What does that mean?' he asked, angry.

'Oh, now and then I get the feeling you've got so used to running, you feel trapped when you stand still.'

'Are you suggesting I'm running away from you? This is work, for God's sake!' This sounded lame even to him, he knew it was not entirely true and a large part of him simply wanted to see Africa. He could not explain to her that he loved her but that this was also a chance to see that bright land, that two months out of their life together would be nothing. Yet he also knew that he wanted a life with Bubbles more than anything: he wanted Africa, but he wanted Bubbles Drake more.

'Sweetheart, I made that leap as soon as I saw you,' he said into the phone. 'I'm not running away, I'm headed straight for you.'

She laughed and then it was over. He was not going to Africa and pushed it from his mind once and for all.

As the time to tell Vernon and Connie he wasn't going drew closer, Billy found it harder and harder to summon the nerve. He wasn't frightened of the actual telling exactly, nor of upsetting their plans: he was frightened of hurting them, as if he were rejecting their very selves for something else. He rehearsed in his head a million ways of imparting this information without offending them, telling them they had been the best kind of friends anyone could want but it was time to move on. Everything sounded insincere and patronizing, as though he were already relegating them to history. He had strong and complicated feelings toward them, contradictory as if they truly had been his own parents, but mostly he felt an embarrassed kind of love.

For some reason he was more inclined to approach Connie on her own, rather than tackle them both at once. He unexpectedly got his opportunity on a buying trip with her one afternoon in Kensington Park Road.

'We really need three of everything,' she said to Billy, holding up boxes of ballet tights. 'What do you think, Billy?'

'You won't need that many,' he answered. 'I'm leaving the Wallabies.'

Connie put the boxes back on the counter. 'We'll be back later, Pat,' she said, taking Billy's arm firmly and walking out.

In a coffee shop they sat facing each other over cups of tea.

'Now, what's all this about? I hope you're not moving to Black-pool to open a shop.'

He smiled at her. 'I haven't really decided what to do.'

'There's not much work out there, you know.'

'Tell me something I don't know,' he said.

'What's prompted this? I hope it's nothing to do with our falling out over your girl.'

Billy touched her hand. 'No, it's not that. Well, it is in a way, but not because of anything to do with you.'

She lit a cigarette and blew smoke in the air. 'It's always tricky being with someone who's not in the business, Billy. Does she understand what you're doing? How we live?'

Billy kept his hand on her arm. 'I think it's best if we drop the subject of Bubbles, OK?'

She shrugged and ashed her cigarette. 'Whatever you say, boss.'

He leant toward her. 'Connie, I'm really sorry about leaving you in the lurch like this. I hope it's not going to ruin your plans for Africa.'

She gave him a wry smile. 'I hate to tell you this, gorgeous, but you're not indispensable. I think we'll manage.'

He was both pleased and horrified: he knew she was probably trying to make him feel better and yet he was felled by how easily she had accepted it. It was as if all their years together had been relinquished in an instant, shed without a moment's thought. He had an image of a pebble being thrown into calm water, sinking quickly, and the water closing over at once.

Outside the Gates

When he finally admitted it to himself Billy saw that he was relying on Reg. He knew that there were other acts he might join, yet Billy couldn't help being captivated by the idea of an act with Reg: he saw at once all the possibilities, the two of them dressed in dinner-jackets, grinning. He had in mind bow-ties and spats, something classy and amusing. It seemed so logical to him that he marvelled he had not thought of it before: they had always worked well together, better than well, they understood each other through the nerves of their fingers. In his head Billy began planning routines they might do, a little comic jousting, an adagio balancing dance perhaps. He smiled because he saw it all, as clearly as if it were before him. The only trouble would be getting Reg to agree: Billy decided he wouldn't push, he would nudge.

He had a day off and sat in the garden thinking about this instead of concentrating on the letter in his lap to his mother. He had owed her a letter for months, but he could never seem to find the the time to sit down and write it. Now he had some real news to tell her, about Bubbles, his changed life; he wished his mother could meet Bubbles straight away yet it was an idle wish, one he could not immediately act on. He had grown used by now to this relationship of delayed reaction, of emotions being received and relayed as a kind of echo. His mother's news reached him as a bulletin from the front: he could no longer smell the blood or hear the bullets. Once he had tried to imagine her fingers holding the pen, the table she sat at, whether she wrote quickly or slow. Now, while there was no doubt she was alive in his head, Saph Hayes felt very far away, and Billy found he could not recall the precise shape of her day. Her letters were always brief, recounting who had married, given birth or moved away, but they gave no sense of the actual rhythm of her life. Billy couldn't imagine any more how she passed her time exactly, the route she took home, where she danced. He had never seen the street where she lived, for instance, or known her as a woman living in a flat on her own, her children grown, her rooms silent. In his mind she was still the woman who had stood on the dock four years before, her large nose red from crying.

Billy no longer gave much thought to going home either, for it seemed his life was now in England. This had not been deliberate, it had simply happened, the tendrils of daily life had grown up to enfold him. He had never actually decided to live his life here, but somehow his mother had stopped asking when he was coming home and his homesickness had mutated into a form of nostalgia.

Billy knew himself to be in voluntary exile now, because he could go home if he chose to. He was the only member of his family ever to live so far away: the rest all lived within three suburbs. In the Hayes family it was an unexamined belief that family members all lived in the same country, as if obeying some law of nature. At odd moments Billy sensed that his exile said something about himself, yet he could not explain what it was or how it had happened. He felt only that it was some kind of natural progression, for he had always recognized himself to be an outsider.

He told himself that he may as well stay outside the gates now, and live fully his outsider's adventures.

Billy was finishing his letter when Vernon came bounding out to the garden; his large frame cast a shadow over the sun. Billy looked up, shielding his eyes with his hand. He could not see Vernon's features properly as the sun was behind his head, but Billy felt rather than saw his agitation.

'What's up?' he asked, squinting.

'You're leaving us, I hear,' Vernon replied.

Billy put his hand down. 'Vernon, at least move around so I can see you.' He didn't budge, so Billy stood up. They faced each other and, to his surprise, Billy saw that Vernon's face was wrenched by strong emotion: he did not look angry as much as in pain. Then Connie emerged from the back door and stood on the steps with her arms folded. 'I thought I should tell him,' she said, shrugging.

Billy looked back at Vernon, who seemed momentarily stranded, uncharacteristically lost for words.

'Well, it's been wonderful . . .' Billy began and suddenly he found himself hugging Vernon, and Connie was running down the stairs and the three of them were in the garden, hugging and tearful, laughing into one another's faces.

In the weeks following they had a number of bookings around London, not consistent but enough. Their date book was sporadically filled over the four months until early November, when Connie and Vernon were due to leave for South Africa. Because of the trouble in Spain, the shipping schedules kept changing, so they booked two passages on different ships just in case. Vernon decided he wouldn't tell the South Africans there were only two Wallabies instead of three until he got there. 'They'll only worry,' he said, winking.

At the end of August Frank managed to fill an empty week with a booking at a number three theatre in Brighton.

'It wasn't so long ago that we were doing number ones,' Vernon complained, but Frank replied that he should be pleased he'd even booked that.

'It's getting worse, my friend,' Frank warned. 'The cinema's what people want to see.'

Against all odds Vernon still did not believe this, for he imagined that nothing could take the place of live artists in front of the naked eye. It was not that he did not acknowledge the power of the movies, he insisted, it was just that he couldn't see how live variety could be eclipsed.

Yet at Brighton they played to small houses, with the second house invariably worse than the first. The programme was good and tight, with a dancing act and a comedian of uncommon charm whose jokes delivered by anyone else would not have been funny at all. Danny Payne was handsome and had great warmth: he did not use a microphone and stood at the very edge of the stage, the tips of his shoes pointing over in his desire to get closer to the audience. When the audience was very small, he asked everyone to move up the front: they did, as if he'd invited them into his loungeroom. One night he even sat down on the stage with his legs dangling over, delivering his gags with great gusto.

On small nights all the acts had fun with each other, pulling private jokes and coming in on each other's acts. Some nights

Billy thought this mayhem reached an unforeseen perfection: if it had been rehearsed it could not have been finer. Usually everyone hated to work a small audience, but this time people enjoyed it: all the acts seemed to bond more quickly and strongly than usual, as if in unity they stood a better chance.

Billy continued to make calls to Bubbles in Blackpool, to feel calm and easy about his life. He should have been in a flap but he did not care in the least: he had a feeling that something would turn up. After shows he walked alone along the pier, along the beach with its pebbles. Already the weather was growing cooler; he hunkered down in the wind. He liked Brighton without so many people. He wondered if it was its true self with its weekend invasions or as it was now, at the closing of the season, slightly sad.

On the train on the way home they sat in companionable silence: Connie did her nails and Vernon read a newspaper while Billy stared out the window. Every now and then Vernon tried to read something aloud to them, but Connie invariably interrupted.

'Oh, do stop it,' she snapped. 'I hate it when people read things out to me.'

This time he tried to tell them about the official opening of the BBC television service which was coming up. 'Television,' he said. 'What next?'

When they got home, Mrs Campbell surprised them by opening the front door.

'This is very nice, Min,' Vernon said, kissing the top of her head. 'I didn't know you cared.'

But Billy had seen her face and knew that something was wrong.

'What's up, Min?' he asked anxiously.

Her chest swelled with self-importance. 'There's a young lady waiting for you in the front parlour, Billy. I'm afraid she's in a bit of a state.'

He pushed past her, calling out Bubbles's name. She was sitting unnaturally stiffly in a chair by the window. He rushed over and knelt beside her. 'Bubbles? What's happened?'

She turned her head toward him slowly, but her eyes did not appear to focus. 'My mother's finally done it,' she said.

'What?' he asked stupidly. 'What's she done?'

'Killed herself,' she answered flatly. 'Although whether or not it was an accident I couldn't say.'

'When?' he asked as if it were relevant. 'When did it happen?'

'This morning. I found her in bed when I brought her a cup of tea.'

He looked at her sitting straight backed and tearless, then pulled her to him, crushing her against his chest. 'My poor baby,' he crooned into her hair, 'my poor, poor girl.' He felt the bristling strength of her, the sheer will which had got her through the day, and then he felt the first shiver and the pain come as the whole of her began to heave and crack.

The Sensation of Solace

That first night they lay apart under the same roof Billy opened his eyes in the dark. He lay on his back, fully alert, his mind working madly, ceaselessly. His body was ready to leap into rescue: it sensed fire, the burn of the flame. He felt the nerves of his body waiting for action, the balls of his feet ready to run. He wanted light so he could begin his new life immediately: he wanted to get out of bed to start now. He thought of Bubbles lying sleeplessly in the room below him, placed on a make-do cot in some girl's room. He had seen she did not like the idea at all, having to share a room with a girl she didn't know whose eyes gleamed at the prospect of weeping. Billy saw that in exchange for her generosity in offering her room, Miss Jenny Pierce was expecting the whole story, bloody and long. But he had closed the door on Bubbles stitched up and resolute and knew Jenny Pierce would barely get crumbs.

He thought, Bubbles is now alone in the world: she has no one but me. This made him feel important and powerful, and stirred within him a great rush of tenderness. He swore to himself that he would love her well, the best he could; he would be everything to her, family and friend. They would make a new family, a bright web of love, joining them to the past and to the future.

But it wasn't morning and he could not begin at once: he had to endure endless hours of waiting. Billy heard the wind blow and pressed his ear against the pillow, preparing for the long wait until dawn.

Bubbles was already sitting at the kitchen table when he walked in the next morning, a plate of bacon and eggs in front of her.

'She won't eat a thing,' Min Campbell said as he came in. 'Tell her to eat something, Billy.'

He stood beside Bubbles, who smiled brilliantly up at him: leaning over, he kissed her mouth and softly asked how she was. Min Campbell stopped moving eggs in the pan and brazenly turned to listen: Bubbles pulled his head close to her mouth and spoke hotly into Billy's ear.

'I love you,' she said clearly: he blushed and reared up as if she had said something obscene. She laughed; Min Campbell made a sort of roll of her eyes before turning back with a cluck of her tongue to the stove.

He looked down again at Bubbles, who seemed in good spirits: she appeared well, her eyes over-bright, curiously ablaze. She looked like she had slept an enchanted sleep and had just come across some unexpected good fortune.

'I think we'll go out and get something, Min,' Billy said, still looking at Bubbles. 'I'll take her for a walk and build up her appetite.' Bubbles immediately stood up and headed for the door; he turned to follow.

'What about your eggs?' Min called crossly, but Billy only shrugged his shoulders in a gesture of apology before following Bubbles out the door.

Outside a snappy wind was still blowing, aimed at their eyes, their clothes, their hair. Billy had never liked wind and he pushed himself into it, holding Bubbles's hand and walking fast. They did not speak; Bubbles seemed to know he was headed for the park, where he could see the necks of trees bending in the wind. The park was empty on such an unpleasant late summer morning; the sky was grey and looked too close.

They continued to walk quickly as if they were going some-where; both had boundless energy propelling them. Billy felt they had so much to talk about he did not know where to start: all the things which had seemed clear and right to him the night before had vanished. He wished to say exactly the right words of com-fort to Bubbles, which she would understand perfectly as soon as he spoke them: he could not at this moment think of what they might be.

'She drank herself to death,' Bubbles said suddenly. 'The doctor said her heart stopped.'

She was holding his hand tightly and spoke with her head down: Billy had to watch her mouth to make out the words.

'I found three empty gin bottles by her bed before he got there. I think she planned it.'

Billy said nothing but moved his arm to encircle her shoulder: they began to drop their speed and walk more slowly. He wondered if Bubbles needed to believe Elsa Drake had died on purpose, that she had stopped her plump and sodden heart by sheer will.

'She was so frightened of dying,' Bubbles said in a low voice: he saw her eyes fill with tears and the effort she exerted to stop them. They walked in silence, past huge trees shaking, past slender plants moving their stems.

Suddenly Billy saw a vivid picture of the corpse of Elsa Drake in Blackpool, her false eyelashes, her rings. To banish it he scrambled wildly to think of something else: anything to chase the picture away. He suddenly remembered that they had not yet discussed the funeral: he glanced at Bubbles, unsure whether it was the right moment. But her face had taken on a new expression: a kind of glow, steady and fierce.

She saw him looking and turned, showing him the whole of her face. 'I'm glad,' she said with violence. 'I'm glad she's dead.' Her eyes were shiny with moisture and effort, she kept walking until she could not go on: suddenly she fell against him and began to keen loudly in his arms.

Billy held her to him, cradling her tightly, and it seemed to him that he was the only still thing in a shaking world.

They walked until they could walk no more, leaving the park to sit in a bleak café. Bubbles's eyes still blazed in her face; she veered wildly between an odd, manufactured happiness and panic. At unexpected moments she grabbed Billy's hand, squeezing hard and peering at him strangely. He had the impression she could no longer see him; he had become for her merely the sensation of solace. She looked at him blindly, reaching out instinctively: he knew she took his comfort for granted. He did not mind, he wanted this: he wanted her to turn to him as if toward the sun.

When he saw that she had harnessed her grief as best she could he paid for the tea and pulled back her chair. On the street the wind was still blowing: he was surprised because he had already forgotten it.

'Oh, look, a seagull,' Bubbles said, pointing to the sky. 'It must be lost.'

They stook looking up at the bird, which darted here and there in the wind. It seemed to ride it like a sea wave, to play as if it did not know it was too far from the sea.

'Stupid bird,' said Bubbles, starting to move: Billy stood still and watched the seagull a moment longer. He began to think again of the funeral, for it would have to be dealt with soon. He told himself that once the bird was out of sight, he would immediately talk to Bubbles: as if it knew, the bird flew away at once, and Billy turned to watch Bubbles's back. Gathering his courage he raced to catch up with her, when he reached her he took her hand.

'Listen, sweetheart,' he began tentatively, 'we'll have to begin making arrangements soon . . . about the burial . . .'

'Oh, it's all been seen to,' she replied matter-of-factly. 'A fellow from the Salvation Army's looking after it.'

'But don't you want to be there? I'll come with you if you like.'

She smiled at him. 'That's very kind of you, but I'd rather not go. We hated each other. Everybody in Blackpool knew it.'

He could not believe this: he had felt the painful letting of her grief. But he also sensed that this was the only way Bubbles knew how to live: to bind herself up and not let anybody act as witness. Because he thought of himself as being like this, he did not pursue it, but privately he considered it monstrous that Mrs Elsa Drake of 26 Osborne Road, Blackpool, should leave the world so unaccompanied.

Vernon was exceptionally kind to them, even suggesting he move out so Bubbles could move in.

'Oh no, there's no need for that, Mr Rome,' Bubbles said politely: Vernon asked her to call him by his first name. Billy saw that he was doing his charm act: it was so natural to him he could not help it. Bubbles seemed oblivious to it for the moment, clearly failing to distinguish between kindness and charm. Billy thought that for once it did not matter which it was: Vernon was offering to help and seemed sincere.

For the time being, they decided to keep the same arrangements, until more suitable accommodation could be found. Jenny

Pierce was willing to share her room with Bubbles, provided it was not for too long. 'I've got a busy life and like to come in at all hours,' she told them, making it clear she was not to be mistaken for a lonely woman. While Bubbles was not entirely happy with this she understood she did not have much alternative: until the house and contents of Osborne Road were sold she did not have a penny. She had brought all she needed in a large battered suitcase, a souvenir of her mother's famous trip to Paris. 'A man took her there,' Bubbles told him as she unpacked. 'She ate caviare and drank champagne out of his hat.'

Billy stood in the doorway watching her remove her worldly goods from the suitcase, watching her arrival in his life. She seemed to be part of it irrevocably now, cast upon him like an orphaned child. This made her seem even dearer to him, a gift with which he had been entrusted. He already knew he did not wish to live with Bubbles Drake without marrying her; he knew he wished to act in the best possible way. Bubbles herself seemed not to have thought of this, she was a fearless girl and did not care about what people had to say. In this she was not like Billy. She held the flag and he could only follow.

In the afternoon Connie came round, bringing a batch of scones she had made herself.

'I don't believe it,' Vernon said. 'The stove would faint if you opened it.'

She ignored him as usual and went about finding a plate, Mrs Campbell showing her to the kitchen. Bubbles went too and Billy watched the women go, the three of them all talking at once. They had instantly assumed the camaraderie of women, although the three of them could not be more different. Billy wondered what it was that let women know certain things about each other, how they seemed to open themselves to each other more readily than men.

'Bubbles doesn't look too bad,' Reg said when they were out of earshot. 'In fact she's in pretty good shape.'

'Women always cheer up when they can have a good natter,' Vernon offered. 'Even Connie.'

Connie's voice came from the kitchen. 'I heard that, Vernon.

And for your information we're not nattering. We're talking about whether there's going to be a war.'

'Not a chance,' said Vernon loudly. More quietly he added, 'How did they get from scones to war so quickly?'

Bubbles came back into the room, carrying the tea-tray: Billy saw that she was enjoying herself. He felt proud of her self-possession amongst so many strangers, her dignity in the eye of the storm. He looked around the room at each of his friends, drawn together for the purpose of bringing comfort: he was proud of them too. He looked at Reg, at Vernon and at Connie. He thought, I have the best friends in the world!

Min Campbell came in last, carrying the teapot, a knitted tea cosy covering it. She was very pleased with herself co-ordinating this wake of sorts for a poor young girl deprived of a mother. She directed everyone to particular chairs and Billy saw she had taken out her best bone china. Everyone sat with fine painted plates in their laps, their cups and saucers resting on the arms of chairs if they were brave or on little side-tables if they were not.

Billy balanced his saucer in the palm of one hand and raised the fine china cup to his lips: the handle of the cup between his fingers seemed excessively frail, like the bones of a very small bird. He took a sip of tea and placed the cup and saucer warily on the arm of his chair in order to free his hands for a scone. They were delicious, just the right texture: he ate two very quickly with jam and whipped cream.

'You didn't really make these, did you, Connie?' he asked, his mouth full.

'I did too,' she declared. 'It's my mother's recipe. I've been making them since I was twelve.'

'Ah, for centuries,' said Vernon, and everybody laughed, taking them cleverly past the inadvertent mention of mothers.

'Yes, I can still turn my hand to the womanly arts,' Connie added. 'I have skills you men can only dream of.'

Vernon raised his eyes to the ceiling. 'Oh, here we go, the unrecognized talents of the ladies. Connie is one of your suffragettes, Bubbles, she's all for having scallywags like me lined up and shot.'

Bubbles smiled prettily; Connie pulled a face, turning toward Min Campbell in complicity. Billy thought Bubbles looked very young between them, unlived in, strangely unharmed. It was this quality of living beneath a whole skin which distinguished her from them: despite her mother's death, life had not rent it.

'I'd keep a close eye on her, my son,' Vernon advised, nodding his head toward Bubbles. 'If I were you I'd make damn sure Connie doesn't get a chance to bend her ear. She'll corrupt her and then you'll be sorry.'

Connie gave a snort. 'Ha! We know who does the corrupting around here, don't we, Min?' Min Campbell laughed, and Connie did too; Bubbles stared down at her tea.

'Oh, now you've embarrassed her. I'm sorry, Bubbles, we're only having a bit of fun,' Vernon said. 'Take no notice.'

Billy smiled encouragingly at her. 'That's right, don't listen to them,' he said. 'Connie and Vernon are full of nonsense.'

'So I gather,' she said in a cool voice. There was a pause.

'And that's putting it politely,' Reg said a little too heartily. 'Tell me, Bubbles, what are your plans?'

All eyes turned to her: she looked back calmly. 'I thought I'd see about a job first – '

'She's an usherette,' interrupted Billy, 'though she's had experience as a secretary too. You can type, can't you, sweetheart?'

She glared at him. 'Of course I can.' For a moment Billy didn't know what he'd done wrong, and was humiliated that she'd snapped at him in public. He had only wanted to help, to ease things along, but realized now he probably sat with a certain zealousness. He made himself sit back and let her fend for herself, let her tell her own story, in her own way.

'I worked for a solicitor's firm in Blackpool. Sanders and Preston,' she went on in her low voice. 'You wouldn't have heard of it in London. It was really boring answering the phone and picking up documents. At least at the cinema I got to see the pictures.'

Billy glanced at Vernon: the cinema was his sorest point. Oh no, Billy thought, remembering his decision: he would have to let Bubbles handle this one.

'The cinema,' Vernon repeated. 'The face of the future, or so they tell me.'

'I think so,' replied Bubbles thoughtfully. 'It's marvellous what they can do.'

'Oh?' Vernon queried, his face assuming a mocking expression. 'And what's that exactly?'

The room fell silent. Billy coughed and shot a furious look at Vernon: it was all he could do to stop himself leaping out of his chair. But Bubbles did not seem perturbed in the least and calmly took a sip of tea, her level eyes meeting Vernon's.

She put down her cup. 'Quite a lot of things actually,' she said with confidence. 'The cinema can do a million things you can't do on stage.'

Vernon had a superior smile on his handsome face, as if Bubbles Drake could not possibly know anything about it. 'And your vast experience as an usherette tells you this, does it?' he asked and Connie abruptly stood up.

'How about another pot of tea. Anyone?' Everyone said yes loudly and she turned to Vernon. 'Come with me, Mr Rome, and I'll teach you some womanly arts.' And with that she pulled him to the kitchen.

Full Rights of Possession

When Billy realized that he finally had Bubbles in London he ceased to think about how she got there and began to celebrate her landing. She had been to London just once before, as a child with her mother and father, and carried only the dimmest memory of an ice-cream eaten in an endless green park, and the shiny buckles of her own shoes. It was Billy's chance to put aside his immigrant's place and take up the role of native: to Bubbles, London was uncomplicatedly Billy's home and it did not occur to her to inquire how or why he came to be there. This freed him for the first time to claim the city as his own, to make assumptions and declarations he saw now he would never voice to a born and bred Londoner. He had never realized before how much time he spent explaining himself and his opinions, how he had come to justify even his mildest complaints about shopkeepers or the weather in order that he be accorded the right to make them. Even to Min Campbell, he was first and foremost an Australian in London, a permanent visitor granted certain privileges. As an outsider he was denied full rights of possession, but Bubbles did not appear to know this and under her eye Billy quickly assumed absolute control.

He felt proud and reckless as he showed her his city, the city he had come to know for himself in a different way from anybody else. He showed her a stone path he knew by the Thames, next to houses with special doors and windows in case of flooding. They drank from a bottle of cider and braved the river, taking off their shoes and socks and stockings in a foolish moment. He showed her the back lanes around Soho, the short cuts to and from all the theatres, a low-ceilinged pub he knew with a large fireplace and sawdust on the floor. He took her to the wood on Hampstead Heath, where the coiled vines met above their heads: they kissed violently amid the damp gloom. He took her to the city and the grand hotels; they had afternoon tea twice at the Savoy. In Oxford Street, Bubbles admired a silk scarf in a window: he rushed in and bought it at once. He handed notes to hoteliers, florists, dressmakers, hatmakers and bakers; he insisted on taxis and tipped extravagantly. As soon as money touched his hand he passed it over, for he was in a flurry of excitement. A meringue tart for supper! A bottle of perfume for Bubbles! A taxi, at once! He could see that Bubbles was impressed with all this, and proud to be seen with him on the street.

'You always look so dashing,' she said, clearly pleased. 'Just like a movie star.'

Billy thought London had never been so beautiful. It had a clean, hosed-down look: all the streets to Billy Hayes seemed shiny. He was struck by the way buildings and lives were constructed atop endless other buildings and lives, and imagined London seen through archaeological layers, revealing its secret history of which only the smallest tip was manifest. He knew his own country to be more ancient, but Australia's history appeared alive in the land itself, in the shape of its rocks, its trees, its mountains. To Billy, London's past seemed alive in the form of manmade bricks, in buildings and in the people who lived in them. He thought of trying to explain some of this to Bubbles, but realized he did not know the language in which to speak of it.

They returned tired and strangely peaceful to the house in Croxted Road each afternoon, in time for Billy to wash up before setting off for the theatre. He was doing two shows a night at the Chelsea Palace: he felt completely exhausted but did not wish Bubbles to know. Each night he collapsed into bed and fell immediately into a sleep full of dreams he could not always remember in the morning.

At first Bubbles came to the theatre every evening with him, sitting where he could see her in the front row. One night she watched from the wings and Billy was conscious of her throughout the act, winking at her and passing comments whenever he could. It was a particularly good audience and Billy felt himself to be in top form; as he moved he could not help feeling that Bubbles must be proud of him. When they came off, he rushed up to her, but straight away she said she'd decided to go home.

'I've seen it too many times before anyway,' she said as she kissed him goodbye. 'Don't you get bored doing the same thing every night?'

He was hurt but kept smiling. 'You know what it's like, sweetheart. You've been on stage, haven't you? You never get bored!'

She raised her eyebrows. 'At least with acting you get to talk,' she said.

He watched her go and suddenly it seemed a long time to wait till the second house, till the show was over and he could go home too.

Bubbles only came once more after that; from then on, she stayed home and read a book. Billy tried to tell himself that no other wife or girlfriend was expected to watch her partner work, but then again, his was no ordinary job. It was not as if he expected her to watch him pushing a pen, or counting money in some shop in the High Street. His tools of work were the dreaming of his muscles, something far more intangible. Nevertheless, Billy tried to weigh up what was fair, and decided it was not fair to expect Bubbles to applaud him every night. He wished Bubbles wanted to come and see him at least once in a while, though. He knew he shouldn't wish it, but he did.

One morning Vernon and Billy were leaving for an appointment with Frank Hurley when Bubbles asked if she could come too. Vernon looked at Billy. 'I don't see why not,' he said, looking pointedly at his watch to indicate the time.

'I won't be long,' she said, dashing from the room: they heard the slam of her bedroom door.

'I wish she wouldn't do that,' muttered Jenny Pierce, who was not finding Bubbles to her taste. She regarded her as chilly and rude, most superior for a girl from Blackpool. Miss Pierce played the piano in cinema pits: Vernon said her long neck must emerge like a giraffe. Vernon Rome had no time for plain women: he barely acknowledged them, or else ignored them altogether. He seemed to think women who were not pleasing had no reason to exist, and consequently treated them as a kind of unnecessary furniture. He did not waste his time getting to know the beauty of their souls; he preferred his beauty out in the open. Miss Jenny Pierce sensed this, or at least his dismissal of her, and was very clear about her reciprocal distaste for Vernon. It was unpleasant to be in the same room with them both: the very air seemed to turn odorous.

Fortunately, Bubbles came smiling back into the room, pulling on her hat and black woollen coat. 'I'm ready,' she said to Vernon and he smiled charmingly at her: Jenny Pierce turned away in disgust. If Billy had ever thought there might be further antagonism between Vernon and Bubbles he soon found out he was wrong: their dispute over the cinema might never have happened. It seemed to Billy only added proof that other people did not take disputes, or indeed life, as seriously as he did.

As the three of them walked to the bus-stop, Bubbles offered Billy her arm: it wasn't till they were at the end of the street that Billy realized Vernon held the other. Bubbles walked between them, a pretty, bobbing thing, oblivious to the jealous rage which suddenly filled him. He almost flung her arm from him and left them to it, only embarrassment prevented him from acting. He felt his walk grow stiff and unnatural, his arm turn rigid with effort: surely Bubbles must feel the stiffness of it, surely she must feel the force of his rage? But she was chattering on about the Ivy, where Billy had taken her to lunch the day before. He ceased to listen, he could no longer hear anyway. If Vernon Rome so much as smiled at her, he swore he would knock him flat: how stupid he had been not to notice Bubbles's flirtatiousness, her inability to control the sweep of her eyes. Of course, it suddenly all made sense: the only woman he had ever loved, taken by his most charming and persuasive friend. Vernon would not be able to help himself, and any girl who had gone out with so many fellows would not know the first thing about restraint. It was so obvious, Billy saw that now, the very moment he had been heading for unavoidably. He hadn't cared about any of the others, and now he had delivered Bubbles to Vernon's door: Billy feared it had a certain fatalistic neatness. He hated Vernon but he hated Bubbles more, for setting him up only to watch him fall. How stupid she looked, needing to be flattered by Vernon Rome, needing to flex her beauty to gauge if it still had muscles. He suddenly understood that getting men to fall in love with her was the female equivalent of Vernon's getting women into bed: she was trying hard, he saw that. All at once, he could stand it no longer: he threw her arm off and walked ahead.

'Billy?' he heard her call in surprise.

'I'll meet you there,' he shouted, hailing a cab. It wasn't until he was in the cab and had slammed the door and the cab was two hundred yards down the street that he realized he might have jumped to conclusions. 'Stop!' he cried and sat for a moment with his head in his hands, before winding down the window and yelling out to them. 'Well, come on!' he shouted and they began to run: he sat back and did not watch them. When she stepped into the taxi Bubbles looked at him questioningly: he turned away, staring at rushing cars out the window.

Just before they got to Charing Cross Road, Bubbles asked if Billy had ever mentioned her to Frank Hurley.

'Sort of,' he said. 'I thought it'd be better if you talked to him about work yourself.'

She appeared small inside her thick coat. Billy was ashamed of himself, for her face seemed to him now so guileless. He supposed she could not help being beautiful; it was a form of power she could not fail to exercise. It must be natural to her, having men smile into her face, she must have learnt early to smile back. He was thinking this as she stepped from the cab, her little hand held out to his.

Frank welcomed them in with an expansive wave of his arm, asking them if they'd care for tea. He had his pencil stuck behind his ear, and Billy saw Bubbles give him a curious glance. He said he had a few details about South Africa to iron out with Vernon and a last contract for the Wallabies to play London. Unexpectedly he also made a few kind comments about the Wallabies being lost without Billy, but Vernon coughed theatrically and said he would not quite put it like that himself.

'So you're embarking on a new life, Billy,' Frank continued, 'leaving the Wallabies, getting married. You're not planning a move to South America, I hope?'

Billy smiled. 'Not at the moment. But I'm not the only one starting a new life.' He blushed and nodded toward Bubbles. 'Bubbles is hoping to find work as an actress. I thought it'd be a good idea if she met you.'

Frank turned to inspect Bubbles candidly, but his long unblinking gaze had finally met its match. She stared back at him levelly, and Frank Hurley was the first to look away.

'So tell me, young lady,' he said at last, 'had any experience?'

Billy smiled helpfully in Bubbles's direction, for he knew that until you got to know Frank Hurley his manner could be daunting.

'The Blackpool Players,' she answered quickly. 'We did *Hay Fever* last spring.'

'Ah,' Frank said, as if this were revealing. Billy knew Frank mainly dealt with variety acts, although he had recently been negotiating movie contracts for certain of his better know comedians.

'I'm interested in getting into picture acting,' she offered boldly. 'I'd do anything to start with.' Vernon let out an audible sigh: Billy looked at him crossly. Bubbles struck him as brave and willing: if he were an employer he would certainly risk giving Miss Bubbles Drake a job. Her small face revealed a strenuous ambition, her large eyes showed a tenacious light. Billy did not know if ambition alone made an actress but he was willing to bet that, as in tumbling, it certainly played its part: he understood that in his case the will to succeed drove him forward, the hot ambition to roll the one perfect roll. The origins of this compulsion were much obscured and did not interest him: he simply recognized its light at once when he saw it. He was not sure yet if Bubbles was a good actress or not but did not doubt for a moment that she had the necessary will.

'As a matter of fact I know Pinewood's looking for extras,' Frank said, 'a costume drama or some bloody nonsense.'

Billy saw that Bubbles was tremendously excited but willing herself to control it. She did not smile ecstatically or even nod her head, she remained calm, her face unmoved. To stop himself grinning foolishly at her, Billy turned his head and found Vernon smiling at him, a smile which veered dangerously close to a smirk. As Billy watched, Vernon moved one hand to his heart and fluttered his eyes heavenward in a parody of love. Billy frowned at him and stood up, then walked across to the window, only partly listening to Frank Hurley's voice.

He forgot Vernon and began to think about organizing work for himself. He was spending his pay as soon as he got it, and already owed money to Reg, Vernon and Connie, plus being behind in the rent. And the wedding was coming up, which he intended to be a wedding like no other, with no expense spared. Why, he should be asking Frank about work for himself, not Bubbles: all at once Billy realized what he had just thought and felt a sharp prick of shame. At the same moment he felt Bubbles come up behind him, the press of her against his back. He immediately forgot everything but the feel of her body, for Bubbles Drake had united his two worlds: his tumbler's world, and the everyday world he traversed on two legs. The everyday world had been transformed, he walked freely, unbound at last. Billy thought, now I have everything. Tumbling, and my own love.

'If only I knew all the thoughts in that mysterious handsome head,' Bubbles whispered into the back of his neck.

He turned around and looked into her eyes. 'I'm going to tell you every one of them,' he said and at that moment he truly believed that he could.

Frank Hurley did get Bubbles a job at Pinewood Studios, but it only lasted fourteen days. Every morning she would rush off, ready to be laboriously made up for a crowd scene in which you could not see her anyway. The film was about great composers and Bubbles obviously thought it was her glorious start. To please her, Billy went out with her one day before his Saturday matinée and stood around for several boring hours in a cold, draughty shed. She pointed cinema stars out to him, but he did not recognize any of them: he thought that compared to a show like his at the Chelsea, making pictures seemed deadly dull. It lacked the tension and nerve of live performance, the human moment of courage and risk. Of course, he did not tell Bubbles this: he saw clearly the pleasure in her face and did not wish to wipe it away.

On the last day of filming she came home slightly tipsy, just as he was leaving for work. She had been out saying goodbye to all her new friends: Billy discovered he did not feel as generous about her pleasure as he had once thought.

'Guess what? I've got another job!' she announced excitedly. 'It's not acting, but at least it's getting there. I'm going to work in a booking agency!'

'Which one?' Billy asked, knowing not all of them were reliable. He was surprised to experience a stab of jealousy, to know that she had broached his territory without first seeking advice from him.

She told him: it was a new firm, Reeves and Butterworth, which Billy had never heard of. It handled more movie people than variety performers and Bubbles would be starting as a sort of secretary.

'They do a lot of work with the studios, and I'll get to hear of everything that comes up. Oh, Billy, I can't believe my luck!' She hugged him: he was happy because she was happy and yet a small grudging part of himself was steadfastly refusing to celebrate. A small part was wishing Bubbles Drake would show as much happiness for him, and cheer for him as hard as he cheered for her.

The Business of Hearts

All of a sudden the wedding was almost upon them: only moments before it had seemed an inordinate time to wait, but now it seemed there was not time enough. There was so much to organize, business to tie up, the busybody nose of the state to mollify. They wanted to get married in the Chelsea Register Office because Billy had passed it one day and admired it, but to his surprise he found that they had to fudge official papers to suggest they lived within the confines of its borough. Later, he did the rounds of all the great London hotels: the Dorchester, the Savoy, Claridge's. Billy wanted to see for himself the best place for a wedding breakfast.

Walking from hotel to hotel, he couldn't help feeling a small burst of pride: that he had come through, that he had made it. He moved with long confident strides through the streets, thinking of how far he had come. He thought of Bubbles, his Royal Command Performance: an entire life carved by himself. I've not done too badly, he thought as he walked: in a flash he remembered the terrified boy who was once himself standing on the deck of the *Kitano Maru*. Unexpectedly tears sprang up in Billy's eyes; he blinked at his shoes and kept walking. *I've done well*, he said fiercely to himself, and did not care if he was committing the sin of pride: let God dare to smite him.

When nothing happened, he crossed the road, looking carefully to the left and right, just in case.

He ordered a new suit from Vernon's tailor in Piccadilly; he ordered flowers from a florist in the Strand. He threw money around as if he were rich; he borrowed money from every friend he knew. Billy still couldn't add up and money was never quite real to him, he only cared that he have some of it in his pocket. But once he began spending he found he could not stop: he would go into a shop to buy one specific thing, and emerge with a silver cigarette case and a new pair of cuff-links. He liked the best, he told himself: why for once couldn't he have it? He had never spent much money before but now discovered he was a spender: once he had acquired the taste he decided to indulge it, and for the first time in his life he wished he was wealthy. In fact, he had nothing to his name: no property, no savings, no nest egg. He knew himself to be in a rickety business but instead of this knowledge promoting cautiousness in him, it prompted a rash disregard. He reasoned that since he would never be rich, he might as well spend what he had.

After much consideration, Billy decided on a small but expensive hotel in a cul-de-sac behind Green Park: it had thick carpets and enormous bowls of white roses, gilded mirrors which were very much to his taste. He had a long talk with the functions manager about what he wanted precisely: the man regarded him seriously and wrote down everything he, Billy Hayes, had to say. Later he took Bubbles there to get her opinion: she loved it as he had known she would. This time, however, the doorman asked them their business, before they had even stepped inside. 'We're holding our wedding reception here,' Billy told him curtly: the doorman opened the door and let them in. This incident threw Billy slightly and he did not feel as confident as the first time: the lush surroundings momentarily swamped him. 'Ah, Mr Hayes, how nice to see you again,' said the functions manager, coming up to greet him: Billy turned, fully restored.

They had to keep the numbers down: the trouble was, Billy knew too many people. They bought him drinks in the Boiling Kettle, they brought bottles of warm champagne to the Express Dairy café. On the last night at the Chelsea, the comedian read out on stage a ribald poem he had composed especially. When he finished Billy was pulled from the wings and presented with a travel bag which the acts had bought after passing round the hat. 'You can keep the baby in it,' the comedian said, nudging Billy. Billy was embarrassed about all the fuss but should have known these people never let an opportunity pass quietly. 'To our young favourite,' someone said, toasting him in the dressing-room afterwards. 'To Billy' they all said, raising glasses. He was surprised to find so many people seemed to like him.

Seven days before the wedding, he sent a telegram to his

mother in Sydney. *Dear Mum*, it read, *Bubbles and I to be married on Saturday, October 28, at 3 p.m. in the Register Office, Chelsea. Reception follows at the Stafford Hotel, Green Park. We'll be thinking of you and send much love. From both of us.*

Now all he had to do was wait. He felt nervous yet at the same time strangely calm.

To his surprise Billy slept very well the night before the wedding: it was morning before he knew it. Immediately he was fully awake: he heard Vernon moving and looked over.

'It's not too late,' Vernon said in a loud stage whisper. 'I've left the ladder under the window.'

Billy sat up: Vernon lay propped up on one elbow.

'You know that old Chinese saying, kid: if you want to be happy for an hour, get drunk. If you want to be happy for a day, kill a pig. If you want to be happy for a month, get married. But if you want to be happy for a lifetime, play the field.'

Billy threw the blankets off, braving the cold. 'I've got a feeling that's the Vernon Rome version,' he said, quickly pulling on his dressing-gown. 'Besides, how many times have you done it?'

'Too often,' he replied, leaning back. 'I don't know why either. I think they hypnotize you.'

Billy pushed Vernon's head playfully as he passed his bed: if he was losing his freedom he did not feel it. He felt instead he was pushing out his world, growing freer than he had ever been before.

In the bath he slipped his head beneath the water, opening his eyes wide. His body appeared before him, a vague embryonic shape; he heard the steady sound of his own blood. He floated in a muffled world until he had to come up for air: breaking the surface, he grinned to himself, thankful that no one could see him. He was revelling in his last moments alone as a single man, relinquishing the last of his boyhood. And yet he had already embraced Bubbles and this marriage, the idea of a shared life. For some reason he was certain that marriage would suit him, and fit him like his own skin.

Reaching for the soap, Billy tested aloud the word 'husband'. He smiled: it sounded fine to him.

Bubbles wanted to do the traditional thing, and had spent the night at a cheap hotel with her friend Nettie from Blackpool. Min Campbell made it clear she thought Billy was the one who ought to have spent the night elsewhere: she was cross with him for not having the reception at her place.

'It's been your home for four years,' she said huffily. 'I could have put on something very nice.'

'That's kind of you, Min, but we wanted something a bit different.'

She shrugged, still miffed. 'I don't suppose you'll be wanting much breakfast.'

But he had already sat down at the kitchen table, preparing for his last meal at Croxted Road, Herne Hill. 'Oh yes I do,' he replied, clapping his hands, 'bacon, sausages, the works.'

He could tell she was pleased with this, for Min Campbell always felt reconfirmed as a woman when a man with an appetite relished her cooking. He was fond of her and her prickly self-importance; this morning he even liked the way she thought she knew everyone's business.

He looked around the kitchen. It reminded him of his mother's kitchen in Glebe, the way everybody tended to congregate there. He thought of all the people who had sat at this table, all the people still to follow. Billy was discovering that there is nothing like a wedding, a birth or a death to concentrate the mind, to allow you to step back and consider the journey. When Min Campbell laid his breakfast on the table, he stared at it in a kind of wonder, at the ordinariness and eventfulness of life.

'It's an egg,' he heard Min Campbell say. 'They come from chickens. Eat up,' He shook himself and smiled sheepishly at her, picking up his knife and fork.

He lay about the house all day, not wishing to go outside and get dirty. He treated himself as a kind of expensive garment, which must not be stained or crushed. He frequently checked his hair in the mirror, and after lunch cupped his hands over his mouth to smell his breath. He chewed a clove bud just in case, a trick Vernon had taught him.

Around this time he began to feel the familiar birth of nervousness, fanning up from the depths of his stomach. Reg had arrived half an hour before, ready to perform his duty as witness. Vernon and Digger Dog Crew had already opened a bottle of stout, the sight of which made Billy ill. Digger still lived in Liverpool and had brought his fiancée with him, a tall red-headed beauty who clearly adored him. They all sat about, dressed to the nines: to Billy their laughter was like a fingernail scraped the wrong way across a blackboard.

'Having second thoughts?' Vernon teased, holding up an empty glass in invitation.

'Oh, leave him alone,' said Digger Dog, who had never quite got over his distrust of Vernon. Digger bent across to his fiancée, Molly, and patted her fondly on the knee. 'It'll be us soon, princess,' he said happily, beaming at her from beneath his famous eyebrows.

'Save me,' muttered Vernon, 'it's a virus.' He himself had asked the delicious June Wagner to the wedding, a woman who, as far as he could tell, was one of those rare creatures who did not think of a wedding ring the minute she rose from a bed.

'They'd have to design a special church for you, Vernon,' Reg said, drawing a plan in the air. 'Instead of one aisle, there'd be five.' There was a knock at the door and Billy raced to answer it, both to escape the room and to do something.

There was a blast of bitter air when he opened the door. It was another telegram; he quickly thanked the postman and ripped it open. It was from Aunt Eva in Sydney and he smiled: he still had the ten Australian pounds she had given him the day he left; he had never spent it and kept it as a kind of talisman. *All the very best to you both*, he read. *Hearty congratulations and best wishes, Aunt Eva and Uncle Arthur.*

He still hadn't heard from his mother.

At 2.45 Billy stood in the vestibule, his mouth dry, his palms wet. He felt his body coiled beneath his suit, the restrained power of his own limbs. His clothes felt good against him: he knew himself to be standing tall. Some moment appeared to be upon him; he sensed change in the vibration of the air. He seemed to be isolated within this moment, for he saw that no one else sensed its shape: everyone in the room looked far away to him, inhabiting some completely different space. He heard their voices but not their words: someone asked him a question, but he sensed rather than heard it.

And then he saw his own love's face. She came toward him and he was delivered.

In the car he had hired to take them to the reception, Billy sat dazed in the back seat beside Bubbles. He was strangely light-headed, as if he had run a hundred miles or turned two hundred somersaults in a row.

'Do you feel like you've just jumped from a speeding train?' Bubbles asked him, and he began to laugh.

'What's so funny?' she said, smiling.

'Oh, Bubbles, you're wonderful,' he said, laughing and pulling her toward him. They kissed, then sat back very pleased with themselves: Mr and Mrs Billy Hayes, passing an autumnal Sloane Square.

As they stepped from the car outside the hotel, Bubbles was presented with an enormous bunch of flowers: roses, Baby's Breath, carnations. She gathered them up close to her face, closing her eyes and breathing deeply.

'Congratulations,' the doorman offered: Billy beamed at him and handed him five bob.

Inside, the wedding breakfast was already laid out: little tarts as insubstantial as cloud puffs, pounds of salmon, gleaming cavi-are. A waiter stood ready with a bottle of champagne wrapped in a linen serviette, filling the glasses of those who had arrived before them. As they stepped into the room, everybody clapped. 'The bride and groom!' announced Vernon. The waiter hurriedly found them glasses and the first of many toasts was drunk: the champagne was icy cold and seemed to burst in Billy's throat; immediately he felt even more light-headed and excited. He saw that Bubbles had two bright spots on her cheeks, and that she never once stopped smiling. He saw Connie for what he thought was the first time that day, although she had been the first to greet him at Chelsea. The room was loud and to Billy it seemed full of good thoughts, for every single person in it had come to celebrate with them. He tried to stay close to Bubbles but found it imposs-ible: he moved around the room, grinning broadly. He was talking to Reg when Reg began to nudge him, calling his attention to a waiter standing patiently beside him.

'Excuse me, sir,' the waiter cried above the din. 'A telephone call for you and your wife.'

Billy was so pleased to hear the word 'wife', he did not immediately respond to this statement.

'The telephone sir,' the waiter repeated: Billy smiled at him and looked around for Bubbles. He saw her and grabbed her by the hand; she was still laughing when the waiter indicated the appointed telephone.

'Hello?' he said loudly into the receiver, as if the receiver could transmit a smile.

'Hello, love,' he heard his mother say, and suddenly the world grew soundless.

'Mum?' he cried into the phone. 'Mum, is that you?' He knew it was but could not believe it: he cradled the phone as if it were a living thing in his hands. All at once the whole of Saph Hayes was there in front of him: her big nose, her laugh, her tiny head.

'Are you there, love?' he heard her shout. 'Tom, are you there?' He realized that Bubbles was standing beside him, one arm raised in alarm.

'I'm here,' he shouted back, 'and Bubbles is here too!'

'Very best wishes to both of you,' she said. 'All the family's here having a drink in your honour. It's the middle of the night for us, but we couldn't let your wedding pass. Are you happy, love?'

A sharp pain passed through his heart. 'Very,' he replied. 'Bubbles is standing right next to me. She's a wonderful girl, Mum! I'll put her on!'

He handed the telephone to Bubbles, who shook her head, miming a furious no. He continued to hold it out to her: she took it and muttered a tentative hello. Billy watched as she began to smile, saying 'yes', and 'Thank you', and finally, 'I hope to meet you one day soon too.' He imagined his mother standing in the kitchen, telling everyone to pipe down so she could hear. He knew that Mary would be pestering her to be allowed to speak too; and Ellen, and Ethel.

By the time Bubbles passed the telephone back he had recovered himself slightly. 'How are you?' he asked. 'You sound well.'

'If I was any fitter I'd be dangerous,' she replied. 'I'm the youngest-looking grandmother in Sydney. We're in the middle of a heat wave, though, and it'd suit me fine if it was ten degrees cooler.'

He smiled, for he suddenly remembered seasons the right way around, the heat of Christmas Day, the long sweltering hours after Christmas lunch. He found he did not know what to say next: his throat ached, and yet he was happy.

'You look after her, Billy,' Saph Hayes was saying. 'There's two of you on the road now.'

The operator asked if they'd like to extend the call and Billy found himself saying goodbye and thank you and take care and look after yourself and then the phone was dead in his hands and he was still holding it. Bubbles cradled him, he felt quite faint; then he lifted up his head and kissed his wife.

PART 4
Over the Border

The Everyday World

Billy had been married almost two months when to his great surprise he realized that he did not actually *feel* married. He could not have said exactly how being married was supposed to feel, but he had certainly expected to feel different. Before he was married Billy had thought his life was about to be cleaved in two, but he saw now he had been mistaken. He waited for change but kept waking up to his own same self. A sense of watchfulness now permeated every aspect of his new life, so that he suffered from an awkward attentiveness and never felt completely relaxed.

They lived in a large sunny bedsit overlooking Peckham Rye Common, not an impossible walk from his old home in Herne Hill. Bubbles spent time arranging new curtains, moving furniture around to suit her tastes. In one corner they had a two-ringed stove for cooking, against the wall a large bed which passed for a sofa during the day. They had taken the room because of its large bay window, which let in light and gave the impression of space.

Every morning Bubbles would get up before him; Billy watched from the bed while she did her face. At first she was embarrassed to be doing this in front of him, and scuttled out the door to the bathroom with her make-up bag. But people started knocking on the door suggesting she was taking too long, so she was forced to apply her accoutrements in the bedroom. He loved to watch her assembling herself, drawing on eyebrows, lips, ruling her hair. She seemed to know she looked beautiful with or without this: she smiled at him in the mirror and once blew powder at him, but missed.

They had not taken a honeymoon, for Bubbles had to start her new job. They began their life instead in the everyday world, a new couple supposed to know the rules. But Billy felt as if he were impersonating this life, awaiting the moment when it would begin to be his own. Bubbles sometimes cooked him an elaborate meal, but both of them experienced a kind of embarrassment in each other's presence and Billy often found himself thinking up things to say while they ate. He was most surprised, for it seemed to him that only a short time before they had been bursting with too much to tell. But in bed at night they relaxed in each other's arms, lying against each other in bodily comfort. At night, when the lights were out, Bubbles's head rested against his chest and Billy felt the flutter of her eyelash on his skin. He held her in his arms and knew the happiness of holding someone he had longed for.

During the long day while he waited for Bubbles to come home, Billy often thought up things he would like to say. He wanted to say: *I have love in my heart, and I have it because of you.* He wanted to tell her exactly how it felt to move through air, how he thought of her a million times a day. He wanted Bubbles to know completely the inside of his head, and to learn the inside of hers. But around the time that she was due home, Billy began to feel terribly nervous: he paced the room or brushed his hair too often; he arranged and then rearranged his posture. He wanted to be sitting looking relaxed in a chair, or busy at the table with some business. But when he finally heard Bubbles's key in the door he found himself jumping straight up, rushing towards her. He kissed her and always talked too much, falling over himself trying to get the words out.

'Slow down!' Bubbles cried. 'At least give me five minutes!' So he had learnt to back off until she had put her bag down and taken off her hat; she always seemed to be tired and out of sorts from her long journey. He watched her as she did all these things, trying to anticipate the right moment. But after she had taken her shoes off and sat down in a chair she began to talk about what had happened that day and quite soon would be thinking about dinner. And then the moment would have passed, and Billy would get up to set the table.

He worked only spasmodically now, since Connie and Vernon had left for South Africa. He tried to convince himself that he was managing all right: a week here and there, a fortnight at a theatre out near Epping Forest. People were good to him, letting him know if anyone was off sick or looking for a replacement. But he still owed quite a lot of money from the wedding, and Christmas was only two weeks away; if he thought about it long enough he began to panic. He began to think seriously about joining Youth and Beauty, who were looking to replace Harry Cook as Youth because he was unable to work following a car accident. But the idea did not completely grab him and Billy had to admit that he was still hoping to persuade Reg. He decided to wait until the last possible moment.

On the days Billy was not working he sometimes took a bus and then walked the rest of the way to Charing Cross Road. There was always someone around who he could talk to: Larry La Fosse perhaps, or Danny Payne, the comedian he had played a bill with in Brighton. Occasionally he dropped in on Frank Hurley, but Frank made him feel as if he should have made up his mind long ago and joined another permanent act.

'There's going to be a war soon,' Frank advised him, looking solemn. 'You won't be in a position to shilly-shally then.'

Billy thought Frank was probably right about a war, for even he sensed an obscure tension. But Billy was someone for whom the inner world was drama enough: in this way, he lived outside the everyday world of men, only noticing its movements when it reared up and shouted. He never read a newspaper, or discussed politics in the pub: Spain only became real to him when a ten-year-old boy befriended him for five days once in Liverpool, following him around and wanting Billy to teach him. He spoke no English and one day he simply failed to turn up: the theatre manager told him the boy was a Spanish refugee. Billy was ashamed of himself: he could have given the kid money; he should have seen the signs of dispossession on his face. He tried to find out what had happened to the boy, and if he could do something, but the boy and his mother had disappeared without trace.

Billy did not really understand how the world was run, who decided whether or not there was to be a war. He could not understand why the world could not live in peace, why its joys could not be shared equally. He had this idea that someone should form a world government, a kind hand which would shield everyone. Privately, he believed that if leaders bent on war could only meet the mothers, sisters and children of their enemies, everyone would shake hands and go away. Lately he had even come to believe that his own father was probably a victim of war, a fresh boy turned ugly by horror. He saw this but he could not quite forgive his father yet: he had been too much of a bastard for that.

Four days before Christmas Billy was lying in bed, worrying about whether he had enough money to buy gifts. They did not have a tree yet, but Bubbles said she'd buy one that afternoon on her way home from work. He felt badly about this, for he some-how felt it was his job. Still, he had made a calculated guess at how far his money would go, and it did not extend to a tree. Bubbles knew he was strapped for cash, and her only advice was that he should not make things worse by borrowing more. 'Anyone would think you were the King of England the way you spend money,' she had said and he had smiled sheepishly because it was true. He still intended to go to Regent Street to buy a paste brooch for her, though: he had seen it in a window but could not read the ticket price. If it was cheap enough, he would also buy her a bottle of Rose of Picardy perfume. He was thinking of get-ting up when there was a knock at the door: he leapt up, embar-rassed to be caught sleeping in, and looked wildly around for his dressing-gown.

'Oh, it's you,' he said when he saw it was Reg.

'It's nice to see you too,' Reg replied, walking in.

Billy hastily pulled up the bedclothes, rearranging the pillows so Reg could sit down. As soon as he himself sat down he realized he should offer Reg something: he jumped up again at once.

'Tea or coffee?' he asked, holding the kettle.

'Tea with two, love,' Reg replied.

Billy busied himself making the tea but he was already thinking of the idea of the double act, of how he might persuade Reg to do it. There had been an almost imperceptible change in his relation-ship with Reg since his marriage, as if Billy had made a decision against his will to shift his loyalty from Reg to Bubbles. While he still regarded Reg as his best friend in the world Billy sensed that it could not be as before, in that Bubbles must now hold his intimacies. He believed that she should be his best friend now, and that it would be disloyal to speak of her to Reg. For the first time since Billy had known Reg Tsang, he was conscious of a certain reserve: he had a private place within him now, and because of this, he felt a little sad. Reg Tsang had always been the only person in the world from whom he kept no secrets: he had always been able to tell Reg everything, and the things he couldn't tell him Reg always seemed to guess. But Billy had since crossed some invisible yet definite line, and he sensed Reg knew this too.

'It's a nice place,' Reg said, taking a cup. 'You've got more room that I have.'

Billy smiled at him. 'There's two of us, don't forget,' he said, looking around: he had to agree, Bubbles had made it look pleasant. He knew that Reg would not ask how things were going; he might wonder, but he would never ask.

'I'm going into town. I thought you might like to come,' Reg said. 'I've got to get a few last presents.'

Billy guessed that with Reg's large family this probably meant at least a dozen more, but the invitation still sounded like fun.

'I'll just have a quick bath,' he said, jumping up too fast and spilling his tea.

The city of London looked the way you imagined it would look in a painting or a dream in your head: snow had fallen only the afternoon before and nestled in the curves of railings and window ledges, turned to immaculate white ice on footpaths. Everyone seemed delighted by the sight of snow for Christmas and on the bus everyone spoke of it. People carefully traced their way along the streets, smiling at one another in surprisingly good humour; the usual frayed tempers of Christmas had been temporarily suspended while everyone made a fuss of the snow.

Oxford Street was hung with decorations; all the shops had special Christmas windows. At once Billy felt the excitement of a child and wished to buy wonderful things: in one window he saw the most beautiful basket of fruit, summer melon and mango and pineapple; in another he saw a row of polished stones which looked as if they might grant a wish if you rubbed them. Reg Tsang, however, was one of those people who knew exactly what he wanted to buy and immediately began accumulating gifts: a length of taffeta for a cousin in the troupe who wished to make a new costume; a woollen scarf for a favourite uncle; a book of Chinese paintings for someone else.

Billy looked upon all this with a certain envy, dying to buy a hundred things himself. Reg had a wallet thick with cash, surely he would not miss a note or two? But Billy restrained himself from asking and stuck to the role of adviser, helping Reg decide on this colour or that. Reg came with him while he bought the paste brooch, though, which turned out to cost far more than Billy had hoped. Of course he did not let Reg see this, and handed over the last of his money with an extravagant flourish.

Around midday Billy began to get hungry but he was loath to suggest lunch. Reg would probably want to go somewhere expensive, or at least somewhere Billy could not afford. He thought about suggesting they buy a sandwich to take away, but it was really too cold to sit on a bench and eat it. He was thinking about steering Reg to a cheap café, or walking down to the Express Dairy, when Reg himself suggested he buy Billy lunch.

'Oh, you don't have to buy,' Billy said quickly. 'Why don't we go down to the Express and pay for ourselves?'

Reg looked at him carefully. 'Think of it as an early Christmas present,' he said after a moment. 'It's on me.'

Billy saw that Reg was not to be persuaded: he allowed himself to be led to a restaurant Reg knew in a lane off Greek Street. It was small, obviously a new variety haunt, for straight away Billy saw several faces he knew. He waved at a few people as they made their way across the room, and after clumsily stacking their parcels in a bright ladder against the wall they sat down.

The restaurant was run by an Austrian couple. The wife came over to take their order and told them they'd better have the potato soup and veal chops before she ran out. The soup was delicious, so thick Billy almost chewed it; the chops came with a sweetish apple sauce. He was just taking his last bite when the woman brought them a large slab of pudding they had not ordered. 'An Austrian speciality,' she said, laying the plates down.

Billy sat back feeling happy and full, glad to be warm and inside. He told himself that his money troubles probably weren't so terrible after all, not half as bad as he had imagined. At least Bubbles has full-time work, he thought, and then felt an immediate flush of shame. How awful not to be able to pay his own way, not to buy a Christmas tree when he wanted!

'Finished?' Reg asked. 'Because I'll eat it if you are.' He leant forward and dipped his spoon into Billy's plate. Billy started, and knocked his spoon away.

'Hey, eat your own!' he said, remembering to smile; Reg pulled a disappointed face.

'Getting much work?' Reg asked unexpectedly, his eyes serious and watching Billy closely.

'Oh, here and there,' Billy replied, concentrating on his pudding. 'I was out Epping Forest way last month.'

Reg did not immediately respond, but continued to make his way through the pudding. After what seemed to Billy an embarrassingly long time, Reg finally laid his spoon down.

'Are you joining Youth and Beauty? I heard Dave Wagner was interested.'

Billy looked at him. 'Actually I was still hoping to do that other thing.'

Reg met his eyes coolly. 'I'm thinking about it,' he said.

Afterwards they walked through the big department stores, Liberty and Selfridges, admiring the way they were dressed for the season: wreaths of holly and painted bells, wrapped packages done up with real cloth bows. Another shop specialized in handmade decorations for Christmas trees: striped candy walking-sticks finished with red ribbon, stars made of tinsel, hand-sewn bells. It also had the most beautiful Christmas messages cut from painted paper, and streamers and ribbons to drape around a room. It was when Billy saw these last that he came unstuck, for he immediately saw a wreathed room overlooking Peckham Rye Common.

'Listen, Reg,' he said before he could stop himself, 'I don't suppose you could lend me a quid?'

And the quid became two, and then three, he owed Reg four pounds, two shillings and sixpence before he got home.

Reg stayed to help Billy decorate the room, to lay his purchases on and around the tree. Billy had bought the tree on the spur of the moment from a fellow near the station: it had looked so plump and Christmassy, and he wanted to hang the decorations right away. It rather appealed to him to have two trees for their first Christmas together anyway: they could have one at each end of the room.

When they had finished, Billy stood back to admire it. There was a sweep of holly tied to ribbons across the bay window, coloured words reading *Happy Christmas* across one wall. From the light hung a silvery orb; hand-painted cherries were pinned around the room.

Just then, Billy heard Bubbles's key in the lock: he held his finger up to his lips in a warning to Reg to keep quiet. He heard her begin to talk as she opened the door, saying something about the tree being at the bottom of the stairs. A silence fell as she entered the room: Billy stepped out from behind the door. Bubbles's face did not have the expression on it he had expected; she looked instead as if she had just had bad news.

'Oh, how could you!' she cried. 'Who'd you borrow from this time?' Reg looked away and Bubbles turned on her heel and walked out the door, slamming it behind her. Billy stupidly stood there, only now realizing his mistake.

In the first week of the new year, Billy decided he would join Youth and Beauty. For the first time since he had left the Wallabies he seriously doubted the wisdom of his decision, but pride would not allow him to express this thought aloud. Privately Billy began to undergo the readjustment which would allow him to accept joining Youth and Beauty, an internal dissembling which when finished would enable him to declare it the best thing.

He sat wrapped in a blanket on the sofa, looking at the remnants of Christmas. The room struck him as lonely, devoid of the noises of life, a strange, silent island on which he had landed. The decorations were already half down and to Billy they represented a wrecked moment: he felt a sharp poignancy at the movement of time, for lost moments which would not pass again. He sighed once, then got up to go downstairs to ring Ida Connolly, who was Beauty, hoping that it was not already too late. At the same instant he heard a knock: he opened the door to find Reg.

'How does the Tsang Brothers sound?' Reg Tsang asked only seconds before Billy hugged him.

The Whole Hog

All at once Billy felt his life had fallen back into place, as if it had again found its shape and direction. He got up now half an hour before Bubbles, creeping around the room in order not to wake her. He and Reg were working out a new routine in a shed in his uncle Augustine's garden at Hammersmith, a new universe created by their own selves. They were aware that as a double act they had to win the audience's hearts and minds straight away, and inspire a happy faith in this universe they presented. To this end, they attempted to convey a world which conjured up amusement and astonishment but also fear and a certain recognition. By now they knew well that an audience wishes first to be amused, to leave for a moment its ordinary place and glimpse that other world the imagination possesses. But an audience also wishes for recognizable landmarks, certain pointers which remind it of its waking life. Billy knew that daring routines worked only because each member of the audience understood what fear was, both the moment of hesitation and its vanquishing. He knew a comedy routine worked only because everyone had fallen flat on their faces, and recognized the furtive look on getting up.

Reg and Billy tried to span as many emotions as they could, to incorporate a humorous skit, a dangerous moment, as well as something pleasant for the eye. Reg agreed at once to the idea of suits and bow-ties, suggesting pale cream with black bow-ties. Very quickly the idea came together, with Reg keen to play the role of earnest but stupid beginner and Billy the seen-it-all, handsome straight man. They fell about the cold shed laughing at Reg's one-oh-eights, which were so good Billy expected to see him stand up with a flattened head: he could fall completely flat on his back without so much as raising an eyebrow, taking the brunt of the fall on his shoulders. They planned to use an oversized book with large letters, HOW TO LEARN ACROBATICS: Billy would read out imaginary instructions from this book, and Reg would attempt and fail them. Reg planned somersaults with his leg accidentally caught up in a chair, and what appeared to be botched attempts to land on Billy's shoulders.

At the end of the routine they intended something extraordinary: balancing head to head perhaps, the top mount rolling down afterwards in a double full-twisting somersault. Billy also thought it would be good to have a smattering of tap: he knew a little from Connie and Vernon, but Reg knew none, so they agreed to look around for a friendly dancer who might help them.

The shed was always very cold; when they spoke they emitted white fog. To begin with they wore woollen mittens which left their fingers free, and long white underwear which afforded them at least some warmth. But after about twenty minutes of work the mittens always came off, then the woollen underwear, until finally they worked in athletic tights and singlets. The shed had actually been built as a garage but now it held all kinds of junk: broken coppers, rusting bedheads, old trunks. Still, there was enough room for Reg's uncle and his troupe to practise: all seven of them, spinning at once. Usually Yuk Fan Ching, Chinese Wonders had no need to practice, since they rarely worked less than two shows a night, but Augustine had got it into his head that Chinese New Year was coming up and it would be lucky to start a new year with new routines. So at eleven o'clock every morning the Chinese Wonders arrived and Billy and Reg left the shed. Before they left, Billy heard the loud song of Cantonese which he remembered well, the end notes wrung out until the last possible moment. They all spoke perfect English, albeit with thick American accents, yet when they worked they preferred their mother tongue, communicating with each other in those dramatically familiar voices. Billy thought he detected a certain chilliness in Augustine, however, and put this down to his having stolen Reg.

'Believe me, he doesn't give a bugger,' Reg assured him. 'He's probably pleased to get rid of me.'

This was the closest Billy ever came to speaking with Reg about his decision: he did not really care how Reg had come to make it, he was simply glad that he had.

After two weeks they picked up their new Sydney Fischer suits, trying them on first in the shop. They stood without speaking while the tailor lifted them from the box, rustling the paper and laying the suits carefully on the counter. He went to fetch matching shirts and bow-ties, then led them ceremoniously to the changing room.

It was only when Billy saw them fully dressed in the mirror that he knew for certain that the idea had worked: they looked witty and elegant, two men for whom life was effortless and amusing, cast over with a glamorous sheen. They stood beside each other, still without speaking, pondering on this new image of themselves. At the same moment, they turned their heads to each other. As if rehearsed, both raised a hand in a co-ordinated handshake, congratulating themselves and breaking into grins.

'I wish my life matched the suit,' Billy said.

'Pretend,' Reg replied.

Clutching their boxes, they took off for the Boiling Kettle, for it seemed they had a million things to discuss. They'd have to make an appointment to see Frank Hurley and get some publicity shots taken which didn't cost a bomb. In fact they had to begin disseminating the news of their birth, announcing that a new life had been created. But the main problem was a name, which they'd have to produce fast for upcoming bills.

For some weeks now Billy had also been privately testing out the idea of a stage name for himself. It seemed to him that he had changed practically everything else in his life over the past few months: he might as well go the whole hog. His own name, Billy Hayes, was common and sounded dull: it did not stand out immediately from the rest. Other names did, such as Tyrone or Blair, which were American sounding and somehow smart. He'd need a strong surname to go with it, perhaps something with the same letter as the first. To tell the truth, Billy was spending an inordinate amount of time thinking up a name for himself, instead of one for the act. He had the feeling that once he came up with his own name, a name for the act would soon follow.

So all the while as they talked in the Boiling Kettle, Billy ran through names in his head. Hank? Chester? He actually had a fondness for the name Clark, but of course it was out of the question, being already so well claimed. Billy wondered if changing his name would somehow alter other things about himself, seemingly permanent traits he had come to believe made up this person known as Billy Hayes. He might spontaneously develop a whole new self, with characteristics known only to, say, Jay Powell, or Rocky Jackson. Billy Hayes might not be capable of pulling someone's leg, but Jay Powell might do it all the time.

Each night in bed he told Bubbles about the steps along the way, for he wanted her to know how much care and work were involved. At night when they lay in darkness, he spoke about the events of the day, the routines they were trying out, how Reg was attempting to balance upside down on one finger. He knew that Bubbles could not possibly know exactly what it felt like to dream an idea from the muscles up, nor could she know the journey from the dream to its expression. Billy was not at all sure he understood it either. The only thing he knew for sure was that his work named him and seemed an act of life.

Bubbles lay quietly while he talked, occasionally asking Billy questions or wanting elaboration. She told him it was a good idea that Reg and Billy had got together, but one night she said she didn't think Billy needed to be so driven about it.

'There are other ways of working, you know,' she said. 'You don't have to prove yourself all the time.'

'But I have to be like this if I'm going to be any good!' he burst out. 'I can't be half-hearted about it!'

She did not say anything and seemed to be thinking: he felt compelled to tell her again what it was like. 'Look, I know tumbling's exhausting and takes up a lot of time and it might seem to you pretty foolish. I know it doesn't pay much considering what I put into it, but that's not the point. It has to be my whole life if I'm going to be any good!'

Still she did not speak and Billy wondered if he had offended her by talking about tumbling as his whole life rather than her. He lifted her chin from his chest; in the half-light he could just see the gleam of her eye. 'You know you're the meaning of life, don't you? And what's the point in being the greatest tumbler in the world if I don't have love?'

His questions remained unanswered in the air; in the dark he heard her make a soft sound.

'But why do you have to be the greatest tumbler in the world? When you talk about tumbling, your voice changes completely, it's like you're on some mission from God. Why can't you be a tumbler without making it sound like it's something of great world importance? Just do it, instead of making a great song and dance!'

He was struck to the core but against all odds remained quietly breathing. A great rage filled his chest: right at that moment Billy Hayes believed tumbling had saved his life and that his own wife was scornful of the means. It was all he could do to stop himself pushing her away, leaping up and walking out the door. He hadn't asked for much, only that she support him by acknowledging that what he was doing was a skilful and worthwhile thing. But the more Bubbles withheld her approval, the more Billy wanted it, so that he was now overwhelmed by the humiliating feeling of having shoved his tumbling in her pretty face.

He lifted his arm and Bubbles rolled away from him; he turned on his side and stared at a sliver of light coming through the window. He was angry, but it was mixed with the keenest disappointment. He told himself that it wasn't as if he wanted Bubbles to tell him he was the greatest tumbler to walk the earth, although in his heart he knew to hear it would be thrilling. Billy did not know why he wanted to be a great tumbler: he knew only that he had some compulsion to show the world his true face.

Bubbles moved and her leg brushed against him. The heat of her body reached Billy where he lay, a human call he could not refuse. All at once he knew himself to be a fool, fast on the way to becoming a foolish old man, all alone, with only a handful of yellowing theatre bills for comfort. He felt a sudden letting go of resentment, the breaking up of something hard and wounding, and wished only that he and Bubbles might lie together again, yielding. As Billy turned to his wife he swore to himself that he would learn to speak of tumbling without making it sound like the most important thing on earth; he would teach himself to ask Bubbles the right questions. He was not the only one with hopes, for he knew that Bubbles was not happy with her job, that it had not led to acting jobs as she had expected. As Bubbles silently settled into his arms, Billy understood all over again what was important: this warm alive love in his arms. Together they could throw a line to the future, weld a shape more solid than the mastery of air. He held his wife and her warm breath passed across his face; the whole length of Bubbles Hayes was pressed against him. When they began to make love, it felt like his body had found its rightful place, and that here was its most important use after all.

His new name came to him out of nowhere. In a moment Billy knew he was going to be called Ben Cannon: he did not know where either the Ben or the Cannon came from, but suddenly the whole name was there. The Cannon part was spelt the only way possible; the Ben was neither Benny nor Benjamin. All at once Ben Cannon was a new being in the room, a likeable, confident sort of fellow, as easygoing as Billy was zealous. This Ben Cannon lay back and let the world wash over him; he did not plot or plan, nor fill his head with grandiose designs. Billy Hayes liked the sound of him very much; he seemed to live the alternative life Billy might live himself if given the luxury of two lives. Ben Cannon did not trouble himself about being the best, and would rather feel the sun on his face than get up from the grass and go to practise; he lived a steady life tending children and gardens, turning an occasional roll in the air only if pestered by the children.

Billy lay on his back and turned his head to see if Bubbles was awake. He already felt himself assuming a restful laziness, and decided to spend an extra half-hour in bed. Ben Cannon's nature belied his name: he did not blast so much as trickle.

Cannon and Tsang opened at the Golders Green Hippodrome, on a bill which included Dorinda Dean, the glamour girl impersonator, and the Six Sharpe Bros, Mr and Mrs Sharpe's Six Little Boys. Frank Hurley had arranged that they had good billing (*Direct from La Bal Tabre, Paris!*) and a choice position on the programme: they were third on the bill and when the time came to begin, the audience was already well primed, expectant and excited in their seats. Bubbles was there, and Digger and Min Campbell: all the people Billy had come to care for.

Billy and Reg felt the thrill of the air: before they went on they grinned to each other, two men alive in their skins. As Billy ran on he felt the push of his body, the burn of the light, and Cannon and Tsang sped toward their arrival.

Perfect Love

If Billy had ever thought that marriage could knock down for ever that wall between his innermost self and another person he soon found out he was wrong. As their first wedding anniversary came up Billy found that although he still loved Bubbles, she no longer felt so known to him, and some wall between them resolutely stood. Sometimes Billy had the oddest notion that Bubbles was a different girl to the one he fell in love with, someone he might never get to know. He could not understand it, for he had been so convinced he knew everything he needed to know about her. Now he had the distinct impression that the hard part was only beginning, that they must learn to live with their flawed, ordinary selves.

At moments Billy felt a sharp grief that ordinariness had claimed them, that their beautiful love had become an imperfect, commonplace thing. Some part of him still wished to fight for heaven, to demand only colour and light. When he felt like this he would insist that Bubbles drop whatever she was doing and come with him: he wished them both to open their eyes to the stars.

Often Billy did not feel at all close to Bubbles; he sometimes thought he knew less about her now than he did that first night at the Tower Ballroom. She still smiled those enigmatic smiles, but the smiles now infuriated rather than enchanted him, and it seemed to him that Bubbles deliberately withheld from him her most private self. She regularly travelled far away, and clearly did not wish to take passengers: at first Billy had asked her what she was thinking, but she had replied, 'nothing' so often he had ceased to ask. It occurred to him that perhaps it was impossible to truly get inside someone else's head, to know what Bubbles felt and imagined. He felt slightly foolish that he had once thought it possible, that two people might exist beneath the one skin.

Occasionally Billy wondered how Bubbles regarded him now, whether she too mourned the passing of perfect love. Lately he had noticed she had begun to roll her eyes a lot, an expression of exasperation usually aimed at him. 'You're not exactly Olivier, are you?' she had said to him once after a show. 'I never said I was,' he replied, hurt. 'No,' she said, a far away look on her face. 'I don't suppose you did.' Many times it had been on the tip of his tongue to ask her if she mourned too but he never did, for he was too frightened of her answer, and could not have borne it if she admitted she was disappointed. Billy tried to tell himself he was not really disappointed, it was only that he was returning little by little to the everyday world after waking from a spectacular dream.

In this everyday world they regularly fought, and Billy clearly saw hatred on her face. He was shocked to discover he sometimes hated her back and wished to leave and never return. The first time they had one of these fights, over how much time he spent practising with Reg, Billy packed his bags and left the house but only got as far as the end of the street. Suddenly he found that they were both rushing toward each other only to collide at the front door: Bubbles running down from upstairs and Billy running fast from the street. 'Don't ever leave me!' Bubbles cried out in real fear: he had never seen her so frightened. 'Sh, sh, it's all right,' he crooned into her hair. 'I'll never leave you. Never.' He was shocked and pleased at this apparent proof that she did really love him and could only conclude that their passions were exactly equal. They parted and collided again and again, an endless motion which came to seem to him the motion of life.

But to Billy the greatest surprise was finding that Bubbles had qualities he intensely disliked and had never before noticed. She displayed a certain meanness of spirit, for instance, that he could have sworn she never had when he first knew her. She had adopted a set against Reg, Billy saw, when Reg only wished to offer friendship. Bubbles had decided without getting to know him that Reg was selfish and saw her as nothing more than an unnecessary encumbrance to Billy. 'He's not interested in me,' she complained. 'I'm not a tumbler, am I?' Billy forgave her this, for he recognized that she was frightened, and he tried to reassure her that she was loved. But he saw that she did not yet feel it, and still lived as if Billy might turn cruel at any time. Bubbles clearly felt even now the need to hoard herself up, secreting her personal news as if from an enemy: Billy would only find out that she had asked Frank Hurley to lunch, for example, if Frank happened to mention it. It was as though out of habit Bubbles could not stop her guard over herself: over her secrets, the events of her day, her very self. He felt as if he were perpetually coaxing her out, encouraging her to share herself little by little. She was an odd, private girl: Billy sometimes caught himself looking at her and it was as if he were looking at a stranger.

Other things about her, though, Billy found more difficult to forgive: he noticed that she was never completely happy when things went well for him, hardly glancing at a glowing review, or looking uninterested when he told her of a particularly successful night. If he did not know better Billy might have thought Bubbles was jealous, but as it was he could not quite put his finger on what caused her to act this way. He knew only that he had learnt to talk about tumbling less and less, and to hide things he once would have shouted.

Their day-to-day working arrangements were not complementary either: Billy would be leaving for work just as Bubbles was getting home. Sometimes they hardly saw each other for days at a time, and seemed in bad tempers when they finally did. In this, their needs were completely different: Billy needed to sleep when Bubbles needed to get ready for work; Bubbles wanted to sleep when Billy arrived home still burning from a show. They made do as best they could, but at times Billy did not feel like creeping around the room when he got home, and Bubbles did not feel like walking around on eggshells in the morning.

At last, toward the end of their first year together, Bubbles finally got more than a bit part in a movie. It was only a supporting role, but a decent one, and she had high hopes that other roles would follow. She did not quit her job at the agency, though, but took holidays she had owing; she said it was better to be cautious.

It was Billy's first chance to see Bubbles act; he found himself feeling nervous. What if she was terrible? What if she could not act at all? Billy realized he had simply assumed she was good, but until now he had not had the proof.

'I'm playing this lovely young mother,' Bubbles told him confidently, 'a regular angel fallen to earth.'

'That shouldn't be hard,' he said and she pulled a face.

'Oh, don't be so wet,' she said with irritation. 'Don't you see anyone without rose-coloured glasses?'

Secretly Billy Hayes believed himself to be an exceptional judge of character. 'Actually I think I see people pretty clearly,' he said with what he hoped was a dignified reproach.

She burst out laughing. 'You! You only see what you want to see!'

He must have looked hurt, because as she passed she ruffled his hair. 'I wouldn't lose any sleep over it,' she said. 'It's too late to trade yourself in now.'

As she left the room, Billy pondered on what Bubbles had said: did he really only see what he wanted?

Bubbles unexpectedly invited him on the set one Friday, for the shooting of her final scene. She told him she'd rehearsed the particular scene a million times already, and that by now she could do it blindfolded.

On the set Billy looked around for the most inconspicuous position he could find so that he would have time to gather his wits if she proved awful. He didn't want Bubbles rushing up to him before he had a chance to think about what he would say, so he stood half hidden behind a false wall. There were a lot of people in between the set and himself: as the cameras began to roll, he felt only apprehension.

Bubbles stood in the set kitchen, a cradle in the corner, beating a cake mix while her mother-in-law sat talking at the table. She was playing a woman who was the only one to believe her lost husband would come back, and whose faith was like a light before her. As Billy watched, the face he knew so well took on a kind of ardour, some bright innocence came into it that he had never before witnessed. All wariness dropped from it, all distrust, so that Billy saw Bubbles Hayes naked as he had never seen her.

As he stood there Billy suddenly became aware of a pain within himself. He could not bear to watch as Bubbles freely and randomly gave herself away, in a manner she had never given herself to him. He had never once seen such an expression of pure love on Bubbles's face as was on it now, never once seen her beautiful eyes so trusting.

Before he could stop himself Billy turned and pushed his way to the door, knocking over a small stepladder as he did so. It clattered noisily to the ground but Billy did not falter; as he reached the door he heard someone say, 'Cut!'

Out in the open he did not know what to think, he felt betrayed by his own eyes. He felt a kind of panic but kept walking, he kept moving because it was the only thing he knew. When he got to the street he looked about but did not recognize any landmarks. Without thinking, Billy turned right, no longer sure in which direction he was headed.

Bubbles was cross with him for embarrassing her. He wanted to explain how it had happened, but that would involve telling her how he had felt seeing her like that, and in truth he was not clear himself. He knew only that he was suddenly less sure about her, that it had cracked open another side to Bubbles and he was no longer sure he knew her. He was now conscious that she was an unknown, separate planet from himself, more mysterious than he had imagined. Billy said only that he thought she was very good; she seemed pleased and some time later he caught her smiling what he had come to think of as her private smile. He felt a sudden burst of irritation.

'What are you smiling at?' he asked crossly.

'Nothing,' she replied, still smiling.

'It doesn't look like nothing,' he said.

She turned to him. 'You don't like it, do you?'

'What?'

'Sharing the limelight,' she said with a kind of smirk. 'You want it all to yourself.'

'That's not true!' he cried. 'I've always helped you!'

She raised her eyebrows and swept from the room: Billy stood stranded in frustration and rage, his fists clenched at his sides. He didn't want the limelight to himself, not at all, he didn't mind sharing it one bit.

But Bubbles was right, he didn't like something, though what it was he wasn't really sure. It had to do with the way he had become aware of Bubbles withholding something vital from him, how her lack of enthusiasm for his work had somehow rendered him unable to be entirely generous toward hers.

Billy felt the unpleasant lurch of dread. He had not longed so badly for someone's approval since his father's: he unclenched his fists, which suddenly seemed small and incapable.

After Bubbles forgave him she asked Billy to accompany her to a party for the film's ending. Before they left, she looked carefully over his clothes, brushed lint from his jacket, then stood back to look again. Billy was wearing his Sydney Fischer suit and knew he cut a handsome figure: he appeared to meet with her approval.

'Do I look good enough for you?' he asked.

'At least I can rely on that,' she replied, turning to the door.

He stopped her hand. 'Is that the only thing I'm good for?'

'Of course,' she said, opening the door.

Billy did not move. 'Oh, come on, you twit,' she said, pulling his hand. 'There must be something I like about you or I wouldn't be here, would I?'

For some reason, this was not comforting.

At the party Bubbles introduced him to several of her actor friends, but he found them quite hard to talk to, and none of them seemed interested in tumbling. A kind of closed-down look came into their eyes when Billy spoke of it and he could not help feeling that they didn't take tumbling seriously. In fact, he had the distinct impression that they regarded only acting as serious, and that they patronized him for being in variety.

'Oh, you're imagining it,' Bubbles said afterwards. 'You worry too much about what people think of you.'

'I do not!' he protested but he knew he did: he looked into faces too hard trying to read them.

'You want the whole world to love you,' she said as they got into bed. 'I can see it on your face when you tumble.'

More and more Billy came to believe that Bubbles did not think tumbling was a serious job, and that tumbling was nothing more than childish showing off. He said this to her now, but she snorted dismissively.

'I can't make you feel anything Billy, no one can *make* you feel like a show-off. It must be something you feel yourself,' she said, turning away.

So Billy began to wonder if he was indeed a show-off, some pathetic man who lived only for the limelight. His pleasure in tumbling was momentarily stilled while he investigated for the first time his own motivations. For a while he could not conjure up the necessary enthusiasm vital to his work; he was not in top form and began to make small but important mistakes.

'What's wrong with you?' Reg complained. 'Come on, Cannon, concentrate.'

For Reg's sake he cleared his mind, working hard and willing himself once more into shape. He wondered whether love of tumbling was enough, if bringing himself and an audience a moment's pleasure was a worthwhile reason to do it. For the first time in his life Billy wondered if perhaps he ought to do something more useful, something less frivolous, less flimsy. He could find a better way to make a more direct contribution, and join the real world at last. But every time he thought of leaving tumbling he felt the most intense devastation: what would be the point in laying aside all he had learnt now, all the knowledge of his muscles he had long strived to attain?

Little by little he won back his confidence, and knew again the joy of fighting air.

About a month after their first anniversary Billy was arranging the cushions on the sofa bed one morning when all at once he realized he felt married. He had an unshakeable feeling that despite everything that had passed between them he and Bubbles had begun to press their shapes upon each other. The wall was still standing and they did not share the same skin, yet it seemed clear to Billy that they were now twin inhabitants of the same domain.

Without him noticing Billy Hayes had turned into a married man: it did not feel the way he expected it to feel, but he was pleased to feel it just the same.

Looking at Houses

Early in the new year Bubbles inherited from her mother's estate what appeared to Billy to be a vast sum. Actually it was quite a modest amount, but still respectable: certainly it was more money than Billy had ever known. If this unexpected reminder of her mother upset Bubbles, she did not show it: she did not talk of Elsa Drake at all now, and seemed to have pushed her to some far place where she could no longer cause pain. Nevertheless Billy watched Bubbles carefully when they went to the solicitor's office to collect the cheque, and listened as she took the unsuspecting man to task over why it had taken so long. 'I'm afraid I can't hasten the law, madam,' the solicitor said. 'No, I'm sure you can't,' Bubbles replied. Outside in the street they did not dare look at the cheque but rushed straight to the bank, where Bubbles deposited it in her account. When the bank clerk handed back Bubbles's savings book, she turned to Billy, beaming, to show him the new balance.

'We're rich!' he cried, gathering her up in his arms. 'We're rolling!'

'Oh, we are, are we?' she asked, pushing his arms away. Billy knew at once this money would not free them.

He was no good with money, he could admit it now: it simply hit his palms and bounced off. Billy could never think about a rainy day while the sun still shone, he could not warm his nest long enough to hatch an egg. If he happened to have money in his wallet he was just as likely to shout the whole cast drinks, or buy a new hat for Bubbles. He enjoyed buying gifts for people more than receiving them, but for the life of him he could not buy a less expensive gift if he happened to be short of money. If it was some special occasion, like a birthday or an anniversary, Billy simply borrowed money and bought the gift he wanted rather than compromise and find something second best. But Billy did not get a reputation as a sponger, for everyone knew when he had money he would be the first to buy a round. People did not seem to mind lending Billy Hayes money: he always paid it back eventually, and probably bought you an expensive dinner for loaning it to him in the first place.

These days Billy mainly lived off the cash Cannon and Tsang were paid at the end of each booking, which was sometimes not enough if they went a few weeks without work. Even after a year Cannon and Tsang were still building a name for themselves, and work was not that easy to come by as more and more theatres were converted to cinemas. When Billy was short of cash he had got into the habit of asking anyone else for a loan rather than Bubbles. She had made clear her lack of belief in his ability to successfully handle his own money, let alone a joint account: in fact it had not occurred to Billy that they could have one. 'You should try living in the real world,' Bubbles said, 'then you'll find that money doesn't grow on trees.' She frowned at the times she had to pay a gas bill: at such moments Billy felt ashamed of himself, his own wife having to pay the gas bill! She took to drawing big red circles around the dates bills were due too, and sometimes wrote afterwards: *Paid, Bubbles*. Billy wished she had more faith that he, and Cannon and Tsang, would eventually make good.

Bubbles had been talking about common sense a lot lately, since Billy had begun a kind of campaign aimed at getting her to leave her job to try acting full time. 'It's the only way you'll really make it,' he insisted. 'You've got to be out there.' She had looked at him in amazement. 'Oh, yes? And what will we live on?' But Billy was privately convinced that because Bubbles did not devote herself to her work full time, it was little wonder she had not been swamped with offers: since her movie role she had done only two further crowd scenes. 'It just shows you shouldn't give up your day job,' she said with the vaguest note of bitterness. 'It just shows how hard you have to work at it,' Billy countered and she groaned.

Then one day, out of the blue, Bubbles said she'd been thinking, and she'd decided they ought to buy a house. Bubbles had made it clear that the money in her account was most definitely hers, so Billy did not expect he would have much say in it. He didn't know anyone in the business who owned a house, and the idea struck him as unnecessary. 'Why?' he asked. 'Our rent's not bad, and we'll never get chucked out. Your mother's money will always be there if we need it.' Bubbles gave him a look which suggested he didn't know what he was talking about, before launching into the reasons why they should. Since economics meant nothing to him, Billy's eyes immediately glazed over.

'You're not listening to a word I'm saying, are you?' she said. He looked away: it wasn't that he was not listening, he simply wasn't interested.

Bubbles gave an audible sigh. 'Thank God one of us is sensible.'

And so they began to look around for a house, a young couple sensible of the future. The trouble was, they could not agree as to where this house should be: Bubbles fancied one of the new London suburbs, but Billy preferred an established house, perhaps around the area where they now lived. 'It's my money,' Bubbles said as if this settled it. 'It's my life too, isn't it?' Billy replied.

The business of buying a house he found impossibly tedious: he wanted to walk into the perfect house, hand over the money and slam the door. But Bubbles turned out to have a flinty eye when it came to a house, and saw at once woodworm, rising damp and suspect walls. He tramped around with her to this place and that, but none of the houses seemed to satisfy her. One afternoon on his way to work he saw a perfectly good one just up the road: the next Saturday they arranged for an inspection, but Bubbles declared it much too old.

'Too old for what?' he asked and she frowned at him: he looked at the estate agent and shrugged.

No, Bubbles was firmly set on the idea of a new house, with shiny taps and fresh lino, empty cupboards she would not have to clean. He knew her well enough to know that when she had made up her mind she would not be swayed: he gave up, and agreed to look at new houses.

The first one they saw looked to him like an empty shell, the kind of structure a child might imagine if asked to describe a house: it had four walls and a flat roof, plain windows and a plain front door.

'It's awful,' Billy said straight away, but Bubbles still wanted to look inside. It *was* her money, he told himself, he just wished she wouldn't keep reminding him.

As spring approached, they were still looking at houses, but Bubbles tended to look more on her own. Billy let her do it, for the fight had left him: he did not care as long as this damn house had walls and a door.

He began to spend his days off on the common, staring hopefully at the sky. Every year as winter turned Billy could feel himself growing excited: it always seemed to him that he sensed the change of season before anyone else did, longing for it with a furious impatience as only someone who grew up in a hot place can. Every spring he began to wear lighter clothes before it was appropriate and then found himself pulling out sweaters he had already packed away. When his face happened to catch a ray of sunlight, he turned toward it greedily, as if desire alone could draw the heat of the sun. On a blanket on the common he lay beneath a weak sun, willing it to grow hotter and more dangerous.

One morning in May Billy was returning to the house from the common when he heard the phone ringing in the hall. Dropping the blanket, he fumbled for his keys, opened the door and ran toward it.

'Hurley here,' he heard Frank Hurley say. 'Is that you, Billy?'

'Ben Cannon speaking,' Billy replied. 'Can I take a message?'

'Listen, Billy, I've got two weeks for you and Reg at the Tabarin in Paris from June 16. Can you come in this afternoon to do the contract?'

'You bet I can!' Billy cried. 'You little corker, Frank!'

He slammed the phone down without saying goodbye and rushed to their room for some coins: he had to ring Bubbles to tell her at once, and Reg, and Vernon, and anyone else he could find.

'Reeves and Butterworth,' Bubbles said, answering the phone, and Billy spilled out his news.

'When do you leave?' she asked. He suddenly felt guilty that she was not coming too. All at once it seemed vital that Bubbles come; he cursed himself for not having immediately thought of it.

'Ask for a week's holiday,' he said quickly. 'Say your grand-father's died or something.'

She did not say anything straight away; he heard the clatter of typewriters.

'Some of us have regular jobs,' she said in a curt voice. 'I can't leave everything at the drop of a hat.'

'Yes you can!' he replied. 'Bubbles, this is a wonderful chance. Come on, sweetheart, take a risk!'

'We'll see,' she said in her business-like tone. 'Look, I have to go now, someone's calling.' And so they said goodbye, but his joy was dimmed: he was suddenly less excited than before.

Bubbles did not come to Paris after all, and Billy felt her absence as a kind of shadow. He could not quite rid himself of the feeling that he was somehow doing something wrong, that he was betraying her by going to Paris without her. He thought of her every morning when he woke, and vowed that one day he would come back to Paris with Bubbles.

He and Reg lived in a small hotel overlooking a square; every morning they were woken by the bells of Notre-Dame. Billy could not believe the beauty of the city, the bleached stone bridges, the glistening water which flowed beneath them. Paris really did seem to have a different light, polished, and somehow whiter. Billy found the buildings which lined the boulevards perfectly proportioned, with their carved stone entrances, tall shuttered windows and black curling rails. They all looked to him as if kings and queens dwelt within, not ordinary men like himself. He loved the scrolled wrought iron of the Métropolitain entrances, the green painted drinking fountains and the grey slate domes of roofs. He loved the gleaming brass and light of brasseries; the red awnings hung deep over pavements; the gold monuments; the million clay chimney-pots on sloping roofs. He walked the streets with his head up, filling his eyes with the fresh spring green of the plane trees, the sweeping flash of pigeons.

Every morning he and Reg sat at a different café on wicker chairs which were always the same, then walked the streets till it was time to go to the theatre. The sounds of a new language washed around Billy's ears, but he found he did not mind living in this strange, mute world: he quickly became a new creature who lived through his eyes. He lived in a speechless place, his own planet. On the afternoons when Reg wished to rest instead of going out, Billy walked alone, sometimes for miles. He would not hear his own language for hours at a time. On the rare occasion he happened to pass someone speaking it the words came to him distilled and loud, as if his ears had suddenly lifted clear of water. He could hear the vowels of English from miles off: the sound hit his ear with precision.

He sat in a café in the sun and wrote postcards to Bubbles and his mother, telling them the work was going well. He left out the part about the beauty of Paris in his card to Bubbles, choosing a straightforward postcard with a view of the Eiffel Tower. But for his mother he bought one of those special folding postcards, with twelve different panoramas of Paris. They fell into his lap, bright bits of the city: Boulevard St Michel, Montmartre, Pigalle.

After he had finished he went off to look for a post office: he finally found one and joined a long queue. He did not know the word for stamp, and could not ask anyone because he did not know how to ask. He waited in line, a dumb mute. At the counter he pushed the cards quickly forward, trusting that a smile had no country.

When Billy got back from Paris late on Sunday night, Bubbles was already in bed. He did not want to wake her, yet he had the impression she was not really asleep: there was something too still about her. Nevertheless he made as little noise as possible and crawled into bed, lying with his eyes open in the dark. Paris was still bright in his head, and he was days away from sleep. He tried not to move too much but was wakeful with excitement, and had to roll over every now and then. After what seemed like hours, he finally fell asleep, but he was woken almost at once by Bubbles climbing out of bed. He tried to grab her, but she only kissed him and continued to climb out.

'Good-morning,' she said, bending over him, wrapping herself up in her dressing-gown. 'How are you?' She seemed genuinely pleased to see him. Billy had noticed before that Bubbles always appreciated him more after he had been away.

He smiled at her. 'I'm very well,' he said. 'I missed you.'

'I missed you too,' she replied, kissing him briefly. 'We'll get a chance to have a long talk tonight.' It appeared she had forgiven him for Paris.

Billy continued to lie in bed while she got ready for work, painting her pretty lips in the mirror. As she did her face she told him all her news, leaving the most important bit till last.

'By the way, I've bought a house,' she said, standing up and coming over to kiss him goodbye. 'It's in Norbury. We can go and have a look on Saturday.'

And that was how Billy came to find himself living in a newish house in Avenue Road, SW 16, miles away from the nearest tube.

And it was where he happened to be on a perfect Sunday morning in September the following year when Bubbles came rushing out of the house toward him. He was sitting in the back-yard on a chair sunk in tender, struggling grass but stood up in alarm as soon as he saw her.

'The war's started!' she cried into his face. 'Billy, the war!'

And he looked up into the sky with disbelief, finding it still blue and defenceless. Bubbles looked up too, then turned to him, saying fiercely, 'How stupid to start a war on such a beautiful day.'

But then the air-raid sirens were tested and they began to run, toward the house and their suddenly rewritten future.

London Fists

For a long time Billy did not really believe planes would come yet at the same time he knew that they would. It was like contemplating the idea of growing old: he could not believe he would turn into an old man yet he also knew that day followed day. Of course he saw neighbours digging holes in their back gardens, and the gathering of people in the street, but he was twenty-three years old, an able-bodied man, not old enough to believe himself capable of dying. He and Bubbles did all the things they were supposed to do, blacking windows and putting together a first-aid kit, stocking up on food in tins: to Billy these were merely anticipatory gestures waiting for meaning, since so many sirens had sounded without consequence. Billy remembered his panic and fright after the first siren, and was embarrassed that he could have thought himself in danger. These days he usually continued with whatever he was doing: having a bath or taking their new puppy Ned Kelly for a walk, practising in the backyard with Reg. It seemed to him that the war was one long false alarm, but then a car would backfire in the street and his heart would stop: he knew his fear was not quenched, only waiting.

Suddenly London was fully alive; everyone had something to do. Because it was not yet fully clear that the war was on, there was a secret feeling that the new interrupted hours were a kind of treat, a lucky break from the plod of more ordinary days. Everyone felt the flush of escape that comes from the fracture of routine: to Billy, people suddenly looked more alert, their eyes had a particular sheen. He thought everyone looked pleased with themselves, proud and willing to hate. The Germans and the war might be very far away, but London fists were clearly already clenched, ready at the first call to swing. Billy knew that fear could not have totally fled, but its face was not yet evident on the street: blood remained the unseen product of a living body, and no one could imagine it escaping.

Still, letters from Australia were full of alarm, as if the London skies could not be anything other than dark with enemies. Sapphire Hayes wrote that they must be frightened out of their wits being so close to Germany and she would organize a parcel at once: Billy hastily sent off a card to reassure her they were safe and well, and that there was really nothing to fear. Because the war was not yet real to Billy, it did not occur to him to dash off and fight for his country: indeed, as no one he knew was being called up, the idea did not even cross his mind. He still watched everything with a kind of disbelieving wonder, not yet fully aware of the implications. Besides, he and Reg were working flat out: suddenly they had more bookings than they could poke a stick at, for the war, or rather waiting for the war, had turned everyone out for a show.

Cannon and Tsang found themselves doing two houses a night, six and sometimes seven nights a week: despite regular air-raid sirens, every house was full. Every night the audience was charged and responsive; the air was shot through with a peculiar tension. To Billy the audience seemed to laugh harder at every joke, sigh longer at pretty songs and gasp louder at Cannon and Tsang's skills. Everything had a heightened quality to it, overwrought, slightly hysterical. Yet hardly anyone went home if a siren sounded during a show, even though announcements were made that everyone was free to go if they wished. The audience sat there while the act continued or a new one came on, not noticeably straining to hear the all-clear.

Everyone in variety was getting work, and could pick and choose for the first time in years. Billy regularly played bills with his favourite comedian, Danny Payne (who had a whole new routine of war jokes), with Larry La Fosse, Karina the Girl Fakir, and once even with Connie and Vernon. Work was so constant in London that Billy and Reg found they no longer had to leave the city and could work theatres closer to home.

Because he was so busy, Billy sometimes did not see Bubbles for days at a time, so they had to formally arrange to meet for lunch, or else Bubbles came to the theatre for a drink between shows. She was still working at Reeves and Butterworth but had recently joined an amateur theatrical group, so she was busy too. The group was not ready to perform any plays yet, but Bubbles spent a lot of time rehearsing: it occurred to Billy that she was only trying to appear as busy as he was, but he chided himself at once for his lack of charity. She had never once expressed disappointment that her movie career appeared to be on hold, but to Billy's unpleasant surprise he discovered he was secretly glad she was not doing any more movies. His worst self was pleased because it only seemed to prove his theory about devoting yourself to the business full time. Also, Billy had not counted on how he would feel when he saw Bubbles's naked face magnified on the screen before him for the first time. He had felt again a confusing pain, yet instinctively recognized it as something shameful. Some dark unacknowledged part of himself had been harbouring resentment against her for not fully believing in him and his tumbling, but his wakeful self was as yet unable to admit it.

One night Billy was waiting for Bubbles in the bar of the Princess Theatre where they had arranged to meet when he happened to see her walking toward him. She did not see him and walked confidently forward, poised and composed. Billy realized with a shock that she was no longer a girl, and that her face had fulfilled its own design. Everything about her looked mature and womanly, from her figure to the way she moved: her small face was still challenging, her mouth full, but the whole effect was more tightly composed, as if every feature had finally finished growing. She was twenty-five years old but might pass for thirty: Billy saw that she had realized her own beauty, and had grown ripe and perfect without him noticing. Just then Bubbles noticed him and gave a wave of her hand: he smiled at her, and was suddenly and inexplicably struck through.

'Hello, Mr Cannon,' she said, kissing him quickly. 'Remember me? I'm your wife.'

'And a very beautiful wife too,' he replied. 'Where would my beautiful wife like to go?' He felt a hopeless rush of love for her, and was ashamed that even for a second he had been less than wholehearted. He swore to himself that from now on he would ignore his ache and willingly watch Bubbles's naked face in a thousand movies.

She lit a cigarette as they began to walk. 'Why don't we try that place near His Majesty's?'

'Isn't it a bit far?' Billy replied. 'I'm afraid it'll have to be somewhere close so I can get back.'

'What about the Interval Club?'

'Oh, come on, Bubbles, you know I don't like it. It's full of actor chappies waiting to have a go at you.'

She exhaled air through her teeth in a way that had grown familiar: Billy shot a quick look at her. Suddenly she stopped and turned to him. 'You decide,' she said, 'only don't pretend you're giving me a choice when I really haven't got one at all.'

And with that she walked smartly off: Billy stood very still and watched her. He wondered why it was always harder to connect than he had planned, and why his most effortless exchanges only ever occurred in his dreams.

A few months after the war started, Billy happened to catch a new angle of himself in the mirror and realized he could not stave off any longer the knowledge that he was going bald. *But, I'm only twenty-three*, he cried to himself. *It can't be*! Yet he could see for himself the thinning hair at either side of his forehead, the way the hair was creeping backwards like an ebbing sea. His beautiful hair with its reddish glints, so thick and yet fine to the touch!

He ran from the bathroom into the bedroom, scrambling frantically in Bubbles's make-up drawer for a hand-mirror. Finding one, he ran back to the bathroom and held the hand-mirror up so he could see the back of his head. He saw at once the tiny circle at the top, the pale skin preparing for its entrance.

Billy sat down on the edge of the bath, a man who has experienced a great shock. Ned Kelly nosed his legs, happy to trespass in the normally forbidden territory of the bathroom. The little mirror was still in Billy's hand, unaware of its secrets. Billy stayed like this while the sirens blew, and Ned Kelly bolted in fright. He stayed without moving, right through the all-clear: every siren sounded to him like the heralding of disaster. Losing his hair was all he could think of: not bombs, not destruction, not war. He was being sabotaged by his own body, which had long been his one indestructible gift. He stood up and looked again into the mirror: with a sense of disbelief, Billy realized that his own body would one day completely betray him, and that baldness served as its warning.

The following summer Connie threw an anti-war party, announcing that people could come only on the condition they did not mention the war.

At the door she kissed Billy and reminded him that any talk of the war was strictly forbidden because she was sick of it. 'Where's Bubbles?' she asked. 'Home in bed,' he replied. 'Alone?' she said, walking off.

Billy and Reg had just finished a show and had brought with them several other acts: everyone piled into Connie's front room, which suddenly seemed far too small. Billy saw Vernon pressing up against a girl in a corner and waved to him: Vernon gave him a curt wave back and Billy understood immediately he would not take kindly to an interruption.

Reg had asked along a pair of dancing twins who were on the same bill: Reg was keen on one of them, but Billy had no idea which one. They both looked exactly the same to Billy and even appeared to have indistinguishable personalities. Both of them giggled a lot and did not talk much, so it was hard to tell why Reg preferred one to the other. To stop himself from calling them by each other's names, Billy tried to pick out some individual trait and saw with relief that one sister had a black mole near her left eye. Whenever one of them talked to him from then on, he looked carefully for the mole and if he found it he called the girl Iris.

Connie's flat was lit by candles standing on saucers in the centre of the room, which looked pleasantly mysterious, far away from the waiting streets of Brixton. She had hung brightly coloured blankets from her African trip along the walls, and wooden masks along the picture rails: all her lamps appeared to be made from the skin of some dead animal: Billy did not dare ask which one. She had strung up a hammock of some sort from the window: Billy saw that Vernon had manoeuvred his girl into it, and the two of them lay side by side, swinging. Billy looked quickly at Connie, trying to guess how the relationship between her and Vernon stood at the moment, but it was impossible to tell, for Connie was as usual ignoring Vernon, and flirting outrageously with any available man for good measure. Billy could not help smiling: he would never understand Connie and Vernon, and could only guess that the relationship had somehow grown necessary to both of them.

Cigarette smoke filled the room; Billy sat down on the floor next to Iris, the twin with the mole, an unknown girl and another man he did not know. The man was saying that he couldn't wait for the bloody war to start, all this hanging about was getting on his nerves.

'Sh, Connie'll hear you,' the girl said. 'She'll throw us all out!'

Iris looked at the girl defiantly. 'I say let's get it over and done with,' she said loudly. 'We're ready if they are.'

Billy was to remember this remark, for a few minutes later the first bombs fell. When the whole party stupidly ran out into the street, the sky was alight and the city of London was burning.

Essential Workers

Bombs changed everything: men grabbed women to their hearts, mothers kissed their children and sent them away. Billy Hayes held his trembling wife beneath the stairs and thought he might die of fear: he wanted to lean against something strong and safe, to close his eyes and not hear a sound. Instead, he sat on a stool and heard every noise: every crash, every pause. He held Bubbles, who sat with her hands over her ears; he felt the nerves shake in her body. At first, they talked all the time: loud, useless chatter about nothing; they sang songs or told each other stories. But as the raids got longer and longer, fear swallowed their concentration, so that they could no longer remember the words of the simplest song. Billy was surprised to find fear so relentlessly physical: he felt bloated and sick, swollen as if he might burst. He couldn't stand being cooped up with a bucket, a gas mask and his own fear; he couldn't stand not being able to run.

If a raid happened to come when he was outside in the street, he did not go to a crowded shelter like everyone else but stayed out in the open, walking fast, and felt more in control. Out in the streets he saw what was happening with his own eyes, the flash of guns, the strange new sky. He could match the sounds with what he saw and was no longer a victim of his own imagination. The streets were empty and brilliantly lit, he walked for miles without seeing anyone. Occasionally a warden would yell at him to get to a shelter, but obscurely he knew himself to be safe.

But one night Billy was walking back from the Prince of Wales when a bomb fell a few streets away: it might have fallen right beside him, for he was instantly knocked off his feet. The earth gave a great shudder and he found himself clutching desperately at the pavement, as if it were pliable and might save him from falling. He had the oddest sensation of dropping into some unknown place, beneath his feet was some endless ravine: he hung on to the footpath as though to life, his nose squashed against the cement. There was a strange sound in the air, a sudden

221

silence and then the clatter of shrapnel. Billy looked up and saw clouds of dust, metal rain pattering on the road. He lay still for a long time: the footpath was warm against his face. After a while he got up and inspected himself: amazingly, he was not hurt at all. Suddenly he experienced the most outrageous sense of triumph: he had been bombed, and survived! He began to run, and felt a weird searing happiness. '*I've been bombed!*' he yelled to the cloudy street. '*I've been bombed! I'm alive!*'

After Billy was hit he was no longer frightened: he felt instead a foolhardy daring and knew he and Bubbles would survive. He did not feel charmed exactly, but more a sense of his own will, some internal decision of dogged defiance. He no longer cowered beneath the stairs if he was home but made sure Bubbles was safe in the basement of the house next door before returning to their own house to watch the fighting from an upstairs window. One morning after a raid he found an unexploded incendiary bomb in the front garden and rushed about trying to dig earth to cover it. A young woman neighbour sobbed uncontrollably; everyone else stood well away as Billy calmly dug a hole and buried the bomb, not once expecting it to go off. It would be a lucky bomb to catch him: sometimes during a raid he even dared walk the streets of Norbury, where he heard dogs howl and smelt fear and wondered what on earth the world was doing. On the radio he heard reports of death and destruction, houses hit, women killed: he looked at the sky in dismayed bewilderment and knew actual men sat in planes. The raids came regularly now at awful times of the morning when Billy had only just got to sleep after a show. Astonishingly, people were still flocking to theatres, desperate now to leave more nervous lives. He and Reg put their whole selves into each performance, keeping going through every crash and bang. Sometimes Billy thought of what would happen if a full house were hit but banished this thought as soon as it came.

Many of his friends had joined entertainment organizations for the services, and Connie and Vernon were being sent next month to the Middle East. Digger Dog Crew was trying to go home to Australia so he could join up there, but was finding it hard to get a ship back.

'Do you think we should go too?' Reg asked one night: Billy

had been thinking the same thing. He knew it was remote that he would be called up by Australia since the authorities would not know where to find him. Instead, he had decided whether to volunteer, to step forward and re-join his country. He glanced at Reg, who was taking off his make-up: Billy picked up the towel from around his neck and pressed it to his face.

'I really don't know,' he finally said. 'I guess we should wait and see.'

They looked at each other, men without weapons, essential workers whose tools of trade were their own limbs. Billy did not know if he would be more useful picking up a gun but decided to wait until it became clear.

Without complaining, Bubbles left her job and began work in a munitions factory; she said Billy should come one day for a laugh.

'You should hear those women,' she said, smiling. 'Anyone would think the main function of the war was to provide them with boyfriends.'

The war had certainly improved their marriage: Bubbles seemed unaccountably happier, and now that she had grown more used to the sound of bombs she no longer seemed frightened. Like Billy, she had obviously set her chin against fear. She looked strong and capable in her new uniform, which Billy asked her to parade for him the night before she started work. Bubbles still complained now and then that she could no longer buy her favourite nail polish, but so did Billy about certain theatrical make-up he could no longer find. He and Reg now made their own concoction of boiled-up lard which passed as a make-up remover but stank unless Billy pinched a little of Bubbles's rose water to put in it. She shouted at him when she found out, because everything was so precious, but forgave him when he brought home an extra pat of butter a kindly waitress at the Boiling Kettle had slipped him.

One morning as Billy watched Bubbles getting ready for work it struck him that the internal workings of his wife were still a mystery to him. He lay in bed and watched Bubbles moving happily about the room, ironing her shirt, putting on her make-up. He had known her now for almost five years and could not say he understood her. He had only the broadest idea of the shape of her dreams (he knew she wished to see New York and Hollywood) but had to guess at what lay behind those unwavering eyes.

In a flash Billy suddenly saw Bubbles as someone else might see her: curiously detached, with no family, no old friends (she occasionally received a card from Nettie in Blackpool), no connections. Apart from himself Bubbles lived unencumbered, unattached to the wider world. All her friends were recent ones, changed often. Except for a moment years ago when Bubbles had broken apart over her mother's death she had not allowed Billy even the briefest glimpse inside.

He sat up in bed. 'Bubbles, do you understand me?'

She gave him one of those looks which suggested forbearance. 'Yes, Billy, I do.' She continued polishing her shoes.

'No, I mean *really* understand me . . . what I feel on the inside.'

She stopped polishing, and sighed. 'Yes, I understand what you feel on the inside, Billy,' she said with only the merest lift of her eyebrows.

He looked at her. 'Well, I don't feel as if I really understand you,' he said.

She had finished the shoes and was putting the brush and cloth away. 'Ah, but do you *really* want to? Are you really as interested as you think?'

He nodded earnestly. 'I wonder,' she went on. 'Most of the time you're more interested in yourself than you are in me.'

'That's not true!' he protested. 'I'm always trying to get you to share things with me! I want to understand you, I really do, I just don't know how to do it.'

Billy noticed then that Bubbles was smiling her private smile.

'See, you're doing it now! I don't even know why you're smiling!'

She turned to him, her smile gone. 'What makes you think I'm smiling?' she asked, standing up and gathering her things.

Not long after this, during a particularly bad early morning air raid, it came to Billy that what their marriage really lacked was a baby. As he sat alone watching the blazing sky, it suddenly seemed obvious to him that this was the missing act which would weld them irretrievably together. All at once Billy had the over-whelming conviction that although the whole world was being shaken up, some natural order was clamouring to make itself known. That's it, he thought wildly, a baby would connect Bubbles to the world like nothing else! Billy immediately stood up and rushed down the stairs: he got to the front door before he realized he did not know exactly what he was going to say to Bubbles. He couldn't simply burst in on her in the middle of an air raid and ask her if she wanted to have a baby! He realized he didn't even know if she wanted a child, for they had not ever talked of it. He himself had simply assumed that one day a baby would arrive and make their love manifest but he saw now he did not have the faintest idea of Bubbles's feelings.

Billy walked back up the stairs to the sound of planes, suddenly sobered. He decided he would bide his time, and wait for the appropriate moment.

It came sooner than he'd expected, when Bubbles complained one morning about the difficulty of buying her favourite brand of sanitary towel.

'I won't tell you what it's like in the lavatories at work. Honestly!'

Billy looked down at his hands. 'I've got an idea and it'll mean you won't need any for a while.'

She stared at him blankly for a moment: he saw comprehension come into her eyes.

'Oh, that's just what I need. No thank you,' she said and threw a cushion at him, but Billy thought he detected a spark of pleasure before she threw it.

Suddenly, it was all he could think of: Bubbles pregnant, their own child! He began to notice babies in arms on the street, the architecture of pregnant bellies. He peered into a rough blanket the night a bad raid stopped a show for the first time: a young mother who had been in the audience looked startled and turned away. He had supposed only women craved a child, yet here he was, hungry as any woman. He spoke of it to no one lest he embarrass himself yet he did not feel ashamed but more human. He jumped on Bubbles every night but would not bully her by leaving off his contraceptive: he wanted her to wish for it too, but was mad with impatience till she did.

One night he turned to her when they finally got back into bed after a siren proved a false alarm.

'Oh, not now,' she said crossly. 'What's got into you, Billy?'

He sighed loudly and slumped back on the pillow. 'I want us to have a baby,' he said at last.

There was a pause. 'You mean you want me to have a baby,' she said. 'Don't you think I should have a say?'

He turned to her in the dark. 'Of course, darling, but don't you want to? Don't you want us to have a child? Bubbles?'

She did not reply at once; the room was very dark because of the blacked-out windows.

'There's a war on, or haven't you noticed? You probably haven't, knowing you.'

Billy did not speak at once and tried to think of the perfect words, but when he came to open his mouth he could not find them. He said instead, 'Well, the war's the reason I thought of it in the first place . . . all this noise . . . people dying . . .' He stopped because his words were wrong: to his surprise Bubbles rolled closer to him without speaking. They lay for a long time until Bubbles fell asleep: Billy did not sleep himself but listened to the sound of bombs far away, his eyes moving ceaselessly in the dark.

Billy and Reg reluctantly began to tour outside London; they didn't want to, but Frank Hurley talked them into it, lecturing them about their duty to the public. 'It's not only the troops who deserve some entertainment,' he said. There were only a few acts of Cannon and Tsang's calibre left now as more and more people in the business were called up, or else joined entertainment organizations for the armed forces. Frank, who was too old to join up himself, was frantically trying to keep business going, organizing shows and keeping as many theatres booked as he could. He rang Billy one morning, practically begging him and Reg to join a show he had organized to go north.

'Come on, Billy, help me out here. I've just been on the phone for two bloody hours persuading a lot of old-timers to dust off their acts. I'm desperate!'

And so it was after this that Cannon and Tsang went out into the country again, first to the ruined city of Hull, where they were shocked to see such devastation: they saw the skeletons of flour mills and power stations, abandoned houses in which the only sign that they had once been somebody's home was a cracked mirror on a wall, or a bright edge of a cushion sticking out from under a fallen beam.

They found that the theatre they were due to perform in had been bombed the night before: Billy and Reg looked at each other, both of them thinking the same thing. Within minutes they had persuaded the rest of the acts to do a free show, along the banks of the river.

Billy remembered this show for the rest of his life: the exhausted faces of the people, the smouldering remains behind them. The violet sky above their heads looked curiously innocent; a great sweep of clouds fanned up from the horizon. Smoke rose from the town; the air was still, strangely dense. People laughed, or tried to; they wrapped themselves in blankets and shook their heads, marvelling at the saving of their skin.

When the show finished, the whole cast took a collective bow, then raised their hands to join the audience: the sound rang loud and seemed to Billy to lift into the sky, floating upwards, higher and higher.

They went to other towns which had not been bombed: everyone wanted to know what it was like in London. 'I wouldn't be there for all the tea in China,' said their landlady in Leeds. 'Hitler's going to smash the place to smithereens.'

Billy had not expected to feel so anxious about Bubbles while he was away: when he was in London he never worried about her, not because he thought his own luck would protect her, but simply because he inexplicably knew her to be safe. He had expected to feel the same way while he was away: he had not counted on worrying about her day and night. He rang her whenever he could, but it was not always possible, and she was not always home. Billy could not quite shake the feeling that she was in danger, and grew more and more anxious until the day came to take the train home. The train was full of troops, many of them

American, and their loud unfamiliar accents got on Billy's nerves.

When he got home, the house was still standing. He burst through the front door, rushing from room to room calling Bubbles's name. She was not home and he sank into a chair: in the silence he heard her call.

He raced up the stairs and found her collapsed on the floor of the bathroom, the only door he had not opened. She looked uncharacteristically frightened and said she had called out, but he had been in too much of a rush to hear: she had fallen over just that minute. It was only when Billy bent to help her up that he saw the bandage on her calf and the fine cuts and bruises up her arms and on her face: she hugged him, placing her arms gladly around his neck.

'I've been in the wars,' she said, half crying, as he carried her to the bed. She tried to tell him about the bomb when she was coming home the day before but she needed more his physical comfort, his live, undamaged skin. And so it was on a clear afternoon in 1941 that a child was conceived, painlessly, amid the pain of war.

Panic's Gun

When Billy found out that Bubbles was pregnant he wanted to run out into the street and tell everybody, he wanted to hold Bubbles fast to his chest. Straight away he imagined the fine conversations he would have, how his child would know only gentleness and love. Billy planned to be the best father in the world, kind and just; he would bend his ear to that innocent mouth, offering only understanding and respect. He instantly pictured himself with a young boy who loved him, who would throw his arms gladly round his father's neck.

And yet as soon as he saw Bubbles's face, really saw it, Billy emerged from this splendid dream. He knew at once it would not be like this, and immediately felt a kind of dread. 'Sweetheart?' he inquired anxiously, lifting Bubbles's trembling chin.

'Bubbles?' he said, and she looked into his eyes for the first time.

'But I'm too young to have a baby,' she said, starting to sob. 'Oh, Billy, I'm too young.'

All at once Billy discovered he felt too young himself, hardly grown into a man. He held his wife close, but his contradictory heart began to beat loud: before he knew it Billy felt the unmistakable lurch of fear, the random shoot of panic's gun. Instinctively he felt he must not let Bubbles know: he stroked her hair and noticed that his hand was trembling.

For nights on end Bubbles whimpered in her sleep while Billy lay awake beside her. Every now and then her body shuddered, sometimes so violently he could not believe she did not wake up. At first Billy tried to hold her, but she shook him off even in sleep, so that there was nothing for it but to wait till morning.

When Billy did sleep, his own dreams were anxious and loud sounds frequently woke him. It seemed to him that the sound of war was closing in, as if the outside world had become nothing more than a manifestation of the fighting within his own head.

Both Billy and Bubbles woke unrefreshed every morning, Bubbles so tired she immediately wanted to go back to sleep. 'Oh, stop it,' she said when Billy tried to hug her. 'I can't stand being touched.'

They argued all the time. One morning, as he had somehow known that she would, Bubbles accused Billy of tricking her into getting pregnant.

'How are you going to support two of us? You can't even support me!'

'I can!' he said angrily. 'I've got more work than I've ever had!'

'And what's going to happen when the war's over? I can guess who'll be paying the mortgage then.'

'Listen, Bubbles,' Billy said in a low voice, 'Cannon and Tsang's the best chance we've got. If I – '

She cut him off. 'Oh, it's always *you*, isn't it!'

Bubbles stormed from the room and slammed the door. Billy stood there: he thought it *was* him they were talking about, his ability or lack of it to support his wife and child. He had been going to say that if Bubbles was prepared to trust him, he would prove himself more than capable of supporting everybody: in a few years' time they would be flush with money and success. It wasn't just a foolish, idle dream but a possibility already pulsing within reach: even now Cannon and Tsang had more offers of work than they could accept.

But Billy saw at once that Bubbles doubted him. She took to staying silent for hours at a time, answering him in monosyllables whenever he asked her a question. From one day to the next she seemed to hate the sight of him: all at once she seemed unable to look into his face.

One morning when Billy was eating his breakfast it suddenly hit him that Bubbles found him repulsive, and he immediately felt self-conscious and ungainly. The food he was eating stuck in his throat: he tried to chew silently so as not to offend her. He felt his mouth to be unattractively pursed, his cheeks pillowed with greed, and quickly got up and left the room, leaving the house hours before he was supposed to.

Before long Billy began to avoid Bubbles altogether, leaving a room when she came in, staying away from the house as often as he was able. He felt a claustrophobia he had not felt since the worst times at home with his father, when his sole ambition had been to escape.

Billy did not tell anyone Bubbles was pregnant but hugged his knowledge to himself so that little by little it might grow less frightening. He needed to get used to it himself first, and for the moment could not imagine telling anyone else. He had never kept a secret in his life and it seemed to him he was differently placed in the world now.

But as Billy was leaving the theatre after a show, he realized he wanted to tell Reg.

'Congratulations!' Reg cried at once, hugging him hard. 'We'll form a family troupe!'

Billy managed a reasonable impersonation of happiness but did not look Reg directly in the eye. He felt ashamed of himself, as if he were being ungrateful, for after all he had been the one to wish for life so immoderately.

Soon after this, when Bubbles rushed out of the kitchen to be sick again, Billy decided to follow her. He watched her leaning over the toilet, and stood waiting with a clean towel which he intended to hand to her. But when she has finished she immediately moved to the sink: Billy saw that her knuckles were white from where she was clenching the sides. She looked at his reflection in the mirror, wiping her mouth with the back of her hand.

'Oh, leave me alone,' she said. 'For God's sake, leave me be!'

And so Billy replaced the towel on the rail, turned and left the room. It was nothing like he imagined having a baby would be like, it was not what he had planned at all.

On a cold Sunday in the sixteenth week of her pregnancy Bubbles unexpectedly sat up and smiled. 'Well, there's nothing I can do about it now,' she said, turning to Billy, 'and it may as well be now as later.'

He smiled tentatively back at her; she put down the book she had been reading. 'It's one way of spending the war, I suppose,' she said, standing up. And with that Bubbles seemed to brush herself down, as if in preparation.

Billy watched her warily, not yet convinced the danger had passed. And yet he saw from her face that some obscure internal adjustment had occurred, some vital private work had taken place. All at once her face looked fuller, softer; her steady eyes had a new, engaged look.

A few mornings later he came across her examining her swelling form in the mirror. He hesitated at the door, unsure whether to say something. 'You're looking pleased with yourself,' he finally said, but this came out sounding less like a declarative statement than a plea.

She looked up at him. 'It's kind of interesting,' she said, 'even if I'm not at all sure what it's going to do for my figure.'

Billy gingerly stepped closer: when she made no move to back away, he gathered her up in his arms. Surprisingly, his self-possessed wife moved closer to his chest, laying her cool cheek against his shirt. He caught a sudden glimpse of her face in the mirror and was shocked by how in need of protection it looked. She suddenly seemed vulnerable, even lost.

Without letting on that he had seen this, Billy continued to hold his wife. He felt that in this one brief moment he had glimpsed the true Bubbles: it was this Bubbles he must remember, and never once give up trying to coax. He told himself that if he could only hold Bubbles long enough, all her barricades, all her anger would fall away. As he held her now he was sure of it, and hugged her harder, the whole of her, his guarded wife for once willing in his arms.

From this moment on Bubbles did not so much invite Billy in as retreat to some far, secret place. He could only watch as she became more and more absorbed in her interior work. But for the second time since Bubbles had found out she was pregnant, Billy felt a rush of hope: he was full of courage, and ready for whatever this baby might bring. His hopes were back, that was for sure, shouting so loud he wondered why everyone could not hear them.

One evening when Reg and Billy were doing their make-up for a show, Reg said he'd had a letter from Lily. Billy had not heard her name spoken for so long that he was surprised by it.

'Oh?' he said. 'How's she going?' He felt the smallest skip of excitement but squashed it at once.

'She sounds all right, considering. She's just heard Vince's a prisoner of war.'

Billy put down his pencil. 'Where?'

'Malaysia somewhere. She's waiting on more news.'

'Poor Lily,' Billy said.

'Poor bloody Vince,' Reg replied. 'I wouldn't trust those Japs as far as I could throw 'em. They're worse than the Jerry.'

All at once Billy felt guilty to be so safe, and was hit by a sudden conviction that he was not doing enough.

'Do you think it's too late to join up?' he asked Reg, who for some reason smiled at him in the mirror.

'Don't worry, Cannon, no one's going to call you a coward. You're doing your job.'

And so Billy did his job, the only one he knew, that night, and the night after. He did not stop thinking, though, about an Irish-Chinese tumbler in a Japanese prisoner of war camp, and Lily Tsang in a Sydney flat, waiting.

A Wigwam for a Goose's Bridle

The night Michael Antony Sly Hayes was born, the city of London was abnormally quiet. Billy Hayes definitely heard a moment's pause as new life found its way to earth: the sky was clear and silent as if ashamed of itself, bombing men felt compelled to stay at home. Billy himself felt alert and zealous, personally capable of stopping wars: behind that door life was moving, a new human being was announcing himself and others would follow after, on and on, through war and peace and human failure. Billy jumped up and ran full pelt down the corridor because he could not help it and had to give his joy a chance to run.

The first time he saw his son's face, Billy stopped in his tracks. It was the face of his father, it was the face of a new human soul.

'You can come closer,' Bubbles said, but he didn't, not yet, he stood at the bottom of the bed uselessly patting Bubbles's foot. His son was wrapped tightly in a sheet, but his head was red and clear in the light.

'He looks like my father,' he said in a quiet voice.

'He looks like you,' Bubbles said, holding her son. She had an expression of triumph on her face which Billy had not seen before: her skin was alight, her eyes had a feverish glitter. She had the unmistakable glow of someone who has gone through a physical ordeal of magnitude and power. Billy saw she was relishing her new body: she looked noble, alert to her body's tiniest nuance, the flow of her own brave blood.

'Oh, come here,' she said, knocking his hand away with her foot. She held the baby out to him, fast, so that Billy instinctively put out his arms. The baby felt heavy, very real: he yawned, a wide, ancient yawn, and Billy looked up at Bubbles in surprise. 'He works all right,' she said, crossing her arms across her still swollen belly.

Billy gazed down upon his son: the pleasure and risk of being alive and breathing seemed suddenly more than he could bear.

He noticed Bubbles smiling at him then, a smile of tenderness and love. It seemed to Billy that she looked at him in the same way as when she first loved him, when she had looked into his eyes expecting to meet the whole world. Billy's heart felt as if it might burst: he was blessed and moving, moving in his big, changing life.

When Michael Antony came home he came equipped with his own infant respirator, a sort of gas mask he was supposed to wear in air raids. Sometimes Bubbles slipped it on his tiny face for a moment; it frightened him so she took it straight off, but, oh, the sight of him for that moment. He looked like some alien thing, with his grasping hands flailing at the sides, his soft squashed ears under the strap. He suddenly did not seem a baby at all but some creature with enormous eyes and an inquisitive nose which looked like it should be on all fours.

'Oh, take it off,' Billy said, 'it's cruel, isn't it, mate?' And Billy would scoop up his son in his arms and lift the mask gently from his face. He did not cry but he looked startled, even shocked, as if he might begin at any time. Of course he could not lift his own head yet, much less crawl: he was a frail, dependent thing of whom Billy was frightened. Billy felt an anxious tenderness toward him, and secretly feared his son was altogether too frail and unprotected for survival. He knew that he held him far too gingerly, and that like a new-born kitten Michael Antony would probably understand if carried off by the scruff of the neck. His eyes did not seem focused yet, as if he had not yet fully made the transition from the place whence he had come: he did not appear used to air instead of water and reminded Billy of nothing so much as a landed fish, its mouth blindly gaping into space.

The baby had only been home three weeks and neither Billy nor Bubbles would claim to be used to him. Billy often snuck into Michael Antony's room at night, peering into the cradle, checking on the rise and fall of his lungs. In the first few weeks he was perpetually asleep, but then one day he suddenly woke up: he began to scream and scream, as if furious about being called to earth. Bubbles's nipples became cracked and sore; she seemed to be crying every time Billy looked at her. In the fourth week she abandoned altogether feeding Michael Antony herself and thrust a warm bottle at Billy.

'Here, you wanted a baby,' she said, slamming the bedroom door.

Billy looked at his son, wondering what on earth he was supposed to do: he was howling uncontrollably and Billy felt like opening the door and throwing him back like a football to Bubbles.

Instead, he sat down on a chair and arranged Michael Antony on a cushion resting on his arm.

'If you shut up for a minute, you'll get something,' he told the baby crossly. 'Here, shut your gob.' He jammed the teat into the baby's mouth, but the baby was crying so hard he could not take it.

Suddenly, having a baby did not seem to Billy one of his better ideas. He looked down in despair at his screaming son.

It took Billy a long time to get over the shock of Michael Antony, far longer than he would have dared say. He settled into their lives as if in too small a boat, so that everyone was forced to rearrange their limbs to accommodate each other. Billy did not feel older, or any less or more himself; he felt only a new and terrible area of vulnerability. Fatherhood was difficult and strange, hardly natural at all. Billy's sleep, if he got any, was disturbed by dreams; images from his past rose up, cruel and overblown, and he frequently woke with a start. He caught himself wondering who his son was, and when he might begin to feel known. Bubbles too seemed suddenly changed: she had a vague, disconcerting look in her eye, as if she were trying to remember something long forgotten. She appeared to shake herself awake if Billy addressed her; sometimes she was still sitting in her dressing-gown at four o'clock in the afternoon, having managed to move only as far as one room to another. She did not seem at all like her old self: Billy often turned around to find her with a lost expression. 'Are you all right, sweetheart?' Billy asked her one morning.

'No, my life's over,' she replied, bursting into tears. He held her as she sobbed, stroking her head for lack of anything else to do: he had never felt so helpless in his life.

To his shame, Billy found he was glad to leave the house, and spend time alone again in a clear space in which his ears were not battered.

He was acutely homesick too, and felt a sharp, physical craving for Australia. It seemed to him that he had not felt like this for years: all at once Billy wished for nothing more than to stand on home ground, to see again the smash of the Pacific Ocean against rocks. He wanted it hot as Australia; he wanted lantana and muscular grass yellow from the sun, to hear cicadas and the screech of proper birds. He was suddenly overwhelmed by a passionate grief that his son had been delivered into bitter English air and would not know his father's own country. Michael Antony would not see a flock of Sydney cockatoos pass across the sky, nor feel the pressure of Sapphire Hayes's grip when excitement ran through her: he would grow all his growing away from his only grandmother, aunts and uncles, away from cousins, the sharp smell of a warmer sea. His days would pile up and then he would be grown, an Englishman, with a constellation different from his father. He would not know what the expression 'a wigwam for a goose's bridle' meant, or that a whole country stopped on the first Tuesday in November until several horses had finished racing around a field. Small things, of course, but big enough to weld a memory, and wear a shape into a man. Australia even shaped a boy's tongue, so that Billy could only pronounce words a certain way: it struck him all at once that Australia lived within him, within his words, within the very way his eyes had learnt to see. He was a fully grown man who had lived all his adult life in England, yet behind his eyes his original landscape was sovereign, he still knew its contours by heart. Only after Michael Antony was born did Billy discover that Australia had built him surely as brick by brick, cast him fully formed from the soil: he was created by language, seasons, customs, and would live all his life with its shape.

It was not that Billy was worried his son would be different to him, for he believed it was every child's right. He mourned instead a whole world Michael Antony would never know, people he would never get to hold. For suddenly Billy Hayes panicked that he would never see Australia again: he tried to tell himself that he was just being silly, but every night he dreamt of Glebe Point.

The war kept on and on, a tired idea whose *raison d'être* had long expired. Everyone was sick to death of it, having given up long ago any notions that its excitements might prove amusing. It meant deprivation and loss now, since everyone knew its intentions were serious; only some children and certain young girls in love seemed capable of uncovering its frivolous side.

Billy and Reg stopped talking about going back, and Billy never once spoke to Reg about his sudden longing to go home: in the circumstances it seemed puny, and shamefully inconsequential. To feel homesick for a country safe and far away was too much like self-indulgence. Billy's own brother Cec was fighting for that same country somewhere in New Guinea; Saph Hayes wrote that Bede could not wait to go too.

In the same letter, Saph Hayes mentioned that she had not seen hide nor hair of any call-up papers for Billy, but could only assume they had been sent to 61 Allen Street where it was anyone's guess what had happened to them. She did not keep in contact with Jack Hayes but wrote that Eva occasionally saw him coming home drunk in the street. Billy found himself feeling pity for his father when he pictured this, a despised old man, left alone. He often caught himself thinking about his father now: had Jack Hayes been as overwhelmed by fatherhood as he now was, for instance, had he too once marvelled at the hairs on his son's head? Billy toyed with the idea of writing to his father, or at least of sending him a photograph. He felt inexplicably compelled to make some sort of connection but did not know yet what the best means might be.

His mother certainly made sure she kept a connection: all through the war she and Eva had sent letters and parcels. Saph wrote that since Uncle Arthur had died, Eva had been thinking of selling up and coming to live with her. Eva and Saph continued to send tins of Arnott's biscuits, jars of Vegemite for Michael Antony to build his nerves, sugar and pairs of badly knitted mittens. Billy knew that there was rationing in Australia too, and wrote again and again telling them to save their coupons.

We don't need much any more, his mother replied. *Your forgetting Eva and I are getting long in the tooth.*

Billy supposed his mother must be getting old, although he could not imagine what she might look like. In July 1943 he sent a photograph of himself, Bubbles and Michael Antony standing outside Avenue Road in the sun. He wrote on the back: *To Mother, Our thoughts are always with you. Our love, Billy, Bubbles and Michael Antony (Tom).* The sun was in their eyes; none of them looked into the camera.

A Small Flag Waving

At last the war was over; the world shook itself, and stood up. There was a strange new stillness, as if a strong wind had blown through and the air was only now recovering from the shock. People got up and rubbed their eyes, straightening curtains and wiping down soot: in the town of Whitby, where Billy had happened to be, people waited to hear the church bells. If the war was over, bells would ring: at the appointed hour Billy could not hear the bells because all the ships in the sea were blowing their horns. The world was ringing, one long, loud, jubilant honk: a young woman with fierce blue eyes and a round face clasped his hand and said, 'It's the peace!'

The peace was here, the new, soft world; the world in which sons and husbands and fathers could come home. Billy saw them stepping off trains and buses, he saw them coming along the road, returning with their hats and their kits, drawn back to the exact spot they were from. All over the world men were coming back: Billy could shut his eyes and see their endless tired figures travelling, over land, over sea. He imagined the dead returning too, speeding homeward, a teeming mass of spirits in the sky. They were headed for England, Germany, Japan; they were headed for America, Australia. Lily's Vince must be speeding toward her, for his ghost would surely know the way home. The whole world was making way for the living and the dead, and Billy Hayes was not the only one to greet them.

Despite himself Billy felt the air move in his chest, the brush of change against his skin. Something alive and hopeful flashed across his heart, he briefly caught the whiff of promise. It seemed to him that some giant background noise had been silenced, as if he had been unconsciously walking around hunched against it and could once again walk about freely.

He had the sensation of unfolding himself into the world once more, as if only now could he afford to stretch himself out fully. Walking down the streets he had known under fire, his body uncurled itself at last: he felt the full force of his fingers and toes, the power in the upward shoot of his spine. His body remembered a carefree world, before loss, before complications: his body remembered everything, every slap, every caress. He used his body now to sense the new peace, to once again lead him forward.

Colour and brightness came back into the world, some inner light switched itself on. Men took their evening dress out at last, their tails and tuxedos, their best silk scarves. Women shone in taffeta and georgette, and it seemed to Billy that every single piece of jewellery in London was taken out and polished. Audiences gleamed again; cut glass once again reflected the light. After years of audiences coming to shows in their work clothes or in army uniforms it was as if flowers had opened: all the acts Billy worked with took to peeping behind the fire curtain, admiring the unexpected flash of silk and stone. Roles for the moment were reversed while the acts looked with pleasure at the audience: rationing might still be going on and things might still be hard to get, but hope had obviously survived undefeated.

One night as Billy looked out from behind the curtain he was struck by how hopeful and willing every waiting face looked, how every face preparing to perform seemed eager and ablaze. It was suddenly clear to him that hope had continued to live below the surface of days, unseen yet all the time still pulsing.

All at once he was hit by the idea that this hope should be honoured, that this human ability to get up again and again should be formally acknowledged. *That's it*, he thought wildly, *a show to honour hopefulness! A show to celebrate hope's survival!* He wanted to jump in the air, to tell someone, he wanted to rush out on the stage right now and throw open wide his arms. He took one last look before turning away, running fast in the direction of Reg. 'Hey!' said a tall girl as he slammed into her. 'Sorry!' he called over his shoulder, blowing her an extravagant kiss.

'I want to put a show together,' he blurted out as soon as he saw Reg, 'something about hope. But it's got to be really big, with tumbling and dancing . . . oh, everything! I want as many people as we can fit on the green. The Palladium's too small, don't you think? What about the Princess?' He almost fell over himself in his rush to get all this out. Reg looked at him in amazement and held up both hands.

'Enough!' he protested. 'What on earth are you talking about?'

Not for the first time in his life Billy realized the great gap between what he felt and its expression: profound and illuminating things were bursting in his chest, great secrets had been revealed to him if only he could find the means to tell. He felt the world had delivered for a moment its meaning, as if he had glimpsed, even briefly, the logic of life.

He tried to gather himself up to a still, quiet place, to sit down and harvest his fever. He placed his hands on his knees and breathed out slowly: he tried to call all his words to his tongue. He had never learnt to truly speak out loud, to bring his inner dialogue out through his mouth. Inside himself he knew all the words, he knew every single right word to say; he knew how to speak comfort, truth, love; he knew the true words of his soul. Inside himself he knew every single thing he needed to know: he sometimes surprised himself by what he knew about being upright and breathing. And yet Billy sat on a hard stool in their dressing-room and words sped from his tongue. He tried to gather them, but they flew by, sensing capture.

After a while he looked desperately at Reg, who raised his eyebrows and smiled in a sympathetic gesture.

'A show, Cannon. You were talking about a show.' Always sensitive to Billy's difficulties, Reg turned away to check the fall of his suit in the mirror, watching Billy's reflection apparently casually in the glass.

'Oh, I was thinking of a kind of salute . . . to the acts and the audience. To all of us who survived by hoping . . .' He looked apprehensively at Reg: of course it sounded absurd spoken out loud; it sounded absurd even to him.

'Try putting that on as bill matter,' Reg said, not unkindly. 'You still haven't answered the question. What kind of show do you mean?'

He tried again. 'I think I mean a show that involves us all, not a show like we do now where we go on, do our act and then another act comes on. Something more flowing . . .'

Reg turned to him. 'More like a play?'

Billy shrugged. 'I guess so. More of a story anyway. Like a pantomime, I suppose.'

For the first time Billy saw he had captured Reg's attention. Reg smiled, a broad, heady smile, and Billy felt his heart lurch.

'It's a great idea,' Reg said after a moment. 'I think we should talk to Frank.'

And so the idea of *The Hope Show* was born, the show to celebrate hope's survival. Amidst the mounting toll of loss and grief, the broken families and peoples and cities across the earth, there was now a small flag waving, a cautious flag, the flag of tentative survival. Of course Billy knew that it was only small, but none the less it was definitely waving.

Frank Hurley took to the idea at once; his phlegmatic self even managed a small smile. Frank had the most immobile face of anybody Billy had met: the funniest joke might perhaps make him raise an eyebrow or almost imperceptibly lift a tiny corner of his mouth. But Billy knew him well enough to know he liked the idea: he even expressed approval of Billy's new role as producer.

'It'll do you good to extend yourself. You won't be able to tumble all your life, you know, Billy.'

Billy feigned polite interest in this advice of Frank's, but secretly did not believe it would apply to him. He felt that Frank Hurley could not possibly know his body like its owner, nor its plans to never give in. His body planned to strive for ever, or at least until death stamped its foot. But even death seemed implausible to Billy, something that might happen to other people but certainly not to him.

He noticed Frank looking at him and rearranged his limbs, bringing his attention back to the issue. Frank took his pencil from behind his ear and leant over his well-used notepad: Billy could not see where he would have any space to write and tried to read what was already written.

'Now, let's see, who's around . . .' Frank chewed on his pencil, then absent-mindedly turned it upside down and sucked the lead tip, his flat eyes wandering to the ceiling.

'Connie and Vernon are back from Cairo next week,' Billy offered. 'We definitely should have them. Oh, and I ran into Danny Payne yesterday. He's just been demobbed.'

'Biggest waste of talent I've ever seen, to drop that lad over Italy by parachute.'

Billy smiled just to think of Danny Payne. 'I'm sure he'll get a joke or two out of it.'

Frank nodded. 'Those dancing twins were in this morning. Flopsie and Mopsie, or whatever they're called. You know, Reg was sweet on one of them.'

'The Delaney Sisters,' Billy said. 'One of them has a mole.'

Frank wrote their names down. 'I took a booking for a hypnotist yesterday . . . or was it a mind-reader. Anyhow, I'll give him a call.'

Before long they had a respectable list of names, a list they would inevitably have to prune. Billy knew this and yet could not help imagining the whole list up on a stage, a great mass of people, jostling and shouting out greetings. He saw a flowing linked line of hands, an endless row of heads collectively bowing. He saw Dave Wagner of Youth and Beauty, who had been fighting in Greece, he saw Connie with her hair piled high, smoking a cigarette, and Vernon chatting up some girl, smiling and angling for her phone number. He saw Larry La Fosse and Danny Payne, Dorinda Dean, the glamour girl impersonator, and Baby Norman, the Ace Ventriloquist. He saw Cannon and Tsang in the middle of it all, voiceless tumblers who had none the less managed to speak. He saw all this, his brightest mission, the job for which he was made. Even Bubbles would see now that tumbling had its use, that tumbling was of the world too.

It took all Billy's will to remain seated in his chair, to stop his muscles from jumping up and starting. He had so much to do, people to call, a whole show to imagine from the muscles up. He sat and listened to Frank for as long as he could, before leaping up and heading for the door.

'I've got to go,' he said, patting Frank's shoulders as he passed. 'I'll give you a ring in the morning.'

'What about the story-line?' Frank called as he opened the door.

'I'm working on it,' Billy replied. As he ran down the stairs he smiled to himself: work to him started as an inexplicable feeling of energy within his muscles, a powerful feeling of movement. Yet it's enough, he thought as he emerged on to the street, it's invisible and yet it's enough.

His limbs carried him fast down Charing Cross Road, past shops, past men and women learning peacetime. He felt himself part of the world's reconstruction, a tiny part, but a walk-on part all the same. An old man unexpectedly smiled at him. Billy knew he must have seen the flag, that small defiant flag now freely waving.

Desperate Eddie

'It sounds like a lot of work,' Bubbles said in a dubious voice. 'Just don't expect me to pick up the pieces when it gets too much.'

'I won't,' Billy replied confidently, still in that happy state of innocence when an idea has yet to be acted upon. Privately Billy imagined that his idea should not be too difficult to carry out, for it seemed to gleam seamless and perfect within him, an unwritten poem which only needed pen and paper. He was about to discover the difference between an idea and its execution, but right now he felt only the secret smugness of beginners.

He sat musing pleasantly on this, fired by his own thoughts. 'I've got a feeling this show's going to be important,' he said aloud without really meaning to, 'I can just feel it.'

'Important for who?' Bubbles said, pushing past him with Michael on her hip. These days everything Billy said sounded wrong, and Bubbles seemed constantly irritated with him, for no reason that he could see. Of course he knew that she was unhappy about not finding work: she had applied for a few jobs but failed to get them, and had had no luck so far with acting roles. The war had broken up her amateur theatre group too, and she had not found anything to replace it. Still, Billy did not see why this should make her cross with him.

'Don't worry, we'll find something for you yet,' he had said to her not long ago, but she had turned on him as if he had insulted her.

'I don't need your help, thank you very much.'

Billy often found himself wondering what he could and could not say: all manner of undeclared rules seemed to have written themselves, and Billy never knew when he was about to break one. He felt himself almost always rendered witless around Bubbles these days, all his words seemed murdered before they left his mouth. Yet despite everything, she was still the one person in the world whose love and respect Billy craved, whose acknowledgement he longed for most of all. Bubbles was the only person who questioned the one shining passion of his life, and who believed he should give it up if it brought in too little money. Even now she did not seem to know that giving up tumbling would be the equivalent of Billy's being deprived of his means of speech, his method of negotiating life.

She was dressing Michael before dropping him off at a neighbour's house, and then catching the bus into town for another interview. Billy fervently hoped Bubbles would get this job, for he sensed that it was somehow critical.

'What time's the interview?' he asked, watching her from his chair.

'Two o'clock,' she replied without looking up. She was seeing someone about a job with the BBC's Light Programme, an actor friend knew someone who knew someone who was looking for a new voice.

'What kind of work do you think it'll be?'

'Don't know,' she replied. 'Knowing my luck, it'll probably be reading the weather.'

Billy suddenly felt he should boost her confidence any way he could. 'You'll make it to Hollywood yet!' he burst out before he could stop himself, only understanding after he had spoken that he had broken another undeclared rule. Billy knew at once he was not supposed to speak out loud of Bubbles's unrealized ambitions, he was not supposed to advertise her unhappiness to the air.

She glared at him, a blistering look, so that he immediately dropped his eyes. 'Pity there's no work for acrobats in radio,' she said after a moment, and he looked up at her again; her private smile was pulling the ends of her lips. It was a line she had used once before when Billy was listening to *Music Hall* and someone he knew came on: such stricken excitement had passed across his face that Bubbles said it made her sick and she got up and left the room.

'Laugh, Billy,' she went on now, exasperated. 'They don't call you Desperate Eddie for nothing.'

Desperate Eddie! Who called him that? He was dying to ask, but pride would not let him. He turned instead to Michael, who had been patiently sitting all this time while Bubbles put on his shoes and socks and tied his laces. Now she was bundling his soft ears beneath a woollen cap and the sight of his son's small patient face suddenly wrenched Billy's heart; he stood and scooped Michael up, holding him tight in his arms.

'I haven't finished!' Bubbles protested. 'For God's sake, he's not a doll!'

'Of course you're not a doll, are you, Tom?' Billy asked as Bubbles grabbed him back. Michael shook his head vigorously as he was returned to the stool, his long unearthly fingers still holding Billy's hand.

'Honestly,' Bubbles said in a cross voice, 'I wish you would call him by his proper name. He has got one.'

Becoming the parents of Michael had somehow driven Billy and Bubbles to the extremes of themselves, so that Billy had come to represent only irresponsible, reckless self-abandon, and Bubbles only repression and denial. Billy did not quite understand how this had happened, yet he suddenly seemed all for truancy and broken routine, for spendthrift days and a small boy doing anything he wanted. Bubbles thought he spoilt Michael; Billy thought she did not spoil him enough.

'There,' Bubbles said, placing Michael on his feet. 'Now, where are your mittens?'

Michael ran to his toybox in the corner of the room, wildly throwing things to the floor.

'Michael!' Bubbles scolded, racing toward him, but he had already emerged triumphant. He held the mittens high in the air, a look of pride on his face. Billy noted his thrill at mastering the world but also how important it was to be seen having done so. He clapped the boy, an enthusiastic clap; Bubbles could not resist a smile too.

'Right, let's go,' she said, heading for the door. The two males held hands and followed.

Billy was early for his meeting with Connie and was idly strolling back and forth in front of the café where he was supposed to meet her when he thought he saw her ahead of him in the street. He wasn't sure if it was her at first, for he hadn't seen her for a few years and the woman approaching him was joined to an unknown man, entwined as closely as possible to him while still making it feasible for her to walk. This was so unlike Connie that Billy assumed it couldn't be her, but as the woman drew closer he realized that it was: her bright hair was unmistakable, her long limbs marked her out from every other woman in the street. Billy stood still and watched her approach: although she was still some distance away, he was immediately struck by some change in her, by some flush of light about the surface of her face. As she came closer, it was clear: Miss Connie Connor was displaying all the symptoms of being in love, Miss Connie Connor appeared at last to have fallen. As if to confirm it, she did not see Billy standing by the door, and would have walked right past if he had not called out her name.

'Billy!' she cried out, rushing up to him. 'Billy, my favourite boy!' She hugged him fiercely, so long he grew embarrassed: he had never known Connie to be so demonstrative. He looked bashfully over her shoulder at the man she had come with, who stood smiling indulgently upon this little scene.

'Why, you're as bald as a coot!' she exclaimed, standing back to look at him. 'The tide's going out quicker than it's coming in!'

He was mortified: lately he had imagined his hair was looking thicker. He felt himself blushing furiously as any boy, but quickly reminded himself that he was a grown man, a father. Right at this moment, though, Connie so vividly brought back his boyhood self that he had to fight against his past and present merging.

'Sweetheart, this is Billy, the boy I nursed from a fledgling. Billy, Captain Ambrose Weinberg of the US Army.'

Captain Weinberg had a kind, lively face and dark eyes which carried a strange pleading. He was not wearing a uniform and was a large man, broad of chest: he held out a strong hand to Billy.

'Glad to meet you,' he said, his other hand coming up to clasp Billy's upper arm. 'Billy, the wonder kid, in person.'

Billy was flattered beyond measure that Connie had even mentioned him, that he featured in any account of her life. He tried to keep this pleasure off his face but was saved by a woman trying to get past them, who said, 'Excuse me' in a huffy voice.

'Certainly, ma'am,' said Ambrose Weinberg, standing graciously back to let the woman pass. 'Honey?' he queried of

Connie, holding the door open with an extravagant wave of his arm.

Connie passed through the door like a princess, the recently proclaimed sovereign of Captain Ambrose Weinberg's New Jersey heart. Billy grinned and followed Connie: the whole café was straining their necks to identify who had come in. Connie sailed past tables, her head high: Billy and Ambrose Weinberg followed in her wake.

Only when they were seated and the waitress had taken their order did Billy get a chance to look steadily into Connie's face. Her eyes looked bright and oddly moist, her skin was flushed, slightly shiny. She did not look a day older than when he had last seen her during the Blitz; if anything she looked more charged, more alive. She kept passing her hands across Ambrose Weinberg's person, over his hands, his arms, his face. She so obviously adored him that Billy was moved: the island of Connie, finally occupied. But he immediately thought of Vernon, for Connie led to Vernon as war led to bloodshed, and he could not imagine one without the other.

'When's Vernon back?' he asked before anything else, before the rush of filling in their lives began.

'I told you, he decided to stay for the next ship.' She seemed hardly interested in the man who usually made her blood jump, who was the red rag to her bull. Instead she traced with her fingernail a plump vein on the back of Ambrose Weinberg's hand, following its course like a diviner.

'So, what's been happening, Connie? What've you been doing?'

She smiled at him. 'Breathing,' she said, leaning over to ruffle Billy's hair. 'Look at you, a middle-aged man! I hate to think how old that makes me!'

Middle-aged! He could have throttled her; he restrained himself as best he could and tried to redirect the conversation.

'Were you working other places as well? Did you get to Alexandria?'

But there was no stopping her. 'Just how old are you exactly? I've lost count.'

He gritted his teeth. 'I'll be twenty-nine in September.'

'Twenty-nine!' she exclaimed loudly. 'Not little Billy!'

He had forgotten how infuriating Connie could be, how her

mind wandered wherever it fancied. He wondered how it was he always came to forget irritating things about people, idealizing them in his heart until he met them again, then remembering at once everything about them which drove him crazy. He looked away from Connie in annoyance only to have his eyes land on Ambrose Weinberg staring at her in wonder, a look of utter enchantment on his broad face. Billy bad-temperedly turned from them in disgust, his eyes sweeping quickly round the room. He suddenly understood how everybody must have felt when he was first in love with Bubbles, how he must have made everyone around him absolutely sick.

His attention was brought back by Ambrose excusing himself from the table. 'Pardon me, ma'am, where's the bathroom?' he asked a passing waitress in a loud voice.

'The Gents is down the hall on your left,' she replied, proud to talk properly the King's English.

'Excuse me,' Ambrose said again as he left the table.

'Polite, isn't he?' Billy said when he had gone.

'All Americans are,' Connie said with satisfaction. 'It makes a nice change too. Ambrose is one of nature's gentlemen, Billy. And he loves me, he really does.'

She looked so pleased he did not need to ask if she loved him back: it was written in every line of her face.

'Where did you meet him?' Billy asked as if it mattered.

'On a ship in a storm,' she replied. She looked down at her hands. 'We're getting married next month,' she said as if in apology, 'and as soon as we can we're moving to New York.'

Billy couldn't have been more shocked: at once he thought of Vernon without Connie. It was unthinkable, absurd: the Wallabies gone, Connie without Vernon, Vernon without Connie.

'But what about Vernon?' he cried, too loud. 'What about the Wallabies?'

For the first time she focused her attention upon him, purposefully putting her cigarette down in the ashtray. 'I want someone who'll love me, Billy,' she said, looking directly into his eyes, 'who'll care if I'm happy or sad. And Rose is so much like me – he wants adventure and risk too. To tell the truth I never expected to meet anyone who wanted the same things. I was happy enough until I met him.'

The paragon himself came up to the table, this adventurer who had against all odds won Connie Connor's risk-taking heart. Billy looked with new eyes at Captain Ambrose Weinberg, who had seemed to Billy not unlike an ordinary man.

'And what do you do when there's not a war on, Rose?' Billy asked a little too aggressively, finding himself regarding Captain Weinberg as a usurper.

Ambrose smiled indulgently at Connie. 'I'm a piano player,' he said, squeezing Connie's fingers. Billy's eyes were inexorably drawn to Rose Weinberg's fingers, which were the unlikeliest piano-playing fingers Billy had ever seen. Blunt and functional, they stroked Connie's hand, growing tender and more lyrical under Billy's eyes.

'Well bugger the sunset,' Billy said. They both looked at him in surprise. All three of them looked at each other and began to laugh. 'Bugger the sunset!' Captain Rose Weinberg repeated, as if it was the funniest thing he had ever heard.

The Hope Show

The Hope Show grew in Billy's limbs at night, growing in his heart and muscles in the light of day. He did not think the show so much as dream it, and slowly it began to assume the shape of a life, an ordinary man's life whose hopes saved him. Billy found the man taking on a name, George Grey, a girlfriend and a job: he seemed to be a timid man easily passed over. Yet George Grey's hopes were his lure: he lived out the war not by clinging foolishly to them but by allowing them to become the means by which he navigated his way forward. Billy suddenly knew the audience must be allowed to see these hopes, that the stage should be divided like George Grey's own life into the life he lived on the outside and the life within. He saw immediately that he would need two men to play George Grey, both as he was and as the hero of his imagination.

Billy sat up in bed, his body alight, and bunched up a pillow behind his back. He flexed his fingers and cracked his knuckles, a deeply satisfying sound. If he had been able he would surely have whistled too, but it was the middle of the night and Bubbles was asleep. He knew he would never sleep now, for his excitation would not give sleep a chance to dock. It occurred to him to check what time it was, so he leant carefully over Bubbles to read the clock. But he couldn't see it and reached out his hand, intending to grab the clock and bring it closer to his eyes. His fingers missed, and the clock clattered to the floor. When it hit the ground, the bell went off, an insistent, terrible ring, so violent Billy jumped clear out of bed.

'What is it?' Bubbles called, waking up. 'What is it? What's wrong?'

Billy was stumbling around in the dark trying to turn the bloody thing off, his stupid fingers flailing frantically to find the right knob. At last he found it, the same instant Bubbles turned on the bedside lamp, revealing him like a criminal, dishevelled and exposed.

She sat up in bed, pushing back her hair, alarm still fresh on her face. 'Oh, for God's sake,' she said as soon as she saw him. 'I might have known.'

He looked down at the clock: it was 3.20, or at least it had been until the clock was broken.

'I was trying to see what the time was,' he said. 'Sorry.'

The door opened, and Michael came in, crying fearfully. Bubbles gave Billy one of her famous looks, before flinging back the bedcovers and picking up Michael.

'It's all right,' she crooned into his hair, 'it's all right, it's just silly Daddy.'

She turned and looked furiously at Billy, holding Michael as if he needed protection. 'If you're going to go on like this for the whole of your bloody show you can bloody well sleep downstairs! All I ever hear about is your damn stupid show and I'm sick of it, I've had it up to here!'

Michael howled. She stormed from the room, leaving Bill alone in sudden silence. All at once his life seemed beyond him, too complicated for his frail skills to unravel. He sat down dumbly on the edge of the bed, a once hopeful man whose own hopes were momentarily beyond him.

The Hope Show did not have a script exactly, it was more a loose collection of ideas. Word had got around, and meetings at the Boiling Kettle got larger and larger as seemingly everyone Billy and Reg knew in the business came forward for their say. They all liked at once Billy's idea of a divided stage, and it seemed the main thing now was to fill in George Grey's story. But as Billy listened over several meetings, George's life and history grew around him: singers and dancers offered their own anecdotes about the war, tumblers turned up with stories about what had happened to them. There were claims and counter-claims, arguments over whose experience had been the worst: in this way George Grey was drawn in, so that before long he represented a bit of all of them. He somehow became an Air Raid Warden, a bank clerk by day: nothing he did went right, his girlfriend Daisy was always going out with Americans and George couldn't even get into the army because he was too near-sighted. Then Billy and Reg found out that Rose Weinberg could write songs, and turn any emotion into words and reason: suddenly the bones of the show rose up, and everyone could see it breathing. *The Hope Show* began to declare itself: it had songs, tumbling, disaster, jokes, a life all of its own. George's modest hopes even began to give him a kind of dignity, a poignancy which had not been planned.

Everyone who heard about the show wanted to be in it. Frank Hurley even began to knock back calls, and three theatres rang unsolicited to ask if they could put it on. People in the business Billy had never met before called him at home or left messages at Frank's, asking Mr Cannon to ring them straight back. As people returned to London, *The Hope Show* became an unofficial meeting point, a way for everyone to get back in touch. And when Vernon arrived home from Cairo he immediately wanted to play the role of the hero of George Grey's imagination, until he heard that Rose Weinberg was writing all the songs.

'Forget it,' he said to Billy, but it was too late: straight away Billy had seen Vernon as imagination's hero, and realized he would be perfect for the part. Vernon Rome was still a handsome man, drawing eyes to himself effortlessly, still passing one hand across his face in movie star grace. Billy suddenly saw that a tumbler would be perfect to play ordinary George Grey as he secretly hoped to be: gallant, unabashed, always moving.

Billy saw too that Vernon Rome would be the perfect foil to the singer Alan Hely, who was playing George Grey as his actual self, for Alan had one of the most naturally poignant faces Billy had ever seen. Obscure losses seemed locked within it, he appeared cruelly defenceless against the burliness of life. When Alan sang one of Rose's songs, it automatically became infused with longing: it seemed to Billy that his tired face, his voice, carried all the private griefs of days, the toll of losses large and small. He unconsciously conveyed a longing for a world everyone once believed in, a light and careless place where bombs never fell and loved people never went away. And Vernon Rome was unquestionably the man to play the buoyant dweller of this careless place, being the very essence of unburdened existence. It was Vernon's insouciance, his blithe insensibility, which somehow allowed him to celebrate life: Vernon Rome was the very incarnation of unblemished survival and Billy knew that at all costs he must have him.

'Why don't you come out to Norbury for a meal?' he suggested, putting his arm round Vernon's shoulder. 'How about Saturday?'

'Will Connie be there?'

Billy hesitated: did Vernon want her to be or not? He took a calculated guess. 'Ah, no . . . she . . .'

'Good. I'll come then,' Vernon replied, nodding and striding off.

Billy did not know if it was pride or not, but Bubbles resisted every attempt to involve her in the show. 'What do you want me to be, a chorus girl?' She did not want a part, she did not wish to sing a song, nor did she want to act as Billy's unpaid secretary. He could not help but admire her stubbornness, her fierce will to make her own way. He was relieved too that she seemed to like her new job at the BBC: it was clear that Bubbles wanted her triumphs to be all her own, earned by her own hard efforts.

Billy was apprehensive while waiting for Vernon to arrive for supper, for he had grown uncomfortable about mentioning the show too much in Bubble's presence. Although he hardly thought about anything else he knew himself to be insufferable: he was trying hard to be less like his obsessive self and more like other people. Only the night before Bubbles had accused him of having no conversation, of not knowing how to converse like everyone else.

'Other people seem to talk,' she said. 'You'd think we'd be able to have some decent conversations too.'

So he had cast desperately about in his head: what *did* other people talk about? The aftermath of war? Economics? Billy knew he felt everything too deeply, caring too intensely for the inconsequential: a faultless sky, the dark and perfect outer circle around the iris of his son's eye. As soon as Bubbles had made this remark, Billy found himself feeling painfully one-dimensional, as if his world were a small and crippled place. He cared about only a few things, it was true: his wife and son, tumbling, his mother, his friends, a few streets in a far-away country. It was a small list, embarrassingly meagre, yet it was the entire circumference of Billy's known world.

This morning he had tried to start a conversation about the

Prime Minister's speech, but Bubbles had simply looked at him and smiled. He saw that this was not what she meant by conversation either, and his confidence collapsed in a heap.

He was still thinking about what Bubbles had said as he brushed his hair waiting for Vernon. When the doorbell rang, he called out, 'I'll get it!' and rushed down the stairs. Vernon stood smiling on the doorstep, his arm around the waist of a pretty girl.

'This is Terry. I thought you wouldn't mind,' he said, stepping back to usher Terry through the door.

'Pleased to meet you, Mr Cannon,' she said, and Billy knew at once she wanted a job.

'Terry's a singer,' Vernon said, patting her bum, 'and a very good little singer too.'

'Oh, Vernon, please,' she said, looking chuffed, smiling coquettishly at both of them.

'And where's that delicious creature? Where are you hiding her? Bubbles?'

Billy took Terry's coat and led her to the kitchen, where Vernon was already embracing Bubbles from behind. She was cutting up something and wore an apron; her wrists rested against a bench while she waited for Vernon to finish embracing her.

'Haven't lost your old silver tongue, I see,' she said testily, shaking him off. 'Still fighting them off by the dozen?'

Billy coughed. 'Bubbles, this is Terry,' he said and Bubbles turned around. 'Ah, yes,' she said, looking at Vernon in mock disapproval. 'Hello, Terry.'

Terry smiled hesitantly and Billy offered everyone a drink. 'I'll join you in a minute,' Bubbles said. 'Everybody out!'

When she came into the loungeroom, Billy was relieved to see she looked to be in good spirits. He realized he lived with one eye always watching her, treading carefully lest he step the wrong way. He looked at her, flushed and beautiful, and listened to what she was saying.

'It opens next month,' she was announcing to Vernon.

'What does?' Billy asked, sitting up.

Bubbles rolled her eyes at Vernon, a gesture of complicity. 'My new play,' she said, taking a sip of her drink.

'What new play?' he continued stupidly.

'Oh, didn't I tell you? I got a lead role in a play of Johnny's. A drama called *After-effects*.'

She looked at him coolly: Billy felt very odd, outside himself, as if he were talking to someone he did not know. And then he felt the unremitting press of anger: the greedy hoarding of her life, the withheld secrets she did not allow him to know! How could she possibly wish to tell such triumphant news to others and not to him, to reveal more to strangers than she revealed to her own husband?

He stood up, as if to strike her: he thought he had crushed the glass in his hand. He felt his heart on the verge of catastrophe, the dreadful impulse to smash his whole life. He turned his head, placing his glass on the mantelpiece, and saw the tremble of his hand. He opened his mouth to let the air rush to him, to stop himself walking for ever out the door.

After a moment he began to be aware of a silence: only deeply ingrained social convention made him breathe once and turn around. The first thing he saw was an unmistakable look of satisfaction on Bubble's face: he dropped his hand from the mantelpiece and walked from the room as quickly as he could without making a scene, as fast as he was able without running.

Pride got him through the rest of the night, a wilful refusal to allow Bubbles to see how much she had hurt him. Only with great effort did Billy turn his attention to Vernon, who proved less difficult to woo than he had expected, for he had underestimated the scope of Vernon's vanity. After Bubbles said she was going to bed and would leave them to it, Billy tried to explain to Vernon what the character of George Grey's alter ego represented, how it demanded someone of style and ease. As he spoke, Vernon sat straighter in his chair and began to smooth the hair at the back of his head with the palm of his hand, visibly preening. He was admiring himself without a mirror, remembering himself without aid. Billy saw the way he glanced at Terry for her reaction, the way he noted the new look of admiration for him she carried on her pretty, unformed face. Billy knew as soon as he saw this that Vernon would agree to take the part: he felt intense dislike for Vernon's strutting conceit, for his overweening certainty of his own attractions. For a moment Billy wished to shove Vernon

Rome's handsome face, to tell him it was this very vanity which had lost him Connie. But he didn't, he only waited for Vernon to tell him he would do it.

He sensed Bubble's presence overhead, her pride and will which were stronger than his own. He saw her small, tenacious face, her fighting eyes, beautiful and unswerving. Billy could not forgive her, but part of him recognized her desire not to tell, to knock him off his feet by her own dazzling efforts. Yet he could gladly wring her dazzling neck, and only wished Vernon would go.

When Vernon at last agreed to take the part, Billy sprung up and unceremoniously led him and Terry to the door. 'Goodbye,' he said, shutting the door in their faces, turning to run up the stairs. 'Bubbles?' he called, a battle-cry in Norbury, a warning to take up defences. He ran full speed ahead, all his blood beating, up the stairs, toward his enemy. He felt anger and exhilaration and opened his eyes wide: he would like to kill her but wanted more to win, to make her realize the enormity of her mistake. He hated her and yet longed agonizingly for her to love him, to see him as a good and worthwhile man.

He reached for his arms and opened the door, ready at the first call to shoot.

Dreaming of Revenge

Billy left Norbury by eight each morning and did not return till late. He and Reg had been forced to abandon any work other than *The Hope Show*, for it increasingly took all their time. This meant of course that Billy had no regular money coming in, and he was forced to borrow from Frank, or sometimes Vernon. He tried to hide this fact from Bubbles, and believed that as long as she didn't ask him outright, he wasn't telling lies. Still, he tried to have cash in his pockets at all times, to throw her off the trail. He rushed about, to various theatres to talk to managers and inspect the stage, to meetings at the Boiling Kettle, to Frank's office to sign yet another form. Billy felt as if he were perpetually running for a bus, a bus within sight forever on the verge of pulling away. It seemed to him he had too much to do, and that he would never get everything finished in time, but he never complained to Bubbles, not once, preferring to remove his tongue than admit she had been right. At night in bed he could hardly bear to close his eyes, to shut his muscle system down: his mind raced ceaselessly ahead with all the things still left to do, it peered endlessly into the crevice between his hopes for the show and the flawed creature it had become. He wanted it perfect but could not realize perfection, yet always when he closed his eyes, the possibility of perfection came to taunt him.

Billy slept on a divan in the loungeroom now, remembering at the last moment to take off his shoes. It did not strike him as unusual to be sleeping there but as a kind of natural progression, a wound in exchange for a wound. He told himself that Bubbles would find out soon enough the dimensions of a double bed, the chilly moment of slipping between unoccupied sheets. Sometimes he was ashamed to find himself thinking up ways to hurt her as she had hurt him. He once imagined not turning up to her opening night: how shocked she would be! But Billy shocked even himself in thinking this, and he blushed alone in the dark. Events had somehow overtaken them, pushing them toward places they had not intended to go yet, at the same time it felt both compelling and inevitable, as if Billy could do nothing in his power to move away from the current in which he was drowning.

Still, sleeping on the couch secretly seemed to Billy a joke; he could not quite get over the feeling that both of them were posturing and might drop their masks at any time. For even though Bubbles had wounded him to the very core, Billy did not believe she had damaged their love in any irrevocable way. He had almost got off the couch and climbed the stairs a dozen times in that first week, but pride always stilled his hand, preventing him from throwing off the covers. He was determined not to be the one to make the first move this time, as he had always done in the past. Bubbles must come to him now, which he felt sure she would do at any time.

So Billy slept on the couch, alternately dreaming of revenge and of a different Bubbles he knew existed, her true self, vulnerable and yielding. If he could reach this Bubbles, what a life they might have: Bubbles with another baby, perhaps a girl this time; the whole family saving up for a trip to Australia. Billy imagined surprising his mother, turning up on her doorstep unannounced.

As he lay there in the dark Billy began to wonder how it had happened that he had stumbled into a life thousands and thousands of miles away from his own country. Only in the middle of the night did Billy ever think about this, when anxiety about *The Hope Show* kept him awake, and every single thing in his life suddenly seemed to come forward for perusal. How had he ended up so far away? Only economics, politics or disaster were supposed to force people into exile: no one ever willingly chose it, or at least not ordinary men like himself. Billy had been fifteen years old when he had boarded a ship: next year he would he would be thirty. In the dark he saw Lily Tsang's face, and wondered what his life might have been. He remembered how slender Lily's bones felt, and how gracefully she had once swallowed clouds.

Five different theatres were vying to put *The Hope Show* on; Billy found himself incapable of making a decision. Just when he had decided on one he would begin to reconsider the merits of another: he supposed it was how Vernon felt when confronted by so many women. One theatre had a larger green, another had better seating, the Palladium had all those beautiful bars. Finally, in desperation, Billy figuratively pulled a name from a hat: it was the London Palladium. He did not tell anyone he had chosen this way, for he was not proud of his decision-making abilities. He seemed not to be able to think things through like other people, it was only the cumulative pressure of indecision which forced him to decide anything at all. And usually by then he might just as well have blindfolded himself and pinned the tail on the donkey, so little rational thought was involved.

And there was war on the site as well, between Vernon and Connie, between Vernon and Rose, between the musical director and the stage manager. Of course no one was getting paid to rehearse, and as everyone was used to doing their act singly and then coming off, several acts on stage at once produced pandemonium. Soon some acts began complaining that *The Hope Show* was cutting into too much of their time.

'Aw, Ben, no!' a magician complained. 'Not Saturday morning too!'

'I'm afraid so,' Billy replied. 'All of you, on the green by nine, please.'

Everyone had to fit rehearsals around their other dates, which was difficult if people had dates outside London. So the show was frequently rehearsed with bits missing, an irritating and sometimes unwieldy adventure. It continued to be a joint creation, with everyone coming up with ideas, quickly growing into a kind of pantomime for adults, lacking only the comfort of a happy ending. Yet Billy intended it to bring comfort of a different sort, being a kind of lifting of the skin from an ordinary life to reveal the recognizable workings within. He wanted everyone to leave the theatre feeling as if their own hopes had been celebrated, as if small unseen moments of defeat and courage had finally been honoured. George Grey's life was supposed to continue in much the same way as when the curtain first opened upon it, but the audience was supposed to feel that this was all right, even noble.

Most of the cast seemed to grasp this intuitively, with notable exceptions, such as Vernon. He played George Grey's life of hope superbly, tapping his way down a shiny staircase surrounded by beautiful women, tumbling his way out of danger gracefully, but

he was always coming up with terrible suggestions and inter-
fering when he was not wanted.

'I really think George's turning into too much of a sop,' he said
one afternoon, watching Alan singing one of Rose's songs. 'He
sounds like Snow fucking White.'

Billy glared at him, but Vernon leant his head closer, whispering
fiercely.

'He's got to have more guts! Only a woman could get away
with singing a song like that. Or Ambrose Weinberg.'

Vernon looked with distaste at Rose, who was playing the piano
in the pit. Billy looked too and saw Rose's large sensitive face, his
eyes closed as he listened to Alan's singing.

'He'll be laughed off the stage!' Vernon continued. 'Look, I've
been in this business longer than you and I can tell a dud song
when I hear one.'

Billy wanted to clout Vernon over the earhole but could not
afford to lose him: Vernon clearly thought he had an ace up his
sleeve because he was older than Billy. This always got on Billy's
nerves, for he believed it was not one's time on earth which
counted but how one used it. And besides, he felt the song to be
one of Rose's finest: Vernon didn't like it simply because it was
one of Rose's.

Billy was about to excuse himself, lest he say something unfor-
givable, when Vernon himself got up in disgust.

'You're too much for me, mate,' he said pointedly in a loud,
surprisingly Australian accent, aimed at the orchestra pit. Billy
always knew Vernon was upset when the homing vowels of Australia rushed to his tongue.

Billy smiled, and settled back, pleased that he could now listen
uninterrupted. *The Hope Show* was no longer that perfect seamless
thing but it was alive, and creaking.

Because he was so busy, Billy feared he would forget Bubbles's
opening night, a week before *The Hope Show*. And because he had
thought about deliberately missing it, he began to fear his worst
self might sabotage him and let him forget. To guard against this,
he wrote the date and time down on as many pieces of paper as
was possible and the morning of the show tied a blue thread
around his index finger. As an added precaution, the first thing

he did on entering the Palladium was to separately ask Reg, Connie and Frank to remind him.

'It's six o'clock,' Frank said at six.

'It's 6.30,' Connie said at twenty to seven.

'You'd better go,' Reg said at quarter to, handing him his coat.

'I'm gone,' he said, running out the door, whistling one of Rose's tunes.

Billy emerged blinking into the street, and raised his hand to flag down a cab. He could not afford to take a taxi and sank guiltily into the back seat, fully stretching out his legs. He tried to tell himself that it was not a long journey and besides he was running late, but the simple truth was that he loved London cabs and took one whenever he could. He had a secret weakness for them, for their cavernous hearts, for the slide of the window between the driver and the back seat. He had never got used to them, no matter how many he had taken, and always felt a burst of guilty joy on stepping in.

When Billy got to the theatre he paid the driver furtively, not waiting for his change, being suddenly struck by the idea that Bubbles might see him. She would chide him for extravagance, or suddenly remember to ask him about his finances. He dashed across the road, but of course she was nowhere to be seen, of course she would be sitting nervous in some dressing-room. He had arranged to meet her at the main bar after the show so did not bother to look around, but bounded up the stairs before he realized he could stop running.

People turned to look disapprovingly at him: he coughed, and looked down at his shoes. He was still wearing his tumbler's pumps, the oldest, most scuffed pair he always wore at rehearsals: no one had reminded him, they had all let him walk out the door looking like a fool. But Billy had to admit that he hadn't even noticed them himself: if he'd seen them earlier he might have asked the cab to turn around.

There was nothing for it now, so Billy handed his ticket to a tall young fellow and allowed himself to be ushered to his seat. He saw some of Bubbles's new friends further down the row: the friendliest of them waved to him and he nodded. He still could not quite get over the feeling that Bubbles's actor friends were condescending toward him, but Bubbles said this revealed more about what he thought of himself than what anyone thought about him: he pondered on this now while he waited for the lights to dim.

When the curtains opened, Billy watched the first actors come on: when Bubbles wasn't among them, he lost interest. It was a story about two effortlessly rich couples who flung devastatingly witty lines at each other and seemed to share a dark secret. Bubbles played the wife in the second couple, talked about but not yet seen. Billy tried to concentrate but knew himself to be straining forward, only waiting for Bubbles to come on. For one brief evil moment he felt malice surge in his heart: he hoped she would be terrible, it would serve her right for all the times she had failed him. Immediately his face flushed with remorse and he quickly looked around, as if someone might have read his thoughts and felt repugnance.

Then, at last, toward the end of the first act, Bubbles walked casually on to the stage: he did not think he was the only one to sit straighter. She was playing a woman everyone was in love with and Billy saw at once she personified this woman's nonchalant grace. She had a sense of power, heedless and compelling, and it seemed to him that all eyes were drawn toward her. But as he watched Billy became aware of a hard unforgiving feeling within himself: he saw Bubbles's face and did not feel happiness or pride, he felt only as if he were waiting for it to be over. When the clapping started at the end of the act, it was mainly shame which made him clap harder.

Perfect Happiness

On the twenty-fourth of September 1945 *The Hope Show*, produced by Ben Cannon and starring Alan Hely, Vernon Rome and June St Leon, opened at the London Palladium. It was an unseasonably chilly night and women wore their fur wraps, men in hats wore checked scarves at their throats. But before these men and women arrived, a balding man, youngish still, took a moment to leave the theatre and walk out on to the street. The cold air hit his ears and he turned his collar up: he looked left and right before running fast across the road. When he got to the other side he looked up, at the push of the Palladium against the early evening sky, at the faces and creatures locked within its stone. The sky above the building had that particular twilight blue, so that the white paint covering the stone seemed sharp and brilliant. He lowered his eyes to read the great sign hanging from the building's neck, his own name written in red paint. He heard every sound around him, every horn, every engine; individual voices came to him, clear and direct. The air smelt of car fumes, winter, food, the particular and unmistakable smell of a London city street. He felt an odd calm within himself, an inner quietness which allowed him to be fully cognizant of the exterior world, to let every sound, every sight come to him pure. All his work seemed to have led him to this one point, all his life seemed to have delivered him to this moment. And then Connie saw him and called out his name; he looked at her, surprised, and every nerve was suddenly awoken.

Billy had only a small role on stage himself, a comedy tumble with Vernon and Connie. Wearing hats, he and Vernon fell over Connie, bank clerks given licence to be foolish. George Grey was on the other side of the stage having a serious exchange with his boss, but he and Vernon were playing out George's escape. He knew it was a funny scene and it seemed to him the audience laughed hysterically. This spurred him on to do a couple of extra flips which were not scripted. It was pure joy that made him do it, an overabundance of happiness rushing in his blood. 'What are you doing!' Vernon hissed at him in passing, for his extra flips had caused Vernon to miss a move. 'Sorry!' he cried, knowing Vernon was a professional and could cover a mistake before the audience's very eyes. Billy was having a great time, bouncing about; his body was sweating, deliriously satisfied. He knew now that the show was going to be a success, he knew without doubt it would be a triumph. Yet right at this moment he cared for nothing but the movement of air: he smiled as he rolled, he smiled all over his face, he smiled as he ran from the stage. As he left he could not resist picking out Michael and giving him the broadest of waves. But it didn't matter, for the audience was cheering, the audience roared, *The Hope Show* was bringing the house down. Billy had hardly hit the wings when Connie and Vernon fell upon him and the three of them jumped screaming in the air.

'We did it!' Billy yelled, loud as the crowd. 'We did it! We did it!'

They jumped and screamed until Vernon realized he was hugging Connie, and dropped his arms, horrified as if she were burning. But nothing could still Billy's joy: he could not imagine feeling anything but perfect happiness ever again.

It was only when everyone was crowded together on the stage that Billy realized his vision had come true. He felt the hot press of live skin all around him, the pulse of human energy surge from hand to hand. Connie was holding his wrist tightly; Reg had one arm round his neck. People were behind him, beside him, crouched in front of him; the whole stage was a moving mass of his friends. The lights were in his eyes, but he could make out people standing before him, standing clapping and not sitting in their seats. He could make out Bubbles, his son standing on the seat waving, Frank Hurley giving him the thumbs up sign. It was so like his vision that he felt as if he had already lived it, as if he had long known these living breaths upon his neck. Then he saw his son walking near the footlights and could not understand how he came to be there, how Michael came to be walking on the stage and no longer standing cheering in his seat. Billy did not understand what was required of him until Connie pushed him toward his son and he saw that Michael held up to him a great sheaf of flowers, their leaves oddly rattling. He bent down on his knees and took the flowers from his son, scooping him up on his shoulders at the same time. He held Michael aloft, the flowers clutched in one fist, and knew what it was to want for nothing.

The reviews of *The Hope Show* were remarkable; there was not a bad one amongst them. Even *The Times* carried one, which declared it to be 'a long entertainment of prodigal copiousness'. Billy secretly loved this review best of all, even though all the others laughed at it. Vernon openly declared he could not make head nor tail of it and wanted to write a letter to the editor asking what was wrong with plain English.

The anonymous reviewer wrote: '*The Hope Show* enabled Mr Alan Hely to sing, without the smallest twinge of self-consciousness, highly moral songs on the theme of hope with a conviction that roused the enthusiasm of a congregation that had no doubts on which side the angels were.' It went on to praise Vernon, 'as elegant a hero who ever wore a dinner-jacket', and 'many other clever people doing other clever things within the tradition'.

Billy carefully cut out this review, dated it and placed it in his scrapbook with the rest. He bought three extra copies of *The Times* so he could send originals to his mother and to Digger Dog, who had long settled back in Sydney. The spare copy he kept in his wallet, taking it out to look at now and then.

Every night both houses were full, and on weekends every matinée. Bookers from various circuits came to check out the new stars: Alan Hely could have as much work in the future as he wanted. He was approached by someone running a radio programme, by a record company; Billy was constantly fending off rival offers from other theatres trying to steal him.

He quite liked his new role of producer, although it did not hold a candle to tumbling. If he had once thought that when the show was up and running most of his work would be over, it did not turn out that way: someone was always sick, or having a spat with someone else, a dancer would want her pay early so he would have to see about getting her some money. He was not sure if this was what a producer did exactly, but found himself doing small, un-producer-like jobs anyway. He had to attend innumerable meetings with Frank and the manager of the Palladium too, for the manager wanted to extend the run till Christmas. Billy had to decide whether to take *The Hope Show* on the road after that, for so many theatres outside London were eager to get it.

In this way weeks sped away, till one day Billy woke up and found Christmas was almost upon him. Bubbles's own run continued until mid-November; they hardly seemed to see each other except briefly in the mornings. Billy had noticed that for some time now Bubbles had inexplicably ceased to be irritable with him: all the fight seemed to have left her, and she had a new air which puzzled him, but which he could only take to be resigned acceptance. Only now did Billy realize how frequently Bubbles must have criticized him, for it was so noticeable when she stopped. She no longer complained about his poor conversation, or the way he spent money; she did not roll her eyes or blow air through her teeth. Instead, she treated Billy with a new kind of polite reserve, bordering on indifference: one morning over breakfast he found himself wondering whether Bubbles knew he was there at all.

'Rose and Connie have decided to stay for a while. They'll leave for New York next year,' he said three times before she heard him.

'Oh. Lucky things,' she said, hardly lifting her head from the paper.

He looked quizzically at her, but she refused to meet his eye: if Billy hadn't known better he might have wondered if she still cared for him. As it was, he could only put this change down to Bubbles's satisfaction with her work, which he guessed had somehow shifted her attention away from him. For Billy's part he was grateful, and had no wish to upset this new equilibrium by asking too many questions. He tried to tell himself that he had got over his own hurt too, and that perhaps this new politeness between them was for the better.

Billy moved back into the bedroom without either of them speaking of it; he simply slid back into some permanent space his body seemed to have created. Bubbles's shape had come to fit his own, made compatible by the sheer wash of days. Although he had to admit that Bubbles was not the easiest person in the world, he could not imagine lying next to anyone else. He was used to her face, her proud will; he was used to the lie of her bones.

Two Sundays after Christmas the whole cast left for Blackpool, where they had a long run booked which would take them well into March. It was the first time Billy had been to Blackpool since before the war and he was looking forward to going. Bubbles and Michael would join him at the end of the month; he'd already booked a dinner at the swank Metropole on the promenade. It would be the first time Bubbles had been back for years, but Billy thought he detected some tremor of hesitation in her as he said goodbye: in fact, he could have sworn that Bubbles Hayes was nervous.

'You'll be able to see Nettie,' he said to her by way of encouragement.

'I suppose so,' she replied. She looked at him quickly. 'Yes, it'll be nice,' she said. 'Her boy's about Michael's age.'

Billy looked questioningly at her then kissed her goodbye: Michael cried and wanted to come too.

'Oh, come now, chin up!' Bubbles said to comfort him.

Michael was three years old and Billy could see him weighing up this advice but, like his father, his heart inevitably won out over logic. He let out an even bigger howl, which had all the hallmarks of a tantrum. Billy raised his brows at Bubbles, picked up his bags and headed off down the path. As he turned she smiled at him, an odd tentative smile which seemed unlike her, before shooing Billy on his way.

At Crewe they stopped to take on passengers and Billy found he knew half the train. He settled back to enjoy the ride, and a feeling of well-being washed over him. His life was going well: he had come to a new understanding with Bubbles (even if he couldn't really figure out how); he had a son he loved, and who loved him back. He had money in his pocket, work lined up, and for the moment saw no reason why this should not continue. Billy did not believe the naysayers who were always prophesying that radio would kill variety, for they had said exactly the same thing about cinema. Suddenly Billy realized he sounded like Vernon: he comforted himself with the thought that unlike Vernon he knew that it was useless to rail against it. The thing to do was not waste your energy getting upset but plan how best to get around it. Billy was thinking this before he fell asleep, a weary man who planned to keep striving.

The show opened to full houses in Blackpool, even though it was off season. The audience included far more children, which had the effect of making each performance lustier, as children screamed and hooted with abandon in their seats. The cast began to improvise more, to add a little something here and there. Personally, Billy found the show growing funnier and funnier; it was like a prism which revealed different colours depending on which way it was held to the light.

Billy had spoken briefly once to Bubbles, to let her know he had arrived safely. She had sounded distracted and would not wake Michael, telling Billy he should have called an hour earlier if he wanted to talk to him. She was usually curt on the telephone, but because he was in Blackpool and reminded of their courtship, her distant manner struck him cruelly: he remembered how he had first learnt about her through her voice, how her true self had come to him over the wires, travelling faster than light toward his waiting ear. She had seemed to tell him everything then, her telling was endless, as if she were going to keep telling herself to him through the course of years. After Bubbles said goodbye, Billy kept holding the telephone, not quite believing more words would not run out. He finally placed the receiver back in its cradle, where it landed with the hollowest of sounds.

Late one afternoon when Billy went back to the boarding-house to have a quick wash before dashing out again to the theatre, the landlady came toward him with a letter.

'It's registered,' the landlady said and it seemed to him all his blood left his heart. He could only think that his mother had died, that here at last was the news he had all this time been expecting.

He took the letter from her and blindly ripped it open and could not see straight to read it for some time. He looked at the words again and again and even after he saw that each typewritten character formed a word he still was not sure what it said. He sat down in a chair, conscious of his legs failing, and stared again at the black words on the page. He looked at the word 'divorce', he looked at the word 'cruelty', he looked at the words 'my client'. But he had to concentrate hard as if it were a foreign language, for the marks were nothing he recognized or understood. He could not understand that this was a letter meant for him, that its words formed a particular intention. For some reason he recalled Bubbles saying that Nettie had a boy of Michael's age and yet he could not remember anything else. For some reason he could not picture exactly how Bubbles's face had looked the last time he saw her, the precise expression that it wore. Billy Hayes sat in the chair and tried to remember but only his body recalled for him the exact feeling of pain.

Crossing Seven Oceans

He did not tell anyone, not even Reg, but went through the motions of being alive and standing. He performed his short tumbling routine as required that night but had to force his body to obey him, calling up the very last burst of his energy. He could feel physical energy rushing away from him, shooting out from him like water from a burst source. He could not protect himself, or staunch the flow, but felt himself to be fading from loss of something vital. A kind of vigour left his body, a vigour which propelled him, so that as soon as he came off the stage all he longed for was bed. At the back of his mind Billy did not believe this was actually happening; some part of him expected Bubbles and Michael to jump out at any moment and surprise him.

'Aren't you coming?' Reg called as they left the stage door, for he had absent-mindedly turned in the other direction.

'Oh, yes,' he said, joining Reg, walking to a well-known theatrical bar in one of the guest-houses off the promenade.

Reg fell back from the group to walk with him. 'I'm only staying for one drink,' Reg said, and Billy did not answer. The wind felt too cold against his face: he almost held up his hands in self-protection. The icy air wormed its way down his neck, blowing its breath across the most tender part of his upper ear. He hunched further down in his own skin, afraid of the cold's power.

After a while he sensed Reg inspecting him, albeit in his casual, underhand way. But Billy could not have borne opening his mouth; he could not have stood bringing actual words to his tongue. He quickened his pace to catch up with the others: Rose Weinberg greeted him and slung an arm affectionately round his shoulders.

The first thing Billy did on waking up the next morning was check the bedside table to see if the letter was still there. But it was, and dread fell upon him: he rushed from the room to be sick.

Leaning over the toilet, bile sprang from his throat; it seemed to spring harsh and pungent from his eyes.

'Oh, dear,' he heard a voice say from the next cubicle. 'I hope we don't all get it.'

Billy stood shaking over the bowl, spitting into toilet paper. 'You'll be all right, Vernon,' he managed to say. 'I'll stay away so you'll be safe.'

He pulled the chain and opened the door to find Vernon laying out his shaving gear, admiring himself at the same time in the mirror.

'Feeling better?' he asked, unexpectedly kindly, stepping away from the basin to allow Billy to wash his face. The water felt cold but good: he kept splashing water up to himself again and again.

'I'll survive,' he said, knowing he wouldn't, knowing he could never bear this loss.

He walked from the bathroom, his face still dripping, and it seemed to him all his love was irretrievably falling away.

He knew of course he must ring Bubbles, to see what the letter could possibly mean. But an unbearable nervousness twisted in his gut as soon as he rose to do it. His palms ran and uninvited air blew about in his stomach: he rose and sat down again at least five times.

Finally, at five to eight on a Thursday morning, he picked up the telephone and dialled. He knew Bubbles would not have left yet for work: she always caught the bus at twenty-five past.

'Hello,' her voice said, the voice which belonged only to Bubbles.

'Bubbles?' he said by way of communication, finding his mouth had gone dry. 'It's me,' he said uselessly, as if she didn't know, as if she didn't know her own husband.

'Yes?' she said, waiting for him to say something, but he could not think of what he must say. There was a long silence while her whole self came to him, the smell of her, the particular shape of her eye. She was breathing, alive, on the other end of the wire, standing with her shoes on in the kitchen.

'Yes?' she said again, offering nothing, and his words rushed crying to his mouth.

'What does the letter mean?' he burst out. 'Bubbles, what does it mean?' He honestly, truly, did not know: he honestly expected her to tell him.

'It's clear, isn't it?' she said in a firm voice. 'I'm going to divorce you.'

'But you can't!' he cried. 'You can't! Listen, I'm coming home straight away, we have to talk about this!'

Her voice came to him angry and strong. 'Talk! You never listen to anything I say! You wouldn't know how to begin!'

'I do listen! I do! It's you who won't tell me anything!'

She snorted derisively. 'Oh, I gave up trying long ago. You're only interested in yourself and your stupid tumbling.'

He could not believe it: it was critical to make her see that their love was in peril. Surely she must see that everything was at risk, that their whole life was about to be smashed?

'Bubbles,' he said desperately, 'do you know what you're doing? I'm coming straight home, I'll pack right now and catch the next train.'

'I don't want you to catch the next train. I don't want you to come home. This is *exactly* what I mean, you never listen to me!'

The line went dead, she had slammed down the phone: Billy stood holding its deadness to his ear. Then he put the receiver down too and rushed upstairs to pack for he had a lot to do before he caught the train.

All the way to London he imagined what Bubbles would do when she opened the door, how this act of flight toward her would make her see. She would see at once that he loved her and was doing everything in his power to keep her: he would fly to Africa if he had to, cross seven oceans, he would never tire till he reached her door. He did not care about *The Hope Show*, tumbling, Australia: he cared only that Bubbles Hayes press him to her heart.

When he got to Euston he jumped straight into a cab: a cab all the way from Euston to Norbury. It would empty his pockets, but he did not care: anything to get him immediately to Avenue Road, SW 16.

At the house no lights were on and no one was home, which was strange because Bubbles was usually such a stickler for routine. She liked Michael in bed at regular hours, even when both of them were working nights, and she had Patricia from down the road put him to bed. Billy had no choice but to go in anyway and surprise them when they came home and opened the door.

He paid the driver and leapt from the cab, slipping all the way up the icy path to the door. At the door he dumped his bag at his feet and pushed the key into the lock, but the key would not turn and kept hitting something. He bent his wrist and tried again, then took the key out to see if he'd picked the wrong one in his haste. But it was the right key, and as he placed it to try again he suddenly realized why it would not turn. *It's not true*, he thought with a sick desperation, *she couldn't do it!* But she could and she had, and he knew then that every door had now been sealed against him.

Billy waited in the cold for two hours without anyone coming home, before bitterly admitting that for the moment at least he would have to give up. A murderous rage propelled his legs along the street as he looked for a cab, fuelling his journey all the way to Brixton. He was consumed by a desire to punish Bubbles, to make her suffer for what she had done. But as he knocked on the door of the first boarding-house he saw Billy was suddenly overcome by the most acute physical exhaustion. He could not think any more but instinctively knew he must lie his cold body down, some place where he would not have to speak. He wanted only darkness, a covering for his head, a soft place he knew would not pierce him. He had never felt so tired in his life, and knew that a kind of false energy must have enabled him to board the train in Blackpool and rush back to London, propelling him for the last time to his front door.

He paid in advance, and could not understand the question being put to him about sittings for breakfast. He looked at the woman's face, but it was as if all his faculties had left him and all he could imagine was lying down. He shook his head at her and climbed the stairs, surprised to see his feet negotiate action.

He closed the door and lay down on the bed, his dirty shoes lying on a folded, freshly washed towel. The ceiling looked far away; the window was slightly open and once again freezing air came to claim his unwrapped face. He knew he should close it but did not have the energy, he could hardly lift his body to take off his shoes and climb beneath the covers.

The sounds of the world came to him through the open window: living people were walking around and talking, the moon was still in the sky. But this thought came to him idly and floated off, it did not seem to him he was thinking. He closed his eyes in this unreal place, gently, as if to move too quickly would activate the pain he knew lurked somewhere, ugly and salivating, greedy to claim him. He did not think or feel anything at all but fell straight into sleep's kind oblivion.

The next morning everything came back to him with clarity before he was properly awake: his frantic dash up the icy path, his hand moving toward the lock. It suddenly seemed more terrible to him that when it had happened and played itself out again in awful slow motion. He sat up, his heart beating fast, and leant over to close the window. The sky was not yet light, but he could make out shapes below: fences, gardens, washing lines. The grey cold sky was close to the ground; a light or two shone from the window of an early riser.

Billy pulled his legs down to the floor and sat straight backed on the bed. *Right*, he thought, *I have to think. I have to think what to do next.* A violent hatred immediately sprang up in his chest, an urge to strike Bubbles dead. *How dare she*, he thought. *How dare she lock me out of my own life*! He stood up and wanted to run there at once, to rush home and smash down the door. All the myriad ways she had failed him came to his attention, how she had not tried in the least to show interest in the things he most cared about, his friends, his tumbling, how she had shown only boredom or contempt. How she was always on at him about money, as if he were not honourable and failed to pull his own weight. He would never, ever let his family starve, he would rather tumble for a hundred years than let Michael go without.

At the thought of Michael, Billy's rage burst so that he ran fast across the room and kicked a chair. It hit the wall so loudly that he was immediately returned to himself. He bent to pick up the chair, inspecting it anxiously as if it were a living thing and might have suffered bruising. But it was not damaged and Billy placed it carefully back on its feet before sitting on it and planning his defence.

How Known to Him She Was

As he waited at the corner to surprise his wife, Billy felt a malicious satisfaction in knowing she could not possibly avoid him. She could avoid him on the telephone by hanging up in his ear, she could avoid him at Avenue Road by not answering the door, but she could not avoid him alive in the street, a breathing man standing before her. Yet at the same time as Billy relished this evil satisfaction he also felt a yearning anticipation, for in some part of himself he still believed that once Bubbles looked upon his live, well-remembered face all her hate would instantly fall away. He knew this possibility was remote, or at least his head knew it, but his heart lagged embarrassingly behind. His heart still ceaselessly waved the flag of hope, no matter how often he ordered it to stop. His heart veered from love to hate with an indecent indiscretion, but always in some far-away corner it continued to bear its flag.

All at once Billy saw Bubbles at the top of the street and it seemed to him he stopped breathing. His mouth was dry, he did not know where to look, his hands in his pockets worked away, clenching and unclenching incessantly. Oh, how known to him she was! How recognizable the swing of her bones! He breathed in deeply and walked toward her, his legs moving as fast as they could. He felt himself to be approaching a creature of easy startle, a creature which might easily speed away.

She had her eyes on the ground and was obviously thinking about something, for she did not see him until he was almost upon her. Her mouth gave a small cry of surprise and her beautiful eyes momentarily widened. And then she recaptured herself and her small face set hard, her small face closed its doors.

'I'm in a hurry,' she said, not stopping, 'I have to catch the bus.'

'I know,' he said falling in with her, 'the twenty-five past eight.'

She kept her eyes on the ground; her gloved hands tightly gripped her handbag. He could have dashed her small head to the ground; he could have grabbed her bony shoulders. But he didn't, he kept walking by her side, intending to stay there like a thorn till she bled or cried out for forgiveness.

He had told himself he would remain calm and lay out before her all the ways she had failed him. He would be logical, concise, state his case coolly, so that she would see that if he had failed her, she had just as surely failed him. If both of them laid out their grievances quietly, reason would save them, and they might begin to make their way back toward each other.

But now that Billy had his chance to speak, his confidence suddenly failed him. Bubbles's face was so hard, her mind so clearly made up, he felt his intentions rapidly wilting, burnt by the heat of her resolve.

They had reached the bus-stop and he saw the bus approaching: he opened his coat to find his wallet. He was going to get on the bus with her, follow her to work, sit in front of her until she relented.

'What are you doing!' she cried as he stepped forward. 'You can't come with me!'

She spoke loudly and several people turned around; the bus conductor smiled and lifted his brows. Billy did not say anything but stepped on to the bus.

'Billy!' Bubbles protested. She stood by the conductor, clearly unsure of her next move, then furiously turned her back, her heels clattering on the stairs to the upper deck. He dashed forward and followed: the bus was crowded and they were pushed close.

'Oh, you're insufferable!' she hissed at him. 'Why can't you just accept things like everybody else?'

'Why should I accept being locked out of my own house!' he cried, louder than he meant to. 'Why did you have to do that!'

People turned to stare, but he did not care, he was angry now, so angry that he felt a sense of physical pressure bursting within his chest. His hate came back, furious and swinging, he could have shoved her intractable face.

'Your house!' she shouted. 'I paid for it! And I locked you out because it was the only way to get through to you. You ignore everything except what you want to see!' She was rigid with rage, her eyes wide and dangerous.

'Me!' he shouted back. 'You ignore everything I care about! You've never once encouraged or helped me!'

For a moment he thought she was going to spit. 'The penny still hasn't dropped, has it? It's not *you* we're talking about!'

He looked at her. 'Is there someone else?'

She let out a derisive laugh. 'God, you're unbelievable!' She suddenly spun around and barged her way past the other passengers, who scowled at her as she pushed roughly through. 'Don't mind me!' a woman said in a loud sarcastic voice. 'Oh, shut up!' Bubbles snapped.

All at once Billy became aware of the sounds of disapproval. 'Why don't they have their quarrels at home?' he overheard someone say and immediately felt the most painful humiliation. He blushed scarlet and moved toward the stairs, desperate now to get off the bus. He could not believe this shameful person was himself and wished to disappear – no, to wipe himself clean, to rise fresh and miraculously purged.

As the bus pulled into the stop, he jumped while it was still moving, stumbling on to the footpath at his most graceless. He felt all grace and goodness had fled from him and stood up to walk as best he could.

For the first time the idea occurred to him that his marriage might indeed be irretrievably lost, vanished as surely as spent days. This knowledge glowed, bright and dangerous, but as yet he did not know what to do with it. Billy looked up at the trees, the sky, buildings, still in place, still resolutely standing.

He did not know where to go, where he might lay his heaviness down. He walked for miles in a kind of stupor, paying no attention to where his feet took him. Once he saw a busy street ahead and determined to cross it whether cars came or not, whether buses ploughed across his path. It was nothing as definite as a wish to die but a kind of throwing of himself to the wind, a throwing of his heavy self away. He wanted no decisions, no responsibilities, no cares, just a blind, dumb walk across a road. When he came to the street he wondered if a car would come but felt only a mild curiosity and stepped out on to the road regardless. As it was, a bus had just passed and a car slowed for him as he reached the other side: he did not speculate on what he would have done if he had actually found himself faced with imminent danger but continued walking, his intention accomplished. He walked for miles although his body was tired and cold; his body issued regular small pleas for mercy.

If he thought at all, he thought about how he had not seen it coming. He knew that they had had their differences, but nothing which couldn't be solved, nothing worth breaking up their marriage. Bubbles's action seemed to him like some weird, unearthly phenomenon, the fall of meteors, the rise of a new inland sea. It did not seem possible that he could have missed its birth, the actual moment when she had decided to leave him. He thought back to the time when she had begun to be coolly polite to him and realized he should have seen it then. He should have seen it that morning she said goodbye to him when he left for Blackpool, or when she had lain that last night breathing in his arms. He could not believe that this terrible secret had not whispered itself to him, that he had not seen it in the surface of her eye. How long had she known? Weeks? Months? What actual moment had finally caused her to decide?

In an awful flash Billy feared Bubbles was right: perhaps he did see only those things he wished to see. He had certainly wished to see love, fruition, survival; he had certainly wished to see those. Perhaps he was like Vernon, hard of hearing when it came to hearts, blind to the small but unmistakable tremor of love's withdrawal.

He almost cried out with anguish that he had not seen this moment when Bubbles had decided it was no longer worth fighting for their love. If he had only seen it he might have been able to shore the walls, to stack sandbags up against the cracks. But he had missed it, for it had birthed itself in a place his eyes could not see.

It occurred to him that once experienced, this moment could not be taken back. He suddenly saw that no matter how loud his pleas were, how terrible his cries, this decisive moment could not be recast.

Billy became aware of how cold he was, how much he longed to sit down. He stopped walking and looked around for a taxi to take him as quickly as possible to his room in Brixton. When he stepped into the cab he remembered the silly joy he used to feel about taxis only a short time ago, and it was this strange useless memory which finally broke him.

On the eighth morning in Brixton Billy woke to the overwhelming realization that he was beaten. He had no eyes, no tongue, no powers left, and all at once knew there was no more he could do. He could not make Bubbles love him, for love could not be willed, he could not shape the movement of flame with his bare hands. She had been unhappy and he had failed her; whatever chance they might have had was now lost. All action had been torn from him, all decisions, all defence: he was forced to admit that his entire life had been lost to him in the blink of Bubbles's eye, but that no amount of fearless fighting could restore it.

For the first time, Billy was forced to think of how best a parting might be achieved, how they might begin to disentangle their lives from one another. For the moment, when Billy thought of Michael, his mind glanced off, as an eye glances off the surface of the sun. He dared not think of him at all, and by sheer will kept his small face away. Instead, he tried to think how Bubbles and himself might remove themselves from each other like dye from a cloth, the dye indistinguishable from the very weave. It took all his intelligence even to begin imagining a separate life for himself, for it seemed to him they had lived for ever in the same rooms and eaten the same food. Bubbles's smell had become as familiar as his own, their daily bed the lair of one living creature.

He tried to imagine himself in a room just like this one, and failed, again and again. His only map was who he had been before Bubbles, and yet he was no longer the same person. He was no longer the young man who had shared a room with Vernon in Min Campbell's house in Herne Hill but a million miles from him and could not fit back into his shoes. His feet had grown, from heel to toe, his arms, his legs; he felt too large even for this room, and could not imagine sharing it with another set of working lungs.

But he tried, he really tried, to think of what to do, where in the world he might go. He thought of Brixton, America, Australia, Herne Hill; he thought of himself cooking in some kitchen. Yet all the while Billy tried to see his unseeable future, a part of him continued to believe that it was not really happening, that he would not really have to decide at all. For part of him continued to view being alive as a kind of story, perpetually able to be rewritten and revised. This part believed that life was eternally redeemable, that no tragedy was too tragic to be healed. It was this part which refused to acknowledge that certain losses might not be replaceable, and that every human heart ceased to beat.

It was only years later that Billy came to see this refusal to believe in what was happening to him as the very thing which saved him. For if he had been forced to look clear-eyed upon his loss, his reason would most certainly have left him. It was only later that he saw that his new family had been torn from him just as surely as the old, the new family meant to stay with him for ever.

But for the moment Billy felt only a frightening propulsion into the unknown, his body's launch into inconceivable tomorrows. He felt the rush of air but could not admit it, and went hurtling into his future oddly disbelieving.

PART 5

Elsewhere

His Alphabet of Love

During that first long year following his divorce Billy feared his courage had failed him. He seemed to have lost entirely his ability to hope, to get up no matter how often he was knocked down. It struck him that he had rushed unselfconsciously through his life, hardly stopping to see in which direction he was going. He had been thoughtlessly, recklessly happy, probably smiling at inappropriate moments. Now for brief fearful moments he felt he had been knocked down for good, and had lost for ever the will necessary to get up. He realized with a shock that he had been an unfailingly hopeful man, lucky in ways he had not suspected. He sometimes wondered if he would ever dare hope again, if joy would rush again in his blood. For the first time in his life Billy Hayes suspected that unfailing hope might not be enough, and that cruel and inexplicable tragedies did indeed happen. He felt he had lived dumb, half blind, a wilfully foolish man who had unthinkingly regarded himself as immortal.

Billy lived in a flat in Westbourne Gardens not far from Bayswater, in a narrow locked-up-looking house facing a square. The square had geraniums and elegant plane trees in summer, and a patch of grass where it was forbidden to lie down. Men like himself lived in flats along the street, sunbaking in shirtsleeves on precarious balconies at midday, nodding to him in passing on the street. Old ladies lived in basement flats, leaving milk-encrusted saucers out for cats. His own flat, though, was mercifully light and cool, painted blindingly white, with remarkably thin walls. Despite its brightness, whole days lurked before him waiting for his decisions, not one decision but many, hour after hour. For the first few months he did not decide anything at all but sat strangely stunned, not really thinking of anything in particular. He felt himself the survivor of violence and wished only to sit for a long time undisturbed.

When Billy wasn't working he did not go out for days, for the outside world seemed far too hazardous. He had not known before that it was such an intolerable, hostile place and it was as if he were seeing the world as it actually was for the first time. It wasn't so much that he feared for himself (although sometimes he feared for himself too), but whenever he went out, his eyes seemed invariably drawn to the broken and the lost, the men and women who had somehow missed their way. Sometimes Billy would only get as far as the end of his street before he was struck by the terrible and unshakeable conviction that something dreadful had happened to Michael and he had to rush straight back to ring Bubbles to see if he was all right. Unbelievably he always was, although Billy no longer trusted the world not to sneak up on him, to deal him a foul blow when he wasn't looking. Bubbles had to put Michael on the telephone before Billy would believe him unharmed, and Billy felt a moment's foolishness only after the first flush of relief.

In the beginning his anxiety transmitted itself to his tumbling, and for the first time ever Billy completely lost his nerve. He lost the capacity to throw himself forward, to free-fall without thinking of the ground. It was this nerve above all which was critical to tumbling, a kind of unselfconscious daring impossible to feign. Billy knew himself to be sheltering his body, protecting it by holding something in: all his muscles seemed reluctant, and there was nothing he could do to coax them out. He tried for hours, practising by himself on the grass in a park near Little Venice, but not even the small admiring crowd was enough to lure his lost nerve back from wherever it had gone.

He and Reg did not talk of it, as if it were bad luck and could only make things worse. Instead, they devised routines incorporating Billy's new hesitancy, without once speaking of it aloud. Reg assumed the bulk of the difficult work and it seemed to Billy that he did the simple, uncomplicated tumbling any talented child could do, work which would have shamed him only a short time before. Yet they continued to get work, they continued to tumble, and for this Billy was embarrassingly grateful. In some part of himself he recognized that he must hang on to his tumbling with all his might, that if tumbling went, the last of him would surely go too.

Billy took fourteen months to write to his mother telling her of the divorce, continuing to send letters all that time signed as if from both himself and Bubbles. He had, of course, been forced to tell Reg sooner, but only because it was too hard to hide. He would have told no one if he had been able, he would have gone on pretending he still lived at Avenue Road, Norbury, till kingdom come. It was not lying exactly, but a kind of protection, although against what he could not possibly have said.

Life moved around him: Connie and Rose finally sailed for New York; a version of *The Hope Show* played at a theatre in Brighton. In the autumn of that first year Reg Tsang surprised him by marrying May Lee Miller in the register office in Acton, asking Billy at the last moment to be his witness. May Lee was a pretty blonde dancer from Texas he had employed for *The Hope Show*. She adored Reg but tried to hide it behind a shy, jokey manner, knocking him gently on the chin and ruffling his hair. At this time Billy still could not trust himself to think of his own wedding, and when he finally got home after the service and reception he discovered his body to be clenched like a fist. It was not that he begrudged Reg and May Lee their fresh hopes, but more that he had no wish yet to recall his own.

Suddenly, after the first few months of not being able to bear going outside, Billy could not bear staying in. He began to spend an inordinate amount of time walking, hardly stopping in case his pain chanced to roar. When he later came to remember this time he recalled himself as being constantly in motion, striking ceaselessly out street after street. He walked through east London, south London, the north, the bloodless heart; he walked to Kew and out to where the river narrowed at Twickenham. It seemed to him he mapped London in the same way he had once mapped a corner of Sydney, imprinting his presence and claiming some private outline for himself. He walked endlessly, tirelessly, after shows, after meetings, on rainy Sunday mornings when the quiet of his loungeroom inexplicably grew too loud. He forgot to take buses, how to use the tube, having no use for tunnels beyond the reach of the sun. His body moved, it did not fail him, and yet its movement was not a comfort but an imperative of personality, and all he could do was obey it.

As he walked Billy sometimes talked to himself, trying to conjure up the smallest flap of the flag. It seemed to him that some test was upon him, a test to determine if he truly believed. He called up now all the will of his blood, all the love in the furthest, deepest reaches of his heart. While he walked he recited lists of all the people he loved, and all the people who loved him in return. He recalled the feel of hands in his own, the joyous jump of himself and Connie and Vernon in the air. He remembered the startling sight of Reg Tsang's face in a London street, the way his whole life moved at the first sight of his son. He remembered all this, his alphabet of love, his swiftest and surest conduit back to hope. He felt that if he could only keep this litany in his heart long enough, it could not fail to win him back his joy.

But for the moment at least this list only rendered him the most acute, poignant comfort, like looking at a photograph of a much loved dead face you will never see again. Like any bereaved person, Billy could not bear to throw the photograph away, and yet it continued to pierce him each time he picked it up.

When he later came to remember this first long year, Billy could not recall himself talking. He must have talked, he must have talked in shops, he must have talked to Reg about a certain tumbling move. But it seemed to him that his tongue lost its muscle through underuse, that the only talking was inside his own head. He could not speak of Bubbles and Michael; he could not wail as if beside the grave. It did not occur to him that talking might release whatever was inside him, let it out of his mouth like so much bad air. While it was certainly true that he sometimes felt himself engorged with poison, so that he once imagined lancing his swollen belly to drain it, he did not think of opening his mouth to speak. He nursed himself, through days and nights, walking, always walking, walking himself and nursing himself his own way.

But one day as Billy was rushing down some unknown street in Parson's Green he suddenly knew he could stop. It was as if he had crossed some frontier inside himself, a frontier he had not known existed. Nothing in particular precipitated this, he simply found he could stop moving. As soon as he realized this, his ears inexplicably cleared as if he had lifted them from water, his skin felt the coolness of the air. He stopped dead, not believing it, having grown used to not trusting his own senses. But it was true, he felt the unmistakable rush of movement beneath his chest, the breaking up of something heavy and sorrowful.

All at once he could bear to stand still and hold what had happened to him in his head, to keep it there without instinctively pushing it away. All at once he could bear to know that he had once loved a woman named Bubbles Drake, with whom he had birthed a son. He suddenly understood that this son would go on being his for ever, even after Michael bore his own son, even after his own body left the earth. Billy could safely go on loving after all, as Michael could go on loving him.

He stood very still, but the knowledge held firm. He looked up at the sky and saw all its colour, the leaves frilled with brown on the trees. Billy Hayes recognized that time had passed, and knew that he was once again moving in it.

The World of Possibility

He did not return to being the same person he was before, he was not returned to himself without a scratch. Billy had lost for ever a certain unselfconsciousness, a sense of luckiness he only now realized he once had. He sometimes suffered too what he came to regard as relapses, little falls into terror and despair. But he could stand them now, because he knew they would not last, and movement would always come again. It wasn't that he stopped seeing the broken and the lost but that he could somehow bear to see them. Billy found that he could brave the world again, and once again dare to look forward.

He began to think of going home, of taking Michael to Australia for a holiday. He had the startling idea that he might face his father, talk to him like any ordinary man. Billy no longer imagined that his father would press him to his heart or beg his forgiveness, he simply felt that looking into his father's face again was something he wanted to do. It struck him as a kind of closing of the circle, some kind of logical completion.

Yet the thought of going back both compelled and frightened him, and his heart jumped even to think of it. Billy could not imagine any more what he might find, for Australia had been reduced to a few images in his head: yellowing grass, a high, far-away sky, the stone lion gates outside the joss-house. He had a photograph of Digger Dog and Molly standing in front of a house they were building in North Ryde, a suburb Billy had not even heard of. They looked to be in some far, unknown place, a different Sydney from any he had known.

But the idea of going home refused to go away, and kept rising up wistfully before him. He still thought of it as 'home' even though he had not lived there for years: he sometimes saw a picture of himself landing and gently pushing Michael forward, his whole family coming up to greet them.

After he imagined this Billy always had to stand up and walk around the room, very fast.

In 1950, Frank Hurley retired and all his friends gave him a party.

'We're the last of the old guard, I'm afraid,' he said to Billy. 'Times are changing.'

Billy knocked him gently on the arm. 'Good old Frank, optimistic till the last.'

'No, Billy, we're the last of an era. In ten years variety will be gone.'

Now Billy knew his date book to be filled, filled in fact till March the following year. Ever since the end of the war Cannon and Tsang had worked when and where they liked, and Billy knew hundreds of other acts who did too. Of course Billy did not wish to point this out to Frank, for he did not want to hurt his feelings. He guessed Frank Hurley felt like a lot of men when they retired, unwilling to believe business could flourish without them.

They were standing at the main bar of the Palladium, which the house manager had kindly allowed them to use. A show was in progress inside the theatre and they had been warned to stand aside at the interval, when warlike men and women would storm the bar.

All of a sudden this prophecy came true as Billy saw the doors open and glint-eyed men and women rush toward them.

'Jesus,' muttered Vernon, who had been standing with his back to Frank until the sudden noise made him turn around. 'The general public!'

Most of the members of Frank's party moved hastily away from the bar, watching in a mixture of admiration and astonishment.

Billy laughed, and turned to Frank, whom he supposed to be still standing beside him. 'If the show's any good, they shouldn't need a drink,' he said, and instantly realized he had addressed this remark to a young woman he did not know.

'Oh, sorry, I thought you were someone else,' he said hastily, looking around in the suddenly swollen crowd for Frank.

'But I'm not,' the young woman said, pushing her hand forthrightly forward. 'I'm Linda Pringle. How do you do?'

Billy quickly moved his drink to the other palm and shook her hand.

'How do you do?' he said, still peering over her shoulder.

'Well?' Linda Pringle said and he looked at her.

'Well what?'

She smiled. 'Do you have a name?'

He laughed. 'Oh, yes, I'm Ben Cannon.' He saw Frank and made as if to move toward him, but the young woman maddeningly kept talking.

'Oh, I know you!' she exclaimed. 'You were the one who did *The Hope Show*. I saw your show when I was at school. I'm a client of Frank's too, a singer.'

Billy glanced at her: she had a pleasant open face, a funny-looking mouth on which lipstick had been badly drawn. It struck him that he had nothing to say to her, that he did not particularly wish to hear a girl express her great ambitions.

'I loved it, I really did. I saw it four times. Are you planning another one?'

It occurred to him that here was a fan of sorts, a fan he might once have longed for. But he felt only a need to get away, to talk to people who knew all about him. This was one unexpected legacy of his divorce: he had developed an aversion to strangers, to anyone who did not know who he was and who he had once been.

'Ah, no, I'm not. I'm in an act, Cannon and Tsang.'

'Yes, I know,' she said, talking to him alarmingly intimately, turning her whole face up to his. 'I've seen your act. Where are you booked at the moment?'

Would she never stop, Billy thought, and made to go.

'Look, you'll have to excuse me, I need to have a word with Frank. I was talking to him before the hordes interrupted.'

She turned to look toward Frank and then back to Billy. 'I'll come too,' she said, moving forward. 'Oh, you don't mind, do you?'

He saw the plea in her eye, and reluctantly shook his head.

As they came up to Frank's table, Vernon gave him a lewd wink. Oh, really, Billy thought furiously, I'm not you, Vernon! He shot a quick glance at Linda, to see if she had noticed, but she was already talking animatedly to Frank.

'So you've met my star, I see,' Frank said, with what passed for happiness on his face. 'This girl's got a booking for television. She's going places, this one.'

Linda Pringle ducked her head in what appeared to be genuine embarrassment, and Billy liked her for it. She seemed impossibly young, recently born, as if she had just cracked the shell. He suddenly became aware of the baldness of his head, the largeness of his nose: lately his nose had been threatening to bloom into a replica of his mother's, claiming naming rights to his whole face. The balder he got, the more noticeable it became: it was not yet a whopper but it erred this side of large, perilously close to disaster.

Billy told himself that of course he was being silly, Linda Pringle could not possibly be interested in him. He was a thousand years old, or at least he felt like it; he had walked the earth for millions of years.

As soon as he reminded himself of this he settled down to talk to Linda Pringle with a certain equilibrium. Since his divorce from Bubbles it had not occurred to Billy to want to try again. Even though he considered himself to be healed in a way that allowed him to go on he did not regard himself as strong enough for that. All women only reminded him of Bubbles, and yet paradoxically all women were not her.

He looked now at Linda Pringle, satisfied that he was safe, and saw that after all she was only a harmless-looking girl.

But Billy was at home one morning when this harmless girl rang him up.

'Is that Ben Cannon?' she asked, and he guessed straight away who it was.

'Yes. Who's speaking?' He could not let her know that he already knew; she had to tell him, he had to let her do that.

'Oh, hello,' he said, sounding unsurprised, his heart thumping all the while in his chest.

'Oh, good, you remember me! It's always so embarrassing, isn't it, when you ring someone up and they haven't got a clue who you are!'

'I suppose so,' he said, already wondering what he would do when she issued her invitation, how he could get out of it gracefully.

'Listen, my flatmate and I are having a party on Saturday and we'd love you to come along. I'm sure there'll be plenty of people there you know.'

'Oh, Saturday!' he exclaimed. 'I can come any night but Saturday. I'm already booked out, I'm afraid.'

Linda Pringle let out a small sound of disappointment. 'Never mind. Some other time, then.'

He hung up but was surprised to feel a little drop of disappointment himself. Though nothing came of this hesitant offering of Linda Pringle's, Billy was suddenly awakened to the world of possibility, to the startling idea that any day now he might once again fall in love.

In the summer Reg and May Lee began to build a house out in the wilds of Hatch End. Privately, Billy thought this was madness, but Reg was so clearly delighted that Billy did not have the heart to express anything but encouragement. It seemed to take half the morning to reach the place and, once there, it did not strike Billy as particularly appealing. He had discovered that he liked to live in the heart of the city, to have life beat incessantly in his ears. Hatch End was altogether too quiet for him, its streets altogether too empty.

But in Hatch End Reg Tsang suddenly revealed a whole new side, making a nuisance of himself on the building site, boring Billy witless with endless ruminations on tiles versus linoleum. Now Billy loved Reg dearly but did not care a jot whether blue was preferable to green, if a bath should be square or oblong. He had always known Reg was a handyman, in that Reg had always fixed anything wrong with their props and had occasionally painted a room he lived in, but Billy had not expected home ownership to cause Reg Tsang to become glint-eyed, weighing up the pros and cons of certain fridges. After Billy's third visit to the building site he began to give excuses as to why he could not go again, finally admitting to Reg that he would prefer to visit when the house had a roof and a door.

Yet Billy had never seen Reg happier, marriage unexpectedly suited him. As Billy grew to know May Lee he liked her more and more: beneath her initial shyness she proved to be a good-natured, unflappable kind of woman who, like Reg, noticed other people without appearing to. This made her kinder than most, and had the lucky result of drawing forth everyone's imaginary best self. People were sweeter and funnier around May Lee Tsang, as if they could not bear to disappoint her.

When the house was finally finished, Billy found himself enjoying his visits to Hatch End, despite the unfortunate surroundings. Reg bought a car, a second-hand green Austin, which first he had to learn to drive. But he was a natural, and soon began to drive all the way to Westbourne Gardens to pick up Billy and drive him back to Hatch End for Sunday lunch. Often Michael came too and the long car trip would be transformed into a kind of adventure as Michael grew excited by the dashboard. Unlike his father, Michael was inexplicably transfixed by anything to do with cars and sometimes Reg let Michael sit on his lap to drive.

Whenever Reg allowed him to do this, Billy anxiously watched Reg's feet. He could not drive himself and although he knew the pedals represented the accelerator and the brake, he was not sure what the other one was for. Billy was not interested in the mechanics of cars, but thought that one day he might learn to drive himself. One Sunday he expressed this desire to Reg.

'You!' Reg exclaimed. 'You'd be a terrible driver! You'd see something and get all excited and run yourself straight off the road!'

Billy was offended but did not show it, and secretly made a vow that he would learn to drive. He was a man who had spent his entire travelling life handing himself over to others, and he wanted to try steering alone.

When May Lee was in the kitchen washing up after lunch one afternoon, Reg asked Billy if he had given any thought to another show.

'Why, no,' he said, taken aback, 'I thought we were doing pretty well with the act.'

Reg sat forward. 'We are, but it can't last. We can't tumble with false teeth and walking sticks.'

Billy laughed. 'I don't see why not. Actually, that's not a bad idea for a comedy routine. We could – '

'Billy,' Reg said. Billy looked at him.

'It's not just age that's the problem,' Reg said. 'The writing's on the wall for tumblers.'

Billy stared at him.

'We'll just have to expand into other areas. Maybe we could produce more shows.'

Billy was not listening. Besides himself, Reg Tsang was the most committed tumbler Billy had ever known: he could not believe what Reg had just said.

A Good Seat

As 1952 drew to a close, it seemed all the world thought of nothing but the coronation. A kind of flush passed over the earth, not only over Britain but America, Canada, Australia too, even far-flung villages in Africa. Suddenly it was all everybody talked about, coronation news was always on the radio, and women everywhere seemed to be discussing the possible proportions of the Queen's coronation skirt. Billy's mother in Australia knew more about the great event than he did, and Vernon Rome claimed to personally know a 78-year-old woman in Birmingham who was in training for the long wait in the street: every time it rained she went out into the garden, just so she could get used to feeling soaked.

'Oh, come on,' Billy said.

'Scoff all you like, doubters,' Vernon cried. 'Her name's Mrs Violet Madden and she lives at 28 Wellerby Road.'

'Yeah, 28 Wellerby Road, Nowhere,' Reg said, smiling.

Vernon ignored him. 'Mrs Violet Madden of Birmingham plans to set up in Trafalgar Square at least fourteen days before the crowning, just so she can get a good seat.'

Everybody laughed and Vernon looked at May Lee, who was planning a trip home to America during the coronation. It would be her first trip home in five years, and her first away from Reg.

'Mercifully, you will be spared the sight of Londoners beside themselves, May Lee,' he said. 'I can't imagine Americans carrying on in such a fashion.'

'Don't you believe it,' she said to him in her soft, singsong voice. 'You should see us when we get anywhere near a president. You'd think it was the very Lord himself.'

They were having farewell drinks for Vernon, who was himself heading off by aeroplane to America. It was the first time Billy had personally known anyone to fly across the Atlantic, and Billy regarded Vernon with envy. Yet Vernon looked as if he did it every day and was sitting back, typically showing off, his coat draped casually over his shoulders. Ever since *The Hope Show* Vernon's career had taken off in unexpected ways, and he now made a handsome living out of guest appearances with other tumbling acts, or brief appearances in musicals where he danced beautifully with the female star. Privately, Billy was disappointed that Vernon had got sidetracked from tumbling into dance, for he remembered how passionate about tumbling he had once been.

'Will you be seeing Connie and Rose?' Billy asked, feeling that too many years had passed to render the subject of Connie anything but safe.

'They'll be in Rio,' Vernon replied with a vaguely dismissive air. 'Ambrose is doing a show there.'

And then Vernon's flight was announced and they all hurriedly shook hands and kissed goodbye, moving to the departure deck to watch his plane take off.

As Billy watched the aeroplace lift into the air he wondered how long it would take to fly to Australia. From the air he might map Sydney's outline below him, long before his feet traced the ground.

Reg and May Lee gave Billy a lift back to the city: Reg offered to take Billy on to Norbury, where he was due to pick up Michael, but Billy thanked him and said it was too far out of his way.

Only when Billy finally turned into Avenue Road did he stop worrying about being late. He looked forward to his weekends with Michael, and would not like him to think he let anything else get in the way.

Billy knocked on the door and Michael opened it at once, his overnight bag festooned with coronation medals.

'Hello, Tom,' he said. 'Been collecting?'

Bubbles quickly appeared behind Michael, resignedly shrugging her shoulders. 'Awful, aren't they?' she said. 'They gave them to him at school.'

Billy forgot about coronation medals: every time he saw Bubbles Hayes again he initially felt a small shock. In this brief shock a sense of their shared history came back to him, closely followed by the realization that Bubbles was a perfectly ordinary woman.

He listened to her going on about coronation medals, but it seemed to him that he was looking at a flawed person much like himself, with ambitions, griefs and disappointments. He saw a woman struggling with her life, who, like anyone else, had her good points. He remembered how he had once believed he could thaw something inside her, but he had also once believed her to be someone else: either Bubbles had changed or he had, and Billy knew unquestionably it was himself. It was not that he had made her up exactly, more that his own needs had skewed his vision: he saw now that he had fallen upon her as if starving. Anybody could have told him that Bubbles Drake was never going to give him what he wanted, nor could he ever have satisfied her.

As he looked at Bubbles, Billy realized that he actually liked himself away from her, who he was, and how he lived his life. He had expanded back to his natural proportions and no longer had to subdue his excessive heart, which loved things Bubbles Hayes deemed unworthy.

'The whole school's got a holiday for the coronation, Dad,' Michael was saying. 'I'm going over to Brent's for a party.' Michael had recently become part of a gang of boys, of which Brent Green was king.

'Brent's got a television,' he continued and over his head Bubbles raised her eyebrows at Billy. Just then a male voice called Bubbles from inside the house.

'Oh, by the way,' she said, 'there's something . . .'

Billy smiled. 'If you're going to tell me you're getting married, I already know. His name's Donald and he takes Michael to car rallies.'

'Dad!' Michael cried, clearly embarrassed. Billy leant forward to briefly lay his hand on Michael's head.

Billy was not sure but he thought he glimpsed disappointment on Bubbles's face. He recalled how jealous he had once been, and felt a pang for his old self.

'Come on, Dad, let's go,' Michael said with impatience, ducking his head as Bubbles tried to kiss him.

Billy looked at Bubbles and shrugged his shoulders, turning to follow his son. He was almost at the gate before he turned around.

'Oh, congratulations,' he said. 'I hope you'll be very happy.' She seemed to search his face for traces of irony before smiling at him and closing the door.

At last, Reg gave in to Billy's request for a driving lesson.

'Come out on Saturday morning, but remember it's only your first time so don't expect to drive back to London.'

When Billy arrived at Hatch End, Reg had not even finished breakfast.

'Eager, aren't you?' he said when he opened the door.

Billy poured himself a cup of tea while Reg and May Lee finished their toast. 'Now explain to me what the clutch does again,' he said and Reg looked at May Lee.

When they finally got into the car, Billy was ready to fly. 'Hang on, don't start yet! There's a few more things I need to explain.'

So Billy listened while Reg told him about the principles of three-point turns, reverse parks and the use of the handbrake. When they finally took off, Billy noticed Reg holding tightly to the seat, and slapped his thigh playfully.

'Keep your hands on the wheel!' Reg cried, and Billy did as he was told. He wasn't very good, as Reg had predicted, for he drove in a strangely blind manner, hunched over the wheel, peering earnestly ahead as if there were a fog. Nevertheless after his one lap around the block he drove into the driveway determined to improve.

'Not bad, eh?' Billy said, following Reg into the house, where the postman had just delivered the mail.

'Here's one from Lily,' Reg said, sorting through the pile.

Billy walked into the kitchen and tried not to appear as if he were waiting for Reg to open it.

'How'd it go?' May Lee asked.

'Oh, fine,' Billy said, careful to avoid looking at Reg.

Reg let out a whoop. 'Lily's coming to England!' he cried.

Something light and felicitous rose up inside Billy: he laced his hands together and warned himself not to raise the flag.

The Way You Go On

It turned out that Lily Tsang was not coming to London to see the Queen: she was going on a tour of the Continent and would be in Ireland visiting some relatives of her late husband's during coronation week. She planned a week in London before she went to Cork, and would return afterwards to board a boat back to Australia. Lily Tsang now taught dancing at a school in George Street in Sydney but still performed every now and then. She had not remarried but had a steady boyfriend, a dancing teacher at her school.

Against his will, Billy Hayes began to wait for her; he waited for Lily Tsang to cross the ocean, he waited for her to cross time. He told himself that he had no expectations, that life did not happen that way, yet he kept seeing Lily's face as if she were already in front of him, and a million things he had not realized he knew came back. He clearly recalled the wandering manner of her speech, its charming randomness and dead ends. He remembered how her hair hung shiny about her face and the way her body had a delirious sway. But most of all Billy remembered how he felt when he had held her, how happiness had bloomed where they lay.

He began to look more often in the mirror to see how much he had changed.

Lily was due to arrive a few days before May Lee left for America.

'I wish I'd known earlier,' May Lee said. 'I feel so bad about not being here for your sister.'

'You'll have a few days together,' Reg said. 'That'll be more than enough.'

Billy smiled to hear the old childhood rivalry between Reg and Lily raise its head.

'Do you want to come with us to meet her train, Billy?' May Lee asked.

A nervousness hit him. 'Ah, I don't think so,' he said. 'I'll catch up with her later.'

The morning of Lily's arrival Billy made sure he was busy. At Westbourne Gardens he cleaned the bath and put away the dishes in the drying rack; he went out and bought some flowers. When he had finished he sat at the kitchen table and idly jotted down a few ideas for routines. He tried not to keep looking at the clock but really he knew what time it was to the closest minute. When he guessed that Lily's train must be coming in Billy stood up and walked to the window, his ear cocked, as if he expected to hear it passing by.

He sat down again and waited for time to move: at 4.15 he was due at Hatch End for afternoon tea.

As he stood on the doorstep waiting for Reg to open the door Billy Hayes told himself to breathe. All his nerves were straining, the whole of his body pitched forward. Time had fallen in on itself so that he was returned to that precise moment on the *Kitano Maru* when he had last looked upon Lily Tsang's face.

The door opened: Lily Tsang stepped toward him and after twenty-one years Billy Hayes felt her slender bones.

He could not look at her, his eyes kept hitting her and bouncing away. Yet it was recognizably Lily, her movements were the same, her frail wrists were the ones he had held in his hands. Her body had imprinted itself upon his own, and all its private details were still his.

He could not speak but followed her into the loungeroom; she held on lightly to his arm as if she remembered how she had once led the way.

When he next looked up she was sitting across the table from him, smoking a cigarette. He saw that she was nervous too by the way she kept taking quick little puffs, sometimes even when she was talking. Lily Tsang was talking in her old chatterbox fashion, telling Reg about people he didn't know.

'I'm sure you met him, Reg,' she was saying, 'a tall guy with sticking-out hair. He married that winska from the Seven Wonders, Nola, the dark one. Well, anyway, Peter's formed a partnership with Tim Ryan and Anona's old schoolfriend Margaret.

Remember her? She lived in Talfourd Lane, behind the post office.'

She appeared destined to go on in this manner: a grin broke out on Billy's face.

'What's so funny?' she asked.

'Billy's wondering why you've travelled halfway across the earth to tell me about Nola the winska I don't know and Margaret who lives behind the post office,' Reg said.

'Oh well,' Lily said, 'you never know who might be interested.'

Billy and Reg looked at her. Suddenly all three of them burst out laughing. May Lee sat in the middle, a newcomer amongst an old crowd.

Later, in the kitchen, Billy had his first opportunity to speak to Lily alone. 'You're exactly the same,' he said hesitantly.

She shook her head. 'I don't think so. I've changed a lot since Vince died.'

He felt himself already stumbling. 'Oh, I'm sorry, I didn't mean it that way. I know all these things have happened but I just meant that you still sound the same, the way you talk, the way you go on . . . if you know what I mean.'

She handed him a teatowel. 'Well, you certainly sound the same. As tongue-tied as ever.' She was teasing him.

He smiled tentatively. 'I used to think you didn't notice, because you were talking so much yourself.'

She laughed. 'I see you've still got the same hopeful face.'

'It's just my hair that's gone AWOL,' he replied. Billy noticed now that there was a sobriety in her, which did not quite disappear even when she smiled. It was a kind of caution which she never had as a girl, he saw it at the back of her eyes.

'Oh, I wouldn't worry about that,' Lily said. 'That hopeful face makes up for it.'

She smiled at him and a sneaky rush of happiness passed through him.

That night Billy could not sleep. He saw again Lily Tsang opening the door, and wondered if it had seemed to her too as if all his hopes had rushed toward her. He had not wanted this to happen, or had he? He lay in bed and thought of his mistakes, and the memory of pain immediately restrained him.

Two nights later Lily came to Westbourne Gardens for a drink. They were going out to dinner but Lily said she'd first like to see where Billy lived.

When she arrived, he was suddenly aware that they were two adults, to all intents and purposes strangers to each other, or at least unfamiliar with each other as grown people. Whole centuries might have passed since they had parted, stars might have burnt out in the sky.

Lily was wearing a cheongsam; her hair was cut short and she seemed to Billy to have that particular Chinese luck of agelessness. Her body had clearly not conspired against her as his own had: her silhouette was much the same, her anatomy still appeared unbelievably insubstantial. He busied himself with the drinks, and discovered he was once again nervous.

'I've got gin, sherry or vodka and that's it, I'm afraid.'

'I'll have a small sherry,' she said. 'You know how we Chinese can't drink.' She winked at him and continued her inspection of the room. Billy watched her reading the bill from the Wallabies Royal Command Performance he had pinned to the wall.

'I live by myself too,' she said. 'I like it now, but it was terrible for the first couple of years.'

Billy handed her the sherry: her hand brushed his as she took it. He felt unexpectedly stranded, with no words to say.

'How old's your little boy?' she asked, looking at the photograph of Michael.

'He's just turned ten,' Billy replied. 'I've started teaching him to tumble.'

She peered intently into the picture. 'I wish Vince and I had had a child, but we kept putting it off.'

Billy did not know how to answer: he felt paralysed by awkwardness. It was as if a stranger had suddenly begun an intimate conversation; he surreptitiously inspected Lily from across the room. 'You should take him home to meet your mum. She's getting pretty toey.'

'Tell me what she said again,' Billy asked.

'She said, "If that Billy doesn't get my grandson over here quick smart, I'll go over there personally and lasso him." I think she means it.'

Billy smiled and sat back on the couch.

'I don't suppose you ever hear anything about my father,' he said, not looking at her.

Lily sat down next to him. 'All I know is the girls have started to see him again. I think Saph sends them around every now and then with a casserole. He's a bit of a sad case really.'

She took a sip of her drink. 'Why don't you come home and see for yourself?' Billy turned: it seemed to him she was asking him more than this. Her hand was resting lightly on his: he remembered exactly the feel of it.

'I think I will,' he said at last.

The stranger that was Lily Tsang leant over and kissed him. 'Good,' she said, 'and not before bloody time.'

When Lily went to Ireland, Billy's hopes unexpectedly galloped ahead of him, planning everything from weddings to fresh starts. He began imagining moving back to Australia, and pictured himself tumbling at the Tivoli. But whenever he got to the part about leaving England, his rush ahead abruptly stopped: he knew he could never move away from Michael, and that there was nothing for it but to stay.

Nonetheless, Billy told himself he would speak to Lily as soon as she got back. She might not want to live in London: she might not want to live with him! Of course Billy realized he was way in front of himself, and that he did not really know what Lily Tsang felt. She had a boyfriend in Sydney, after all, a life of her own: there was a chance she might only see him as an old friend. And yet Billy instinctively knew that she did not, but since he no longer believed in guesswork, the only way to definitely find out was to ask.

Billy decided he would do this the moment he saw her again. In the meantime there was the coronation to get through, a whole week in which there was nothing for it but to wait some more.

Coronation Day

Coronation day was almost upon them before Billy and Reg discussed their own plans. Great crowds were descending on London, and there was an unmistakable sense of moment in the air.

'I'm all for leaving the country,' Reg said. 'Lily and May Lee had the right idea.'

But they couldn't leave the country because Cannon and Tsang had a booking in Kilburn the night before the coronation, on a programme which insisted on styling itself a coronation revue.

'We could go to some remote village,' Billy suggested; 'take the car to Kilburn and leave from there.'

Reg shook his head. 'No, the traffic'll be terrible. The entire population will be converging on London.'

Billy sighed. 'We could just give up and join the cheering crowds. Join old Mrs What's-her-name in Trafalgar Square.'

Reg looked at him: Billy shrugged. 'It was just an idea.'

Billy put his head in his hands. 'Let's face it, Tsang, we've been abandoned. I'm afraid it's just you and me.'

They decided to spend the day holed up in Hatch End, comforting themselves with food and drink. The weather had turned unpleasant anyway, and Billy Hayes was too old to stand in line to see the face of the newly crowned Queen.

With both May Lee and Lily away, Reg took to coming around more often to Westbourne Gardens. Billy talked Reg into giving him a few more driving lessons: he hoped to personally drive Lily about London when she got back. Without May Lee around Reg was clearly at a loose end: after a show he was reluctant to go straight home, and three nights running he asked Billy to go for a drink with him. It was not unlike the time when he had first known Reg, when the two of them had spent practically every spare moment together. Billy remembered the fever to get out his front gate to practise full twisters on the joss-house lawns.

He began to think of how he might tell Reg how much their

friendship had meant to him, but every time he thought of the right words he was overcome by acute embarrassment at such tender declarations of manly love.

In the end, he did not say anything. He felt Reg Tsang knew that the most important human messages were not always delivered by mouth.

The day before the coronation Billy got a postcard from Lily. *Ireland's beautiful*, she wrote. *One day we should see it together.*

He read these words and it seemed to Billy Hayes that he had received his answer.

On the morning of the coronation, on what would prove to be the coldest June day so far this century, Billy woke early in Reg and May Lee's spare bedroom in Hatch End. His nose was cold, so he burrowed further beneath the covers.

Despite himself he felt a sense of occasion. He thought of Lily and smiled hugely, then took a quick breath and threw off the blankets before dashing to the bathroom where he turned the hot tap on full blast.

Before he stepped into the bath Billy Hayes inspected himself in the full-length mirror. Granted that he was bald and his nose was rather large, he still reckoned he did not look too bad for a man who was about to turn thirty-six. The calves of his legs were solid and round, his stomach taut and flat. He told himself that if Lily Tsang could bear to look at him, he still must be all right.

As he looked at himself he thought of the words Lily had written and could not believe his luck in having wrested love from unforeseen sources. He felt ready to burst from an over-abundance of fortune: blessed with this late chance, the world's finest friends, a son, the gift of work to love! Even his small useless talent had brought him immeasurable joy and enabled him to feel the very essence of himself and, through it, the living pulse of other human creatures.

Billy Hayes turned up his head to the unseen sky on the coldest June day of the century, and felt the whole of his life, the big life of the spirit, alive and moving.

He stayed in the bath for what seemed like hours, feeling happy and warm. He wondered if the Queen was in the bath too, growing nervous beneath soapy water. He and Reg had sworn not to mention the coronation all day, to close their eyes against any show of glee. Unlike his neighbours, Reg had not bought a television set especially to watch the live coverage.

When Billy finished dressing he carefully made his way past Reg and May Lee's bedroom, down the stairs and into the kitchen. He was making a pot of tea when he saw the car keys and an idea suddenly hit him.

He would drive himself! He would drive alone before anyone else was on the roads, before the whole of England rose to go to London.

When he got into the car, it started at once: he stared intently through the rainy windscreen. He remembered to turn on the windscreen wipers before the car took off, leaving the driveway in odd little jerks. Billy held the wheel and peered uncertainly out through the streaked window, driving the car slowly forward. He went willingly, completely unburdened: he did not once feel his own moment descending.

He rounded the corner and took off down the road, unaware of anything but his own happiness. He began to whistle tunelessly, counting the joys of his life, looking around him at the moving world. It seemed to him that happiness had turned out to be not some flawless unbroken whole but the full weight of life, perilously balanced.

He went on whistling, thinking how he might talk to Lily about this, when all at once he realized his attention had wandered. Before he could prevent it, the car was caught in a long graceful skid and the wheel was spinning in his palms and time began to rush and move slow. Without warning Billy saw the earth tip, the flash of grey cloud, his own moment speeding toward him. Only then did his hands fly up, a useless gesture, curiously beseeching, as if he were about to turn a last roll in the air, and begin the long reach out to God. There was no sound, only Billy's surprised mouth protesting, even as he knew himself to be leaving. He was not ready and fought as he went, finding no time left for favours. He had no time to think, no time to plead, but thought he saw the shape of a tree, the rim of the world, before he shut his eyes against what was to come.

Billy Hayes's body rose in one great surprised swoop before it felt the final pull of the earth and abandoned the world for the skies. For one brief moment a certain buoyancy quit the air and an elderly woman in Sydney, Australia, felt something pass over her so that she gathered her cardigan up, looked quizzically into the darkening sky and went quickly inside.

And as the light grew brighter on the coldest June day of the century, men and women watched the newly crowned Queen receive from the Archbishop of Canterbury the sceptre with the cross in her right hand, and the orb into her left.

The Queen was in Westminster Abbey, London, but for the first time in history she was also in loungerooms all over England, and every single person watching television could clearly see into the eyes of the Queen.

A Boy Rolling

It is the sky that decides him. His mother made him promise to stay inside but the sky is mauve and teetering, hovering on the cusp of night and day. At such moments an eleven-year-old boy might believe in his own earthly powers, in the ability of his will to transform the whole world.

Billy Hayes passes through the front gate of 61 Allen Street, Glebe, with his head up. He feels as if there is something undeclared inside himself, a coil of secret, ready to spring. He walks quickly, on the very balls of his feet, believing everything is about to happen. The world seems about to open itself up, and Billy is rushing to receive it. Above his head birds fly in arcs; around him is the noise of settling heat and cicadas.

He knows his mother will be angry but he does not stop: the sky is drawing him forward, his secret also, his body full of energy and hope. As he turns into the street with the joss-house, Billy turns his head: against the twilight sky he sees a pyramid, a constellation of human bodies arranged by perfect laws of balance and weight.

He is conscious as he walks forward that his secret is about to uncoil. He looks out over the grass, over the sky, over the world, and sees a boy rolling, glad in the air, waiting for the future to reach him.